WHEN BABY STARTS TO TEETHE,
IT'S HARD TO KEEP ACTIN' *NORMAL*

Us Hogbens is quiet folk  and lead quiet lives in our comes near withouten we folks in the village are us try hard not to act consp

If Paw gets drunk, lik middle of Main Street in his red underwear most people make out they don't notice, so's not to embarrass Maw. They know he'd walk like a decent Christian if he was sober.

The thing that druv Paw to drink that time was Little Sam, which is our baby we keep in a tank down-cellar, startin' in to teethe again. First time since the War Between the States. We'd figgered he was through teething, but with Little Sam you never can tell. He was mighty restless, too.

A perfesser we keep in a bottle told us once Little Sam e-mitted sub-sonic somethings when he yells but that's just his way of talking. Don't mean a thing. It makes your nerves twiddle, that's all. Paw can't stand it. This time it even woke up Grandpaw in the attic and he hadn't stirred since Christmas. First thing after he got his eyes open he bust out madder'n a wet hen at Paw.

"I see ye, wittold knave that ye are!" he howled. "Flying again, is it? Oh, sic a reowfule sigte! I'll ground ye, ywis!" There was a far-away thump.

"You made me fall a good ten feet!" Paw hollered from away down the valley. "It ain't fair. I could of busted something!"

"Ye'll bust us all, with your dronken carelessness," Grandpaw said. "Flying in full sight of the neighbors! People get burned at the stake for less. You want mankind to find out all about us? Now shut up and let me tend to Baby."

Grandpaw can always quiet the baby if nobody else can. This time he sung him a little song in Sanskrit and after a bit they was snoring a duet.

—from "Cold War"

BAEN BOOKS by
DAVID DRAKE & ERIC FLINT

BAEN BOOKS by RYK E. SPOOR

For a complete listing of Baen Books
by these authors, please go to our website:
www.baen.com

Mountain Magic

David Drake,
Eric Flint,
Ryk E. Spoor &
Henry Kuttner

MOUNTAIN MAGIC

This is a work of fiction. All the characters and events portrayed in this book are fictional, and any resemblance to real people or incidents is purely coincidental.

"Exit the Professor" was first published in *Thrilling Wonder Stories*, October 1947. "Pile of Trouble" was first published in *Thrilling Wonder Stories*, April 1948. "See You Later" was first published in *Thrilling Wonder Stories*, June 1949. "Cold War" was first published in *Thrilling Wonder Stories*, October 1949. Reprinted by permission of Don Congdon Associates, Inc. Copyright © 1947, 1948, 1959 by Standard Magazines, renewed 1977 by C.L. Moore. *Old Nathan* was first published by Baen Books, October 1991, copyright © David Drake. This is the first publication of *Diamonds are Forever*, copyright © 2004 by Eric Flint and Ryk E. Spoor.

A Baen Books Original

Baen Publishing Enterprises
P.O. Box 1403
Riverdale, NY 10471
www.baen.com

ISBN: 0-7434-8856-3

Cover art by Gary Ruddell

First paperback printing, October 2004

Distributed by Simon & Schuster
1230 Avenue of the Americas
New York, NY 10020

Production by Windhaven Press, Auburn, NH
Typeset by Bell Road Press, Sherwood, OR
Printed in the United States of America

CONTENTS

To Henry Kuttner (1914–1958) and
C.L. Moore (1911–1987)

DIAMONDS ARE FOREVER

Eric Flint and Ryk E. Spoor

1. Calling Mamma

"You're getting MARRIED?!"

I had to pull the receiver away from my ear. Father always said if Mamma was in full voice she could break window glass over in the next county. "Yes, Mamma. I asked Jodi yesterday and she accepted."

"Well, that's WONDERFUL!" Another ear-saving reaction. Her voice shifted to *No Nonsense* mode. "Now you've put this off long enough, Clinton Jefferson Slade. You're bringin' that girl home to meet your family this very week, you hear? I know you can take that time off if'n you try, in that big fancy job that you're so important at."

When Mamma uses your whole name, there isn't anything for it but you'd better do as you're told. "Yes, Mamma. It's just . . . Mamma, she's city."

"Well, now, I know that, boy. What other kind of girl would you be meetin' in New York? We're not completely uneducated out here, you know."

3

I lowered my voice. "Mamma, I'll come. I'll bring her, okay. But . . . is everything okay there?"

"Well, of COURSE it—" Mamma cut off short, then sighed. "Oh. Yes, Clinton, ain't been none of *that* in quite a while. Daddy Zeke said you might be tryin' to hide *that* from this girl and that was why we hadn't met her."

"From anyone, Mamma, not just Jodi. Family's never told anyone, and I didn't aim to change that." I was slightly embarrassed to hear the Kentucky accent getting stronger; it always did when I talked to family. Not that I was really *embarrassed* about my family, not really, but . . . sometimes they were so weird. "So everything is okay?"

"Just FINE, dear. Now, we'll be expecting you when?"

I did a quick calculation in my head. "Say, Monday evening? We'll be driving and I'll have to make some arrangements before we go."

"That will be just fine, Clint dear." I was back to Clint now, so that was good. I hadn't been at all sure how they'd take me marrying a city girl, even though they really thought I was more than half city myself now. "We'll do you proud, boy, because we really are all proud of you, first Slade to finish college this century and all, and you done so well."

I blushed, and I know darn well Mamma could tell, even over the phone. "Aw, Mamma, ain't any big deal, really. Anyone in the family coulda done it."

"Don't you go selling yourself short, Clint dear. Even Evangeline knows perfectly well you're the genius in our family, and she's no dummy herself. Take care, and the whole family will be looking for you!"

We exchanged kisses over the phone, silly though that sounds, and I hung up.

"So," Jodi said, coming over, "were those bellows of fury, or was she happy to hear about it?"

"You could hear her?"

"*Oy vey*, Clint," she said, smiling. "Thought she'd break your eardrums with a couple of those."

Jodi was something of an anachronism. Her grandparents were immigrants who still spoke more Yiddish than English and had maintained an intimidatingly firm emphasis on the link between the old and new traditions. Linguistic traditions, anyway, if not religious ones. Jodi's grandfather had been active in the needle trade unions, a follower of Max Shachtman's brand of socialism. He had no use for religions of any kind, but that hadn't stopped him from maintaining a number of Jewish habits and customs. Jodi's family was almost a time capsule of clichés from the '40s and '50s, and Jodi had inherited enough to sound like a near-parody of the New York "Jewish American Princess." So why did I find her Yiddish, of all things, endearing? Especially when spoken with that New York accent that reminded me of nails on a chalkboard?

Probably just the blindness of love, I had to admit. I'd known Jodi Goldman for four years, though, so hopefully the blindness (or, in this case, deafness) would last for many years yet. "She was ecstatic," I said, answering her question. "I guess I should have more faith in my family, but they are still, well . . ."

"About as rustic backwoods as you were when you first showed up?"

I laughed. "Worse, sweetheart. I'd gone through college before that, remember. First Slade—"

"—this century, yes, I know, my fave *nebbish*. You mentioned it a time or two, probably because your whole family mentions it every time you go home, yes?"

"And on the phone. Look, I sorta committed us to go visit. You don't argue with Mamma."

"Yeah, sounds like my mother. When are we supposed

to get there, so they can get a good look at what a horse you're bringing home?"

Jodi's sensitive about her height—she's taller than me by two inches or so, and I'm almost six feet tall. This doesn't bother me, but when she's nervous she tends to fret about it. As well as her weight, which for her height is just fine. "Don't you worry about that, Jodi. When they get a look at you, Father'll be tellin' me how lucky I am, and I'll have to watch so Adam doesn't try to steal you. Next week."

"What? Are you totally *meshuggeh*? What about work?"

"Mamma knows I can take the time off. What about you?"

She made a sort of growling noise in her throat, and then hummed several bars of a Streisand tune—a sign she was both thinking and calming herself down. "Okay, yeah, I think I can do that. They won't be thrilled, but if we want to make your Mamma happy, I can live with it. Oy, I have packing to do! Do you have electricity where you live?"

I managed to keep from laughing. "Yes. We have our own generators, actually. Every month Father or Adam trucks in to town to buy the fuel. Had to have the phone line run in special; these days I suppose we'd have done something like get a satellite link, but not back when the family first decided to get one."

Jodi blinked. "Running out a phone line just for you? That's pretty pricey, Clint."

"I said we was backwoods," I drawled, emphasizing my Kentucky accent. "Didn't say we was *poor* back-woods. If the Slades ain't the richest family in Crittenden County, it's only 'cause we've spent a lot of it the last few decades."

"I never knew, Clint." Jodi looked at me with surprise. "How'd your family get rich?"

I realized my big mouth had me dangerously close to the secret. Time to follow the honorable Slade tradition of ducking the truth. "One of my ancestors, Winston Slade, made a ton of money mining, and brought it with him to the homestead when he settled down." That was, as one of my online friends would put it, "telling the truth like a Jedi"—it was true "from a certain point of view." If I'd done the casual voice right, though, she'd never suspect a thing. Once we were married, we'd be living near New York and just visit the family homestead once in a while, so the chances were she'd never have to know.

"Well, that'll be a relief for my more cynical relatives," Jodi said, throwing back her long black hair. "They were kinda worried about just what your background was, especially with your nickname."

I wasn't very surprised. "I suppose 'Crowbar' Slade does sound either like a real honest-to-god Good Ole Boy, or like a wannabe wrestler." Truth was, I'd gotten the nickname in college because my roommates noticed I had a crowbar in my baggage when I moved in, and that I had that particular bag with me most of the time.

"Look," Jodi said, "if we're leaving to get there Monday like I think I heard you say, I gotta get moving. We just got tomorrow to get ready. And like I didn't already have a busy schedule tomorrow? You know what sort of planning I have to do for the wedding, and now we have to schlep all the way to Kentucky." She leaned slightly down and we both shut up for a while for the good-bye kiss, which lasted for several kisses as usual before she finally got out the door.

I sighed and grinned. Hey, maybe this would be fun.

2. Meet the Slades

"Ow! I see why you have this oversuspended monster now." A larger bump than normal jolted Jodi against the harness. "And boy am I glad we put the equipment in those transport cases."

"I wouldn't have pulled out of the driveway if you hadn't. You want to keep doing work on our vacation, I'm at least going to make sure you can't wreck half the lab's equipment getting there. 'Sides, that one weren't nothing. Right after winter you should see the potholes we get and have to fill in afore—I mean, *be*fore—we can really drive the road well." I kicked myself mentally. One night sleeping over in a southern West Virginia motel on the way and a few stops at regional gas stations and I was already falling back into dialect. Pretty soon Jodi wouldn't even understand me.

"No bigger than the one on Seventeenth last month," Jodi said dismissingly. I had to remember that New Yorkers are like Texans: their potholes are worse, their taxicab drivers more dangerous, and their people tougher than anyone else, damn what the facts might be.

"Construction areas don't count as potholes." I responded. "*Holy—!*"

I slammed on the brakes just in time to keep from going over into the ravine that now cut squarely across the packed and oiled rock-dirt roadway leading to the Slade homestead. Last time I'd been here there hadn't been a sign of such a thing; now it yawned, a raw gash in the earth, fully forty feet from the edge I sat on to the other side, eight feet deep on the right dropping to ten or twelve on the left as it passed out of sight into the old-growth forest.

We sat there for a few moments in silence, me waiting for my heart to stop pounding before I slowly backed the truck a few more feet from the edge, just in case. Jodi turned to me. "So you *had* to prove me wrong. Okay, that is bigger than the one on Seventeenth." She looked at the ravine with slightly wide eyes, the only sign she was going to let this disturb her New York sangfroid. "So, what, are we supposed to fill that in with our bare hands?"

"Stay here a minute." I reached down into the bag and grabbed the crowbar.

I walked to the edge, so I could look to the left and right. I could see, down below, the mound of jumbled dirt, trees, and rocks which marked the slide. The thing that bothered me—really, *really* bothered me—was how straight and selective this was. The slide started about fifty feet up the slope, cut across the road in a perfect right angle, and ended about a hundred feet below. I poked at the dirt with the crowbar; it crumbled like normal, not too wet, packed hard where the road was. There wasn't any sign of the usual slumping you get when the earth's moving because it's gotten too soggy and all. The road looked like someone had just cut a piece out of it with a giant knife, like a Bunyan-sized slice of earth pie. I listened. Not a sound except some water dripping off the trees in the fog—and the fog wasn't common this time of year, either. Seemed like the air was colder here than ought be. No animal sounds, the critters were quiet.

Maybe Mamma had been premature. This sure 'nuff looked like *that* kind of trouble to me.

Well, no help for it now. I studied the lay of the land. Awfully steep in parts but . . . I could probably make it around the upper end. Old-growth forest has some advantages, like usually bigger distances between the trees. I got back into the truck. "Jodi, get out and wait a ways down. I'll try and drive around."

"If you aren't scared to drive it, I'm not scared to ride it. And it's chilly out there."

"I *am* scared to drive it, but I ain't leavin' the truck parked here neither!" I heard my voice head all the way back home. Shoot, this wasn't good. "Look, Jodi, sweetheart, this kind of driving's really tricky, and I'll do better if I'm not worrying about you as a passenger while I'm trying to hold her steady on the slope."

Jodi rolled her eyes, then kissed my cheek and got out. I knew she would if I put it that way; it made practical sense, sure, but more importantly, it told her I didn't doubt her courage, just my concentration.

There was one really sticky moment when the earth near the top of the gouge started to give, but I gave her the gas and bounced clear before I could get dragged sideways. With only a couple of minor scratches to the side panels, I made it to the far side of the road. "YEEAH! Try 'n' stop a Slade that way, willya? *Ha!*" I shook the crowbar at the silent woods. "Okay, honey, you can come on over. Walk around the way I drove."

"Walk? You need sidewalks here, Clint! This isn't walking, this is an obstacle course!" Despite her complaints, Jodi was making her way through the woods at a respectable clip. She'd done hiking before. "I— *yow!*" Her figure seemed to vanish into the earth.

"Jodi!" I shouted in horror. Damnation, I should have made *her* take the crowbar! I had the whole car to protect me!

"Calm down, Clint!" Relief flooded me as I saw her rise back into sight, brushing leaves and dirt off. "I was just being a *schlemiel* and looking at you instead of where I was putting my big feet. Honestly, you worry like my grandmother." She emerged from the forest and got back into the car. "Well, so much for my perfect grooming."

"Don't worry none about that." I dropped the crowbar back into the bag and put the car in gear. "It's their fault for not watching for the slide and preventing it." That wasn't true, of course, if it was really what I suspected, but either way the family wouldn't blame Jodi for not looking her best. And as far as I was concerned, she'd look as good in jeans and a dirty T-shirt as in a formal gown.

There were no more incidents on the way up. We crested the last hill, came around the much smoother bend that led to Slade's Hollow, and came down through the woods into the open. "Whoa!" said Jodi involuntarily.

I couldn't repress a grin. "Yeah, y'all expected a couple log cabins and an outhouse, didn't you? Admit it, the Slades don't have a half-bad spread."

The Slade House really is something of a mansion, even if it is more spread out than up. Every generation adds a room or two somewhere, sorta like Lord Valentine's Castle. We try to keep a sort of style to it, but you can still tell where one generation left off and another started. The main part used for living these days was a massive mansion whose architecture was natural-looking logs and hewn stone—sort of a magnified version of what the earlier stuff had been, but if you knew anything about building you could tell that this thing hadn't been raised up by two farmers and their families; serious construction work had gone into the three-story, semicircular building.

"The original house is that small squarish part, off-center," I told Jodi, pointing. "That's where Winston Slade put his house back in 1802. It's used mostly for storage now. The funny addition over there is our generator shed, and on the other side's storage for tools, stuff like that. Got farm equipment in the barn there, even though we don't use it all that much— don't have to do much farming, so it's mostly just for the family."

"It's a mishmash all right, but pretty, you know? And this valley!"

"Yeah, the Hollow's pretty. One reason old Winston chose it was because it was already clear for building; figured it was a sign and built his house smack in the middle of the Hollow, on this little rise. And here we are."

I killed the engine and got out, Jodi doing the same on the other side. Our feet barely touched the ground before the front doors burst open and the Slade clan came running out, Mamma in the lead as usual. She was wearing her best dress, which was a pretty lace-embroidered blue and white affair that she'd only had to let out a size or two since she got married to Father and which set off her complexion and dark brown hair. There still wasn't a trace of gray in that thick hair. Either she just aged well or used dye that no one caught her at, but no one would have the guts to ask her.

"CLINT! Clinton! Welcome home, boy!" She gave me the usual huge hug and a kiss on the cheek, and turned to Jodi. "And this must be your Jodi! Welcome t' the Hollow, dear. Come on in, come on in, you're just in time for dinner!"

Adam clapped me on the back. "Quite a looker!" he murmured in my ear. "What's she see in you, Clint?"

I stuck my tongue out at him and crossed my eyes the way we used to when we were kids. "Maybe some-day I'll tell you my secret. After I've got her safely tied down with a ring!"

Adam chuckled at that. The girls have always loved

Adam. Standing six foot four and built like Conan the Barbarian, with the best of Mamma's softer rounded features tempering the edges and planes of the typical Slade face, he practically had to beat the girls off with a stick. I glanced towards my fiancée, to find that Mamma had taken charge of Jodi—well, as much as anyone can take charge of Jodi—and had her inside already.

I noticed that the gate had now rolled across the entrance to the Hollow, and heard the faint change in sound from the generators. Someone—probably Father—had engaged the electric fence.

Father was in the big family room when Adam and I got in, trailing behind everyone else. He gave me one of his usual nods. "Clint."

"Father." I gave him a hug, which he returned, then clasped hands for a moment.

"Been a while."

"Sorry, Father. I try to keep in touch."

He nodded. Not angry. Just quiet, as usual. Father didn't talk much, thought a lot, and acted when he had to. He was actually a tad shorter than me, but built as solid as the rock of the mountain; Father didn't have an ounce of fat on him but still outweighed me by about thirty pounds. Still, almost no one paid him mind when they first met him, on account of his being so quiet.

A booming laugh momentarily silenced everyone else. Grandpa Marlon was Father's opposite—he filled a room with his voice and his figure, standing taller even than Adam, with snow-white hair hanging to his shoulders and a rough-hewn face that reminded almost everyone of Charlton Heston. Evangeline, all long dark hair and pale face, was in the corner curled up on the padded armchair as usual, reading and watching. I didn't see Nellie or Helen, but that didn't really surprise me. Helen was going to be married herself soon, so she was probably out, and Nellie was trying to match her stride for stride, so to speak. Jonah was staring a bit too much at Jodi, but I remembered being fourteen myself, and in her New York getup Jodi was a pretty stareable sight.

I looked at Father again. "Road was out, Father. Down near Snake Rock."

His lips tightened. "Not the weather for slides."

"My thought, too."

"Fence is up. Don't worry for now." He looked at the dining room and started to head in that direction.

Mamma noticed. "Zeke! Ezekiel Slade! No one at the table yet!" Father stopped immediately; you didn't trifle with Mamma's directions. "Evangeline, could you be a treasure and help me set the table?" She noticed Jonah. "And stop standing around like a lump, Jonah Winston Slade! You and Adam go out and get Clint's truck unpacked and get their things to their rooms."

Jonah shook himself, looked at me enviously, and then nodded. "Yes, Mamma."

Jodi followed them out. "Whoa, boys, there's special equipment in there!"

Mamma seemed to think about protesting that she shouldn't do any work, but thought better of it. This was the opening I'd been hoping for. I went with Mamma into the kitchen to help her with the food— as usual, there was enough to feed an army. "Mamma . . ." I said, letting a warning tone creep into my voice.

She blinked up at me. "Something wrong, Clint dear?"

"The road was out. And it wasn't no landslide, neither."

She busied herself with the roast.

"You told me there wasn't any of that going on."

"Well, dear . . ." she said, in the voice she used when

she was trying to get around Father, " . . . there *wasn't* any of that when I told you *then*. Just seems to have started in the last couple of days."

"I know that voice, Mamma! Don't try no dancin' around this one! Just what—"

"Clinton! Don't take that tone of voice with me! I can still tan your hide, boy, and I won't need no help to do it, neither!"

I backed down; getting Mamma mad wouldn't help. "Sorry, Mamma. Did anything happen that might have . . . started it again?"

"Clint, we've got your wedding and Helen's, and ain't going to be no surprise if Nellie's and even Adam's come pretty quick. And of course we're going to do you proud, son."

For a minute I was completely befuddled. What the heck did all that have to do with . . . "Oh, for the love of—Mamma Bea, you *didn't*!"

"I just sent Adam down for a little extra."

I couldn't believe this. "Mamma, you can't possibly be telling me we were broke again?"

She was slicing the roast in perfectly even slices— something I never did learn how to do, even though I was in some ways a better cook than Mamma. "Broke? Clint, darling, of course not. But ain't nothing wrong with thinkin' ahead, is there? Takes a powerful lot of money to keep the Slades running, and what with building Helen her new house—"

I closed my eyes and rubbed my temples. I could see where this was going. The Slades had always been rich, but never learned to keep it. Spend it like water, that was the Slade way. Why learn about investment and things like that? Need more money, just go get some. I suppose I should have expected something on those lines—the last time the family refilled the vault was, as Mamma said, when Grandpa Marlon

took his last trip, and besides all the living expenses
there'd been additions and enhancements to the
house, all the gadgets that the Slade clan loved—
Mamma couldn't get enough of the home theater and
DVDs (she had just about the complete *Dark Shadows* collection, an expense big enough to show up in
the budget of any third-world country), and even
Father seemed to enjoy his own time with a computer
almost as much as he liked doing his woodworking—
and of course putting the first Slade in a century or
more through a real expensive college with no schol-
arship.

" . . . so you see, Clint dear, weren't much choice.
And no point putting things off, so I sent Adam off."

"You knew I was worried about this happening!
Couldn't you have waited a week or so, until after me
and Jodi left?"

"Clint. Enough, now."

I hadn't heard Father enter. "Yes, Father."

Father took up one platter, I took up another and
followed him out. "Your Mamma is who she is. Works
hard to be a Slade even though she weren't born one.
Sometimes that's not all to the good. 'Taint no point
worryin'. Trouble usually doesn't come here, even bad
times. Scared of the Hollow. Keep her busy here,
shouldn't see anything. Right, son?"

I smiled reluctantly. Father always reminded me of
Unc Nunkie from the Oz books; this was a long and
involved conversation for him. "Right, Father."

Mamma's voice suddenly boomed from the intercom
she'd had strung through the whole house. "Dinner!
Come an' get it!"

Even though Jodi was an extra, Mamma had taken
out one leaf from the table since Nellie and Helen
weren't here, so it wasn't hard to join hands to say
Grace. Jodi looked slightly uncomfortable, but the

Slades knew a lot of people who weren't of the Faith, so it didn't cause a bad moment like it might with some families—no pressure on her to follow along with the prayer.

Then we all got to eat, which was what we'd all been waiting for. The roast, as should have been obvious, was only the centerpiece. Potatoes, green beans, salad (which didn't used to be a fixture, but me and the girls pushed for it), sweet potato pie, biscuits, well, just so much food we had to eat fast before the table broke. And then there were the desserts! When Mamma set out to show off her cookin' skills, she didn't stop until you surrendered. Luckily, one thing Jodi wasn't traditional about was food; I hadn't had to face the horror of tryin' to tell Mamma that she'd have to change the way she cooked.

Jodi had done the wise thing, and eaten small servings of everything. I just plowed ahead and ate from one end of the table to the other, and paid the price with pain in my stomach later. Then again, I always eat more when I'm nervous, and damn-all but I was nervous tonight. Bad enough I was watching them decide what to think about my fiancée, but I had to worry about what Adam had stirred up at Mamma's orders.

I started to relax as the dinner wound down. Jodi got up and insisted on helping Mamma clean up. Even though cleanup's a lot easier with an industrial-sized dishwasher, there's still work to be done after a king-sized feeding like that one, and Jodi was scoring big points with Mamma by showing that, city girl or not, she'd do her share. I just hoped she didn't end up washing the actual pots and pans. Willing Jodi might be, good at cleaning dishes she wasn't. I always ended up having to rewash the ones she thought she'd scrubbed. And if Mamma found a spot of food left on one of her big pans . . . well, it'd be the Big Lecture for me.

Apparently that passed without incident, because Jodi and Mamma came out with Mamma reeling off her recipe for the sweet potato pie and leading Jodi into the big family room, where the instruments were being dragged out from the huge closets on the sides or taken down from the dark-paneled walls. The family room was just about large enough to play tennis in, but what with all the little tables, big comfy chairs and couches and all, it seemed right cozy.

"I hear tell from Clint you're a damn fine singer," Grandpa Marlon said. "The Slades always been a musical family too; mind if we indulge?"

"No, please do," Jodi said.

"Join in if you feel like it, dear."

I sat down to watch and join in the singing. I liked listening, and I felt too rusty to just join in right away. Mamma was on the piano—Nellie was better than she was, but of course Nellie wasn't here—Grandpa had his banjo, Father a guitar, Adam the big standup bass, and of course Jonah had an electric guitar, as might've been expected. Without Helen, we were short our main vocals. The family did several numbers Jodi didn't know, though I could hear her start to hum along with the choruses, but when we started up "Amazing Grace," she sat up; I knew she liked that song. I'd wondered about that, like how she could perform in Handel's *Messiah* with her background— to which she'd replied: "*Oy*, don't be silly. First, I'm a terrible Jew—I eat *trayf* sometimes. Second, beautiful music is beautiful music. I even like Wagner, which my grandfather would be like to explode over if I said it to his face. But Wagner was a great musician, just a complete *schmendrick* as a person."

I've always liked "Amazing Grace" myself; but once

Jodi started singing it, you could see that even the rest of the Slades hadn't heard anything like it before. That voice, that could fill a concert hall without a single bit of electronic assistance, took the old spiritual and made it Jodi's own song of joy and thankfulness. There was a hush in the family room when the song ended, everyone else having stopped playing to hear her last notes. Grandpa spoke, finally. "Young lady, if'n I were wearin' a hat, I'd take it off to you. As it is, I have to say Clint didn't do you justice. Sing just like the angels, you do."

This time it was Jodi who blushed crimson. "More like a bellowing angel. I'm a belter, not a real singer."

"Don't sell yourself short," I said. "You're the best singer I know, Jodi."

"Can she do the glass trick?" Mamma wanted to know.

"Mamma!"

Jodi laughed. "Don't worry, Clint. Believe it or not, singers like me do sometimes get that question. I could, Mamma Slade, but it usually only works with pretty good glasses, and I wouldn't want to break anything valuable."

"Nonsense! I can always get more glasses—why, with all these young 'uns I've had through the years, I've gone through more'n one set of them anyways. But I've always thought that was just some fancy trick on stage."

"Well, it takes just the right pitch, and if your voice is off, it won't work. But if you really want . . ."

Mamma went to the cabinet and got out one of the leftover glasses from the set she'd had when I was young; yeah, I remembered breaking one of those. Only two left. "That one good enough?" she asked.

Jodi tapped the rim of the glass while everyone was silent. "B-sharp," I said automatically. She nodded. "In my higher range. But I think I'm loosened up enough . . ."

She put the glass down on the table, took a deep breath, and then opened her mouth wide, letting a single note build upward from a gentle hum to an almost deafening single-toned sound that escaped being a shriek only by sheer purity. As it built, you could hear an answering undertone, as the glass's resonant frequency was found, building, rebuilding upon itself, a positive feedback loop that caused the crystal to vibrate, blur, and with an abruptness that startled all of us even though we knew what was happening, it virtually exploded in a shimmer of transparent shrapnel.

"HooooEEE!" Grandpa and Mamma said at the same time.

"Wow!" Jonah exclaimed.

Jodi giggled. I grinned. "Luckily you use your powers for good and not evil."

"What about you, Clint?" Father said, as Mamma and Evangeline set about cleaning up the shattered glass; they wouldn't let Jodi help, of course, since Mamma had asked her to do the trick in the first place. "Haven't made a note yet."

"Aww, I'm too rusty, Father."

"Fiddlesticks, Clinton!" Mamma retorted, going to the trash bin. "Jonah, you get Clinton his fiddle."

Jodi looked at me. "That's right, you mentioned you used to play violin some."

"Some?" Adam laughed. "You know that song about the Devil? If'n the Devil came to Kentucky, it'd be Clint he'd be after."

"And he'd whip me good, too," I said, taking the fiddle from Jonah since Mamma weren't taking no for an answer. "But what the heck."

The lights flickered. A moment later I heard the backup generator come online. The family relaxed, but I could see Jodi was surprised by the change; for a moment, she'd seen the family in a completely different way. Every single Slade had stood, poised for action, and both Grandpa Marlon and Father had long iron bars in their hands—taken from concealed locations under their chairs. "Dang it all, Adam!" Grandpa said. "Who's forgotten to make sure the main generator's supplied again?"

It had broken the mood, for the time at least. I went to help Adam put more fuel into the generators. "Grandpa forgot that we drew almost twice normal load all day," Adam grumbled. "Mamma's been working everyone overtime. Shouldn't have had to refill until tomorrow."

"'Don't think ahead, can't keep ahead,'" I quoted at him, checking the oil levels; I noticed that one of the generators was a new model, put in since last year; Father wasn't taking any chances.

"Yeah, yeah, I know. No excuses, just results." He tightened the cap down. "Okay, now we're done."

We went back inside, where Mamma had gotten Jodi to take her on in chess. I hoped she wasn't suckered into a bet; the only person who ever beat Mamma was Grandpa Marlon, and I more than half suspected that she let him win sometimes because his pride couldn't take the constant humiliation of having his daughter-in-law take him to the cleaners every time they played. I'm not that bad, but Mamma could beat me while she was busy watching TV. I studied the board, realizing that I'd actually never played Jodi. They were already past the point where I tended to concede to Mamma; looked like either Jodi was a heck of a lot better than I'd guessed, or Mamma didn't want to embarrass her by beating her too soon. Seeing the way Mamma was pursing her lips, though, I had to grin. Nope, she wasn't taking it easy; Jodi was making her work for it.

"Mate in five moves," I joked; Mamma knew I

couldn't see more than three moves ahead even if I worked at it.

"Six," Jodi said absently. Mamma blinked and stared at her, then bent over the board with renewed concern. I repressed a snort of laughter, as I could see the little twitch at the corner of Jodi's mouth that she always got when she was having someone on.

As that game was probably going to last a while, I went and joined Evangeline and Jonah at the entertainment center for a bit, taking turns beating the heck out of each other in the latest *Virtual Fighter* game. Just as Evangeline kicked me out of the ring, I heard Mamma's clear voice: "Well, now, I know when I'm beaten," followed by the clicking sound of her king being tipped over.

"Well, if that don't beat all," Marlon muttered from his armchair.

Evangeline finally spoke. She generally was even quieter than Father. Turning to me, she said, "You keep her."

"Oh, believe me, I mean to."

3. Night Movements

"Usually I'm up for a nosh before bed, but your mamma stuffed me so much I think I'm like to roll down the hall." Jodi stared at the three-decker BLT I was eating. "Clint, you keep eating like that and you'll look like Elvis."

"Thank yuh. Thankyuhverramuch," I said, with the proper accent. "I've been eatin' like this all my life. I exercise a lot, you know. And I know we'll be doing a lot of luggin' equipment around tomorrow, right?"

"Right. This is actually a good place to test. The

New Madrid zone runs right through part of this county."

Jodi's current project was based on acoustic engineering research funded partly by NYU and partly by some interested commercial firms with some government backing. My main skills lay outside of that—I was a dual major, geology and compsci—but they intersected perfectly with the intent of the project, which was actually what had brought us together. It'd long been noted that some animals can apparently sense approaching earthquakes, and some work had been done showing that the Earth emitted varying levels of sound at different wavelengths ranging from infrasound—acoustic waves below about 20 cycles—and up to a bat-level ultrasound in the hundreds of thousands of cycles. Our team had modeled a number of possible interactions of the layers of soil, stone, and so on involved in fault systems, and it seemed to indicate that you should be able to detect both the main movement of an earthquake, and some of the precursors to it, through sound waves (rather than the related shockwaves recorded on seismographs). If the precursors could be detected, we'd have a possible way of actually predicting earthquakes. So if Jodi's sensor packages seemed to be getting reasonable readings, she'd probably just leave a set of them operating here; it was, as she said, a good potential location, with the fault system responsible for the greatest quake in the history of the United States passing by this very area.

"I notice," she continued, "we've got separate rooms."

"You had better believe it."

She grinned. "Hey, I'm not really *kvetching*; you wouldn't be getting the same room as me if we were staying at my house either." She looked out into the darkness. "Your family seems really nice, Clint. Okay, they are kinda weird, with this strange combination of hick and twenty-first-century gadget freaks, but they're trying to make me feel welcome, and I can tell they love the hell out of you. So why didn't you bring me here earlier?"

I looked down. Part of it of course was *that* problem, but it wasn't the only thing. "I guess I should've had more faith in them. I wasn't sure how they'd react to you. I mean, let's be honest, you're a—"

"JAP. Jewish-American Princess. I know, you can't say it because I'd knock your block off, but I can say it, because it's true. But I'm not like some of the others, and you know it. We work good together as a team, and did before we started dating. You do the modeling work and I do the tinkering and we and the rest do the brainstorming. So what's to worry about?"

"Some of the family's still pretty . . . fundamentalist. I didn't know how they'd take a Jewish daughter-in-law."

"You're right, you should have had more faith in them," she said tartly. Then she shrugged. "But I guess I wasn't sure how I'd introduce you to my family at first, either, and if they'd been like seven hundred miles away maybe I wouldn't have taken you to meet them yet."

I suspected she would have anyway, but I wasn't going to argue about this—since it might then get back around to what *other* reasons I might have for not bringing her to meet the folks.

"Well, you may still be hungry, but me, I'm just tired."

I walked her to her room, which was just down from Mamma and Father's. They might be being friendly, but they weren't taking any chances on anything happening under their roof.

Afterward, I went outside to take a look around the homestead. The lights from the house and the ones dotted around the property nearby let me make my way. Let me tell you, if you're from the city, you have no clue as to what dark is. The only thing darker than an overcast Kentucky night is a cave, and having been in both many times since I was a kid, there isn't much difference. Without the faint light from the homestead, I could've gotten lost fifteen feet from the front door.

A darker shadow against the night showed me where Adam was standing.

"Hey, Adam."

"Clint. Congratulations again."

"Thanks. Look, I hear Mamma sent you down."

"Yeah. S'pose that was a mistake?"

I shrugged, but nodded. "I think she should've waited until after we'd left. Nothing that desperate."

"Well, you know Mamma; once she gets an idea in her head, three wild bulls couldn't drag it outta her."

"Hadn't the place moved?"

"Well, sure 'nuff, but you know almost as much as me about that. Only so many places it gets moved to. Won't no one need to go down for a time now, anyway."

"You got a lot?"

He chuckled. "Grandpa Marlon was a little jealous. Got more than he did, last trip."

That startled me. "You got the biggest haul in our whole history?"

"Sure 'nuff. Three double handfuls. Stuffed the bag I had."

"Jesus!" The word was shocked out of me involuntarily. "Sorry, Adam. But . . . Jeez. That's going to actually take serious time to convert."

He laughed. "Not hardly. Sure, in the older days it was kinda hard but now with the markets open an' all? And the Internet connections and international market? I'd placed 'em with potential buyers 'fore you ever got here. Only a few left for us to keep for jewelry 'n' such."

I blinked. Yeah, things had changed that much. "Two things for Grandpa to be jealous over, then."

"Yep." He stared out at the fence. So did I. Was that movement?

"Father said something about the road," Adam said after a minute.

"Have to get it fixed. Forty feet got taken out by a slide."

"*They* did that."

I did the shrug-and-nod again. "That's my guess."

"Darn. Sorry, Clint."

"Guess we'll have to just hope nothing happens we can't explain to her."

"Or that we can hide it fast."

We both knew how important it was. If anyone else knew, the Slade gravy train would probably come to a screeching halt.

"Well," I said finally. "Guess I should head to bed."

"Me too. Forty feet of road . . . good thing we've got the equipment and supplies already. Might even need some cement to make concrete with, reinforce it you know."

"Might could. Won't protect the rest of it, but the whole area might be in need of that kind of stability. I'll help."

"If your lady'll let you off, we won't turn down another pair of hands."

"Heck, she'll help herself. She's got her own calluses."

Adam followed me in. "Guess she might, at that. Sure didn't have trouble carryin' her bags herself."

I went to my room. Undressing with the light off as usual, I kept an eye out the window. The moon showed now through an occasional ragged break in the clouds. Suddenly I saw movement.

Yeah. They were there, looking at the house almost as though they could see me looking back, two of them. Looked like they might be armed. But still, they didn't try to pass the fence. Not yet, anyway. I saw other movement near them, but didn't look too closely. There are things that give me the creeps when I see them, so I try not to. I pulled the steel shutters over the window and locked them. Even with that and the door locked, it was a while before I fell asleep.

4. Echoes of the Present

"Are we getting a signal now?" Jodi asked, having adjusted the reception parameters again and checked the fifth probe's functioning.

"We get signal," I said in a monotone. "Main screen turn on."

"You run through that stupid routine once more, wise guy, and all your mouth is belong to duct tape."

"What you say???"

"I mean it!"

"Anybody want a peanut?"

"C'mon, Clint, stop the comedy, I want to see if this works!"

"So do I," I said seriously. "I was making the last adjustments. You do the honors."

It had been, for me, a tense couple of days, as she'd seemed almost on the edge of asking questions I couldn't have dodged well, and *they* had assuredly been active. Like asking about the steel shutters, which we'd explained with older history about local feuds and some later paranoia born of the Cold War and survivalist themes. Fortunately she'd been with Mamma, talking nonstop about dresses and color schemes, when Jonah had come running in to me and Father to give us the news about the hole in the storage shed and the concrete all going missing. I'd made a virtue of that necessity, heading into town with Jodi so we could be together while picking up the concrete—and while Father and Adam fixed the shed so it looked okay. After getting the road repaired the last two days—well, making new road, really—Jodi and I had finally gotten around to setting up SUITS, the Subterranean Ultra-Infrasonic Tracking System.

"Here goes," she said. "Igor, throw the switch!"

The screen flickered, then began to show a multicolored jumble of lines and dots all over the place. There was a big central blob, some dark and light areas, and so on. To a layman, it would look like a modern art piece, but we could tell there was some kind of structure there. "*Oooooooy vey*," Jodi moaned. "Look at that, the signal's such total *schmootz* I can't make out anything."

"Hey, don't worry. That's the raw signal. Looks like the gadget's working just fine. I just have to clean up the signal. I could do averaging, but if we're looking for individual signals that might really screw up things."

"We're sampling at two GS," she pointed out. "We could probably take five, ten and average them without losing too much, unless all the signal we want is on the really high limit."

I nodded. "Probably. And it's already sorting by band . . . maybe I can take each band separately and focus on individual strong-signal regions."

We started fiddling with the various algorithms I'd already coded into SUITS. Slowly a more clear-cut image began to appear on the screen, although it would have been no less arcane to a layman.

Jodi stared at it. "What sort of cockamamie signal is that?"

I had to admit it had me stumped too. There was a huge zone under the Hollow that was . . . different. Signals changed going through it. I tried some analysis on it. "Dense. Really, really, really dense, Jodi. Specific gravity over five, at least."

"Totally *meshuggeneh*, Clint. There's almost no natural rock even close to that density, except—" Suddenly she stood and stared around her. Then she bent back to the display. "Clint, look—gimme a better look at some of the signals coming in from here. Yeah. Now, what's that say to you?"

I was starting to get her drift. "I think I see. That's why the Hollow looks like it does."

"One big mass of nickel-iron. Your Hollow is a meteor crater."

"Darned if you ain't right." I caught myself before commenting on how much sense everything made now.

"And look here, around the area—these deader spots. Clint, I think you've got caves running through your property!"

Ice seemed to pierce my heart. I tried to act casual. "Where?"

"Look. You know there's karst all over around here, it isn't unlikely. Isn't this part over near the road? Maybe that's why it slid, some kind of small cave-in or sinkhole."

She wasn't far wrong, of course. "Yeah, that would make sense."

"Maybe there's even an entrance around somewhere!"

"I'd think we'd have found it in the past few centuries."

She looked crestfallen. "I guess you would, yeah. Darn, but I would've loved to see a new cave! Well, at least we're stopping by Mammoth Caves on the way back, right?"

"I promised, didn't I? Didn't I know you were a caver? Just didn't want to stop on the way up, we'd have spent a day and a half there, I know you."

She nodded, grinning sheepishly.

"Anyway, this isn't helping us check out the real signals. I'll have to clean 'em up from the interference here, start trying to sort out different patterns, all that, and then correlate them with tremors in the area."

"Right, right. It's running good now."

"Sure is."

We left SUITS to gather data for a while, and went to join Adam, who'd invited us to go fishing. While fishing wasn't Jodi's favorite thing, she was a good sport about it. Me, I was just glad to have a distraction while I recovered from yet another near miss.

That evening, I filled in Father, Helen, Grandpa, and Adam on our discovery.

"By thunder, that explains it! No wonder they almost never tread on the home ground!"

Father nodded. "Good thing."

Couldn't argue with that. I'd seen what the back of the storage shed looked like. If that was what they could manage in a desperate raid, half blind and stretched to the limit, I hated to think what would have happened if they hadn't been slowed up.

After everyone went to bed that evening, I had my own portable crunching away at the signals. There were some interesting patterns turning up. I was trying various signal envelopes, filters, and so on to see if I could make any sense of them. They were clearly signals, not random noise, but it's always hard to figure out what a given signal is if you don't have a prior reference point. And these were pretty faint; processing could pull them out of the noise floor, but they weren't big, clear signals that I could rely on correlating with something else. Something about their general patterns seemed vaguely familiar, but the familiarity just wouldn't gel. Oh, well, I'd figure it out eventually.

It was the middle of the next morning that Jodi came running out of the house to where Adam, Father, and I were doing maintenance on the generators. "Clint! Clint, come on! You have to see this!"

"What?"

"Come on! You'll love it! I was looking over the whole signal plot and I think—well, never mind, we'll see when we get there!"

I looked at Father and Adam. They'd looked interested when she first came over, but their eyes started to glaze over when she said "signal plot." Father gave a tolerant nod and let Jodi drag me off.

To my surprise, we went straight past the house and started up Cold Breeze Hill. "Hey, I thought you found something on the plot!"

"I did!"

I followed her, a sense of foreboding building as we went up. Her footsteps slowed as she found herself walking a well-defined path, worn by feet that had climbed those very stones hundreds—maybe thousands—of times since the dawn of the nineteenth century.

Her eyes narrowed and I swallowed. "I found a signal pattern that seemed to indicate that a cave came very near the surface here," she said quietly as she continued to walk.

I was silent. We rounded the last corner, passing between Winston's Gap—two huge boulders that forced you to walk single-file.

And there it was, a yawning hole in the ground with the massive iron grate secured across it with a heavy steel bar and chained with a hardened steel padlock.

The big metal sign across it blazoned SLADE FAMILY
PROPERTY. KEEP OUT.

Jodi stared at the barrier, large enough to make a
decent bank vault, and finally turned to me. "Okay,
Clint. What in hell is going on here?"

I closed my eyes. Was there any way . . . ?

Not a chance, I answered myself. Too many mysteries, and this one just couldn't be explained away. Not
with her caving enthusiasm and my evasion of the
subject only yesterday.

"I think you'd better come back to the house. We've
got a lot of talking to do."

Jodi followed me. It was not a companionable silence.

5. Wealth of History

Father started out. "All begins with Winston Slade."

Winston Slade had been quite a character. Son of
a butler for one of the English nobility (family legend
differed on just who), he'd run away and ended up in
Holland, where he made a sort of living performing
odd jobs until one of the local jewelers gave him a
chance to apprentice. Winston didn't mind the work,
but after a while his restlessness got the better of him,
and he took his accumulated savings—what little there
was—and got a boat to America. He arrived in 1795
and immediately started working his way across the
country, doing whatever jobs came to hand. He had
a reputation as a man who'd try anything once, and
never complain no matter how hard, dirty, or dangerous. He fought Indians in the mountains, caught at least
one outlaw himself, was suspected of smuggling activities, and joined a traveling group of performers (who
might, some said, be a fancy group of thieves) for a

few months. Finally he reached the interior of Kentucky and decided that now, at the age of thirty-three, he was getting tired of the constant movement. He found a girl who could put up with him—Genevive Vandemeer—and the two of them packed up everything they owned and set out to find a homestead. When Winston found the Hollow, he knew he had arrived. He built the house with his own hands and started working on becoming a settled farmer.

"Winston weren't exactly a wanderer," Grandpa said. "He wandered because he wanted excitement. When he settled down, he meant to do it. But it wasn't easy on him."

This made the cave he found some years after they settled a godsend. It gave him a dangerous and challenging place to explore that nonetheless kept him near home. Genevive didn't like it, of course, but it was better than Winston either forcing her to move every few years, or just running off into the sunset.

By the end of 1811, Winston Slade had explored a considerable stretch of cave, methodically working his way inward, taking different sources of light and taking far fewer chances than might be expected. He enjoyed doing his explorations especially during the winter, as the underground passages were actually warmer than the air above. On December 2, 1811, Winston descended into the darkness for a two-day exploration jaunt. By this time, Genevive had grown accustomed to his periodic explorations. She was no shrinking violet and as long as he left her a gun, plenty of firewood, and food for the time, she was perfectly content to take care of things for a few days. On at least one occasion Winston had come back to find a bear laid out for skinning, Genevive having shot it when it got too close to the family holdings.

Winston took a new path downward which, after a

short steep run, led into a number of magnificent caverns whose extent he could hardly grasp. While exploring the side passages, he came across a cave dotted with fascinating pools filled with various types of stones. This puzzled Winston. He had seen "cave pearls" before, but this wasn't the same thing; each pool had a particular sort of stone in it, rounded as though from water flow. He wondered what sort of process would sort out minerals like that.

It didn't occur to him at that point that there was anything intelligent behind the pattern. While he'd occasionally heard odd sounds and movements in his explorations, he'd never seen anything to give evidence that there was really anything down there. He was the only man who'd ever descended this far into the earth that he knew of.

One particular pool, filled with translucent pebbles, attracted his attention. With the shimmering, pure cave water pouring down into the pool, the stones seemed almost like landborne clouds or ghosts of pebbles. Idly he reached in and picked up a few, rolling them around in his hand.

It was at that moment that he noticed something— a particular glint of light, a feel, he was never quite sure—that tugged on memories from twenty years before. Hardly able to believe it, he tried the pebbles on his jackknife; the knife scratched. The file he carried in his pocket, hardened in his own hand-forge, couldn't make a mark on them.

Winston let out a whoop which could have been heard for miles in the caves, had there been anyone to hear it, and scooped out the pebbles, stuffing them into his pockets. He considered checking the rest of the pools, but he was too eager to get out and show Genevive.

As he turned to go, Winston suddenly felt his blood

run cold. He saw something moving at the edge of his light, where nothing should move at all. If he could have, he would have extinguished the torches, but he knew that if he ever lost the light, he'd never get it back. And did he want to be alone in the dark with the shape he could barely see?

So he tried to hide behind a large stalagmite. The shape came on, carefully stopping at each pool and waiting a moment before moving on. It paid no immediate attention to the torches or Winston, and it dawned on the ancestor of the Slade clan that the thing was blind in the normal sense. Clearly it could make its way around without help, but it wasn't using sight or smell. Winston began edging slowly away from it, and received confirmation that it could not, in fact, see him. Winston still moved very carefully, as he suspected the thing had other senses—possibly hearing, or something more outlandish.

The creature was making its way methodically along the array of pools, and Winston realized it wouldn't be long before it reached the pool he'd just emptied. It was then that it dawned on him that these pools must be something special to this creature. Maybe it was a miner, as well. What it might do when it found one of its pools emptied was something Winston didn't care to find out. The thing might be shorter than him, but its color and the way it moved gave him the impression of something with the solidity of stone. Winston grabbed up one of the torches, made sure the rest of his equipment was secure, and headed for the exit as quickly as he dared.

His foot struck a pebble just as he reached the tunnel, and the rattling, clicking sound echoed like thunder around the cavern. Instantly the creature's head turned in his direction, and it began walking purposefully towards him.

Seeing that stiff-limbed mockery of a man shambling towards him, Winston panicked. He spun and dashed off, hearing something like an unoiled gate screech behind him.

"Winston got out, of course, or we wouldn't be here to talk about it," I finished. "He and Genevive darn near moved out that day, momentarily wondering if he was atop a stairway to Hell, but the lure of money was stronger. Plus, with the relief born of escaping the things, Winston's curiosity returned."

"Whoa, whoa, whoa!" Jodi said. "What, is this the reverse of the old bit where the city slickers play tricks on the country rube? Are you serious?"

For answer, Adam pulled on one of the fireplace bricks, which opened a concealed vault. He reached in and tossed what he found to Jodi.

Jodi looked at the rough pebble. "Diamonds? Here? Isn't that crazy talk?"

I shook my head. "Turns out there's three places you find kimberlite pipes in Kentucky. One of them is in this county, not far from here. No one's ever found a diamond in Kentucky, but as near as I can figure it, the Nomes can dig into 'em at a level no one's ever reached before and there's diamonds down there."

Jodi looked at me. "'Nomes'?"

I blushed while the rest of the family laughed. "Ayup, Nomes indeed!" Grandpa Marlon boomed. "Old Winston called 'em kobolds, or somethin' close to that, but when little Clint saw 'em first he was readin' them Oz books an' so he started callin' them Nomes, and their leader, assumin' they got one, Ruggedo."

"Okay, so it's silly. Still the way I think of them."

"So," Jodi said, "these 'Nomes' or 'kobolds' have been after you guys ever since for stealing their diamonds, like a leprechaun and his gold or something?"

"Something like that," I said. "Winston figured out

a lot of stuff about them in the next few years. The reason they had a hard time tracking him was because he carried iron with him. Cold iron, he remembered, was one of the ways of dealing with the faerie folk. Most of their senses didn't do well around iron and steel. I guess they're doing some kind of electromagnetic sensing. They could hear some things and make sounds—pretty creepy ones. They don't do their tunneling themselves, they've got some kind of rockworms that do that for them. And their tunneling creates things that look just like natural caverns, complete with the formations. We're not sure yet what they actually want all those minerals for; maybe they eat them or something."

Mamma handed me the secret album, and I flipped to the centerpiece. Jodi sucked in her breath. The things in the picture could be faked by modern technology, but the picture was clearly from twenty, thirty years ago. The thin-looking legs and arms attached to the more massive body were very like Baum's Nomes, while at a distance the head with its mass of crystals atop and fluted tube below could look like something with a head of hair and pointed beard. The crystalline "eyes" were located about where a human's would be, so overall the effect was very bizarrely humanoid, in a creepy way. The thing had a braided crystalline harness around its body, holding what looked like a sword sheath and some other crystal-and-stone accoutrements.

Next to it was a low-slung thing, apparently of the same general order of living creatures by its gray-rock luster, but otherwise unrelated. It was much more reminiscent of centipedes in general construction, but the head glittered with points and tubes and glints of grinding structures. It was a clearly alien thing with an even more alien purpose.

"I took that shot," Mamma said proudly. "Second time down, first time seeing them, never let out a peep."

"Developed it herself too," Father said. "Mamma Bea insisted we get pictures."

"*Oy!*" Jodi shook her head. "So, these things are real. I believe you. So what did you mean 'something like that,' when I asked you that question?"

"The Nomes lost track of Winston when he ran away, and for a while nothing happened. Winston found he could sneak around and spy on them, sometimes, without them noticing. For the next few years Winston didn't go down much, though, because there were the New Madrid Quakes which made anyone going underground awfully nervous. About 1816 he started regular trips again, this time focused on scouting out the Nome territory. Either he got clumsy or they got lucky, but this time they followed him to the exit. They don't seem particularly inclined to violence, but they seemed to want something from him and made a nuisance of themselves for a few days, though they never seemed able to actually approach the homestead."

"After the second time Winston got himself some diamonds, though," Helen continued, "they changed their approach. Even tried to get into the house, though they clearly were almost blind here. Winston found he could bash them senseless with an iron bar and they were almost unable to hit back."

Jodi glanced at me. She'd finally made the connection between my habit of carrying a crowbar and the family history. "So, you've been dropping in on these poor people every few years and stealing their diamonds, and then you have the *chutzpah* to beat them over the head when they object? Have I got this straight, now?"

The family stared at her open-mouthed. While, upon

reflection, I agreed with her assessment, I don't think anyone else had ever put it that way before.

Father got his voice back first. "Point," he admitted.

"I'm impressed," she said sarcastically. "And here I'd thought all the eminent domain conquests and oppression of the native population had been finished years ago."

"It wasn't as if they were doing anything with the stones, girl!" Grandpa objected. "Just leavin' them sit in pools o' water. We had better use for 'em."

"And if someone decided you weren't making use of your furniture, what, you think they could just come in and take it?"

"Hold on, let's not get in a big argument here," I said, to head off an explosion by Grandpa. "For what it's worth, Jodi, I agree with you. I didn't think it through before. So what do you think we should do?"

"Have you geniuses ever thought of talking to them?"

"Not recently," I admitted. "But several times people have tried to communicate. They don't seem to be able to see writing the way we do, and admittedly both sides are either mad or scared whenever they meet, which doesn't dispose them towards expending lots of effort to understand us. On our side, well, if they've got a language we haven't noticed it yet. They carry some things that look like tools, but darned if anyone's ever seen them making one, so we don't even know how they do things in their civilization."

Jodi frowned. "Well, it's a *furblungit* mess, I'll say that. But Clint, you tell me: is that picture one of an animal or a person?"

"Person," I said without hesitation.

"Well, then?"

The family was silent for a long moment. Then Grandpa heaved a long sigh. "Girl, you have a tongue for sure, and I don't know whether I envy Clint now. But damn-all, I guess you're right. Can't keep going down there takin' a man's stuff without even askin'. Even if the man's made of stone."

Jodi failed miserably to hide a look of superior triumph. "So you'll go return this last batch, right? Maybe that will start a communication going with them!"

We winced, and Adam bit his lip. "Um, Jodi? Can't rightly do that. Don't have them any more."

"What?"

"Most of 'em are already sold. We kept some as a reserve, but given the way they work it's not like we're gonna try to hide 'em in the cellar. They're in the safety deposit down to the bank."

She grabbed my keys off the table. "Okay, then, Clint, let's head on down to the bank and make that withdrawal."

There was a distant rumble of thunder. I opened the door, expecting to see clouds, but the sky was clear blue. "What in—?"

Then I saw the cloud of gray-brown dust rising from the trees. "Father!" I started running towards the forest. Jodi and the rest of the family followed.

I skidded to a halt a hundred yards into the forest. "Holy Mother!"

The prior damage to the road had been nothing. A yawning pit over a hundred feet wide dropped straight into the earth, edges surrounded somehow by upthrust rock that formed a barrier that even my truck would never pass. It would take weeks to make a new way around.

Grandpa came puffing up behind everyone else, his bum leg having slowed him up. "Kids! Kids! Get back to the house now!" He caught sight of the hole in the mountainside and cursed. "Listen!"

We listened. The forest was as silent as a grave.

Then we heard faint, deliberate movement. Heading towards us.

Slades aren't cowards, but we're not stupid either. The Nomes couldn't drop the homestead, sitting on that massive, unsuspected foundation of nickel-iron, but they could take the ground where we stood out from under us. And they were aboveground, in force, in the daytime.

"Something about this last raid," I said, "seems to have really pissed them off!"

"Never done this before?" Jodi asked.

"Nothing on this scale," said Mamma Bea, handing Jodi a length of steel bar.

As we rounded the bend towards the gate, something burst from the underbrush, a shining stone weapon leveled at Jodi, screeching like a berserk set of rusty springs running over potholes. In bright daylight, there was little human about it—sparkling crystals on its head, faintly fluorescent violet eye-crystals, and that howling screech from the tube in its face which made me and Father jump back.

Jodi didn't even flinch. Her steel bar parried the stone sword and carried it around in a disarming arc that sent the weapon spinning away.

"What, don't get pushy with me! I've seen taxi drivers scarier than you!" Her New York accent was strong enough to cut, the only sign of how scared she really was. Jodi poked her bar in its stony chest, making it shrink back in disorientation, holding its arms up defensively. "Back off!"

It stumbled backward, bumping into another one that had belatedly decided to try to back up its buddy. We took advantage of the delay to make it through the gate and lock it.

"Power on, boy!" shouted Grandpa.

"Way ahead of you, Grandpa!" Jonah shouted, outsprinting me as he streaked towards the house. We saw a dozen—two dozen—gray figures at the fence, pulling at it. Strong and well fastened as we'd made it, I could see that they'd be through it in minutes.

Then tearing-metal shrieks echoed from stone throats and the Nomes leapt away from the now-electrified fence. A few of them shook weapons in our direction, but I swore that I heard a note, not of fury, pain, or anger, but desperation in the voices.

Voices?

We all collapsed to the ground, catching our breath. Finally I turned to Jodi. "It looks like we go to Plan B."

She drew a very shaky breath. "Okay, yeah, we're now surrounded, the road's gone, and they're waving sharp stone things at us. Let's do that Plan B." She looked at me. "Just what *is* Plan B?"

"Talk to them," I said, grinning. "I think we just might be able to do it now."

6. Voices of the Earth

"Tell me again just how this is supposed to work, Clint?"

I should have expected Mamma to ask again. I was never sure how much of her cluelessness was an act and how much was sincere lack of understanding. I compiled the subroutine, tested it with the main one, started running it on some test data. "It's what I do, Mamma. Signal processing is, well, it's teaching a machine to do some of the same stuff that we do naturally. If you figure out how, sometimes you can eventually get the machine to do it better than we do."

She continued making sandwiches for Jodi and me. "Can you give an example your silly mother could understand, dear?"

"You're not silly, Mamma." I thought for a minute. "Okay, try this. There's a big party here, everyone making a lot of noise. Evangeline spills hot water on herself and gives a holler. Do you think you'd notice?"

"Well, sure enough I would! Don't you think I could tell when one of my own children might be in trouble?"

"I know you could, Mamma. That's what we can do with our built-in signal processing. You've got twenty voices, all making a ton of noise, but somehow our brains can sort out the different voices and notice when one specific voice is doing something unusual, like shouting in pain, even if the actual volume in the room should, by rights, be drowning that voice out."

She nodded slowly. "Never thought of it that way, but you're right. A mother can hear even a small sound by her baby over a powerful lot of noise."

"Right. So we can program a computer to do that, too, if we know how to tell it the tricks of the trade. Turns out there's a lot of different ways to do that.

"For what we're doing, the important thing is that there's different kinds of sound, what we call frequencies; high-frequency sound's high-pitched, low-frequency's low-pitched. I had a project I was on, once, that had to sort out human voices that were whispering at a distance of, oh, about three hundred yards. The kinds of signals I got from that looked a lot like some of the ones I was getting from Jodi's sensors, except that these were up in frequencies you only see bats screeching on. So I'm guessing the Nomes talk way up out of our hearing range. This converter setup will shift ultrasonic frequencies down to our range, and kick ours up to the ultrasonic."

"And I hope you've got everything set, because I

don't think our neighbors are going to wait much longer." Jodi set down the heavy packs.

"Got everything?"

"Steel weapons in case they stay hostile, three sources of light—caver's lamps, flashlights, candles and matches—radio relays, walkie-talkies, food, clothing change, rope and climbing gear, hey, you name it, plus the stuff we cobbled together out of our gear. This isn't the first of these hikes I've been on, you know. Just that this *mishigas* changes some of the extras we need to bring. You got the code for our little universal translators, Geordie?"

"Mr. Scott, pléase. You know Next Gen was a weak, pale imitation. Yeah, the code should work. It's not all that complex and I could adapt a lot of the code I already had. But it ain't really a translator, remember; we're not going to understand them." I took two smooth alloy cases in rubberized jackets from her. "Oh, that's right, we already had some of these set up for long-term monitoring."

"What else could I use? We don't know how long we'll be out or where we'll be, so it's a good thing we had ruggedized, sealed cases for this kind of thing." Jodi was right—in the cave environment we expected, the gadgets we brought had darn well better be awfully tough.

"I've got the code just about set. You've got extra battery packs?"

She patted me on the shoulder. "Hey, have a little faith in your techie fiancée, *neh*? I pirated all the batteries from our stuff. Taking no chances."

She glanced over at the rest of the family. "I admit, all the gadgets you people have not only surprised me, they'll come in handy. Wouldn't have expected you to have short-range radio repeaters."

Grandpa laughed. "Hain't much difference twixt this

adventure of yours and some of the ones we've thought 'bout doing over the years. Never had to use 'em yet, but Adam durn near did for this last trip. If most of us come with you an' provide relays with our own radios, those relays should take y'all a good long ways in before we gets out of contact."

Radio, of course, would be attenuated real fast through all that water-soaked rock, but relays could really stretch that, especially if we used the family to stretch it farther. Evangeline, Grandpa, Mamma, and Helen would be staying topside; the rest would follow us down. We knew the Nomes hadn't—and couldn't—come up through the Slade entrance, not with all the iron around and below the entrance. The only question was whether they'd try to kill us when we got out of that area.

I transferred the code into our equipment and spoke into it. There was a faint sideband of whining high-pitched noise, but the instruments showed most of the output centered around the same waveband as the signals I thought were the Nomes' voices. I put the outdoor headphones on and walked out into the night, pointing a parabolic mike in the direction of the besieging force.

"*Choura mon tosetta. Megni om den kai zom tazela ku,*" I heard, or something very much like that. The voice was tenor, with an odd, scraping quality to it.

"*Zom moran! Zettamakata vos bin turano,*" replied another, deeper voice. Chills went down my spine. It was one thing to have figured it out intellectually, another to actually hear the voices of nonhuman creatures. I pulled the headphones off and turned back. "I was right. Voices. Damn!"

Jodi nodded. "Didn't have any doubt myself, love."

Jodi and I each clipped one of the little boxes that contained the signal processors, memory, and whatnot that did the conversion to our belts, ran compact headphone wires up inside our clothing, and put on the slim-profile headphones that fit under our caving helmets. No one goes caving with a bare head, unless they want to end up with lumps or worse. We tested all the connections, made sure all the power packs and other gadgets—repeaters, lights, and so on—were well distributed, and then turned towards the door. "Let's do it. Time's getting short. They've started testing the fence again."

I led, Jodi followed, with Father, Jonah, Nellie, Adam, and Grandpa bringing up the rear. In the darkness the huge grating seemed even more grim and forbidding, and opening it was like watching a mouth opening up in the earth. We turned on our lights, checked all our equipment again, and descended the iron ladder set into the living rock; as agreed, Grandpa stayed topside to keep the exit secure, just in case, and to be the topside relay.

It's a long, solemn climb at the best of times; the iron ladder drops straight down into pitch blackness that first muffles the sounds of the outside and then starts amplifying the echoes of your descent into a cadence of solemnly echoing drumbeats. Ninety feet down, my feet touched stone. I looked around, saw nothing in the immediate vicinity, and stepped away to let everyone else get down. The sounds of people and equipment echoed through the tomblike silence of Winston's Cave, silence normally only broken by water dripping from the ceiling.

"Okay. Everyone ready?"

"Ayup," Father answered. "Nellie?"

"Yes, Father. I'm first relay. I'll be right here at the base of the ladder." She took out her iron truncheon, swung it around, and leaned back against the iron ladder. We heard her checking reception with Grandpa topside as we moved down the Snake's Belly, a twisting passageway with scalloping where swift-moving water had carved it out. The lights glinted brightly off water-slick rock, giving back highlights of yellow, brown, and white from the flowstone that coated parts of the wall. We moved cautiously, waiting to make sure we could see as far ahead as possible.

A flash of light ahead. I stopped, then turned one of our Mag-Lites on and aimed it down the corridor.

Across the tunnel, just where the Snake's Belly exited into the Crossroads, five Nomes stood, weapons aimed at us, rockworms waiting at their feet. By now, only Adam and Father were with us, Jonah having stayed back about halfway down the Belly because the signal was starting to fade. We'd probably have to leave Adam at the beginning of the Crossroads. I took a deep breath. "Guess this is it."

I put on the headphones; Jodi did the same. We walked forward, Father and Adam following some distance back. As we approached, I heard *Turano! Turano zom ku!* in a sort of whispered voice, and the figures tightened their grip on their weapons.

When we were within twenty feet, I stopped. My heart was pounding awfully fast, and for a minute I couldn't convince my hands to let go of my trusty iron bar. At this range, in this light, the Nomes and their rockworms were too eerie to contemplate for long. I forced my grip to relax and handed the weapon to Jodi, then took another slow couple of steps forward. They muttered something and gathered themselves. Something about the tone of voice and the way they almost bunched together actually heartened me. Why, they were afraid of us too!

"We don't want to fight you," I said, the microphone taking my normal voice and catapulting its sound to seventy-five thousand cycles higher.

The reaction was everything I could have hoped for. They literally jumped backward in startlement, and I couldn't even sort out separate word-sounds from the gabble of Nome-talk that erupted from the headphones. Finally they settled down and one of them stepped slightly forward, stone sword still in his hand but lowered to a much less threatening position. "*Rennka ku? Mondu okh wendasa hottai rennka?*"

I shrugged. "Hey, I don't understand you, but I get the idea you're surprised I talk. We just found out that you did ourselves." I reached very carefully inside one of my pockets and took out a small bag. I put the bag down on the ground and backed up a few paces to where Jodi waited.

Whatever senses they had, they'd been able to tell I did something there, at any rate. The spokesman came hesitantly forward and stopped, staring at the bag with his weird crystal eyes. Then his face snapped up, looking at me with a very human startlement visible in his pose despite the stony immobility of his features. "*H'adamant! H'adamant huran zom!*"

Jodi and I looked at each other, startled. "Adamant?"

It clapped fists together in what was somehow an exultant or agreeing motion. "*H'adamant! H'adamant!*" It scooped up the bag and emptied the three diamonds into its palm—last of Winston Slade's original cache, saved for sentimental reasons in our safe—and held the palm out to us. "*H'adamant, vu!*"

"I'll be damned," I said. "Wonder if they got that word from us, or we got it from them?"

Jodi shrugged. "Don't have any idea. But he looks like he's coming down from his ecstasy."

Indeed, the spokesman was now looking in his palm, and loosed a steady stream of words which included "*H'adamant*" as a frequent occurrence.

"Sorry, sir, but we don't have any more of them."

I tried gestures to get the point across. "Maybe we can reach some kind of understanding?"

He finally seemed to realize no more diamonds were forthcoming. He then pointed down the corridor—clearly, whatever senses they had must have some analogy to sight, at least when used for that purpose—and made emphatic motions that I couldn't interpret as anything except "Come with us."

"Well, it's what we wanted," I said, not feeling all that comfortable with the idea.

"So long as what they want isn't to cut us open to see if we have the rocks inside us."

"You just had to bring that idea up, didn't you?"

"Clint. Best get along now."

"Yes, Father." We started following the Nomes. Adam stayed behind at the beginning of the Crossroads. When we reached the entrance to the Corkscrew, Father knew he would have to stay behind also. He gave me an unexpected hug. "Be careful."

"We will, Father."

The Nomes talked with themselves in low undertones. They'd clearly realized we didn't understand them, and at this point had stopped trying to talk to us. We followed farther into the bowels of the earth. After a while, I keyed in the radio. "Father?"

The Nomes and the rockworms spun around at that, staring at me again.

"Hear you, son. Getting faint. Figure a few dozen more yards."

The Nomes relaxed slowly, then continued on, but they were now talking with great intensity and animation. "Something about the radio really set them off."

Jodi nodded. "Well, makes sense, doesn't it? You said they must sense things in the electromagnetic, and that's why the iron throws them off. That radio might be like a flashbulb or something to them."

I dropped one of the relays. The rearmost Nome stopped, turned, and came back towards us. It picked up the relay. I stepped towards it, it backed up, studied the relay for a moment, then put it back down and glanced at me. I let it move away and then continued walking.

Soon we were entering areas of the cave that even Winston had never seen, past the Hall of Mysteries and obviously deep into what was the Nomes' territory. Now I really started to get worried. We were seeing other Nomes around us, who would stop and point and start to gabble amongst each other, just as prisoners being marched through a city would start to see the citizens point and whisper.

There were only two of our eight relays left. We were now in an immense cavern that I couldn't even see across. The Mag-Lite hinted at its great expanse, reaching the roof overhead, bearded with stalactites that were twenty feet long or more and still ended with well over a hundred feet of air between them and the ground. When we lowered the light it touched on more wonders: gargantuan columns, dozens of tunnel openings, flowstone curtains that glittered translucently, a shaggy forest of helictites beneath a high-up opening that obviously vented air into this area.

Since the cavern was effectively open air, we wouldn't need a relay until we were all the way across it. As we reached the far side, surrounded by the eerie rusty-gate hissing and screeching that was the audible-edge component of the Nomes' speech, something massive came slowly into view. We slowed down and stared for a moment in awe.

If we'd had any remaining doubt that this was a civilized species, we would have lost it then. For the first time we saw an undeniably artificial construct in the depths of Winston's Cave. Towering before us, over sixty feet high, were a pair of what could be nothing but titanic doors. In a way they still seemed to belong here, their surface as smooth yet naturally flowing as the rest of the caverns. They were composed of what looked like marble, but with strange, almost interwoven components of a semitransparent black stone which looked like obsidian. They were covered with shimmering alien symbols that appeared to have been grown there as a natural part of the stone. We could not grasp what the symbols meant, though they were clearly the work of intelligence.

None of our guides made any attempt to open the door. There was a sound of rushing water, and the great slabs simply pivoted up and rose smoothly out of sight as we approached; almost noiselessly, without any visible sign of the truly impressive force that must be needed to move. I saw the thickness as I passed . . . four-foot-thick slabs of stone. I did a quick mental calculation. Mother Mary, together those doors must mass over a thousand tons! I dropped the next-to-last relay just outside the doors.

Jodi evidently decided that it was time for a clearer look, because she pulled out the big electric lantern and turned it on.

Beyond the huge doors was . . . the Throne Room.

Even if I hadn't been half expecting it since I was a kid, there was no way I could have called it anything else. The penetrating beam of the portable lantern barely made its way across the room, maybe over a thousand feet in diameter. Circle upon circle of Nomes, each with its weapon and companion rockworm, stood in what looked like a military attention pose, with a narrow gap through which we marched. The great domed cavern sparkled everywhere with the same alien designs. I wondered, vaguely, how they saw such designs, and what they "looked" like to their eyes; surely what we saw was at best only a part of their symbology. In the center of the cavern, a series of concentric terraces were laid, with rough-surfaced ramps curving in a spiral fashion to each level. And at the top of this raised formation, on a perfectly circular polished dais of stone over fifty feet wide, was a throne, hewn from the living rock it sat upon, with a single Nome seated in it.

This was the meeting I'd half dreamed about, half feared for almost twenty years. I couldn't think of *this* Nome as "it." He looked down at us from an elevation of fifteen feet, counting the height of the throne itself. His crystalline crest seemed finer and higher, the fluting on his chin longer, and he looked to me to be somewhat larger than the others around the room, or those escorting us. In the shadowy light of the stupendous throne room, with my overexcited imagination working at double time, I could almost see the halo of white hair and long beard. This was Ruggedo, sometimes called Roquat, the Red—the Nome King.

I shook my head to clear it. I might not be able to keep from giving him the name in my mind, but there wasn't any other connection. This was a first contact between humans and whatever this race really was, and I wouldn't help matters any by letting kids' stories influence my behavior. And whatever they were, they had a lot of things in their civilization that we hadn't the faintest clue about. Behind the throne we could see bizarre and distorted shapes; things that looked like they might have been living things of the same general sort as the Nomes and rockworms, but jammed together, intertwined and almost sculpted in ways that hurt my eyes to look at.

"Father," I said into the radio. "We're about to meet the Nome King."

"Then mind your manners, son."

Ruggedo (as my mind still insisted on calling him,

lacking any better name) had leaned forward with
interest as I talked with my father. He leaned back
slowly and studied us as we were brought up the ramps
until we stood before him, a mere twenty feet from
the being who was clearly in charge of this entire
underground world. His head tilted slightly, as though
he were a bird trying to see us with one eye, and then
another. Now I could see there was, in fact, one strong
similarity between the real and the fictional Nome
King: Ruggedo did, indeed, hold a heavy, elaborate
scepter with a great glittering red crystal at its end.

"That thing gives me the creeps, Clint." Jodi spoke
in an undertone, having wisely shut off her high-
frequency transducer.

I just nodded. She wasn't talking about the King,
but about the shapes behind the throne which we could
now see much more clearly. This was not a good thing.
It was something inherently unsettling, seeming a blend
of the living and the living rock, shapes almost like
attenuated Nomes blending into rockworms and
other . . . things of even less familiar outline, like an
unholy blending of Bosch and Giger. My earphones
hummed and murmured with whispered sounds of the
Nome language and with other things, like barely
audible whines, interference, and subliminal voices.

We stood there a moment, each side regarding the
other in motionless silence, broken only by the sounds
that even our transducers couldn't render into rec-
ognition. I took the time to study the King closely.
Even though he was clearly larger than his subjects,
the Nome King still wouldn't stand taller than
Evangeline; I guessed him at no more than five feet
tall. The body was almost spherical, with variegated
geometric patterns of black, green, brown, and yellow making it look almost as though he wore clothing, at least from a distance; up close, it was much

more a natural mottling of the skin. Round, slender arms and legs, with rocky sheathing that had the appearance of thin clothing on their bodies, completed the resemblance to Baum's Nomes, as envisioned by John R. Neill. The crystal growths on the head, up close, didn't really bring hair to mind. They shimmered with multiple colors—the King's seemed predominantly violet, amethyst perhaps—and the immobile eyes and stony tube jutting from the chin emphasized the alien nature of the creature.

Finally, the Nome King leaned forward on his scepter and spoke.

"So, *you* are the people who speak in the air!"

7. Underground Understandings

Neither Jodi nor I really know precisely what we did in that moment. That clearly spoken English sentence stunned me so much that all I know for certain is that we stood there for a while, staring at him with our mouths literally hanging open. Just as we started to recover, the King suddenly began to emit a series of whooping noises which, after a moment, we realized must be laughter.

"Hooo Hooo Hooo Hooo! OOOoohoohooohoo! You really do appear that way! Pardon, I mean, look like that—when surprised."

"You speak English?!" I finally got out, rattled enough to slide into dialect. "What th' hell's goin' on here? Weren't four hours ago I first heard a word of your language, an' from their reactions I'd thought was the first time y'all had heard ours!"

That sent him into another fit of laughter. Jodi and I exchanged glances. This wasn't even vaguely what we'd expected. It didn't help that I actually recognized the voice. Well, not really recognized it, exactly, but I knew I'd heard that voice before many times.

Finally he settled down. "In a way, you are quite right. And in another way, no, I do not speak your language. That"—he gestured to the twisted structure behind him—"speaks your language, through me."

That brought all sorts of icky possibilities to mind, just looking at the thing.

"Are you the ruler here, or is it?"

The shrieking snort seemed equal parts amusement and annoyance. "I am the High Spirit here. That is a ..." He seemed at a loss, finally saying, "*makatdireskovi*. There are several words in your language which seem to partly apply, none of them actually meaning what I am trying to say."

"So what do you mean by saying you hadn't heard our language before?" Jodi asked.

"Never before have we heard your voices speaking in our manner," the Nome King—well, High Spirit— said. "But there were those of us who ventured into *Tennatu*—the Land of Fast Changes—who, in past cycles, began to *turan* certain signals which we realized were not natural. We made this *makatdireskovi* to help us understand what we sensed, and eventually did. But we never realized it was your people who were doing the speaking."

It took some considerable back-and-forth exchanges before we finally realized that they'd managed, over a period of many years, to derive our language from television broadcasts. That explained the voice—it was a combination of several TV anchormen, most notably Peter Jennings and Tom Brokaw, with a hint of Walter Cronkite. They had realized that part of the transmissions could represent a depiction of objects in some way. But because they didn't see at all the way

we did, and within their own "sight" spectrum had a
different arrangement of seeing intensities and "colors," they could translate the signal but the "image"
they got did not resemble the "image" their regular
senses got of us at all. So they had no idea that the
babbling in the air came from the same people that
sometimes raided their caverns. That was also why it
had taken the King several moments to verify that we
really did look "surprised" in the same way as the
images they had previously extracted from the signals.
The *makatdireskovi* and he had needed to find the
translation between the signal-images and what he was
seeing.

"Okay," I said finally, realizing how much time
had passed, "I think we need to at least cover a
little business before we go back to this discussion,
sir. We came down here to see if we could try to fix
up the bad blood that's been built up between us over
the years."

He sat still for a moment, head tilting in that birdlike
fashion again, and then gave a nod. The gesture was
clearly deliberate, something he must have learned
from the transmissions they monitored. "I had hoped
this was true. You do not seem to be suicidal or hostile, despite the formidable reputation you have among
my people. What do you propose?"

"Well, first off, you've got us in your power, so if
you'd be so kind as to pull your people back off our
land topside, and then I can tell my folks to relax—
that we're talkin'?"

He considered that for a moment, then raised his
staff and barked out several commands in their own
language. "It is done. Tell your people that mine shall
bother them no more, at least so long as we remain
in council."

I keyed up the mike. "Father?"

He responded instantly, even though it must've been a good hour and a half, maybe two hours of nothing but waiting before he heard anything. "Yes, Clint?"

"We're having a good conversation here and might be here a long time. But we're able to talk together— don't ask me to explain the ins-and-outs right now— and the King has agreed to pull back his people. Can you check that for me?"

"Hold on, son." A few minutes passed, then: "Clint, all disappeared a short time back. Looks like everyone's playing on the level."

I relaxed. The situation could still get bad, but it looked like we were past the worst. "Good, Father. You guys pull back too, then. Me and Jodi can find our way back if we have to, and I don't think we're in any danger here."

"Will do. Be back every few hours to check on you, though."

"Okay, Father. Take care."

"You take care of that girl, hear me?"

"Yes, Father."

"Good luck."

I put the transmitter away. "You know, I think we've forgotten all our manners. I'm Clinton Slade. This is my fiancée, Jodi Goldman."

The Nome King had apparently seen plenty of introduction scenes. He rose up on his slender pipestem legs and gave a low bow. "A pleasure, Mr. Clinton Slade, Miss Jodi Goldman. I am *Rokhasetanamaethetal*, the High Spirit of the *Nowëthada*."

We returned his bow. "Rokasta . . . ?"

"*Rokhasetanamaethetal*," he repeated. Jodi frowned, and I caught the impression of sounds involved in that name that I couldn't even describe.

"I'm not sure I can even say that properly, sir," Jodi said.

"Ah, yes. I recall that the vibrations that formed your language did seem to have, relatively speaking, great simplicity. We can reproduce any such vibration very easily, but you seem to be more limited. Choose another name for me, if you wish. I will see if it suits me."

I was strongly tempted to call him Ruggedo and see if he'd take it, but it was time to drop that line of thinking. "Let's just shorten it a bit, sir. How about Rokhaset?" The name sounded vaguely Egyptian, said that way, and the tube-beard did kinda look like the tight little beards you saw on the Egyptian statues.

"That will do well enough. Come then. You have stood long before my throne, and in the images your people send through the air the *makatdireskovi* has noted that you prefer to sit, as do we if the time is overly long."

He gestured with his great scepter, and the other Nomes parted along the line of the gesture. It was a smooth and well-practiced movement that simultaneously gave me great respect for their attentiveness and reaction time, and a bit of wariness about our so-far genial host. That kind of coordinated, instant obedience I'd only seen in humans when the boss was a pretty hard-assed tyrant . . . or in a very heavily drilled military establishment.

At the far end of this pathway, a passage was visible in the light of our lantern. Noticing the beam again for the first time in a while brought something urgently to mind. "High Spirit, sir?"

"Just call me Rokhaset, as you have named me. Might I call you Clinton Slade and your friend Jodi Goldman, instead of by formal terms? Yes? Very well, then. What is it?" The High Spirit led us down this new course.

"Your people see using senses we don't—I guess the word you're using for it is '*turan*'—and we see using ones you don't. The problem is that our light's going to go out in not too many hours, and we'll really be pretty helpless without it." This was something of an exaggeration, as we had several light sources on us which would enable us to manage some kind of illumination for quite a while, but I wanted to see what his reaction was.

He tilted his head. "Rather as I am *matturan* near you and your iron and steel, eh? Give me this lantern of yours for a moment."

"Be careful with it," Jodi admonished him.

"As though it were a child, I assure you."

Reluctantly she handed him the lantern. He took the hard-plastic-cased giant flashlight and examined it carefully, running his fingers across it. "How do you activate it?"

Jodi indicated the on/off switch, then had to physically place his fingers on it, as he couldn't actually see the gesture. While his people often gave the impression of sight like our own, things like this constantly reminded us that what we were seeing wasn't what they saw.

Rokhaset moved forward. As we went to follow, he stopped and held out a hand. "Wait a moment, please. I wish to be able to examine this clearly, and your presence with all of your iron makes that impossible."

We waited as he moved about thirty yards on, then stopped and examined the light again. There was a click and we were in darkness. "Hey!" I said.

"Just testing. So it is now no longer giving you illumination?"

"It's off."

He verified this by switching it on and off several times, then brought it back to us. "I believe I can arrange something, if I understand the operation correctly." Rokhaset screeched some orders to his people, and then gestured for us to follow. "There are many things for us to discuss, I believe, but first it is time for us to speak together as friends. It has been a very, very long time indeed since my people and yours spoke as one people."

"I wondered about that. There are legends among our people about spirits who live in the earth and who fear the sunlight or who are vulnerable to iron."

"The 'sunlight,' as you call it, merely confuses some of us, and can damage our eyes over time by causing them to fog. There are some beings that avoid your sunlight for more pressing reasons." Rokhaset spoke those words as we passed along a polished-looking corridor. "But I am surprised by your people even having legends, for the time when the *Nowëthada* and the *Tennathada* walked and spoke together is many generations past even for my people. Indeed, it was thought to be no more than legend by many of the *Nowëthada,* as none of them could even tell whether your people spoke at all."

We emerged now into another large hall, but this one seemed oval and had what appeared to be a long table and chairs of odd designs in it, with many Nomes going back and forth. The others formed into an honor guard as we approached. The High Spirit seated himself in the center of one long side of the table, and indicated we were to sit directly opposite him on the other side. The table was about five feet wide, allowing for plenty of room. The chairs were a bit short for us—not unexpected—but after a few minutes of sitting in them seemed surprisingly comfortable, though my legs did feel that they had very little clearance below the top of the table.

"I've been thinking about what you just brought up, Rokhaset," Jodi said finally. "The problem is that there's no way you could have talked with us before.

It wasn't until the past, oh, fifty years or so that we could've built gadgets that would let us hear you, and you hear us."

" 'Gadgets'?" Rokhaset repeated, puzzled. "Gadgets . . . Do you mean these 'machines' like the ones you carry that make your voices sound like ours?"

"Yes."

"Ah. Well, in those days, there was no need of such things. As our legends and histories relate it, we were a much closer people in the ancient time; that is, you and I would have seemed less alien to one another, and we would have had ways of speaking together that would be considerably more simple. But then came the *Makurada Demagon* . . . the, hmm, what would make sense in your language . . . the 'Senseless Shattering'? Ah, no . . . Darkness? Hmmm . . . Perhaps the best expression would be something like 'Plague of Blindness.' But that implies a disease, which this was not; it was a disaster which struck the whole world and affected it in different ways for each of the peoples who then inhabited it. The *Nowëthada* lost contact with *Nowë*, who was sore injured by the *Makurada*, and with your people, and while apart, we changed."

"Who is *Nowë*?"

"You would call *Nowë* our patron deity, god or goddess of the Earth. That is what *Nowëthada* means, the People of *Nowë*. It is at *Nowë*'s will that we exist. We are the servants of the Earth, made to oversee the interaction of the living rock with those other things that live upon it." He sat up a bit straighter. "Ah, tell me how this seems to you."

Light began to fill the room, shining out from several stafflike objects being carried into the room by other Nomes. It was light of a brilliant blue-white color, not exactly what I'd have chosen for lighting; but it saved on batteries and our host had apparently had this whipped together just for us. "That's just great, Rokhaset!"

"You had your people do that up now?" Jodi asked. "Well, I'm impressed. Can I take a look?"

"By all means, Jodi." It was still pretty strange to hear such courteous and very well-spoken English coming out of that unmoving mouth. The only oddity to the sound was a slight hollow resonance, but in this cavern setting it was hardly noticeable.

Jodi studied the twisted stony shaft, which ended in a crystal that produced the light. "How do you turn it on and off?"

"I suppose I could instruct it to turn off, but do you not still require the light?"

"Oh, sure, sure. What do you mean, instruct it? Is this gadget voice-activated?"

Rokhaset tilted his head a few times. "There you are, using these words oddly. Tell me, would you call our pets gadgets?"

"You mean those things we call rockworms? No, they're creatures."

"Then what you hold there is not a gadget either, if I understand you correctly."

Jodi nearly dropped the rod. "Are you saying that this thing is *alive*?"

"As alive as I am," the High Spirit agreed. "Not, I confess, nearly as capable of other activities as I. We grew that very quickly for one purpose only, to make that crystal *hevrat* in the same *gos* as your 'lights' . . . how would that be in your language . . . hmm . . . Yes, we made it to glow in the same way as your lights do. It provides little for us to sense, but for you it appears to suffice quite well."

I shifted uncomfortably, then glanced down at the chair. "And what about . . ."

I almost got the impression of a broad smile. "Ah,

you have noticed that they grow, have you? Yes, certainly! How else could we have chairs that all would be comfortable in, for my people vary in size as do yours?"

Jodi and I exchanged glances. I could see her mind following the same path. We kept getting deceived by the Nome's human-sounding voice and his—or, to be more accurate, the *makatdireskovi's*—grasp of our language, derived from the past forty years of broadcasts. Clearly we had much in common with the Nomes, and there was no reason we couldn't be friends. But, just as clearly, there were some very, very alien aspects to their civilization. The thought that even the furniture I was sitting on, the lights I was seeing . . . "Is everything here alive?"

Surprisingly, that made Rokhaset pause; almost I could see him frowning in thought. "In a sense, yes . . . but not in the same sense as these things, no. The Earth itself is alive in its own way, but certainly there is a difference between the ordinary stone about us and ourselves, or these chairs or your new lights."

Servant Nomes moved to the High Spirit, and other Nomes came in and seated themselves—leaving a respectful, and possibly fearful, distance between us and their leader. The servants placed several stony bowls, plates, and platters on the table. There was a quick discussion with some glancing at us, which Rokhaset resolved with a gesture. "I presume you have brought at least some of your own food, Mr. Slade, Ms. Goldman? For it is time for me to eat, but I suspect our food is not to your taste."

"We've brought some stuff, yeah."

Five huge covered platters were carried to the table, heavy enough to require two Nomes each, and placed carefully in front of the diners. The one in front of the High Spirit unfolded its top like a flower at his touch.

In the brilliant blue-white glow, the dishes within shimmered with the colors of the rainbow. There were slices of some rich brown and yellow rippled stuff that looked almost like a chocolate and yellow swirled cake, some brilliantly red fruitlike things, some really peculiar transparent sticks, and other things like noodles, puddings, and crumbled croutons.

"Are those . . . rocks?" Jodi asked tentatively.

The High Spirit gave us a deliberate nod. "Properly prepared by the finest chefs, of course."

"How do you cook a rock?"

"Not using the trivial methods shown in your media, if I understand them correctly. Your people lost, in some ways, far more than we in the *Makurada Demagon*."

"So," I said, studying his plate, "What are those? The reds . . . garnets, maybe. The stuff that looked like cake slices at first must be layered limestone—the main rock around here."

"You have an excellent eye for one of your people," Rokhaset said. "Though I am not sure of your first identification, your second is quite correct."

Suddenly Jodi began laughing almost hysterically.

"What's so durn funny?"

She finally got a grip on herself. "You . . . you Slades! And the Nomes! All this time, you big, strong frontiersmen have been sneaking in and robbing the Nomes' pantries! You're nothing but overgrown mice with iron bars!" She went off into another fit of laughter.

I blinked. Now there was a completely humiliating thought. "Is she right, sir? Have we been stealing your caviar—special food or something?"

"In a manner of speaking, yes. I admit to having a fondness for *H'adamant* when I can afford to have some prepared. But I would hardly have sent out a legion of warriors to Tennatu just for my stomach!"

"So why did you send your warriors after the diamonds?"

"Not diamonds—*H'adamant*."

"Same thing."

He shook his head, emphasizing his disagreement by using our own gesture. "Ridiculous. I have seen these 'diamonds' in your television advertisements. They are nothing like *H'adamant*."

"We weren't anything like what y'all got out of those broadcasts either," I pointed out. "There, Jodi's got herself a big diamond on her hand, you tell me that ain't the same thing."

Jodi held out her engagement ring. Rokhaset studied it for a few minutes, then slowly raised his head and gazed at us with those weird crystal eyes for a long time in silence. Finally he reached out and placed one of the stones we'd returned to the Nomes on the table between us. "I return your question, Clinton Slade. You tell me that these two things *are* the same."

"Shoot, I know they are. I've studied geology for years, and hell, it ain't hard to tell a diamond. Jodi's ring was cut from one of the ones we got down here."

He stood bolt upright and shrieked out something that I couldn't make out because the transducer's volume cutoff killed it. Jodi and I jumped back, fumbling for the iron bars, sure that we were about to get mobbed.

But no one else moved in a way that seemed hostile. If anything, they huddled together a bit more. Finally Rokhaset got himself under control. He sat down slowly and selected another morsel off the plate. I could see now that the mouth was located under the sound-tube he used for speaking—sort of where the chin-neck juncture would be in a human. He didn't seem to eat this with enthusiasm, but more like a man doing something while thinking.

Finally he looked back at us. "I must beg your pardon. It is hard for someone such as myself to suddenly realize how alien your people are. I had foolishly permitted myself to think that because your words are translated to ones I understand by the *makatdireskovi* that we are really essentially the same, aside from a few minor differences." I got the impression of a long, shaky breath being drawn, though all I could see was a faint movement of the stony skin on the rounded torso. "To give you something you might understand, telling me that the . . . stone in the ring that Ms. Goldman is wearing is the same as this *H'adamant* would be the same as my holding out one of your skeletons and telling you, in all seriousness, that I could not tell the difference between the skeleton and the living, breathing *Tennathada* before me."

He shuddered, a movement rather similar to our own. "Your people have lost more than I had ever imagined. This"—he indicated the natural diamond—"is a living stone, Clinton Slade, Jodi Goldman. The *H'adamant* is precious because of that living essence within it. Now that I know your people cannot see the difference, and that you call both by the name 'diamond' . . ." He shook his head again. "What a terrible waste. You cannot even see what it is that you destroy by cutting the stone in the way you do. We had foolishly thought that you needed the . . . diamonds for the same reasons we did, for their special properties."

"Well, since we're on the subject," I said, after a moment's pause, "we'd like to come to a more peaceable arrangement. Maybe a trade, something you'd like for stuff we'd like. Maybe we can bring you stones like aren't around here?"

Rokhaset nodded thoughtfully. "Yes, there are ossibilities—many crystals and minerals that we know of, yet cannot find here. But we would have to give you some way of making sure you brought us live stones, not ones whose essence had been damaged or destroyed. However, there are more pressing matters. You returned these few stones as a gesture of your goodwill, and so I have accepted it. But it is essential that you return the ones you took recently."

I shifted in my living chair. "Well, sir, we can't exactly do that. For two reasons."

"That would be extremely unfortunate. What reasons are these?"

"Well, firstly, your people kinda wrecked our road. Really bad, this time. It'll take a week, at least, before we have a chance of getting out of here and making it to the bank where we keep the stones."

Rokhaset's eyes flickered—literally—but the tone of his voice was warm and perhaps slightly amused, so I guessed that the flicker might be something like a smile. "What the *Nowëthada* can destroy, the *Nowëthada* can rebuild, and just as swiftly, Clinton Slade. If that is all that stands between us and the *H'adamant*, lay your fears to rest."

I sighed. "Sorry, sir, but that's the smaller problem. Y'see, most of them are already sold. We've got some left, but not even a tenth of what was took."

The whole room seemed to go silent. Rokhaset sat utterly immobile, as did the other Nomes, and for a few minutes it looked like we were stuck in some lunatic sculptor's workshop, surrounded by macabre statues.

When the silence broke, it was by a hurricane of sound, gabbling Nomish voices all talking at once, with one alien word repeated so often as to be recognizable even in the Babel of noise: *lurizata*. The Nomes had risen from their seats and were now shouting back and forth at each other, sometimes gesturing unsettlingly in our direction.

Just as it reached a new crescendo, Rokhaset's voice boomed out: *"RATCHOTAI!"*

Dead silence fell again. It only lasted a split second, however, because the quiet was instantly broken by the High Spirit talking to his people. Well, I say "talking," but it sounded more like a lecture—or a tongue-lashing. He laid into them but good. We couldn't understand it, of course, but we could pick out *"lurizata," "H'adamant,"* and some of the other words we'd heard before. His people shrank back, just like humans getting bawled out by the boss, as he continued his tirade. It must've lasted a full five minutes before he stopped, seemed to take a breath, and turned back to us.

"My apologies, Clinton Slade, Jodi Goldman. Your news is very disheartening, and it seems some of my people were unready for such bad news. We had always believed you kept the *H'adamant* on your property. With all the *H'kuraden* that underlies it, we could not of course sense the crystals at any distance to see if they were in fact there. I should have realized the truth once I understood the diamonds of your transmissions were what became of our *H'adamant*. Unlike some of my less courageous subjects, however, I refuse to view the situation as hopelessly lost."

"I think," Jodi said, "it's about time you told us just what the real problem is, *neh*? What's so vital about this particular batch of diamonds that you've just got to have them?"

The High Spirit looked over at her, then gave one of his deliberate nods. "Yes, you are correct. But let us finish our meal first. A few more minutes should make little difference, and the story is long and not entirely pleasant."

I was never so anxious for a meal to be over.

8. Assault of the Earth

"Ours," began Rokhaset, "is not the only city of the *Nowëthada* in the Earth."

We were seated in another set of chairs, which were slowly adjusting to become more comfortable in their creepy way, in a smaller and obviously more private room, a circular cave about thirty feet across and twenty high, hung with hundreds of delicate straw stalactites dripping water on most of the area; we'd pointedly stood near the two dry spots in the room and waited for the Nomes to move the chairs for us. While we were getting seated, I'd finally asked Rokhaset why he was excluding the other Nomes, which seemed to amuse him.

"Few of my subjects can hear what the *makat-direskovi* sings to me, Clint. It was designed for me alone. Therefore, any with us cannot understand you, nor speak to you, and would thus be of little use in our deliberations. The only reason they understood some of what we discussed while dining is that one of those who can, somewhat, hear the *makatdireskovi* was summarizing what he heard, something as one of your reporters or sports announcers. This would be somewhere between clumsy and useless at this point in our discussion. Now that it has become clear that the signals involved are important we shall have to make something which will speak to—or perhaps to be more accurate, translate for—all our people as the *makatdireskovi* does to me. But that is a project far more complex than simply making you lights." This relieved me to some extent. Rokhaset didn't seem to be the tyrant type, although military leader still seemed likely.

"Yes," Jodi said, returning to the subject, "I wouldn't expect you were the only city."

"The problem is that the *Nowëthada* are no longer the unified race we were. Those who survived the *Makurada Demagon* . . . all of us changed. But some changed more than others. Our task was always one of balancing the way of the Earth with the way of the life on its surface. But as we became less like you, and the powers of *Nowë* faded, the old senses which used to tell us how to perform this duty also weakened and faded." He rubbed his hands, a gesture which seemed like a slow shaking of the head. "To allow your form of life to survive and prosper, of course, it was always important that the world remain overall peaceful. But changes must happen to the world as well, and so it was our job to ensure that these changes were sufficient for the world's purposes, and to minimize the injury to people such as yourself. This task we continue to this day."

I could not help but be tremendously impressed by the *makatdireskovi's* work. Oh, now I could understand how it was possible; the thing was a living construct, probably with the brainpower of a hundred Nomes but all focused on the single task of translating. Still, the way it was taking two separate languages and even apparently conveying accurate nuances of emotion . . . hell, there are career actors who can't handle that job in their own language!

"Like all spirits, however, we had our opposites, those charged with the release of destructive impulses from the Earth, the eradication of other life through disasters, and so on. While *Nowë* was active, both sides had the great Senses that told us when each approach was correct or incorrect. And so we cooperated with each other and with your people in ensuring that the great dance of *Nowë* was carried out properly. Over the span of millennia, however, that was lost, and the *Lisharithada* were changed horribly by the *Makurada Demagon* into a race of creatures who enjoyed the destruction they could create and sought ways to make it worse, if possible."

"So you're at war with them, then?" I asked.

Rokhaset began another of those sudden shrieks, but cut it off. His voice was heavy with sadness when he continued. "War? By *Nowë's* heart, never! We try to negate their efforts. We are made to cooperate, to assist, Clinton Slade. Killing and fighting is tremendously hard for us. We have warriors, yes, and they are formidable in their own way. But they do not kill except in self-defense or by accident, even such creatures as yourself. Kill our own people? It is not even to be imagined easily."

"So you try to sabotage their efforts, sorta undoing their work, but you can't fight them directly?"

"In most cases, yes. We can directly fight them, in small numbers, under very specific circumstances—when what they are trying to do is of sufficient destructive scale that it is not merely our lives, but those of countless others involved. It is then that we truly need the *H'adamant*."

"For . . . ?" Jodi prompted.

"In your language, I suppose the best term would be 'potion' or 'elixir.' Your own people understand certain symbolisms with *H'adamant*, now that I realize you call them by the name 'diamond.' The basic symbolism is not far from correct. If the Earth wills it, we can extract the essence of *H'adamant* and preserve it in an elixir which will make us stronger in virtually all ways—more capable of withstanding injury, and quicker, physically and mentally. In this way we are able to utilize small numbers of our people to oppose their vastly larger forces, to cut through their defenses, and to neutralize the rituals in which they invoke such massive powers of destruction."

"They can fight you, right?"

Rokhaset nodded deliberately. "Oh, yes, Jodi Goldman. Enough of our old instinctive accord survives that even they will not attack us for no reason—there will be no genocide here, despite our opposition. But if we are actually intruding on their territory and interfering with their work, they most assuredly will fight us, and can and will kill our people. As you can see, this places us at a grave disadvantage without *H'adamant*."

"Okay, I get you. And right now they're planning one of their big parties, right?"

"One which, if you will pardon the use of one of your own idioms, will assuredly bring down the house." Rokhaset seemed grim. "And for the second time, your people, Clinton Slade, have made it impossible for us to stop it . . . and both your people and mine will pay the price."

"Second time?" Now, I was getting really nervous, as I started to get a glimmer of the horror that was waiting behind Rokhaset's account.

"Second time, Clinton Slade. When your ancestor first entered our caverns and stole our entire cache, cloaked by the *H'kuraden* he carried, he did so at the worst possible moment; the times and powers had aligned so that the *Lisharithada* could carry out one of their greatest destructive rituals, and suddenly we were powerless to stop it. For a time we believed that somehow they had found a way to bypass the mystical defenses that surrounded our most secure caches. It was almost a relief when the next theft's source was traced to your forefather. But that did not repair the damage from the first theft. For a while, we had convinced them to moderate their behavior, but then your people truly began your intrusions upon the Earth, and their anger grew. Now the same forces have aligned once more, and the *Lisharithada* prepare to unleash them with even more fury than they did a short time after your ancestor had robbed us for the first time."

"Holy Mother of God." I heard myself whisper, unable to stop myself. "You're talking about the New Madrid Earthquakes!"

What Jodi said at that point I can't repeat. Rokhaset simply bowed his head.

"Look, Rokhaset, we gotta try to stop 'em at least! We'll head topside and you guys will help us get the road back, so's we can get you the diamonds that're left. We could try to buy some more back."

Rokhaset nodded. "We shall try, Clinton Slade. We shall hope the *H'adamant* you still have shall suffice, but I have grave doubts. We do not have the time for you to buy some more, I am afraid. To make the elixir will take two and a half days, as you measure time. They will strike in four days, as that is when the forces will be at their peak of alignment. Do you truly believe you shall be able to locate so many *H'adamant*, arrange for their purchase, and deliver them to us, in time for us to make the elixir and then carry the battle to them? Even as things are, it will be difficult, leaving aside the fact that, as your people do not know or respect *H'adamant* for what it is, there would be no way of telling whether the ones you purchased retained their true virtue until they had actually arrived."

There wasn't any arguing that. Four days . . .

I tried not to think about it, but anyone in my profession has already visualized the consequences of a Richter 8+ quake east of the Mississippi, and the New Madrid fault has always been the chief suspect. The area of effect of a major quake in this area would be monstrous: ten, fifteen times that of a comparable quake on the West Coast. It would level almost everything manmade in at least three or four states, cause heavy damage in adjoining ones, and be felt from the Rockies all the way to Vermont, maybe even Maine.

"Waitaminnit!" I said, suddenly thinking of something. "These *Lisharithada*, they live underground like you do, right? Well, if they set off a Richter eight quake right here, what's gonna keep 'em—and you, for all of that—from being squished when the quake brings the caverns down?"

"We are spirits of the Earth, Clint. We have our ways of preventing our own homes from breaking. Unfortunately, this is not true of your homes, or of caverns which we no longer inhabit."

I stood up. "Well, sir, seems to me we've both got work to do. We need to get topside so's we can get the *H'adamant* back, and you'll need to get your people to rebuild our road."

"Indeed." He stood as well and after a moment offered his hand, another gesture he had clearly been shown by the *makatdireskovi*. I took it; the skin was cool and hard, like shaking the hand of a rough-hewn statue, but no statue ever squeezed back that way. "Clinton Slade, Jodi Goldman, it has been a pleasure, truly. I regret we have met in these circumstances, yet perhaps *Nowë* shall smile upon us and somehow we shall stop the coming disaster." He shook Jodi's hand as well. "Shall I send an escort with you?"

"No offense, sir, but you people don't seem to be the fastest sorts. I remember the route, and I think me and Jodi can make it back a lot quicker on our own."

Jodi nodded. The route was long, but it was actually pretty direct, and we had blazed our way with more than just dropped relays whenever there was a doubtful intersection.

"As you will. My people can move quickly, but not for long distances. There you have the advantage of us."

❖   ❖   ❖

We left the throne room with hundreds of Nomes lining our path, holding their weapons in a very different manner. Clearly the word had spread that there was now an accord between us, and they were expressing their understanding as clearly as they could without their ruler's peculiar advantage.

Once out of the throne room, we made time, pushing as fast as safety would allow. "Father, I don't know if anyone's listening, but we're on our way out."

"Clint!" came Jonah's voice. "Y'all okay?"

"We're fine, and the Nomes are right nice folks, but we've got ourselves a powerful lot of trouble. Tell you about it once we're up."

Jonah said he'd get the family, so I signed off. The next four days were sure going to be interesting, but like in the old Chinese proverb way.

9. Too Little. Too Late?

"We might be 'bout four days from Armageddon, or leastwise that's how it's going to seem around here," I started out.

The whole family was gathered around the table this time, from Evangeline through Helen and Adam on through Grandpa.

"But you said the Nomes isn't our enemies, right, Clint?" Mamma asked anxiously.

"Right, Mamma. But it turns out they've got relatives of their own that there's a feud with. These boys play on a bigger scale than we ever figured, and we Slades have gummed up the works but bad." Jodi and I went on to summarize what Rokhaset had told us. "So unless we can do something to help 'em out, in four days the New Madrid's going to cut loose with a

Big One and ain't nothing going to be left standin' for hundreds of miles, least of all the Slade homestead."

The family sat there in silence. It was an awful lot to take in at once. And somehow it sounded a lot more fantastic here, in the comfortable electric lights of the family room, than it had in the blue-white glow of Rokhaset's domain.

"You think they can do that?" Father said finally.

I exchanged glances with Jodi. "It's hard to say, Father. But . . . yes, I guess I have to believe it. What reason would they have to concoct such a silly story if they had a more reasonable motive for wanting the diamonds? We sure didn't show any sign of needing anything that outlandish."

"Well," Evangeline pointed out, "y'all did say they learned how to talk with us from listenin' to the TV and radio. Lord only knows what they think is normal, Clint."

I chuckled despite my worries. "You got a point there, Evvie. Jodi?"

She tossed her dark hair back, then shook her head. "I think Rokhaset's pretty clear on how we think. No way he'd waste his time making up some *bobbe maisse* like that one; he's got more important stuff to do."

"Well, then, we give 'em all the diamonds we have left and hope it's enough." Mamma said.

"Do more than hope, Mamma. Pray. If this doesn't work, those destructive cousins of the Nomes are going to cause the biggest disaster the States have ever seen."

"What can we do, Clint?" Adam demanded.

"Grab our tools and get out there for when they start trying to get the road back. It's easy enough to wreck something, but they don't drive cars, and I'm not sure they'll know what has to be done to really make it driveable. And shut off the fence. They're not going to come after us now that they know us." I felt my eyes trying to shut. "But me and Jodi have to get some rest."

"Lord, of course you do," Mamma said. "Why, it's been almost twenty-four hours you've been up, and most of that either hiking the caves or facing Mr. Rokhaset, which must have been about as scary as anything!"

"Get up to bed," Father agreed. "Need your strength later."

Jodi and I didn't argue. We knew there wasn't any way we were staying awake much longer. I stumbled up to bed, feeling my feet get heavier with every step. The clothes I peeled off seemed to be made of lead, and I don't really remember hitting the mattress.

I woke up with a hoarse shout, as the ground quivered underneath the house. *"JODI!"*

"A *CHORBN*!" I heard the Yiddish curse echo all the way down the hall. *"What?* Did they move up the schedule?"

By then, I was out of bed and down the hall, bursting through Jodi's door. The shaking was already over. "No, no, that was just a little one. But Holy Mother, did that scare me!"

"And I was calm, you think? *Oy!*" She was still in the bed, nude from the waist up since the sheets had slid down when she sat up abruptly. The view was on the spectacular side. Her long, curly, lustrous black hair was spilling over her shoulders, framing her chest. Jodi was basically a slender woman, but not everywhere. I was a little transfixed, for a moment. Memories . . .

She looked me up and down, suddenly grinning. "You look as nice as I remember, too, *neshomeleh*. But you might want to put some clothes on before your family decides *we* caused all that shaking and bouncing around."

I looked down. I was nude from the soles of my feet up.

"Oops. Hey, look, I was startled. Gimme a second."

By the time I got back to her room, with my bath-robe on, Jodi was already out of bed and wearing her own robe. In that respect, if nothing else, she certainly didn't fit the stereotype of a Jewish-American Princess. Jodi was always punctual and could get dressed faster than a fireman. How she manages that, I'll never know, because the end result was never sloppy. Every item of clothing was on right, buttons square, zippers zipped, hair brushed, the works. Even the many times I'd watched her do it, I'd never really been able to fig-ure out her secret. She just seemed to pour herself into her clothes, shoes and all—hell, *work boots* and all—and she had the kind of magic hair that, despite its length and thickness, immediately fell into place at the touch of her fingers.

When I walked in, she was muttering something to the effect that the much-vaunted stability of the nation's conservative inner regions compared to decadent Manhattan was obviously a be-damned lie. About a third of the words were in Yiddish so I didn't catch all of it. But the last phrase came through clear as a bell: "—least the *ground* doesn't mug you!"

"C'mon," I chided, "what's the big deal?" I imitated her accent. "'The trucks on Fifth shake my apartment harder than that!'"

She giggled despite herself. "Okay, wisenheimer, you'll get yours. But only after I get a shower."

We both needed showers badly after the last day. If I hadn't been so dog-tired I'd have showered before going to sleep, but collapsing in a shower isn't the best idea.

So, half an hour later, we met downstairs. A frus-trating half hour, since Jodi and I like to take show-ers together which maybe accounts for why we usually take such long ones. I was finding this *be-proper-before-the-family* routine was getting old really fast. Even the prospect of continental catastrophe in four days wasn't enough to squelch all my normal *I-want-Jodi* enthusiasms.

I guess I muttered something to that effect. "Stop whining, Clint," Jodi instructed me, as we headed for the kitchen. "Look at it this way. Soon enough we'll either be dead or we'll be married and either way you won't have to worry about it any more. Getting laid, I mean. You'll still have to scrub my back—don't think for a moment I'll let you off the hook on that just 'cause you're my husband. Or a corpse."

Her stern and stoic words would have been more effective if she hadn't goosed me as I started through the kitchen door.

Mamma was in the kitchen, looking exhausted herself, but with enough food to feed four of me laid out. "Nice to see both of you up, Clint dear, Jodi. Father and Adam are up to the road, along with Helen and Evangeline. Everyone else just went to bed, which is where I'm going now."

"How's it going up there?"

She gave a tired smile. "Lord, they're devilish looking things, but those rockworms and their keepers can work miracles. We just might get this done in time, Clint. Might could. Best eat up and go see for yourselves."

I gave Mamma a hug, which she returned—a little tighter than usual. She kissed Jodi on the cheek and then headed upstairs. I turned to the table and dug in.

"We slept ten hours, Clint. Down to three and a half days or less now. We have to get into town, get back with the diamonds in less than a day."

I nodded, wolfing down some ham. "I know, I know. Let's get up to the road, see what they're up to."

It wasn't a long hike, and in the sunlight it was less eerie, though no less strange, to see the hurrying pipestem-limbed Nomes and their centipedal assistants.

As we came to the edge of the huge scar in the earth, I sucked in my breath. Buttresses of limestone were forming, curving in rippling bands to create supports for the stone that would lie atop them. It was the rockworms which were doing most of the work, chewing up rock in one place and depositing it, changed and molded, in another. I looked around and saw Adam, Father, and Rokhaset under a large spreading oak at the far edge.

We hiked around to them. Looking down, I could see that the rockworms came in differing sizes, from the little ones about two feet long up to one nightmare-inducing monster nearly twenty feet long, with horns and spikes of crystal adorning its head and a mouth that looked more like a rock-crusher than anything living.

"Father, Adam, Rokhaset." I said in greeting.

"It is good to see you again, Clinton Slade, Jodi Goldman," Rokhaset acknowledged us.

"Clint. Jodi. Work's going."

"And fast, too," Adam said. "Their . . . what was the name again, sir?"

"*Seradatho H'a min*, or you might call them simply *seradatho* for short."

"*Seradatho*, yep, they just make the rock as we stand here. Ain't maybe as fast as a full construction crew, but it's plenty fast enough. I think."

"Is it safe for me to go down and look?"

Rokhaset gave a deliberately human shrug. "The *seradatho* will not harm you on purpose, Clint. But some may not notice you immediately, even with their handlers present, so take care."

I slid down into the pit and walked carefully up to one of the medium-sized *seradatho*, which was starting to put some kind of joining stone between some of the buttresses. I examined the resulting stone carefully, then climbed back up. "Sir, that looks just like standard cavern limestone! I swear, if I took that back to a lab I wouldn't be able to tell the difference!"

"And nor should you. We are part of the Earth, Clint. How many times must I say this before you truly understand? Nothing that we do may be apart from her. Except in our own dwellings, it must not even be recognizable as our work, but be fully in harmony with *Nowë*, as much a part of her as we are."

I shook my head, still trying to comprehend it. "But it looks like standard flowstone—deposited over thousands and thousands of years. How the hell can you possibly replicate that?"

"I could attempt to explain it," Rokhaset said, after some consideration, "but in truth, without taking much time indeed to instruct you, all that I could tell you would boil down to saying 'it's magic,' a most unsatisfactory explanation. Suffice to say that this is the way it must be for us."

"So some of those natural-seeming caverns we see around the world are really your doing?"

"Undoubtedly. Sometimes your people intrude upon us by exploring what you think are natural caves and are, instead, our dwelling places. Only in the great cities and central places of the Earth do we build places such as the throne room and its nearby environs."

I rubbed my temples. Running into the Nomes themselves, well, I'd always known they were there. So it was more like just meeting some aliens. This, though, was magic—a kind of magic that affected stuff I really did know a lot about, and direct enough to hit me in the gut. The threat of the *Lisharithada*'s great quake was real enough, but too huge to grasp, really. Seeing stone that, by rights, ought to have taken a million years to form be spat out in seconds by some crawling centipede-thing, that was different.

I remembered, suddenly, the rushing water I'd heard when the great doors to the Throne Room opened. "You don't even use machines like we do. You just channel water and maybe use levers or something to move those doors and other things."

"Correct. In nature, sometimes water does move great boulders, so we can construct a device that takes advantage of that."

"Well, Clint, now we know why we've never seen any traces of these things before in caves around the world."

I nodded to Jodi. "Ayup. We *did* see traces, more'n likely. Problem is that there was no way to tell the traces from the original stone. Y'all even make stalactites and stalagmites and all the trimmings, right, and make sure the water's there to keep it alive?"

Rokhaset seemed pleased that I'd picked up on the last part. "Exactly right, Clint. I see you have finally penetrated the significance of your original ancestor's find."

"In a cave, water flowing represents life to you just like to us. So you keep your diamonds and other stones in those pools so they stay a part of *Nowë*'s essence, right?"

"Very good. Yes, precisely so."

I noticed Rokhaset was staying carefully in the deepest shadows under the tree, and remembered his prior comments. "Hey, you said your eyes might suffer in the sun. I could get you something that probably will help."

"Indeed?"

"Yeah. I've done some work with multispectral optics, off and on, and you mentioned your eyes get messed up slowly. I'll bet the crystals are being affected by the ultraviolet rays, which you'll never run into underground." I handed him a pair of UV-blocker sunglasses.

He put them on and glanced around with his odd sight. "Extraordinary. There is minor interference from these glasses in how well I *turan*, but I can tell that the faint pain from the light here is considerably lessened."

"I wasn't sure if the plastic would interfere with your own senses, but the fact that it blocked UV made it worth a try. UV's generally the culprit in most damage sunlight does."

"I believe you are correct in this case. Thank you." Rokhaset glanced into the pit. "I do not suppose you have a few dozen pairs of these?"

I chuckled ruefully. "Nope, and can't get any until we get to town."

"Then let us arrange that as swiftly as possible."

The next few hours passed quickly. Rokhaset drove his people and their seradatho twice as hard, pausing only to listen when we clarified how the terrain would have to run in order to permit the cars to pass. Before our eyes, the landscape healed; it was the only way to describe that incredible sight. Stone and soil literally growing up out of the bowels of the Earth, a foundation of limestone covered by soil, and trees and brush somehow moving in over the scar through careful manipulation of the soil and roots.

Finally, the hillside was solid again. "Now, Clinton Slade, it is time for you to fulfill your part of this bargain."

"I'm on it. C'mon, Jodi, we've got a withdrawal to do up to the bank, and darn little time to do it in. We've gotta get to town in less than an hour or the bank will close!"

We dashed to the truck and got in. "Strap in tight, Jodi—y'all's in for a hell of a ride!"

Fountaining gravel, we pulled out of the gateway and

thundered downhill, plowing over the newly-laid earth
and leaving its first set of tire tracks. The new road
around the first gash slowed me down some, being as
it had to make a sharp curve, but I opened her up
again and had all four wheels off the ground at the
first drop on the straightaway. We jolted against the
harnesses and even with the heavy shocks she nearly
bottomed out. "*Oy*, Clint, slow down! We can't make
any withdrawals if we're dead!"

"Ain't no slowin' down, sweetheart. If'n you remember when we drove through last time, takes all of an
hour and ten minutes to get to town. And we can't take
that long nohow."

"Your accent's getting worse, Clint."

"Yeah, I know. It's 'cause o' th'truck," I said stoutly.
"A pickup jest naturally brings out th' inner hillbilly
in a man."

Pavement, albeit pretty crappy, was now under the
wheels and I opened her up as much as I dared.
There's places where you can make over 70, and others where even a nutcase wouldn't go past 30 on those
roads, unless he was stone drunk. I drove like a stone-
drunk nutcase and Jodi just hung on to the doorframe
and said nasty words in Yiddish.

We came screaming down the main street with me
riding the brake to get down below the limit as we
passed the town line; I think Sheriff McCloskey almost
lit off his lights before he saw it was me. I skidded
us into a spot in the parking lot and jumped out for
the doors, just as I heard the soft but final *click* of the
bank door being locked for the day.

"Son of a—" I couldn't quite stop in time to keep
from whomping the doors. Arlene Ebsen, the manager,
gave me a stern look, but turned around. "Clinton
Jefferson Slade, I've known you since you were in dia-
pers, and I know your mamma raised you better'n that!"

"Sorry, Miss Arlene, really sorry, but I've just gotta get into the deposit vault. Please!"

She pursed her lips. "Clint, you know we like the Slades as our customers, but I can't just go openin' and closin' at someone else's convenience."

"*Please*, Miss Arlene, I'm beggin' you. I'm right here on my knees, I mean it." And I was. We just couldn't miss it by this much, we just couldn't!

She rolled her eyes. "Well, Lord, if it's *that* all-fired important . . . just this once. But don't try this again!"

The sound of the door unlocking was like the whole weight of my truck lifting off my back. "Hurry up, y'hear?" Arlene said. "That there vault's on a time lock. Locks itself down in half an hour after closing, less'n someone's in it, but if someone is in it, it screams fit to wake the dead."

"Don't you worry!" I said, racing ahead of her, key already out. "Be gone so fast you'll think I wasn't even here."

Jodi waited back by the doors. After Arlene took my key, matched it with hers and opened the safety deposit box, she marched out of the vault heading for the phone. She was probably going to call Father to make sure there wasn't some reason I might be trying to make off with the family treasures in secret. It didn't take me long to get out the diamonds, since they weren't loose but stashed in three little bags. I slammed the box shut again, locked it hastily, and hurried out of the vault towards the outside door. Passing Arlene, who was just hanging up with a slightly bemused expression, I said: "Thanks a million, Miss Arlene!"

I took a bit more time on the drive back. It'd be awfully stupid to get us both killed now that we actually had the diamonds Rokhaset needed and weren't racing against a specific deadline. But it wasn't easy, because my foot kept wanting to hammer the gas, and from her expression I think Jodi felt the same way. We were going to be in good time overall, but still, it felt like every second counted. It was getting dark by the time we made it back to the homestead. I parked the truck and jogged to the front door.

I then faced what might have been the oddest sight I'd ever seen in my life: Rokhaset was sitting at Mamma's big table, everyone else eating her cooking and him with slices of some kind of stone on his plate, as though he was no stranger a dinner guest than some new neighbor. Strange, yeah, but I felt a huge swell of pride in my family. Okay, so we Slades had been barbarians to these people, but damned if you could call us barbarians now. I wouldn't bet that one in a thousand families could have a Nome at the table and treat it—him—like proper company.

Rokhaset stood as we entered. "The *H'adamant*—do you have it?"

"Right here. Hope it's still alive, like you call it."

As I put the bags in his hand, he nodded. "I can hear it. Weakened slightly by time away from the heart of *Nowë*, but still there." He fumbled with the bags a bit, examining what was inside; he didn't need to open them. I wasn't an expert in Nome body language, but it seemed to me he slumped a bit.

"My thanks to you for a valiant effort, Clinton Slade," he said finally. "But it is as I feared. There is not enough here—not nearly enough—to provide us with a force to overcome what the *Lisharithada* will have to defend them. We shall do our best, of course; it is our calling and destiny. But we shall never triumph."

I stared at Rokhaset. "No. We can't let it end like that."

"Of course we can't, Clint dear. And we won't," Mamma said tartly. "Mr. Rokhaset, we've come invisibly into your homes and taken your diamonds; it's about time we made it up to you. How do you think a few Slades might change the odds, down there in your little war?"

The High Spirit turned around to face her. "You would fight for us?"

"Well, it's for my family too, isn't it? And it's our fault, as Jodi showed us. Now, I only married into the Slades, but what I was taught was that a Slade admits when he's wrong and fixes it until it's right."

"And that's the God's honest truth," Grandpa said forcefully. "Damn this bum leg! I'd come if I could, but I'd slow y'all down."

"Only a few," Father said. "Not like Nomes; can't live without light, need lots of spares."

"I'm going," I said.

"And so am I." At the reaction of the others, Jodi snorted. "What? You think I'm not tough enough? I've lived in New York for years, that's more than tough enough to take care of some *shlemiels* who think they can just start an earthquake whenever they want to. I'm tough enough to keep Clint here in line. You just try me."

Debate in this argument wasn't going to last long. We knew we had to field a pretty strong team, but a lot of the family had to stay behind, both because of the limits on equipment and because if we failed, the rest of the family had to stay behind to get everything out of the house and save as much of the homestead as possible when the Big One hit. So it was me, Jodi, Father, and Adam.

Rokhaset nodded slowly. "It may work. Never in all these centuries have your people helped us, and with your ability to use the *H'kuraden* as both weapon and cloak . . . yes, it could be enough. I—"

He froze suddenly. I was puzzled for a moment, then realized that he must be getting news through the same kind of link he had with the *makatdireskovi*. A few moments later, he looked back at us, and I could tell just by the way he stood that it wasn't good news.

"It appears that the *Lisharithada* want to make sure we are not able to interfere." Rokhaset sat down slowly. "They have deliberately sealed off *Nowëmosdet* between our area and theirs. While we can, especially with the power of *H'adamant*, pass through, they will doubtless have forces waiting there to slow and harass us. There is no way that a *Tennathada* could possibly reach them."

The room that had been optimistic a moment ago now seemed utterly sunk in gloom. After a few moments in silence, Rokhaset forced himself to his feet. "I must take the *H'adamant* to my people. It may not suffice, but I must at least make the attempt, and none of my people can come here to fetch it. It requires quite extraordinary efforts by myself and the *makatdireskovi* to maintain my communication at all. Others of my people would be crippled in the attempt. Farewell, Clinton Slade, Jodi Goldman, and all of your kin."

Something was nagging at me as he left, but it refused to gel. The door closed.

Grandpa slammed a hand on the table so hard it upset three glasses. "Damnation! So close!"

Mamma sighed. "I suppose we shall have to prepare for the worst now. If only there was another way."

Suddenly it clicked. *Another way!* I raced out the door. "Rokhaset! Wait!"

He turned, a dark shadow with faintly glowing eyes. "What is it, Clint?"

"Listen, some people have had a theory for a while now that most if not all of the caverns in this state, maybe farther, are connected somehow. Would you know if that's true?"

He nodded. "It is true, Clinton Slade, though finding the connections could be difficult for your people, and not all connections are direct. Why?"

"Then we come at them from a different direction, if you can tell us the right route to take! Mammoth Caves, Rokhaset—if there's a route through there, we can hit 'em from behind!"

He stood very still for a moment. "It is possible. Barely possible, Clinton Slade, for the route shall be long even if I can find such a route that you can pass, but . . . it is worth a try. Get out all the information you have on these 'Mammoth Caves' while I deliver the *H'adamant*. I shall return and we will see if, perhaps, there is one last chance for us all."

10. Paging Arne Saknussemm . . .

"I *really* don't know about this," I found myself saying for the twentieth time.

Rokhaset waved a hand at me to be quiet, so I shut off the transducer that bounced my voice into his range and turned to Jodi. "I meant Mammoth Caves as an example, I guess. I mean, look how far away it is. You know how long it takes to get through anything except a tourist section of a cave—a lot of the time you wouldn't measure things as miles per hour, but more like hours per mile. Or hours per hundred yards, in really hairy terrain."

Jodi nodded. "But Rokhaset has some idea of what we're able to handle, I'm sure. He's not *narish*. Maybe he knows something we don't and that's why he asked for more maps."

"Maybe. But I think I'd best make sure." I got up and went over to where the High Spirit was standing, seeming to look into thin air, and turned the transducer back on. "Rokhaset—"

"A few more moments, Clinton Slade, and then I will answer your questions."

Rokhaset was actually looking at our maps, which hadn't been easy to arrange. Once more, the fact that the *makatdireskovi* allowed us to talk as though we both actually understood each other's language had tripped us up. We'd gathered all the info we had on Mammoth and other, more nearby, caves, only to realize—the next day, when he arrived—that Rokhaset could neither see the pictures and diagrams nor read the words on paper. It had taken a couple hours of panicked discussion, and then a few more of hours of jury-rigging by Jodi, to arrive at a solution. But with the help of an old video camera and some low-power broadcast kit-bashing, Jodi had made it possible for Rokhaset to receive images of the books and maps in the same way they had been intercepting transmissions all along. Another hour had been required to help Rokhaset interpret the diagrams in a way analogous to our own so that he could then try to coordinate what he was seeing with what his people knew about the underground world. Now the High Spirit was trying to put together what he knew with what we knew and see if there was, indeed, any chance of us reaching the *Lisharithada*'s domain in time via another route.

A few moments later he turned. "I believe it can be done."

"Are you sure?" I asked. "No offense, sir, but you gotta remember that we're surface people, and makin' our way through underground passages takes time. Hell, that's something like a hundred miles from here. Even topside I'm not sure we could cover that distance on foot, an' that's straight-line distance, which ain't what you're dealin' with underground."

He made a weird sound I interpreted as laughter. "True and more than true, Clinton Slade; and yet it can be done, I think, though it shall be far from easy." He turned to Jodi, who was testing connections on her latest improvisation. "Are you ready, Jodi Goldman?"

"Try it, Rokhaset. If you can duplicate the transmission pattern, we should be set."

Given the manner in which Rokhaset and the *makatdireskovi* communicated, and the fact that the *makatdireskovi* received and interpreted TV and radio broadcasts, Jodi had wondered if it could, through Rokhaset, replicate the transmission in the other direction. After some consulting with the semisentient geobiomystical device and his advisors, Rokhaset had announced that it should in fact be possible; if so, he would have an ideal way of communicating the chosen route to us.

For a moment, the TV in the room just showed wavering patterns of static. Then, so suddenly we jumped, a test pattern and sound appeared, just like on any standard broadcast station. Except, of course, this was on one of the channels that shouldn't show anything but dead air.

I swore I could almost see Rokhaset grin. "Ah, so it works. Excellent. Then I can show you and you can record this into your portable computers."

We hooked our laptops up through the RF modulator and checked to make sure the signal was being recorded. "Let 'er rip, Rokhaset."

A map of Kentucky appeared, with purple highlighting the Slade homestead and bright green marking Mammoth Caves. The highlighting was shaped like an octagon instead of a circle, the way we usually do it, but aside from that and Rokhaset's apparent preference for using our colors in painful ways, it looked just like one we would produce.

A bright red dot came into view, looking to be somewhere in Muhlenberg County. "The *Lisharithada* are based here, very nearly halfway between the great cavern complex you call Mammoth Caves and our own homes. You must disrupt their operations here in order to prevent the ritual from being carried out.

"Now, I fully realize the distances involved, and if you indeed had to travel in the normal fashion through ordinary caverns, there would be no way for this to work. However, one of the reasons both we and the *Lisharithada* have remained in this area for so many ages is simply that more remnants of the Old Ways have survived here than in nearly any other part of the world. One of these remnants is a portion of *Nowëmosdet*."

I remembered the word from earlier, but I'd presumed it was just a term for cavern. "What's that?"

"You might call it '*Nowë*'s Road,' I suppose. In the old days there were many interconnected tunnels, like cities, and passage between them was made easier by a sort of network of canals invested with *Nowë*'s power—the *Nowëmosdet*. Two long segments of it still exist in this area. One connects our area with that of the *Lisharithada*, and this is of course what they have closed off to make it difficult to traverse. The other section was traditionally used only by the *Lisharithada* as it goes in the other direction. It is ironic, in a way."

Jodi and I looked at each other. "What do you mean?"

"One could say that it is the *Nowëmosdet* that is responsible for our current emergency. You will recall that I did not question you as to what 'Mammoth Cave' was; this is because I am all too familiar with that system of caverns, at least in general. While the *Lisharithada* are, as I have described, now very hostile towards your people, the thing that finally pushed them into action is that your people's exploration of the great cave system is fast approaching the point where you might discover *Nowëmosdet*, which would be potentially disastrous even though you could not normally use it as we would. No matter how natural looking, your people would become curious about a straight-line cavern so long and even in design, and would quickly arrive at the *Lisharithada*'s domain. Thus, despite the fact that parts of what you call Mammoth Cave are of historic significance to us, the *Lisharithada* have determined that they will destroy it all to prevent your continued intrusions."

"And just incidentally kill thousands—maybe tens or hundreds of thousands—of us along with it. Nice people."

Rokhaset gave a humming sound that carried the same force and tone as a sigh. "Once they were. In some ways, they are still very much like us. But without *Nowë*'s guidance . . . No matter." The image zoomed in, showing the network of caverns that made up the longest, if not the deepest, cave system known to man, a duplicate of one of the maps we'd shown him. Suddenly, an entirely new network of caverns spread across the map, filling in areas never explored by humans, extending across most of the state and beyond into every area that had stone to support caves—and some, near as I could tell, into areas that normally shouldn't have caves at all.

Rokhaset didn't need to tell us where *Nowë*'s Road was. Even without his highlighting it was sharply obvious, a geometrically perfect line running from near the intersection of Flint and Mammoth's networks directly to the west-northwest almost half the distance to the homestead. It terminated in another tangle of caverns, and then started again on the other side to end somewhere below our feet.

"As you can see," Rokhaset said, "if you can reach *Nowëmosdet*, you will be able to proceed straight to the realm of the *Lisharithada*. Taking into account your size and what I have been able to deduce of your abilities, I here trace the path you must take to reach the Road of *Nowë*."

We watched as the route started at the Historic Entrance, following the route for the now-defunct Echo River tour through the Rotunda and the Historic Tour route to River Hall before diverting to pick up the River Styx and the Echo River. Then it suddenly jagged off towards the connection to Flint Ridge, which was near the middle of Cascade Hall.

"Wait up there," Jodi said. "Looks like the connection that leads to the Road is more over to the Flint side, Rokhaset. Why come in through Mammoth?"

"Two reasons, Jodi Goldman. Firstly, if I am not mistaken, Mammoth is more open and will permit you to make better time in all likelihood, even if you must approach over a somewhat longer route. Secondly, the approach from the Mammoth direction will make it easier for you to reach the tunnel here, which is unexplored by your people and eventually leads you to *Nowëmosdet*. This tunnel will be found at the very top of the chamber. While maps such as this are terribly inadequate for showing elevation, on the Flint side you would be ascending quite steeply before you even reach the level of this known passage. And then you would have a further difficult climb to reach the critical tunnel."

"Whee. Abandoning the tour in mid-stride. That'll liven up the tour, sure 'nuff."

"Get ourselves banned from the cave too. Oh, well, not much we can do about that, *nu*? Just remember to have everything packed and move fast. It'd be embarrassing to have the whole state devastated because we were too slow and some well-meaning tourists caught us." She studied the map. "Still, I don't want to be a *nudje*, but that stretch of *Nowëmosdet* is like to be forty miles long. And filled with water. What, you think we're fish? We're not doing that in two days, that's for sure."

The High Spirit nodded. "I understand this completely. There is a way to give you the endurance and speed needed. But it may not be entirely safe."

"*Give* us endurance and speed? How—" I broke off, staring at him. "Are y'all out of your mind? I don't doubt the stuff works on your people, but it's prob'ly pure poison to us! 'Sides, y'all need it, right?"

"You are quick in grasping the idea, Clinton Slade. Yet you are not entirely correct. The elixir, made according to the ancient recipes, is said to have been the same for your people as well as my own. It is born of the power of the world that sustains us both." He shifted his stance slightly. "It is true that the Powers have changed, so there may be some difference in effect, which is why I say there may be some risk. Yet I sincerely believe it shall produce the requisite effect, and, most importantly, surround you with the aura of one who belongs in the Earth, so that *Nowëmosdet* will accept you and assist you."

"And the fact that you won't have time to make it before we have to leave—which will have to be in very few hours, to be honest—and that y'all need it for your people?"

"If you can be of assistance at all, Clinton Slade, it will be because one of your people, wielding *H'kuraden* and striking from invisibility, will be worth many of my warriors combined. But the true drawback is this: I have but two elixirs at this time, for as you have so correctly noted we shall need far more time to finish making any from your own *H'adamant*. So only two of you may go, and no more."

"That's gonna be me and Jodi, then," I said, before she could say anything.

She looked surprised. Pleased, but surprised. "Hey, look," I continued, shrugging, "I've given up trying to keep you out of it, Jodi. And to be honest, you're probably better at the caving end of things than anyone else here. Ours is a pretty specialized knowledge of how to rob Nomes, not explore caves. That was Winston's gig, more or less, and he's been dead quite a stretch."

"Well, what do you know. Maybe you can be domesticated after all," Jodi said smugly.

Ignoring the gibe, I turned back to Rokhaset. "Okay, let's say we get there. Where, exactly, do we go in this area they obviously control, and what'll we be fighting? How many, what's their weaknesses, that kind of thing. Jodi's done some fencing, as one of your warriors found out, and I'm not too bad in a scrap, but we still probably ain't going to be taking on a whole army at once."

"In the main, their troops will be very much like our own in appearance, but more willing to inflict injury. Still, they have avoided your people over the years, while we have grown used to you. They will be very disoriented by the fact that you cannot be sensed easily, if at all, with *H'kuraden*, and you have advantages of reach and height which, in the caverns they favor, you will be able to exploit."

He fingered the Egyptian beardlike tube on his chin. "Your goal, as I mentioned earlier, is to disrupt their ritual. You must work your way inward along this path from *Nowëmosdet*; in one way this route works in our favor, as the center of their mystic workings is located considerably closer to this branch of *Nowëmosdet*. Once there, you must shatter all crystalline items you see with your iron. This will completely negate the ritual and their power will be broken for many years to come, in which period perhaps we shall, together, find some means of returning sanity to *Nowë*'s realm. It is of course possible that they can overwhelm you if you are slow or unfortunate, but I think you have an excellent chance. The only thing that might stop you . . ." He trailed off, evidently having thought of something quite unpleasant.

"Go on, might as well know the worst."

"The *Lisharithada*, Jodi Goldman, like ourselves, are capable of *wëseraka*—life-shaping, causing the life of the Earth to take the form which best suits our purposes. Alas, in this as in all other things they have turned their power to destruction. They have developed the *seradatho* into efficient creatures of war. Most of these will still pose little greater threat to you than their masters; many of their offensive abilities are designed to deal with our people, not yours. However, if by bad fortune you encounter a *Magon* . . ."

"If we do, how will we know?"

Rokhaset gave one of his eerie laughs. "I assure you, Clinton Slade, you will know. A *seradatho H'a magon* is more than twice the size of the greatest of the *seradatho* you saw rebuilding the road, and is a being bred purely for destruction. It can strike us *matturan* at its approach, leaving us helpless before it. Even if its powers cannot directly affect you, it is huge, armored, equipped to tear and break and dissolve. Flee if one approaches."

That was a nasty image. "And why shouldn't we expect one?"

"Because they are extremely difficult to breed, and even more difficult to control, given their temperament and peculiar abilities. I do not believe they have more than one or two *Magon*, and they will almost certainly concentrate these major weapons at the area they expect us to attack, not the opposite direction. With any luck whatsoever, you should reach the ritual center and destroy it before they could even decide to redeploy the *Magon*, let alone have it reach you."

I winced. "I don't like trustin' to luck. I'm bringin' everything I can."

"We can't bring too much with us, Clint. That's a long hike, with a war at the end."

"Sure 'nuff, but I ain't goin' to a war unarmed. May not be able to smuggle a rifle past the entrance staff, but might could do some other stuff."

Rokhaset shrugged. "I have seen the power of some of your . . . gadgets, Clinton Slade. But the problem will be to have the chance to bring them to bear. Still, if it does not slow you down, there is no harm in bringing whatever you think might aid you." He reached into a pouch in his woven harness and extracted two octagonal crystal vials and a blue crystal, broken in half. "The *mikhsteri H'adamant*—the diamond elixir. Save it until you arrive at the entrance to *Nowëmosdet*, for we do not know how long it will last for a human, in this age of the world."

Jodi and I took a vial each and stowed them away in side pockets of our packs. Rokhaset then handed Jodi the broken crystal. "Keep this with you; it is attuned to its other half, and with it I can follow your progress and time the arrival of my forces to coincide with yours; perhaps we shall even meet in the domain of the *Lisharithada* and see victory together."

"I sure hope so." I shook his stony hand again, then turned to my fiancée. "C'mon, Jodi. Let's do this thing."

11. Three-Hour Tour

"You sure they'll let us take this stuff in?" Jodi asked.

"F'cryin'—Jodi, stop askin' the same question again

every few minutes. I wore a pack the last time I went in, no one said nothing."

"Yeah, yeah, I know, but I'm nervous! Me, okay, I'm not carrying anything all that bad except a couple nasty iron bars, but you—*oy*, if you trip—"

"It's not nitroglycerine, Jodi. It won't blow up without the right trigger. I could carve little doggie statues out of it if I wanted to. No one's gonna search me—unless y'all look so nervous that they think there is somethin' wrong, and then we're in big trouble. I got a permit for my gun, so that shouldn't be a problem. Not that I wanna use either if I don't have to, seein' as how big noises in caverns could lead to cave-ins which would ruin our party right quick."

"Right, right."

Leaving had been hurried. We had to pack everything we could fit into a reasonable space—we couldn't afford to draw too much attention—and picking and choosing while arguing with Grandpa, Mamma, and everyone else about why we were going and no one else hadn't been easy. Easier than the goodbyes, though, since none of us knew if we'd see them again. Even Father had gotten pretty choked up, which doesn't happen, and so that'd set me going, which got Jodi to start in, and I guess pretty much everyone ended up with sniffy noses and red eyes before it was all over and we drove off.

Fortunately for our hoped-for future, Jonah had asked what I was going to do about my car. Given that we were planning on violating federal law in breaking off on our own and all that, it would probably be pretty stupid to leave my truck parked overtime in the lot. Father and Adam would be coming after us about an hour later to pick up the truck and bring it home; if we lived through this, we'd come back home with Rokhaset and the others, rather than suddenly show up back at Mammoth anyway.

Mammoth Caves wasn't hard to find, at least. Major parks get good publicity like signs and all, which I appreciated, as it wasn't going to be likely we'd find anything like that down in the caves. In fact, we'd have to move fast through areas we only knew from tour maps and photos at first. While lagging behind might get us the chance to split off from the tour group at the right point, we didn't dare take the chance that someone might catch us. Put bluntly, if someone *did* try to catch us, Jodi and I would have to stop them instead.

The whole situation was really pretty annoying. If this disaster had happened back around 1991, we'd have been able to get right down to Cascade on the tour, but economics and conservation concerns had put an end to that one. At least one thing was in our favor: the past month or so had been pretty dry and the Green River was low. That meant we'd have dry path to run down for most of it before the splashing started. According to what I could gather, we probably wouldn't hit water much over five or six feet, leastwise not in too many places, which was good; not that me and Jodi couldn't swim, but in hiking clothes with packs, that was a different story.

I ran my finger around my neck; it was getting hot in here, even though I had the air conditioner on. We both had wetsuits underneath the hiking clothes. Any serious caver has them, though I'd only needed mine once. The water in caves at this latitude averages down around 55 degrees, and that's more than cold enough to give you hypothermia right quick.

We pulled into the parking lot, found the entrance and schedules, paid our tickets, then had to sit around for twenty nerve-racking minutes as the next tour prepared for departure. No one questioned our packs, which I thought was a near miracle, given that Jodi looked so jumpy. Maybe they just thought she was claustrophobic or something. Finally, the guide called us together and we all started the long hike—down a path, the two of us trying to hide how hot we were getting now while the guide pointed out the occasional squirrel. About the point when I felt like I was getting set to melt, we started down the stairs through the huge, vegetation-fringed opening that yawned darkly to swallow the staircase and us tourists whole: the Historic Entrance to Mammoth Cave.

Despite our hurry, I had to appreciate the sights. Mammoth is a damn impressive place. The Rotunda, a massive hall, opened up before us, and Colin Blair, the guide, began describing the operation that had taken place in the early 1800s to extract saltpeter for gunpowder from the mines. It seemed a bit ironic to me that the operation began somewhere around the time old Winston had grabbed his first big score from the Nomes. I resisted the temptation to ask how the quakes had affected the cave; the last thing Jodi and I needed was to draw attention to ourselves.

After a monologue that seemed, to my stressed psyche, to be hours long, Blair finally turned and began leading us along through Broadway—only to pause almost immediately to describe the Methodist Church. This was a large cavern with a pulpitlike formation which actually had been used as a church in the past. Jodi and I were slowly permitting others to pass us. Eventually we intended to end up at the very back, fall behind, and hopefully make our getaway without anyone noticing until it was too late to catch us.

"Look at that!" Jodi exclaimed.

As we neared Gothic Avenue, one of the weird phenomena Mammoth was famous for had materialized.

Within this giant confluence of caverns, a genuine sheet of clouds had formed and was trailing into the Avenue overhead. I pulled out the camera and took a couple of shots; we might be on our way to save the world, but what the heck.

We continued, past the Giant's Coffin, over the yawning mouths of the Sidesaddle and Bottomless Pits, and then through the maze of the Fat Man's Squeeze. By now we were used to the cavern's impressiveness; it was too thoroughly tamed here to continue to carry the impact, and some of the features we had seen in Rokhaset's domain overshadowed it. Now we were approaching the moment of truth. As we passed through the Great Relief Hall, Jodi and I fell back even farther, finally reaching the very tail end of the group. We lagged to look at some of the features in River Hall, then appeared to head towards the group again as Mr. Blair did the usual glance backwards to make sure all his sheep were following him in the direction of Sparks Avenue. He turned the corner, and we slowed down. No one was looking at us.

Jodi turned and walked quickly towards the pathway that led towards the River Styx. A moment later, still with an eye on the tour group continuing on, so did I. Then we both ran lightly down the path until we were out of sight of River Hall.

"Whew!"

"Shh!" Jodi put a finger to her lips. "We're not nearly out of it yet. Sound carries and they can chase us down fast. Keep moving!"

Move we did, heading farther and farther down. But when we got near Cascade Hall we encountered two things: water, which we expected . . . and voices, which we hadn't.

"Clint? What's going on?"

Belatedly, I remembered one of the National

Speleological Society articles I'd come across. "Damn, damn, damn. Must be the NSS team that's helping remove all the old stuff left by the tours over the years. Didn't know they were down here now." I was, like Jodi, whispering to keep from being overheard.

"Well, now what, genius?"

"We go forward, what else?"

Go forward we did. Lights ahead of us showed where the team was working; somewhere quite a ways out in the hall. "Maybe we can make it. We have to angle over that way, through the water. Try not to splash."

Jodi put her foot in, winced as the cold hit her clothes and the wetsuit. "Fun, this isn't. The things I do for love."

"Well, and for the sake of all mankind too."

"To heck with mankind!"

"Shh!"

The water got steadily deeper, until we were both hopping on the bottom with our toes to keep our heads above water. So far, though, no one seemed to have noticed anything. I would've crossed my fingers, but I needed everything I had to keep my balance and keep moving forward. The cold prickled on my hands and neck, but at least the wetsuit had now adjusted and was keeping me from really getting chilled.

Halfway there. In the reflected glow of the lights I could make out the entrance to the tunnel that led to the Flint Ridge cave system. We just might make it!

Just as I thought that, my foot found nothing at all under it and I plunged completely underwater, bouncing back up after having hit a pothole that dropped to eight feet. But that had been enough; my ungraceful entry had made a splash even a deaf man would have had a hard time ignoring.

"What?"

"Who's there?"

"What the hell was that?"

Flashlight beams were probing the darkness and sweeping over us.

"Go, Jodi, move it!" I snapped. "No more point in sneakin'."

"Hey, you! Stop! You can't go in there!"

Some of the NSS team were heading in our direction. I found myself standing a bit higher now—a low ridge of rock was under my feet. Good enough. I reached into the top of my pack, unzipped it. "Y'all just go back to what you were doin'. What we're doin' is our business."

"Look, Jack, you can't come down here! Now both of you get back—*holy shit!*"

His lapse into bad language was probably excusable, as I'd just hauled out an old .45, still nice and dry from inside the sealed pack and the Ziploc I'd put it in. "I said, y'all really do want to just go right back to what y'all were doin' and y'all *sure* don't want to follow me."

"Clint?!" hissed Jodi from behind me. "Are you completely *meshuggeh*?"

"C'mon, man, what's the matter with you? There's nothing worth getting out a gun for here!"

I aimed and fired. The thunder of the Colt was like the voice of the Lord telling Moses to get down off the mountain, and a fountain of white water exploded between the two in the lead; one of them jumped back and went under for a moment, while the other just froze. "Maybe y'all are right on that, but ask yourselves if there's anything worth getting shot for here."

"Christ, David, let the fucking lunatic go wherever the hell he wants!" said an older man from further back. "The cops can catch 'em when they come out."

The NSS people backed off. I grinned, bowed, and followed Jodi into the Flint Ridge connection.

12. The Road of Nowë

"Ow!"

This had been a pretty standard refrain for the past couple of hours. The passages were often tight, some so filled with water that there were only a few inches of breathing space between the water and solid rock. I don't normally get claustrophobic, but there were a few moments there where I got the willies thinking of the millions of tons of rock overhead, waiting to fall on us.

This time it was Jodi saying the "Ow!" and I looked up at a view that I was unfortunately way too tired to appreciate, as I was crawling right behind her. "You okay?"

"Just another rock in the way of my head."

"Is it opening up ahead?"

"Looks like it. It should be, from the map we have . . . yes, there it is. Flattening out."

"I say we take a break for lunch. No one's chasing us, that's for sure." We'd been going for a long time, and even if the NSS team had decided to try pursuit later—which I doubted very much—they hadn't been prepared for a long-term caving expedition and would've had to give it up a while back.

Jodi nodded, though I could barely make that out, and a few minutes later we emerged into a room large enough to stand in, with some flat spots to sit down. "Whew. That'll be a relief."

"I'm starved," Jodi admitted, shrugging off her pack and turning. "I—*oy*, Clint, your face!"

I flushed, which probably didn't make me look any better. "Just my dumb feet. Went under again and tried to come up for air a little fast. Which would've been fine if there'd been two feet of air instead of four inches."

"Are you all right? Jeez, you look terrible!"

I didn't really mind Jodi fussing over my face. It probably did look pretty bad, and it actually felt better after she was done cleaning it off, maybe just because it was her doing it. "Thanks, Jodi. Hey, I love you."

That got one of her best smiles. "I love you too, Clint. Hell, you sure know how to show a girl an . . . interesting time."

"We Slades are never boring." I killed the LED-based light I'd been using—sealed, efficient, water-proof—and got out a few candles to light us during the meal. We didn't talk much for a while, seeing as we were both tuckered out. Finally I put away the sandwich wrappers and drink bottles and put the pack back on. "Not too much farther to go, eh?"

"To the *Lisharithada*? A long, long way. To *Nowëmosdet*? A couple more crawls and then we have to make it to the top of a tall, skinny room. After that, we'll be in pure virgin cave for a ways, and then we get to the Road of *Nowë*."

"Let's do it. Either we're past the worst of it, or we'll find out we're completely screwed. But we'll be done with this stuff in any case."

The "tall, skinny room" was the worst of it. We had to ascend nearly forty feet, some of it chimneying. I had to put in some pitons, just to be sure we wouldn't fall. Finally I reached the top.

Blank rock greeted my gaze.

"Shit! There's nothing here!"

Jodi gave a little sound halfway between a sigh and a groan. "There has to be something!"

I shook my head, raised the light higher. Nothing, nothing . . .

Wait. That shadow up on the side didn't seem to move much.

What looked like a shadow was a dark, narrow opening that took us another five minutes to reach. We finally wiggled into it, crawling down a tunnel that Jodi said reminded her of the Gun Barrel in Knox Caverns for about fifty yards. This dropped out into an almost perfectly circular cavern with completely bare walls, with the large scalloping of slow-running water showing on the limestone. At this point I pulled out the laptop and checked the map, because there were three exits from this circular cave. Taking the leftmost one, we entered a chimney that sloped downward and, with water trickling constantly, was utterly treacherous. I backed up, with my white face reflected on the nearby rock, to hammer in several pitons to secure our descent. There was no way we could've made that descent alive otherwise, and I'd been lucky I could even back up when I did.

Fifty feet or more down we finally hit a sloping floor and were able to relax a bit. This tunnel had a small stream running along one side in a channel about three feet deep, and as the rest of the tunnel got lower we started wading through the stream for extra headroom. After a while this degenerated to our having to wriggle through pretty tight, mostly water-filled spaces; believe me, ordinary claustrophobia is nothing compared to the fear you have to fight back when you're hundreds of feet under solid rock, possibly about to get stuck in a water-filled passageway miles from any help. Without warning, I rounded a corner—it was my turn to lead—and dropped over the edge of a small waterfall, plunging into an icy pond over nine feet deep. I heard Jodi splash down about the time I came up and felt the water of that impact douse me again. Fortunately our sealed lights still worked, so we were able to flounder our way to mostly dry rock and get our bearings.

"We've got a ways to go." I said wearily.

Jodi flopped down beside me. "Well, I'm beat. If we don't rest, it won't matter if we get there or not. Time for dinner and some rest."

I couldn't disagree with that, so we took the time, and gave ourselves a few hours' rest. When the electronic whine of the alarm went off, I painfully dragged myself upright, seeing Jodi do the same. My face ached terribly, and from Jodi's expression I knew it must actually look worse now than it had before; bruising often works that way. "Once more unto the breach."

We passed through several caves filled with subtle ornamentation of flowstone and stalactites, waded a shallow underground lake with green water as clear as glass, climbed a twenty-foot chimney, followed a set of narrow crawlways for a long distance, then scrambled up a huge dome and wriggled through a short passage into a winding tunnel just far enough across for us to walk single-file.

With a startling suddenness, the tunnel opened onto a wide, flat shoreline of a watercourse that extended, ruler-straight, as far as our lights could see. *Nowëmosdet* was huge—a great semicircular hallway nearly two hundred feet wide, with even, flat banks about thirty feet wide on either side of the glassy-smooth emerald-glinting water. It felt slightly warmer here, and there was a hint of air moving.

We stared at it for long minutes, our breathing steadying after all the effort we'd gone through. Then I reached into the pocket of my pack. "Guess it's time."

Jodi got out her vial.

We struggled a bit with figuring out just how they opened, but eventually realized they had to be squeezed

and then twisted before pulling off. That over, we
stared at each other for a moment. Then I shrugged
and tossed the elixir down my throat in one swallow.

I immediately regretted that. Not that it felt bad—
it was in fact the opposite. The taste of *mikhsteri
H'adamant* was like nothing I'd ever tried before, and
I tipped the vial back again, letting the last drop of
it linger on my tongue. Sweet, cool, sharp, subtle, cold
and warm at the same time . . .

"Clint . . ." Jodi's voice held something close to awe.
"Your face!"

I touched my face. I could literally feel the scabs
falling away, leaving new skin where there had been
raw wounds minutes ago. More than that, I felt exhaustion falling away from me as well, as though I had just
put down a hundred-pound backpack. I felt I could
jump across that entire giant reflecting pool. "Yeee—
ha! Try it, Jodi, you'll love it! Shoot, now I'll have to
see if Rokhaset's got any other goodies like this in his
recipes!"

Jodi swallowed her elixir, and now I got to gape. You
could literally see the change, the head lifting, eyes
shedding their tiredness, cuts and scrapes fading away
like bad dreams. Jodi looked more gorgeously alive than
she'd ever looked before, worry lines smoothed away,
uncertainty lifted. I knew that I must look the same
way—confident, happy, and ready for anything.

"*Oy!* I'd start a war to get more of this stuff. I'm
surprised you Slades didn't get yourselves killed."

I couldn't help but grin, and stepped forward. We
hugged, kissed, then I laughed and spun her around
with another whoop. "All *right*! Jodi, let's see what the
Road is like!" I jumped off the ledge towards the water
two feet below.

And I didn't sink into the water. It supported me,
Jodi goggling wide-eyed while I stared back at her.

Then, as though a decision had been made, I began to descend, but as though it were transparent quicksand. The feeling was something entirely different, though.

If you were lucky, you had a wonderful, loving mother who was never too busy for you, who always knew the right thing to say whenever you were sad, or scared, or hurt. If you weren't, you probably wished you did. And if you had a mother like that, you might remember a morning or two when you, as a little child, were scared or lonely and crawled into bed when mommy was sleeping. And mommy, even though still asleep, somehow knew you were there, and her arm reached sleepily out and hugged you close, and you knew everything was completely and utterly right with the world, and nothing could hurt you as long as she was there.

That was what *Nowëmosdet* was like. The presence here slept . . . yet She knew us, and somehow we knew Her, and Her Road was ready for us.

Jodi stood next to me in the water, both of us standing on the bottom, our heads just above the surface, and once more we just stared at each other. Then we took a step forward.

It was as though there was no water there at all—except that we seemed to be somehow supported by it. Walking together, we seemed not to walk really, but to float, carried onward by our intent, not by muscles. We didn't really move very fast at all, but it was without effort. No matter how far we traveled this way, we sensed we would arrive completely rested and ready. Even more odd . . . I didn't feel wet. The dirt had washed from us both, yet otherwise we seemed as dry as if we were walking on the bank.

"Rokhaset, you've steered us right so far," I muttered under my breath. "Let's hope this last leg works out the way you planned it too."

We continued on, through the darkness, towards the enemies we had never met . . . yet.

13. Stone and Steel

"I just keep noticing weirder and weirder things."

"What is it this time, Clint?"

"Ripples. We're not leaving any."

Jodi looked down, then behind us. "You're right. No wake. Like we're not even here."

I thought a moment. "No, more like we're just a part of the water. The Road is taking us along just like we were part of the flow. Unless we hit something to cause the flow of the water to be upset, there won't be ripples."

"That makes . . . hold it."

"What?"

Jodi's forehead furrowed as she stared ahead. "The echoes. Something's different. I think we might be finally getting to the end."

I glanced at my watch and received a bit of a shock. We'd been following *Nowëmosdet* for nearly ten hours—which seemed to be no more than fifteen minutes or so to me. "I guess so!"

"Shh. They can't hear most of our talk, but some of the high harmonics might get through."

Ahead, the darkness seemed to thicken, then lighten up into the yellow-gray of limestone. The water of *Nowë*'s Road continued on into the wall, through a passage completely filled with water, but we felt the impetus which had carried us along weakening. The water still supported us, but clearly this was the end of the road.

On the right-hand side the walkway opened up into

a huge tunnel, and on either side of the tunnel—
Lisharithada.

They looked very much like the Nomes, but as I
studied them, I could see some differences. The crystal
crests which served as hair grew in a subtly three-
ridged pattern. Their faces were slightly broader and
more sharply pointed towards the chin. And they
wore stony armor and carried weapons in a much
more . . . comfortable fashion than the *Nowëthada*.

I glanced at Jodi, who nodded. We turned towards
the bank.

Even as we made the decision, the Road sensed it.
We rose up out of the water and found ourselves stepping easily to the stone above, gripping the iron bars
which seemed strangely light now.

As we had hoped, the *Lisharithada* seemed as oblivious to our presence as the Nomes had been when first
we met. Rokhaset's people had learned ways of sensing us to some extent—maybe, if by no other way, by
paying careful attention to pockets of "air" that seemed
even emptier than usual—but the *Lisharithada* apparently didn't have knowledge of, or use, such tricks.
Anyway, why would they? No human being could
possibly come down this far without them knowing it.

Neither Jodi nor I saw any point in conflict when
it wasn't needed. Before we passed between them,
though, Jodi caught my arm and pulled me back up
the walkway some distance. "Check our route."

I nodded, and we got out the portable. Rokhaset's
map glowed up at us from the screen. The *Lisharithada*
city was large and complex. I carefully compared the
version on the screen with the printed version and
made a couple annotations to be sure I could tell which
ones were supposed to be above the others, tracing the
route in highlighter and checking to make sure Jodi
agreed with me. Then I shut the machine down again.

While so far there was no sign we were being sensed, given how little we knew about their senses I didn't want to take any chances with having more electronic equipment running near them than I had to.

We passed between the two guards, maximizing the distance between us by entering the large corridor directly in the center. After that, though, we moved to one side, figuring that, like most people, the *Lisharithada* wouldn't generally crowd into the side of the corridor unless they had to and therefore wouldn't be likely to bump us.

As we moved onward, this became a very real concern. The tunnel leading from the Road was empty, but soon it joined with another, and there were many of the city's natives using it. The *Lisharithada* were a busy people. Maybe preparing for this destructive ritual demanded a hell of a lot of work, or maybe they just liked to keep busy, but whatever it was, there were dozens—hundreds—of them in the main corridors. It would have been funny if it weren't so deadly serious—watching how we contorted, jumped, and twisted keeping out of the way of hurrying contingents of rock people. Once one of them passed within inches of me and stumbled, barely catching itself before hitting the ground. Its companion helped it up. *"Pokil mondu ku?"*

The fallen one responded with a quick spurt of language that I couldn't catch, but I did get the word *matturan*, which made me hustle out of there. Clearly he'd gone momentarily blind near me, and that was something we definitely didn't want anyone thinking about too much.

Jodi was more worried about their *seradatho*. Some of the creatures were clearly more formidably designed than those of the *Nowëthada*—guard dogs, so to speak, rather than work dogs. It seemed that these *seradatho* also didn't have any clue we were there, but I made a point of tracking their whereabouts more closely as we moved farther inwards.

"So far, so good." I muttered. "We're about halfway there. Maybe we can make it all the way into their inner sanctum without them catching on. Then we can trash the equipment and get the hell out of Dodge."

Jodi shook her head. "I wouldn't bet on it."

Another great cavern opened up before us, this one similar to the one we had seen back in the Nome's area—clearly a living or gathering place, with lots of traffic. It might have been my imagination, but I thought I could see some of the patterns in their movements and the shapes of the natural-stone areas that served them as . . . what, shop stands? Houses, without roofs because of the lack of weather? Offices?

"Y'know, I think I'm seeing better."

"You only noticed already? I'm like to be seeing twice as far as I usually can."

"I just hope this stuff doesn't wear out too soon."

We came into sight of the next intersection. "Aw, shit."

The free ride had evidently come to a halt. Probably the next area belonged to their ruling class. Whatever the reason, this one had a door on it, and the door was guarded by three *Lisharithada*, who were being given a wide berth by the others. Even if the direction they were going would make it sensible to cut close by the doors, the others—civilians, I supposed—would detour quite a distance around instead.

"Can you see how to open the damn thing?"

Jodi and I studied the area for a few minutes. Then she pointed; after a moment, I nodded. Like their less warlike brethren, the *Lisharithada* tried to use natural approaches even to technological problems. There were, barely visible from where we stood, a pair of channels in the stone floor where water could run down and into holes in the wall. The channels actually connected with each other, but there was a stone that sat—perfectly fitted—in the connection area, preventing water from the one channel from reaching the other. Just moving that stone would divert the water from the first channel to the second, presumably causing something to fill with water and lever the door aside.

There was no way we could avoid causing some kind of stir here, but maybe we could still avoid combat. Moving carefully around the guards, I positioned myself near the door, while Jodi walked over and considered the fitted stone. I saw her shrug, then stick the claw end of her crowbar in and lever the stone out. To my surprise, she then picked the stone up and carried it over, joining me by the door. Jodi's a big woman, and because of her very active lifestyle she's a lot stronger than her slender build would lead you to think. Still, I wouldn't have thought she could handle that large a stone so readily.

I didn't give it much thought, however, because I was watching to see how the *Lisharithada* would react. As far as I could tell, we weren't so much invisible as just effectively a blind spot in their field of vision. Humans have a blind spot in each eye, but we virtually never notice them. Our brains cover up their existence, filling in the area with appropriately non-distracting "stuff" so we perceive our field of view as being complete and uninterrupted even though there's a significant hole in it. Apparently the same phenomenon applied here. They simply weren't *aware* that anything was happening where we were.

"Why didn't you just move it to the 'open' position?"

"Because I could just see the comedy routine if I did! They can't see me, right? So they see the water going, come over to check it out, I back away so they don't go blind and realize what's up, they push it back in place, door doesn't finish opening, I schlep back over and push the rock: lather, rinse, repeat."

By now the guards had noticed the water flow had shifted and were gathering around the valve area. I couldn't understand the words, but the tones were so very familiar I could almost interpret it anyway.

What the heck's going on? Hey, where's the damn rock? Who's the joker? Dammit, that's going to stick the door open!

And open was exactly what the door was doing, rising up smoothly on its unseen lever arm which was now weighted down by the water pouring into some hidden bucket. I had to concede Jodi had done the right thing. Given how ponderously slow these doors opened, we'd never have gotten it open wide enough to get through without Jodi's tactic, at least not without ending up having to lay the guards out. "Good call, Jodi."

Jodi looked smug. She does "smug" awfully well, too; it's probably her worst major character flaw.

The new tunnel branched out to left and right; we took the right-hand branch, which was narrower than the tunnels we'd been in earlier. Jodi stowed away the crowbar and got the longer, straighter rod of steel that she'd made up for a weapon—like a blunt sword with a wooden and leather-wrapped handle. There weren't quite as many *Lisharithada* in this corridor as there had been in the other, but it was enough smaller that neither of us had much hope we could continue undetected for very long. We were getting close to the ritual area, though. Just maybe we'd get away with it.

Suddenly a mob of fifteen of them came charging down towards us, weapons out.

I was in the lead. They were coming so fast I figured I could hurdle the first line of them and sow confusion in the middle, so I jumped just as they got to me.

I damn near cracked my head open on the cavern roof, which wasn't less than twenty feet up. I was so completely stunned that I landed like a sack of potatoes. I had to be helped up by Jodi, who had followed my example but kept her head a bit more.

I looked back; we had leapt completely over the entire troop, which was continuing on its headlong charge. Whatever they were after, it wasn't us. "Son of a . . . How the hell did we *do* that?!"

"Well, isn't it obvious, genius? That *H'adamant* stuff works! How else do you think I could have hauled that bloody great stone. What? Do I look like a lady weightlifter?"

The look of chagrin combined with outrage on Jodi's face was comical, even under the circumstances. With her elegant, fine-boned features, she looks about as far removed from "lady weightlifter" as possible.

But I didn't dare even crack a smile. "This could take some getting used to," I said gruffly. "We'd better be careful about really pushing ourselves."

"Wonder where those guys were going?"

I thought about it. "Only one real possibility, I'd guess: Rokhaset's kept his word and followed our timing. They're drawing off the *Lisharithada*'s forces. Who else could be down here that they'd be chasing with armed men?"

"Point. Unless they have really tough mice."

The hallway curved around a bit farther to the right. As we rounded the corner, we could see our luck had just run out.

The next room—a pretty darn large one, decorated with flowstone and helictites in one corner—was filled with *Lisharithada*, all armed, ready for the Nomes to try their assault. There was no way we could cross that room without fighting. Even with the superhuman strength the *H'adamant* elixir seemed to have conferred on us, we couldn't even jump halfway across, and we'd get way too close to a lot of them on the way for them to ignore it.

"This is it, Jodi."

She took a firm grip on the handle of her weapon. "You know, we don't actually have any proof that these are the bad guys."

"*What?*"

"Rokhaset seems nice and all, but he could still be handing us a line. Or even just turning things around. His people could be the ones making the quakes, and these guys the poor schmucks he's setting up for the fall."

I stared at her with my mouth open for a moment. "Well, god*damn* it, girl, y'all chose a hell of a time t' come up with that theory!"

She shook her head. "I don't really believe it myself, Clint . . . but, *oy vey*, we're here about to declare war on a bunch of people we've never met, all on the say-so of someone we just met day before yesterday."

I guess I wouldn't have been so aggravated if I didn't share her worry, somewhere deep down. We really didn't have any proof of what Rokhaset said, and with the *makatdireskovi*'s demonstrated ability to interpret and help Rokhaset express our language like a native-born actor . . .

"So what th' hell do y'all want to do? Sorry, Jodi, but—damnation! Ain't we kind of committed now?"

We dodged a couple runners coming from the other direction. Jodi bit her lip. "I guess we are. I just . . . it hit me, when we were about to walk in and start beating up these poor *schlemiels* who can't even see us."

We'd been so focused on our dilemma that we'd only

subconsciously noted the increase in the gabbling language around us. Now it reached a crescendo that broke through our indecision as, suddenly, another detachment of *Lisharithada* burst out of the room in front of us.

There was no chance to dodge or jump. They plowed straight into Jodi and me, knocking us down before they tumbled to the ground themselves in blinded consternation. Scrambling to my feet, I swung my steel at the next *Lisharithada* soldier with all my strength.

The bar bent on impact as though it'd been a willow wand instead of a half-inch of spring steel, picked up the rock-man and flung him a full ten feet backward. A crumpled, oozing line showed where the steel had caught him, as my weapon rebounded into straightness again. Jodi's matching blow knocked over her opponent and the two behind him. Crystal-edged swords chopped blindly at us. I parried one so hard it shattered, raining stone fragments everywhere, but a second one, swung flat and hard, got through my guard.

I staggered sideways, my side on fire. "That hurt!" I snarled, and backhanded the *Lisharithada* who'd hit me hard enough to send him tumbling head over heels. They were trying to crowd in and find us, and I figured giving them that advantage would be bad. "Jodi—into the big cave!"

"Got you!"

We could maneuver better in there, even though there were more opponents. With our height, reach, and effective invisibility—not to mention our magnified strength—our weapons started to take an awful toll. Every swing I made put one of the enemy down—broken legs, shattered chests, crushed skull or arms—and Jodi matched me swing for swing. Worse for them, even when they hit us it didn't smash our bones or cut our limbs off. The blows stung, sometimes really hurt, and I could feel bruises, but nothing at all like the damage they ought to be doing. Two of their guard-*seradatho* scuttled towards me, met the steel coming the other way and flew twisting through the air, shedding pieces as they went.

There was something utterly macabre and horrid about it all. These rock-men were desperately fighting something they couldn't see, something even stronger and tougher than they were—that killed and maimed them, broke their weapons, moved like lightning, and smashed aside any defense. I felt a little sick as we continued to fight our way towards the far side of the room, where just one door stood between us and the ritual room Rokhaset had told us we would find. Even if we were fighting enemies of our people, this was their home, and we were the invaders, slaughtering them without warning, without even showing them the faces of their adversaries. It was as if Jodi and I were the monsters in some kind of underground legend—the rock-people's equivalent of trolls or werewolves.

Still, sheer numbers count for an awful lot. For every one I took down, I could see another one running forward—sometimes two. And while one blow from their weapons wasn't enough to take us down—or even five—in the end you can beat a man to death with a rolled-up newspaper if you hit him often enough.

Two more *Lisharithada* went down, then three of them jumped me and I staggered. A fourth, knocked reeling by Jodi, fell down and tripped me. The three on top were blind, but now they could feel someone under them. They were punching and kicking for all they were worth, their shrieks carrying terror and revulsion along with anger.

"*Clint!*" I heard Jodi scream, and a barrage of

impacts erupted from her direction. Two of the ones on me suddenly departed involuntarily, and the third let go and backed off. I got painfully to my feet and smacked a *seradatho* into its handlers.

Jodi's eyes held a desperation I'd never seen before. "We're not going to make it, *tei-yerinkeh*." She almost never used that word; it meant "sweetheart" or "dearest one," but it was a private thing, a silly little private word we used only alone together.

I looked over my shoulder. We weren't even half-way across the room, and in the dimming light—half the LEDs on our lights were broken now—it looked like even more *Lisharithada* were coming in to reinforce the others. She was probably right . . . The ring of *Lisharithada* that had drawn away for a moment was gathering itself for another lunge.

I shook my head. "Maybe, but damn-all if I'm givin' up." I hit the transducer switch. "YEEE-HA! C'mon, then, let's see if y'all can take a Slade!"

And in the stunned moment as the *Lisharithada* heard our voices for the first time, another voice boomed out from across the great cavern:

"*Well said and well met again, Clinton Slade!*"

14. The Sound of Music

No sound had ever been so welcome as that deep, reassuring voice. "Rokhaset! You made it!" Jodi shouted triumphantly, taking three *Lisharithada* out with the accompanying swing.

"Indeed, Jodi Goldman." I could now make out that at least part of what I'd taken for reinforcements of the *Lisharithada* were Rokhaset's assault forces, driving towards us like a wedge against the increasingly

desperate *Lisharithada*. "And it gives me great joy to
see that not only have you arrived, but that also the
mikhsteri H'adamant has worked surpassingly well on
you."

"OW!" I shoved the one that had just hit me out
of the way. "Yeah, and without it we'd have been dead
before we got here. Great stuff."

The enemy were now in serious disarray. They
couldn't decide whether the two invisible slayers or the
larger number of *Nowëthada* were the biggest threat,
and that made them hesitate at the wrong time. Jodi
and I turned and started plowing our way towards the
door on the far side, knowing that Rokhaset and his
troops were backing us up and if the ones behind us
tried to drag us down, he'd carve right through them
and get 'em off our backs.

Now there wasn't any mistaking the panic in the
voices of the *Lisharithada*. The situation had gone
from bad to impossible. There just weren't enough
of them left to deal with Rokhaset's forces on top of
the unknown, invisible killers that had devastated their
guarding force. Seeing how Rokhaset and his people
proceeded onward—steadily, but nowhere near as fast
or efficient as our devastating attack—it was pretty
clear that he'd told the truth about just how little
chance he and his people had stood alone. That, to
me, confirmed we'd chosen right to take his word on
this mission. There wasn't any way he'd expected
events to take the turn they had, but he'd clearly
planned on this assault anyway. Plus, his people had
had several chances to do us in at different points,
and hadn't.

Suddenly, the *Lisharithada* morale broke. The ones
in front of us threw down their weapons and sprang
aside, running for the exits—there were, I could see,
three ways out of here besides the sealed door we were

headed for. And even the ones behind us and around Rokhaset's people were now fleeing, stampeding out the doors with desperate speed.

"Well, I think they've decided that's enough."

Rokhaset joined us. His posture had not relaxed. "They do not usually retreat even when being beaten."

"And how often have you had invisible, superhuman, apparently invincible assistance? C'mon, Rokhaset, everyone has a breaking point."

"True enough, Clinton Slade. I find your presence unnerving, and you are my ally. Perhaps indeed it is that invisible assistance which overwhelms their courage."

"Last door. I hope we can get it open from this side."

Rokhaset nodded deliberately. "I assure you it can be opened, especially by those assembled here. Be prepared; the interior guard will have been alerted, and they will fight to the end."

"Let 'er rip. Let's blow this joint and see if we can get home in one piece."

The Nomes gathered around the door, poking at the mechanism, which was apparently jammed. After a jabbering conference, Rokhaset turned back to us. "The door is not entirely disabled. They did not have the time to do so, and those inside cannot do so without considerable effort. Stand by; we shall open the door—now!"

Something broke inside the wall—we could hear it and feel the vibration through the soles of our boots—and the door ground its way upwards. The doorway to our destination was open.

Stepping forward, Jodi and I peered in. It was a low but tremendously wide room, maybe ten feet high but with regular buttress columns supporting a span so large that our weakened lights couldn't reach the other side, even with the increased sensitivity of our eyes. At regular intervals around the room were crystalline shapes of bizarre design. The nearest one was a sort of curved double-trumpet shape rising from one side of a six-foot-high dais, thirty feet across, carved in a spiral fashion with rippled indentations along it. I started for it, raising my bar and watching for the interior guard.

No one came forward, no attackers, nothing. "Rokhaset? Where's the welcome wagon?"

"I admit my bewilderment, Clinton Slade. I cannot—"

But at that moment, the dais began to uncurl. The crystalline shape sat at the crest of a head fully five feet long, armed with black-shining spines, cutting blades of blue stone, a crushing maw, and grasping talons. It gave voice to a grinding screech like the unoiled hinges of Hell and turned towards us.

"*Magon!*" Rokhaset gasped. His shocked cry was echoed by his fellows, all of whom, the Nome King included, began backing away as fast as they could.

"Figures." I stared at the monstrous thing as it continued to uncoil. "They brought one here as a last-ditch defense."

The *Magon* shrieked again, and a steady humming began to emanate from it as it stalked towards us on many sets of legs.

"*Matturan!*" I heard Rokhaset shout. "Run, all of you, for we cannot fight if we cannot see!"

"Well, I can see perfectly—what the . . . *YOW!*"

My steel weapon had brushed my hand; that fleeting contact had burned me.

"*Gevalt!*" Jodi cursed.

The zipper on my wetsuit was heating up. If you have never experienced the sensation of a rapidly-heating zipper, my advice is simple: avoid it at all costs.

Jodi grabbed me and dragged me backward, away, running as fast as we could from the *Magon*. We both tore the earphones from our heads, as they were starting to burn our ears.

"The damn thing's radiating electromagnetic waves!" Jodi said disbelievingly. "That's why it makes the Nomes blind—it's overloading their senses on some level. But for us, it's inducing eddy currents and heating every bit of metal on us!"

"Damn! Damn, damn, *damn*! No wonder the *Lisharithada* bugged out. They knew this thing was waiting back there as a last-ditch weapon." We stopped for a breather on the far side of the cavern we'd been fighting in for so long. Two of the exits had been closed off, but one was still open. That gave me an idea.

"Hey, Rokhaset! Our real goal's to get inside that room and break up all the crystal things, right?"

"Correct."

"Well, that being the case, why don't we have one group of us keep the thing chasin' us, and the other group runs inside? That *Magon* thing sure doesn't look up to opening doors, so if we can all get inside ahead of it and close the door, we're set."

"A worthy plan," Rokhaset said after a pause.

"Why isn't Rokhaset answering?" Jodi demanded. "Is he okay?"

"He *is* answering. I guess my electronics survived, but yours fried."

"Some of them, anyway. Lights and all are still working."

I glanced in the direction we'd come from. Nothing was moving in the range of the lights. "Speaking of that, I'm swapping out for the spare lights and new batteries. I can't see the thing at all."

That did the trick nicely, but I didn't like what I saw. "Shoot. The darn thing's stopped with its head right in the doorway. Rokhaset, y'all said these things were hard to control, but looks to me like this one understands 'guard dog' just fine."

Jodi gazed at it speculatively. "Wonder what its range is?"

"We should probably find out. Though to be honest I dunno what we're going to do. My pistol's just a popgun to something like that, and no way I'm gonna get close enough to hit it with the explosives—hell, I was lucky the detonators and my pistol rounds didn't go off when it started doing its metal-heating trick."

"Well, I don't have any explosives on me, and most of my stuff that's going to fry is already toasted." Jodi dashed forward before I could stop her.

The *Magon* raised its head a bit as she got closer, and that eerie, high-pitched, monotonous hum began again. Jodi snatched up her weapon, which was about thirty feet from the thing, and ran back, juggling it like a hot potato until she got back to me and dropped it on the floor to cool.

"*Oy!* Looks like it's got a range around seventy-five feet. At least, it didn't seem to be cooling off until I got out about that far. You didn't feel anything back here, did you?"

I shook my head. "Nothing. Though I'd bet the range for just blinding our Nome friends is much longer."

"You are correct, Clinton Slade. We dare not get even as close as you are now to the *Magon*. Although . . . Perhaps, if we were to all rush it at once, we might still defeat it. There are twelve of us all told, plus the two of you."

"No, you're outta your mind, Rokhaset! That thing's even bigger'n you said; I think I eyeballed it at something close on eighty feet long. It'd kick our asses even if y'all weren't blind, which you will be." I studied the thing from our current distance, about a hundred and fifty feet away. "Jodi, do you want to try that run again and see if you can get my weapon too?"

She looked at me. "You've got something else in mind, haven't you?"

"Maybe. More a matter of I need to get a better look at something." I moved forward until I was about a hundred feet away from the thing.

"Here goes nothing." Jodi sprinted back in. The grotesque head rose, the humming started up again, and Jodi gave vent to Yiddish curses as her clothing started to heat up. She had to get within twenty feet of the *Magon* to get my weapon, and at her closest approach the thing stirred uneasily, almost began to move forward, jaws and grinder working.

But I'd noticed something else. I focused my flashlight squarely on the crystalline growth on the *Magon's* forehead as Jodi sprinted back. Sure enough, the light looked vaguely defocused until she got far enough out and the humming sound faded, and then the reflection was as sharp as could be.

"I think I've found its transmission antenna."

"The things I do for love! What? Where?"

"That crystal thing on its head. That humming noise coincides with its vibration." I shook my head. "I suppose I could try to shoot the thing off, but it's a sucky target in this light and at this distance."

Jodi stared at it with a look of revelation that startled me.

"Jodi? Sweetheart, what is it?"

"Clint, tell me: doesn't that thing look almost exactly like a couple of wineglasses from here?"

I looked. "Well, yeah, it does. So?"

"I'd put that hum right up around my high B."

My mouth dropped open and stayed that way. "You can't be serious!"

"I'll bet you twenty bucks it'll work."

"You're nuts! You'd need to get right up to it—twenty, thirty feet at the outside—and it's looking kinda antsy already."

"So, like you have a better idea, Mr. Genius?"

I thought about it. "No," I finally muttered. "But hold on a second. I'd better get stuff ready, in case this crazy idea of yours does work."

I pulled stuff from the pack, sorted it out, fitted things together, checked the connections. "Okay." I looked over at the monstrous creature and turned, grabbing Jodi tight. "You be damn careful, y'hear? I ain't lookin' to see you eaten by some rockworm."

The slight quiver in her voice answered my concern. "Hey, don't worry, it's no big deal. You should see the rats on a New York subway."

"I *have* seen the rats on a New York subway. They aren't anywhere near as bad as—"

She clucked her tongue disparagingly. "That was just Manhattan, you tourist. I'm talking about Queens. Now stop distracting me."

She took a deep breath and hummed to herself for a few moments, running scales up and down, loosening her throat and lungs so they could deliver when needed. As she did so, she started stripping off all the extraneous metal. Her backpack hit the floor as she started a run of *do-re-mi* and her shirt and pants (with metal rivets) joined it a few moments later as she ran back down the scale, followed by the wetsuit.

Being human—okay, male human—I could at least appreciate the view, which was magnificent even if stopping *just* short of being indecent. Jodi's sports bra and panties had no metal in them, so she left them on. Still, there was a definite exotic charm in the setting, especially with the waiting monster in the background. Any fantasy illustrator in the world would have been in seventh heaven.

Jodi stood still for a moment, muscles just a bit too tense, then took a deep breath and started walking forward.

As before, once she got within seventy feet, the creature raised its head and started humming. But this time Jodi wasn't wearing anything metal to be affected. She kept moving forward slowly, forty feet, thirty, twenty-five, twenty . . .

At twenty feet, the *Magon* hissed and moved slightly. Jodi stopped and opened her mouth. A pure note issued forth, one matching the eerie hum precisely in pitch. The hum instantly sounded louder than ever, and Jodi's voice responded, increasing volume steadily.

The *Magon* must have encountered caverns in which it had heard feedback. The hum started to fade for a moment as it stopped generation. But nothing had ever tried this trick on it before; as Jodi made a step forward, its instincts forced it to begin the defensive signal generation again.

Jodi's face was as set as a marble statue, giving out an unending, unwavering tone that I knew could not be sustained much longer, a crescendo of echoing sound that was answered in the swiftly-building hum that she was trying to drive out of control. The *Magon* moved jerkily, trying to shake its head and drive away an indescribable sensation, starting a lunge forward but drawing back as the movement increased the resonance. Even from this distance I saw Jodi's face changing color slightly, reddening from the effort of wringing the last dregs of air from her lungs to maintain the feedback cycle. She was running out of air, it wasn't going to work—

And then the sound of her own pure voice echoed out from behind me, doubled and redoubled, as the *Nowëthada*, having caught on to her plan, all joined together to imitate the same precise sound.

Though they were much farther away, there were twelve of them, and they were putting all the strength into it they could; with their ability to imitate other sounds perfectly, they did exactly what was needed. They maintained the resonance as the *Magon* gave a frustrated whine and finally moved, in fits and starts, towards Jodi.

But by maintaining the resonance, the Nomes had given Jodi a breather. She backed up two steps, her lungs refilled, and this time her voice seemed to split the room with a single note of high-pitched thunder. The resonant hum from the *Magon* rose with her volume, becoming louder, the creature scrabbling now to reach its own forehead with claws just a bit too short—and the crystal antenna exploded with enough force to send shards flying thirty feet.

The *Magon* gave a shriek that pierced my ears like an icepick and lunged at Jodi; no longer under control, just berserk and out to kill the one that hurt it. Jodi ran.

I stood still and let her run past me. As the *Magon* followed—ignoring me completely in its mania to get Jodi—I swung the iron at one of its legs hard enough to break it. There was no heating; Jodi's trick had ended that problem. The monstrous centipedal creature skidded to a halt and whipped around, screaming at me—and that's when I pitched the ball in my other hand down its throat.

For a moment only I saw it, sparkling silvery in the LED light with its duct-taped surface. Then I flung myself flat behind a low, domelike stalactite.

The blast deafened me and shattered helictites sixty feet away. When I rose up, I could see that the *Magon* was writhing on the floor, headless and dying. All Jodi and I had to do was dance like madmen to stay out of the way of the rocky coils until they juddered slowly into stillness. Two pounds of C-4 makes for a hell of a case of indigestion.

Rokhaset and the other Nomes moved forward slowly. Even though they didn't have expressions, everything about the way they moved shouted out their incredulity. "Clinton Slade, Jodi Goldman . . . you have defeated a *Magon*. I did not think it possible."

"*Nishtkefelecht*, it's nothing. Without you singing backup, my main performance would've bombed. We did it together."

"Perhaps, perhaps. Still, such a thing has not been done in my memory."

"Enough time to congratulate later. Let's finish this job and get out of here before they come back to check on us."

As we turned towards the door, a quiver ran through the floor. Then another, stronger shake that jangled the remaining helictites.

"*Jh'amos!* They know we have won out here. They seek to complete the ritual now, though it will be slightly weakened!"

"Oh, no they don't!"

Into the room we ran. There were some guards now, running to stop us in these last desperate minutes, but this time I had the pistol out and was shooting. It probably wouldn't kill them, but the impact of the slugs startled them, knocked them off balance, broke armor where it hit. I ran past, kicking over a tall stone with an intricate crystal atop it, and then I saw him—like Rokhaset, bigger than his subjects, surrounded by crystalline structures, mumbling incomprehensible sounds. His personal guard swung at me, but I bowled him over and grabbed the *Lisharithada* ruler, swinging him right up against the wall. "Rokhaset!" I shouted. "Tell 'em to cut it out right now, or I'm about to break their king in half!"

Rokhaset and the *Lisharithada* exchanged hurried words. "They say it is all over for them in any case, now that you monsters have found them. They might as well take us all with them."

"It's all over! Tell 'em, Rokhaset—we only got here because you showed us, and we ain't told anyone else!"

A shattering sound told me Jodi was finishing off the crystals. The *Lisharithada* king struggled desperately in my grip; then, as the sound of crashing crystal faded, went limp.

"It would seem, Clinton Slade, that he has recognized a losing position, now that Jodi Goldman has destroyed the channeling crystals."

I dropped the king. "Okay. So they can't do the earthquake now?"

"No, Clint. It will be a long time before they can regrow such a mass of channeling crystals and even attempt such a ritual again."

"Good. Let's go get your stuff, Jodi, and go home."

The *Lisharithada* king suddenly whirled around, yanking a long staff of stone capped with a green-glowing gem from its hiding place in the depression from which I'd yanked him. I threw up my hands instinctively, but the gem hit me like a wrecking ball combined with a cattle prod. Concussion and seething energy catapulted me backwards, twitching.

The room erupted in renewed combat as the king directed his next attack, a sickly emerald bolt of energy, straight at Jodi. She tried to block it with her steel rod and had no more success than I had. Seeing her collapse, I tried desperately to get up, but my legs and arms wouldn't move.

Rokhaset roared something I couldn't make out, and there was a confused exchange of lightnings, red and green clashing as though the rainbow was having an internal debate. A glittering, three-crested head loomed

above me, then fell as Rokhaset's own scepter came
down on it.

Everything was dim, silent. I wondered why it was
growing so dark, realized that I must be losing consciousness.

"Clinton Slade! Can you hear me?"

I made a supreme effort, managed to force out the
word, "Yes."

"It is over. Their ruler is dead, they will have to
select a new one, and we can escape."

"Guess . . . over for us . . . too."

"No, Clinton Slade. We shall bring you home."

I felt strong, slender rods of stone . . . Nome
arms . . . slide under me. "Jodi . . ."

"We have her too. Save your strength."

I tried to tell him that I wasn't lying down here
while Jodi might be hurt, but my lips wouldn't move.
The light faded, and then everything was dark and I
fell away into nothingness.

15. Some Slight Side-Effects.

Consciousness returned in fits and starts. I vaguely
remembered shouting Nomish voices, and a feeling of
sudden comfort overwhelming me as we entered
Nowëmosdet again. Darkness giving way to light and
Mamma crying. Being forced to drink something that
stank like rotten eggs and tasted . . . well, it was a good
thing I couldn't fight it then or someone woulda gotten hurt.

I opened my eyes. It was dim in the room. Shades
were pulled over the windows. I tried to get up, but
just getting to a sitting position took the wind out of
me. "Hello?" I called.

The door flew open and Mamma ran in. "Clint? Oh, thank the Lord, Clint, you're awake! How do you feel, boy?"

"Like I've been pulled through a knothole and wrung out. And like I could eat a bear whole, without salt."

Tears glinted in her eyes. "Well, I'm sure we can find something to eat for you! Just stay there and take it easy and I'll be right back!"

"Jodi, Mamma! What about Jodi?"

Mamma hesitated. "She hasn't woken up yet, Clint, but now that you've come back to us I'm sure she'll be up and about in no time."

"But she's alive?" I felt a huge weight lift off my chest.

"She is indeed alive, Clinton Slade." Rokhaset entered the room. "Did I not give my word that we would get you home and that we had Jodi as well?"

"Yeah, and I didn't doubt you meant it . . . but sometimes the world can make liars of the best of us." Mamma, seeing that I had someone to talk to, headed on out, presumably to round up some food.

It suddenly dawned on me that I was not wearing any transducers. I glanced around and saw speakers on the bedside table. Obviously someone had decided to distribute the ability to talk to the Nome King around the house. Probably Adam, I guessed.

"She is recovering, I assure you. Though it was indeed a near thing for you both. It took the medicine of both worlds to bring you back from the edge of death."

"So you were the one making me drink that stuff."

"You needed the *Nowë H'wadalo*, the True Fire of Her spirit, and the elixir gave it to you. *Mishtarkistekh' orametanerala* intended for both Jodi Goldman and yourself to never return from the paths below the

Earth, and tried to extinguish the fire of life within you. Had you been of our people, you would have died on the spot; had you been ordinary *Tennathada*, I doubt it would have affected you any more than an ordinary blow. But by being brought closer to *Nowë* by the *H'adamant* elixir, you were in a unique state and his attempt to destroy you neither entirely failed nor entirely succeeded."

"Dang. Slades don't usually do anything halfway. Well, better half dead than all dead, that's what I say."

"That would be my assessment as well."

"So . . . no big quakes then?"

Rokhaset nodded slowly. "For now, no. Yet it is true that the *Lisharithada* shall recover in time, and the Earth still builds its tensions which will need careful release if they are not to harness its strength for destruction. But that will be a problem for a later day. Your deeds this time have struck fear and confusion into them, and there is no need to worry; I shall know when they begin to think of the great rituals again."

Mamma came in with a tray piled with everything from soup to drumsticks. "Now that's enough jawing, Rokhaset. Let my boy eat."

I ate, as directed; by the time I was done, my eyelids were sagging again. I don't really remember putting the tray down.

When I woke again, it was nighttime, the moon shining through the slits in the window and lighting the room up so it looked almost like daylight. I tried to move and found I could get up, though I felt like Grandpa on a bad day. I tottered across the room and almost fell over Evangeline, who steadied me. "Careful, Clint. Nice to see you up, though. You wanna see Jodi, I bet."

"You'd win that bet."

"Well, c'mon. Mamma would probably try to keep you in bed, but that wouldn't be fair."

Evangeline led me down the hall—which seemed 'round about five times longer than usual—and opened the door to Jodi's room.

Jodi's eyes were open, and I felt tears suddenly well up in my own. I staggered to her bed and hugged her tight. "Jesus, Jodi, I thought we were dead."

"You weren't the only one, boychik. That nasty green light laid me right out."

We sat there for a few moments, just holding each other and absorbing the fact that we were still alive.

"Hey. It just hit me. We saved the world."

"Oy, don't go exaggerating. Just part of the country. Not even the most important part. Manhattan wouldn't have been touched."

I laughed. "Okay, yeah, but . . . in a way, it might not be exaggerating. A big enough disaster to the USA . . . I'm sure the rest of the world economy wouldn't like it either."

"They'd get by. Hey, are you saying it's not enough?"

"Heck no. It's just a lot more impressive to say 'I saved the world' than 'I saved Kentucky, Tennessee, Missouri, southern Illinois, and chunks here and there of a few other states in the area.'"

Jodi thought about it. "Especially where I come from. Most New Yorkers think Kentucky and Tennessee—forget Missouri—are just suburbs of Hoboken."

Over the next few days, Jodi and I got better. Finally we felt like ourselves again and Mamma threw a heck of a party, which Rokhaset attended, wearing his sunglasses and bringing two of his court along—*Tordamilatakituranavasaiko* and *Mesh'atarasamthimajistolath*, whose names were promptly shortened in our *Tennathada* way to Tordamil and Meshatar.

The new arrivals were the first of their people given a connection to the expanded *makatdireskovi* so as to be able to talk with us. It was nice to hear new voices; Meshatar sounded like Lauren Bacall, which certainly helped us remember she was female, as there weren't any clear visible indications of sex among the Nomes. Tordamil had evidently selected Richard Dean Anderson as his voice model, making it occasionally sound as though MacGyver had come to dinner.

The Nomes brought their own food with them, to the family's great interest. Though Mamma realized that making *Nowëthada* dinners would probably be impossible for any of us, she still ended up talking to Tordamil after dinner, trying to understand just what it was that the Nomes did when they "cooked." As Tordamil turned out to be Rokhaset's head *sirakster H'ista*, which apparently meant something between "master chef" and "head shaman or alchemist," he was definitely the one to ask about these things. He was just as interested in our methods of cooking—or at least convincingly faked an interest in it—so the two were kept happily occupied for a long time.

We went out to look around the grounds with Rokhaset after dinner.

"Man, it's nice to be outside again."

"I like caves, but after that long trek, okay, yeah, I'm glad to be aboveground again too."

"I will admit, Clinton Slade, that there are enjoyable aspects to *Tennatu*. You will forgive me, I trust, if I still prefer *Nowëtu*."

"Wouldn't expect anything else, Rokhaset. A man should always love his home best, no matter what sights there are to see elsewhere." I glanced at him. "Speakin' of sights, I thought you people were damn near blind here in the Hollow?"

"We are indeed *matturan* to some extent whenever

we are here, Clinton Slade. But other senses can be used to appreciate the world; and it is, I think, not entirely a bad thing for myself and my people to accustom themselves to this, in case they must deal with your people."

"Can't hurt to be ready to deal with it, I guess. But we ain't planning to spread the word about your people around."

Rokhaset nodded emphatically. "As individuals your people have proven to be, as you would say, decent folk. I am however very much afraid that were your country as a whole to become aware of us—and especially of the *Lisharithada*—that it would become a matter for politicians of your sort . . . and eventually for warriors, once they realized what the *Lisharithada* were capable of."

"Oy, no doubt about that one, Rokhaset. They'd be dragging half of you to the labs and declaring war on the other half. Clint may be a backwoods boy, but he's pretty enlightened. There's plenty of other people that'd be perfectly willing to ignore the fact you can talk and just call you monsters."

I didn't want to get off discussing the flaws of the entire human race which Rokhaset, having derived his understanding of us from forty years of TV, was undoubtedly all too aware of. "Besides," I said, "it'd be just plumb stupid of us. The Slades have got some tradin' to do with your people, right?"

We had gotten past the edge of the Hollow now, and Rokhaset was moving a bit more easily. "That is a matter I have been discussing with your family during your convalescence, Clinton Slade. While the initial problem was certainly caused by your blind thievery, even the most reactionary of my people—and make no mistake about it, Jodi Goldman, the *Nowëthada* are just as capable of anger, deliberate prejudice, and judgmental behavior as your own—as I say, even the most reactionary of my people must admit that the two of you risked everything—your lives, your freedom, and your souls—to atone for the involuntary wrongdoings of Winston Slade and his descendants.

"We are, accordingly, quite interested in establishing a peaceful trade between the Slade clan and our own. Yet we still find ourselves at the same impasse that we encountered when first we spoke of this problem."

"What d'you . . . oh, yeah."

"You grasp the issue, Clinton Slade. We have no need for the devices your people manufacture, at least not in any significant quantity, and many of your machines would have to be specifically redesigned to make them worth our while. So the only reasonable trading goods we have are crystals—we supply you with diamonds, as we can, and you bring us gemstones and other crystals which cannot be found in this part of the world. Yet your people are as blind in this area as we are in what you call the visible spectrum. You cannot tell whether a crystal is *hevrat* with life, or is as dead"—he gestured at the brilliantly-sparkling diamond on Jodi's finger—"as that. And clearly you cannot afford to purchase many rough stones, hoping they will be worthwhile, and have them rejected—at least not often."

"Well . . . depends. If your people can shape stones like I've seen, you ought to be able to cut gems to order. That'd raise the value of the reject gems an' we could still recoup."

"Sure he could, Clint," Jodi said, with the air of a teacher explaining something to a really slow student, "but to make it worth his people's while we'd have to, well, make it worth their while . . ."

"D'oh!" I smacked my forehead. "Okay, yeah, that was dumb."

"Alas, Clinton Slade, mine are a busy people indeed and truly we cannot perform much labor for you unless we can establish equitable exchange. I do, however, have one thing to give you."

"Oh?"

He withdrew from the woven-crystal pouch at his side what looked like two medallions suspended from strings made of the same material as his pouch. "As, I suspect, nearly all people, the *Nowëthada* recognize and honor bravery, willingness to aid others, strength in battle, and so on. It took considerable courage for the two of you to come to us, into our stronghold, and hope to make peace—perhaps, if I read your personalities aright, more than it took to face the *Lisharithada* and the *Magon*."

"Well, I don't rightly know about that. Even walking into your throne room wasn't as scary as fighting a stone monster the size of a house. But still, we appreciate the kind words."

"To recognize you for bringing our people together, and standing with us against a common foe, I have had fashioned these amulets. They have little mystical significance to one such as yourself, but similar devices mean a great deal to my people, and I know that you award similar, um, medals, to courageous members of your own species. So take these, at least, as . . . what is the phrase? Ah, yes, as a token of our esteem and gratitude for bringing our sundered peoples together. May we one day find a way to bring peace to the *Lisharithada* as well."

"I'm all for that, though I admit to not bein' overly hopeful." We each stooped low to let Rokhaset, who once more had clearly watched the similar rituals on movies and TV shows, put the medallions around our necks. Straightening up, we then got a chance to look at them.

"Oooy!" Jodi breathed. "Rokhaset, these are just beautiful!"

I had to agree. The medallions were shaped—or maybe grown—transparent crystals with traces of glittering metal in them that looked like gold, surrounding a core of what had to be solid silver, covered with intricate designs that looked like completed versions of the symbols we'd seen on the Throne Room walls. I wondered if silver gave them problems to work, or if it was just the ferromagnetics that did. Overshadowing all the other features, though, was the crystal set in the very center. It, too, was transparent, but it didn't merely pass light; it radiated light, a soft but unmistakable polychromatic glow that pulsed and flickered gently like a candle in the gentlest of breezes. As I admired it in the slowly-gathering dusk, I realized the whole medallion had a faint glow to it, though nothing like the glorious luminance from that central stone.

"What *is* that stone, Rokhaset? It's incredible!"

"I am surprised, Jodi Goldman, Clinton Slade. How can you not recognize the stones over which we nearly shed blood? They are *H'adamant*, of course. The only appropriate choice."

"Okay," I said, "but what'd you do to 'em to make 'em glow like that?"

Rokhaset froze, looking almost comical. "Glow? Clinton Slade, I assure you—we have done nothing to them at all, save to shape them so they are faceted in a way that would reflect the light pleasingly for your eyes."

"But . . . these look nothing at all like Jodi's diamond! Well, yeah, they're both transparent, but . . ."

I trailed off, a chill going down my spine as I realized what I was saying.

"Clinton Slade," Rokhaset said, with a quiet intensity

that showed how serious he was, "Look carefully at me and tell me what you see."

We stared at Rokhaset. "Oh, my," Jodi whispered.

In the dimming light, looking hard at Rokhaset, we could see that he glowed like our medallions. It was dim, yet with a sense of being contained—like being in a dark room and seeing the glow under the door from the brightly-lit hall beyond.

It was only then that I glanced at my watch, remembering just when we'd started eating. Twilight? At this time of night it ought to be damn near pitch black. Yet it only seemed to be late twilight—easy enough to see in, even if the shadows were pretty thick under the trees.

"*Nowë Ro'vahari*," Rokhaset said in a tone of reverence. "Such things are mentioned in legends, from before the *Makurada Demagon*, but how they happened none could say. Perhaps the *mikhsteri H'adamant*, combined with the change in our peoples, has done this itself; perhaps the treacherous attack of the *Lisharithada* ruler, or our desperate treatments of its effects on you, has wrought this transformation. But somehow *Nowë* has seen fit to make you *turan*, at least in some way, as we do."

"Then I gotta apologize, Rokhaset. I thought you were overreacting when you realized we couldn't see what happened when *H'adamant* died. Now . . . I think maybe y'all almost didn't get mad enough."

I wondered what else had changed about us. "I sure hope there aren't any nasty side-effects waiting. Don't want to go blind around metal, that's for sure."

"It is as *Nowë* wills it, Clinton Slade. Yet it would seem to me that her blessing is, for you, working as your normal sight, only . . . more so. It should, therefore, not be so sensitive to *H'kuraden* as ours, if at all."

"I'm going to have to get to the lab!" Jodi exclaimed.

"Clint, an entirely new sensing modality—even if we're the only ones with it, just imagine what we could learn this way!"

"Whoa, whoa. One thing at a time. The important thing is that this solves our trading problem."

Rokhaset laughed. "We spoke and the World heard us, and answered. So it has ever been, Clinton Slade, in the times when it was crucial. *Nowë* is pleased with you, Jodi Goldman, Clinton Slade. It is important to Her that we be friends. So She has provided."

I was starting to realize that our pragmatic friend was also about as religious as a preacher. But if he wanted to see this as a miracle, what'd it matter? Heck, he might even be right! "Let's just hope it doesn't wear off."

Rokhaset nodded slowly. "Yet this, in itself, gives us an answer. If the effects of the elixir remain with you for this long—even if only the senses are affected— then at the worst you merely need take one before you go on a . . . shopping trip. With careful planning, even taking into consideration the costs we would have to charge you for the *mikhsteri H'adamant*, I am sure it would remain a very profitable venture on both sides."

He tilted his head in that birdlike fashion. "Clinton Slade, I must return home now. In the wake of our battle I have spent far too much time here, though I do not regret that time. I have informed Meshatar and Tordamil that we must go; they are taking their leave of your family. Send them my apologies, but I can no longer ignore my people. Please, come visit us soon, however. I would be honored to entertain your family in my home."

We shook hands and went with him to Winston's Cave—where the iron grid had been removed and the handholds down replaced by *Nowëthada* stone-shaping. Meshatar and Tordamil came hurrying up just as Rokhaset entered, so we got to say goodbye to them too. Then we headed back down the path.

"So, Clint . . ."

"What?"

"We'll have to be pretty careful."

"You mean to not let people know we can see in the dark—and maybe see other things, too? Yeah."

"More than that."

I turned to see what she was talking about, as we emerged from Winston's Gap. "Holy Mother of God!"

Jodi was carrying the gate, which had been left way off to the side as no one had wanted to carry it down the hill at the time. It weighed in at something like five hundred pounds.

"You just better hope that it doesn't wear off while you're pulling stunts like that, girl!"

"I'd bet I'd feel it happening."

I reached out, wondering if I had the same ludicrous strength. She relinquished her hold, and I hefted the mass of steel. The gate felt more like forty, fifty pounds, if that. "Well, shit fire and save matches. You know, this is even weirder'n it looks. I haven't felt like Superman at home, an' the chairs I was draggin' into place before dinner didn't feel any lighter, so what gives?"

Jodi the scientist answered. "We'll just have to experiment and find out. Maybe Rokhaset's a little off— maybe these abilities *will* go away when we're around a lot of iron."

I lifted the gate a bit higher. "Counterpoint: just what is it I'm holding, then?"

Jodi studied it, frowning. "Okay," she admitted a bit grudgingly, "I'd say that counts as a falsified theory. Maybe it's expectations; we don't get the high-end strength and toughness unless we're either trying to use it, or maybe panicked into using it. We can test that. And see whether it's decreasing or staying steady. Remember, we never had any chance to test out exactly how strong we were back in the *Lisharithada* caverns. So it may be—probably is—slowly fading in effect. We just need to know how long it'll take."

I chuckled suddenly. "Nope. I can tell you it's going to be staying steady. However it happened, we've got 'em for the rest of our lives."

"What? Clint, how can you say that?" She stared at me as my smile widened.

"Because it comes from the *H'adamant* elixir."

"And? What's your point?"

I couldn't help letting my smile turn into an evil grin. "Why, Jodi, everyone knows that."

I paused for dramatic effect.

"Diamonds are forever."

THE HOGBEN STORIES

Henry Kuttner

Exit the Professor

We Hogbens are right exclusive. That Perfesser feller from the city might have known that, but he come busting in without an invite, and I don't figger he had call to complain afterward. In Kaintuck the polite thing is to stick to your own hill of beans and not come nosing around where you're not wanted.

Time we ran off the Haley boys with that shotgun gadget we rigged up—only we never could make out how it worked, somehow—that time, it all started because Rafe Haley come peeking and prying at the shed winder, trying to get a look at Little Sam. Then Rafe went round saying Little Sam had three haids or something.

Can't believe a word them Haley boys say. Three haids! It ain't natcheral, is it? Anyhow, Little Sam's only got two haids, and never had no more since the day he was born.

So Maw and I rigged up that shotgun thing and

peppered the Haley boys good. Like I said, we couldn't figger out afterward how it worked. We'd tacked on some dry cells and a lot of coils and wires and stuff and it punched holes in Rafe as neat as anything.

Coroner's verdict was that the Haley boys died real sudden, and Sheriff Abernathy come up and had a drink of corn with us and said for two cents he'd whale the tar outa me. I didn't pay no mind. Only some damyankee reporter musta got wind of it, because a while later a big, fat, serious-looking man come around and begun to ask questions.

Uncle Les was sitting on the porch, with his hat over his face. "You better get the heck back to your circus, mister," he just said. "We had offers from old Barnum hisself and turned 'em down. Ain't that right, Saunk?"

"Sure is," I said. "I never trusted Phineas. Called Little Sam a freak, he did."

The big solemn-looking man, whose name was Perfesser Thomas Galbraith, looked at me. "How old are you, son?" he said.

"I ain't your son," I said. "And I don't know, nohow."

"You don't look over eighteen," he said, "big as you are. You couldn't have known Barnum."

"Sure I did. Don't go giving me the lie. I'll wham you."

"I'm not connected with any circus," Galbraith said. "I'm a biogeneticist."

We sure laughed at that. He got kinda mad and wanted to know what the joke was.

"There ain't no such word," Maw said. And at that point Little Sam started yelling, and Galbraith turned white as a goose wing and shivered all over. He sort of fell down. When we picked him up, he wanted to know what had happened.

"That was Little Sam," I said. "Maw's gone in to comfort him. He's stopped now."

"That was a subsonic," the Perfesser snapped. "What is Little Sam—a short-wave transmitter?"

"Little Sam's the baby," I said, short-like. "Don't go calling him outa his name, either. Now, s'pose you tell us what you want."

He pulled out a notebook and started looking through it.

"I'm a—a scientist," he said. "Our foundation is studying eugenics, and we've got some reports about you. They sound unbelievable. One of our men has a theory that natural mutations can remain undetected in undeveloped cultural regions and . . ." He slowed down and stared at Uncle Les. "Can you really fly?" he asked.

Well, we don't like to talk about that. The preacher gave us a good dressing-down once. Uncle Les had got likkered up and went sailing over the ridges, scaring a couple of bear hunters outta their senses. And it ain't in the Good Book that men should fly, neither. Uncle Les generally does it only on the sly, when nobody's watching.

So anyhow Uncle Les pulled his hat down further on his face and growled.

"That's plumb silly. Ain't no way a man can fly. These here modern contraptions I hear tell about—'tween ourselves, they don't really fly at all. Just a lot of crazy talk, that's all."

Galbraith blinked and studied his notebook again.

"But I've got hearsay evidence of a great many unusual things connected with your family. Flying is only one of them. I know it's theoretically impossible— and I'm not talking about planes—but—"

"Oh, shet your trap."

"The medieval witches' salve used aconite to give an illusion of flight—entirely subjective, of course."

"Will you stop pestering me?" Uncle Les said, getting

mad, on account of he felt embarrassed, I guess. Then he jumped up, threw his hat down on the porch, and flew away. After a minute he swooped down for his hat and made a face at the Perfesser. He flew off down the gulch and we didn't see him fer a while.

I got mad, too.

"You got no call to bother us," I said. "Next thing Uncle Les will do like Paw, and that'll be an awful nuisance. We ain't seen hide nor hair of Paw since that other city feller was around. He was a census taker, I think."

Galbraith didn't say anything. He was looking kinda funny. I gave him a drink and he asked about Paw.

"Oh, he's around," I said. "Only you don't see him no more. He likes it better that way, he says."

"Yes," Galbraith said, taking another drink. "Oh, God. How old did you say you were?"

"Didn't say nothing about it."

"Well, what's the earliest thing you can remember?"

"Ain't no use remembering things. Clutters up your haid too much."

"It's fantastic," Galbraith said. "I hadn't expected to send a report like that back to the foundation."

"We don't want nobody prying around," I said. "Go way and leave us alone."

"But, good Lord!" He looked over the porch rail and got interested in the shotgun gadget. "What's that?"

"A thing," I said.

"What does it do?"

"Things," I said.

"Oh. May I look at it?"

"Sure," I said. "I'll give you the dingus if you'll go away."

He went over and looked at it. Paw got up from where he'd been sitting beside me, told me to get rid

of the damyankee, and went into the house. The
Perfesser came back. "Extraordinary!" he said. "I've had
training in electronics, and it seems to me you've got
something very odd there. What's the principle?"

"The what?" I said. "It makes holes in things."

"It can't fire shells. You've got a couple of lenses
where the breech should—how did you say it worked?"

"I dunno."

"Did you make it?"

"Me and Maw."

He asked a lot more questions.

"I dunno," I said. "Trouble with a shotgun is you
gotta keep loading it. We sorta thought it we hooked
on a few things it wouldn't need loading no more. It
don't, neither."

"Were you serious about giving it to me?"

"If you stop bothering us."

"Listen," he said, "it's miraculous that you Hogbens
have stayed out of sight so long."

"We got our ways."

"The mutation theory must be right. You must be
studied. This is one of the most important discover-
ies since—" He kept on talking like that. He didn't
make much sense.

Finally I decided there was only two ways to handle
things, and after what Sheriff Abernathy had said, I
didn't feel right about killing nobody till the Sheriff
had got over his fit of temper. I don't want to cause
no ruckus.

"S'pose I go to New York with you, like you want,"
I said. "Will you leave the family alone?"

He halfway promised, though he didn't want to.
But he knuckled under and crossed his heart, on
account of I said I'd wake up Little Sam if he didn't.
He sure wanted to see Little Sam, but I told him
that was no good. Little Sam couldn't go to New York,

anyhow. He's got to stay in his tank or he gets awful sick.

Anyway, I satisfied the Perfesser pretty well and he went off, after I'd promised to meet him in town next morning. I felt sick, though, I can tell you. I ain't been away from the folks overnight since that ruckus in the old country, when we had to make tracks fast.

Went to Holland, as I remember. Maw always had a soft spot fer the man that helped us get outa London. Named Little Sam after him. I fergit what his name was. Gwynn or Stuart or Pepys—I get mixed up when I think back beyond the War Between the States.

That night we chewed the rag. Paw being invisible, Maw kept thinking he was getting more'n his share of the corn, but pretty soon she mellowed and let him have a demijohn. Everybody told me to mind my p's and q's.

"This here Perfesser's awful smart," Maw said. "All perfessers are. Don't go bothering him any. You be a good boy or you'll ketch heck from me."

"I'll be good, Maw," I said. Paw whaled me alongside the haid, which wasn't fair, on account of I couldn't see him.

"That's so you won't fergit," he said.

"We're plain folks," Uncle Les was growling. "No good never come of trying to get above yourself."

"Honest, I ain't trying to do that," I said. "I only figgered—"

"You stay outa trouble!" Maw said, and just then we heard Grandpaw moving in the attic. Sometimes Grandpaw don't stir for a month at a time, but tonight he seemed right frisky.

So, natcherally, we went upstairs to see what he wanted.

He was talking about the Perfesser.

"A stranger, eh?" he said. "Out upon the stinking

knave. A set of rare fools I've gathered about me for my dotage! Only Saunk shows any shrewdness, and, dang my eyes, he's the worst fool of all."

I just shuffled and muttered something, on account of I never like to look at Grandpaw direct. But he wasn't paying me no mind. He raved on.

"So you'd go to this New York? 'Sblood, and hast thou forgot the way we shunned London and Amsterdam—and Nieuw Amsterdam—for fear of questioning? Wouldst thou be put in a freak show? Nor is that the worst danger."

Grandpaw's the oldest one of us all and he gets kinda mixed up in his language sometimes. I guess the lingo you learned when you're young sorta sticks with you. One thing, he can cuss better than anybody I've ever heard.

"Shucks," I said. "I was only trying to help."

"Thou puling brat," Grandpaw said. "'Tis thy fault and thy dam's. For building that device, I mean, that slew the Haley tribe. Hadst thou not, this scientist would never have come here."

"He's a perfesser," I said. "Name of Thomas Galbraith."

"I know. I read his thoughts through Little Sam's mind. A dangerous man. I never knew a sage who wasn't. Except perhaps Roger Bacon, and I had to bribe him to—but Roger was an exceptional man. Hearken:

"None of you may go to this New York. The moment we leave this haven, the moment we are investigated, we are lost. The pack would tear and rend us. Nor could all thy addlepated flights skyward save thee, Lester— dost thou hear?"

"But what are we to do?" Maw said.

"Aw, heck," Paw said. "I'll just fix this Perfesser. I'll drop him down the cistern."

"An' spoil the water?" Maw screeched. "You try it!"

"What foul brood is this that has sprung from my seed?" Grandpaw said, real mad. "Have ye not promised the Sheriff that there will be no more killings—for a while, at least? Is the word of a Hogben naught? Two things have we kept sacred through the centuries—our secret from the world, and the Hogben honor! Kill this man Galbraith and ye'll answer to me for it!"

We all turned white. Little Sam woke up again and started squealing. "But what'll we do?" Uncle Les said.

"Our secret must be kept," Grandpaw said. "Do what ye can, but no killing. I'll consider the problem."

He seemed to go to sleep then, though it was hard to tell.

The next day I met Galbraith in town, all right, but first I run into Sheriff Abernathy in the street and he gave me a vicious look.

"You stay outa trouble, Saunk," he said. "Mind what I tell you, now." It was right embarrassing.

Anyway, I saw Galbraith and told him Grandpaw wouldn't let me go to New York. He didn't look too happy, but he saw there was nothing that could be done about it.

His hotel room was full of scientific apparatus and kinda frightening. He had the shotgun gadget set up, but it didn't look like he'd changed it any. He started to argue.

"Ain't no use," I said. "We ain't leaving the hills. I spoke outa turn yesterday, that's all."

"Listen, Saunk," he said. "I've been inquiring around town about you Hogbens, but I haven't been able to find out much. They're close-mouthed around here. Still, such evidence would be only supporting factors. I know our theories are right. You and your family are mutants and you've got to be studied!"

"We ain't mutants," I said. "Scientists are always calling us outa our names. Roger Bacon called us homunculi, only—"

"*What?*" Galbraith shouted. "Who did you say?"

"Uh—he's a share-cropper over in the next county," I said hasty-like, but I could see the Perfesser didn't swaller it. He started to walk around the room.

"It's no use," he said. "If you won't come to New York, I'll have the foundation send a commission here. You've got to be studied, for the glory of science and the advancement of mankind."

"Oh, golly," I said. "I know what that'd be like. Make a freak show outa us. It'd kill Little Sam. No. You gotta go away and leave us alone."

"Leave you alone? When you can create apparatus like this?" He pointed to the shotgun gadget. "How *does* that work?" he wanted to know, sudden-like.

"I told you, I dunno. We just rigged it up. Listen, Perfesser. There'd be trouble if people came and looked at us. Big trouble. Grandpaw says so."

Galbraith pulled at his nose.

"Well, maybe—suppose you answered a few questions for me, Saunk."

"No commission?"

"We'll see."

"No, sir. I won't—"

Galbraith took a deep breath.

"As long as you tell me what I want to know, I'll keep your whereabouts a secret."

"I thought this foundation thing of yours knows where you are."

"Ah—yes," Galbraith said. "Naturally they do. But they don't know about *you*."

That gave me an idea. I coulda killed him easy, but if I had, I knew Grandpaw would of ruined me entire and, besides, there was the Sheriff to think of. So I said, "Shucks," and nodded.

My, the questions that man asked! It left me dizzy. And all the while he kept getting more and more excited.

"How old is your grandfather?"

"Gosh, I dunno."

"Homunculi—mm-m. You mentioned that he was a miner once?"

"No, that was Grandpaw's paw," I said. "Tin mines, they were, in England. Only Grandpaw says it was called Britain then. That was during a sorta magic plague they had then. The people had to get the doctors—droons? Droods?"

"Druids?"

"Uh-huh. The Druids was the doctors then, Grandpaw says. Anyhow, all the miners started dying round Cornwall, so they closed up the mines."

"What sort of plague was it?"

I told him what I remembered from Grandpaw's talk, and the Perfesser got very excited and said something about radioactive emanations, as nearly as I could figger out. It made oncommon bad sense.

"Artificial mutations caused by radioactivity!" he said, getting real pink around the jowls. "Your grandfather was born a mutant! The genes and chromosomes were rearranged into a new pattern. Why, you may all be supermen!"

"Nope," I said. "We're Hogbens. That's all."

"A dominant, obviously a dominant. All your family were—ah—peculiar?"

"Now, look!" I said.

"I mean, they could all fly?"

"I don't know how yet, myself. I guess we're kinda freakish. Grandpaw was smart. He allus taught us not to show off."

"Protective camouflage," Galbraith said. "Submerged in a rigid social culture, variations from the norm are more easily masked. In a modern, civilized culture, you'd stick out like a sore thumb. But here, in the backwoods, you're practically invisible."

"Only Paw," I said.

"Oh, Lord," he sighed. "Submerging these incredible natural powers of yours . . . Do you know the things you might have done?" And then all of a sudden he got even more excited, and I didn't much like the look in his eyes.

"Wonderful things," he repeated. "It's like stumbling on Aladdin's lamp."

"I wish you'd leave us alone," I said. "You and your commission!"

"Forget about the commission. I've decided to handle this privately for a while. Provided you'll cooperate. Help me, I mean. Will you do that?"

"Nope," I said.

"Then I'll bring the commission down from New York," he said triumphantly.

I thought that over.

"Well," I said finally, "what do you want me to do?"

"I don't know yet," he said slowly. "My mind hasn't fully grasped the possibilities."

But he was getting ready to grab. I could tell. I know that look.

I was standing by the window looking out, and all of a sudden I got an idea. I figgered it wouldn't be smart to trust the Perfesser too much, anyhow. So I sort of ambled over to the shotgun gadget and made a few little changes on it.

I knew what I wanted to do, all right, but if Galbraith had asked me why I was twisting a wire here and bending a whozis there I couldn't of told him. I got no education. Only now I knew the gadget would do what I wanted it to do.

The Perfesser had been writing in his little note-book. He looked up and saw me.

"What are you doing?" he wanted to know.

"This don't look right to me," I said. "I think you monkeyed with them batteries. Try it now."

"In here?" he said, startled. "I don't want to pay a bill for damages. It must be tested under safety conditions."

"See that weathercock out there, on the roof?" I pointed it out to him. "Won't do no harm to aim at that. You can just stand here by the winder and try it out."

"It—it isn't dangerous?" He was aching to try the gadget, I could tell. I said it wouldn't kill nobody, and he took a long breath and went to the window and cuddled the stock of the gun against his cheek.

I stayed back aways. I didn't want the Sheriff to see me. I'd already spotted him, sitting on a bench outside the feed-and-grain store across the street.

It happened just like I thought. Galbraith pulled the trigger, aiming at the weathercock on the roof, and rings of light started coming out of the muzzle. There was a fearful noise. Galbraith fell flat on his back, and the commotion was something surprising. People began screaming all over town.

I kinda felt it might be handy if I went invisible for a while. So I did.

Galbraith was examining the shotgun gadget when Sheriff Abernathy busted in. The Sheriff's a hard case. He had his pistol out and handcuffs ready, and he was cussing the Perfesser immediate and rapid.

"I seen you!" he yelled. "Your city fellers think you can get away with anything down here. Well, you can't!"

"Saunk!" Galbraith cried, looking around. But of course he couldn't see me.

Then there was an argument. Sheriff Abernathy had

seen Galbraith fire the shotgun gadget and he's no fool. He drug Galbraith down on the street, and I come along, walking soft. People were running around like crazy. Most of them had their hands clapped to their faces.

The Perfesser kept wailing that he didn't understand.

"I seen you!" Abernathy said. "You aimed that dingus of yours out the window and the next thing everybody in town's got a toothache! Try and tell me you don't understand!"

The Sheriff's smart. He's known us Hogbens long enough so he ain't surprised when funny things happen sometimes. Also, he knew Galbraith was a scientist feller. So there was a ruckus and people heard what was going on and the next thing they was trying to lynch Galbraith.

But Abernathy got him away. I wandered around town for a while. The pastor was out looking at his church windows, which seemed to puzzle him. They was stained glass, and he couldn't figger out why they was hot. I coulda told him that. There's gold in stained-glass windows; they use it to get a certain kind of red.

Finally I went down to the jailhouse. I was still invisible. So I eavesdropped on what Galbraith was saying to the Sheriff.

"It was Saunk Hogben," the Perfesser kept saying. "I tell you, he fixed that projector!"

"I saw you," Abernathy said. "You done it. Ow!" He put up his hand to his jaw. "And you better stop it, fast! That crowd outside means business. Half the people in town have got toothaches."

I guess half the people in town had gold fillings in their teeth.

Then Galbraith said something that didn't surprise me too much. "I'm having a commission come down from New York; I meant to telephone the foundation tonight. They'll vouch for me."

So he was intending to cross us up, all along. I kinda felt that had been in his mind.

"You'll cure this toothache of mine—and everybody else's—or I'll open the doors and let in that lynch mob!" the Sheriff howled. Then he went away to put an icebag on his cheek.

I snuck back aways, got visible again, and made a lot of noise coming along the passage, so Galbraith could hear me. I waited till he got through cussing me out. I just looked stupid.

"I guess I made a mistake," I said. "I can fix it, though."

"You've done enough fixing!" He stopped. "Wait a minute. What did you say? You can cure this—what *is* it?"

"I been looking at that shotgun gadget," I said. "I think I know what I did wrong. It's sorta tuned in on gold now, and all the gold in town's shooting out rays or heat or something."

"Induced selective radioactivity," Galbraith muttered, which didn't seem to mean much. "Listen. That crowd outside—do they ever have lynchings in this town?"

"Not more'n once or twice a year," I said. "And we already had two this year, so we filled our quota. Wish I could get you up to our place, though. We could hide you easy."

"You'd better do something!" he said. "Or I'll get that commission down from New York. You wouldn't like that, would you?"

I never seen such a man for telling lies and keeping a straight face.

"It's a cinch," I said. "I can rig up the gadget so it'll switch off the rays immediate. Only I don't want people to connect us Hogbens with what's going on. We like to live quiet. Look, s'pose I go back to your hotel and change over the gadget, and then all you have to do is get all the people with toothaches together and pull the trigger."

"But—well, but—"

He was afraid of more trouble. I had to talk him into it. The crowd was yelling outside, so it wasn't too hard. Finally I went away, but I came back, invisible-like, and listened when Galbraith talked to the Sheriff.

They fixed it all up. Everybody with toothaches was going to the Town Hall and set. Then Abernathy would bring the Perfesser over, with the shotgun gadget, and try it out.

"Will it stop the toothaches?" the Sheriff wanted to know. "For sure?"

"I'm—quite certain it will."

Abernathy had caught that hesitation.

"Then you better try it on me first. Just to make sure. I don't trust you."

It seemed like nobody was trusting nobody.

I hiked back to the hotel and made the switch-over in the shotgun gadget. And then I run into trouble. My invisibility was wearing thin. That's the worst part of being just a kid.

After I'm a few hunnerd years older I can stay invisible all the time if I want to. But I ain't right mastered it yet. Thing was, I needed help now because there was something I had to do, and I couldn't do it with people watching.

I went up on the roof and called Little Sam. After I'd tuned in on his haid, I had him put the call through to Paw and Uncle Les. After a while Uncle Les come flying down from the sky, riding mighty heavy on account of he was carrying Paw. Paw was cussing because a hawk had chased them.

"Nobody seen us, though," Uncle Les said. "I think."

"People got their own troubles in town today," I said. "I need some help. That Perfesser's gonna call down his commission and study us, no matter what he promises."

"Ain't much we can do, then," Paw said. "We cain't kill that feller. Grandpaw said not to."

So I told 'em my idea. Paw being invisible, he could do it easy. Then we made a little place in the roof so we could see through it, and looked down into Galbraith's room.

We was just in time. The Sheriff was standing there, with his pistol out, just waiting, and the Perfesser, pale around the chops, was pointing the shotgun gadget at Abernathy. It went along without a hitch. Galbraith pulled the trigger, a purple ring of light popped out, and that was all. Except that the Sheriff opened his mouth and gulped.

"You wasn't faking! My toothache's gone!"

Galbraith was sweating, but he put up a good front. "Sure it works," he said. "Naturally. I told you—"

"C'mon down to the Town Hall. Everybody's waiting. You better cure us all, or it'll be just too bad for you."

They went out. Paw snuck down after them, and Uncle Les picked me up and flew on their trail, keeping low to the roofs, where we wouldn't be spotted. After a while we was fixed outside one of the Town Hall's windows, watching.

I ain't heard so much misery since the great plague of London. The hall was jam-full, and everybody had a toothache and was moaning and yelling. Abernathy come in with the Perfesser, who was carrying the shotgun gadget, and a scream went up.

Galbraith set the gadget on the stage, pointing down at the audience, while the Sheriff pulled out his pistol again and made a speech, telling everybody to shet up and they'd get rid of their toothaches.

I couldn't see Paw, natcherally, but I knew he was up on the platform. Something funny was happening to the shotgun gadget. Nobody noticed, except me, and I was watching for it. Paw—invisible, of course—was making a few changes. I'd told him how, but he knew what to do as well as I did. So pretty soon the shotgun was rigged the way we wanted it.

What happened after that was shocking. Galbraith aimed the gadget and pulled the trigger, and rings of light jumped out, yaller this time. I'd told Paw to fix the range so nobody outside the Town Hall would be bothered. But inside—

Well, it sure fixed them toothaches. Nobody's gold filling can ache if he ain't got a gold filling.

The gadget was fixed now so it worked on everything that wasn't growing. Paw had got the range just right. The seats was gone all of a sudden, and so was part of the chandelier. The audience, being bunched together, got it good. Pegleg Jaffe's glass eye was gone, too. Them that had false teeth lost 'em. Everybody sorta got a once-over-lightly haircut.

Also, the whole audience lost their clothes. Shoes ain't growing things, and no more are pants or shirts or dresses. In a trice everybody in the hall was naked as needles. But, shucks, they'd got rid of their toothaches, hadn't they?

We was back to home an hour later, all but Uncle Les, when the door busted open and in come Uncle Les, with the Perfesser staggering after him. Galbraith was a mess. He sank down and wheezed, looking back at the door in a worried way.

"Funny thing happened," Uncle Les said. "I was

flying along outside town and there was the Perfesser
running away from a big crowd of people, with sheets
wrapped around 'em—some of 'em. So I picked him
up. I brung him here, like he wanted." Uncle Les
winked at me.

"Ooooh!" Galbraith said. "*Aaaah!* Are they coming?"

Maw went to the door.

"They's a lot of torches moving up the mountain,"
she said. "It looks right bad."

The Perfesser glared at me.

"You said you could hide me! Well, you'd better!
This is your fault!"

"Shucks," I said.

"You'll hide me or else!" Galbraith squalled. "I—I'll
bring that commission down."

"Look," I said, "if we hide you safe, will you promise to fergit all about that commission and leave us
alone?"

The Perfesser promised. "Hold on a minute," I said,
and went up to the attic to see Grandpaw.

He was awake.

"How about it, Grandpaw?" I asked.

He listened to Little Sam for a second.

"The knave is lying," he told me pretty soon. "He
means to bring his commission of stinkards here anyway, recking naught of his promise."

"Should we hide him, then?"

"Aye," Grandpaw said. "The Hogbens have given
their word—there must be no more killing. And to hide
a fugitive from his pursuers would not be an ill deed,
surely."

Maybe he winked. It's hard to tell with Grandpaw.
So I went down the ladder. Galbraith was at the door,
watching the torches come up the mountain.

He grabbed me.

"Saunk! If you don't hide me—"

"We'll hide you," I said. "C'mon."

So we took him down to the cellar.

When the mob got here, with Sheriff Abernathy in the lead, we played dumb. We let 'em search the house. Little Sam and Grandpaw turned invisible for a bit, so nobody noticed them. And naturally the crowd couldn't find hide nor hair of Galbraith. We'd hid him good, like we promised.

That was years ago. The Perfesser's thriving. He ain't studying us, though. Sometimes we take out the bottle we keep him in and study him.

Dang small bottle, too!

Pile of Trouble

We called Lemuel "Gimpy," on account of he had three legs. After he got his growth, about the time they fit the War Between the States, he was willing to keep his extra leg sort of tucked up behind him inside his britches, where it would be out of sight and people wouldn't talk. 'Course it made him look a little like one of them camel critters, but then Lemuel never was vain. It was lucky he was doublejointed, though, or he might of got cramps from keeping his leg tucked up thataway.

We hadn't seen Lemuel for some sixty years. He was living in the southern part of the mountains, and the rest of us was up in northern Kaintuck. And I guess we wouldn't of got in that trouble if Lemuel hadn't been so blame shiftless. It looked like big trouble for a while. We Hogbens had had plenty of that before we moved to Piperville, what with people peeping and prying and trying to find out why the dogs barked so

much for miles around. It got so we couldn't do no
flying at all. Finally Grandpaw said we'd just better pull
up stakes and move down south where Lemuel was
staying.

I hate moving. That trip to Plymouth Rock made
me sick to my stummick. I'd ruther of flew. But
Grandpaw's the boss.

He made us hire a truck and load everything in it.
We had trouble getting the baby in; he don't weigh
more'n three hundred pound, but that tank we got to
keep him in is purty bulky. No trouble about Grandpaw,
though; we just tied him up in an old gunny sack and
shoved him under the seat. I had to do all the work.
Paw had got at the corn likker and was plumb silly.
He kept hopping around on the top of his haid and
singing something called "The World Turned Upside
Down."

Uncle wouldn't come. He'd dug himself in under
the corncrib and said he was gonna hibernate for ten
years or so. We just left him there. "Allus traveling
around," he kept complaining. "Cain't stay put. Every
five hundred years or so, bang! Traipsin' off summers.
Go on, git!"

So we got.

Lemuel, the one we used to call Gimpy, was one
of the family. Seems there was a dust-up when we first
came to Kaintuck—the way I heard it. Everybody was
supposed to pitch in and help build a house, but not
Lemuel—he wouldn't. Plumb shiftless. He flew off to
the south. Every year or two he'd wake up a little and
we'd hear him thinking, but mostly he just sot.

We figgered we'd live with him fer a while.

That's what we did.

Seems like Lemuel lived in an old water mill in the
mountains up over a town called Piperville. It was kind
of ramshackle. Lemuel was on the porch. He'd been

sitting in a chair, but it had fallen down some while before, and he hadn't bothered to wake up to fix it. So he sat there in the middle of his whiskers, breathing a trifle. He was having a nice dream. We didn't wake him up. We toted the baby in the house, and Grandpaw and Paw started carrying in the bottles of corn.

That was how we settled in. It warn't exactly convenient at first. Lemuel was too remarkable shiftless to keep vittles in the house. He'd wake up enough to hypnotize a coon, back somewheres in the woods, and purty soon the coon would come wandering along looking dazed, ready to be et. Lemuel had to eat coons mostly because they're clever with their paws, which are sort of like hands. You can call me a weasel if that shiftless Lem didn't hypnotize the coons into building a fire and cooking themselves. I never figgered out how he got the critters skun. Maybe he spit out the fur. Some people are just too lazy for anything.

When he got thirsty, he made it rain a little over his haid and opened his mouth. It was shameful.

Nobody paid no attention to Lemuel, though. Maw got busy. Paw, natcherally, snuck off with a jug of corn, and I had to do all the work. 'Twarn't much. Main trouble was we needed some sort of power. Keeping the baby alive in his tank uses up a lot of current, and Grandpaw drinks electricity like a hawg sucks up swill. Ef'n Lemuel had kept the water running in the stream, we'd of had no trouble, but that was Lemuel! He just let it dry up. There was a trickle, no more.

Maw helped me build a gadget in the henhouse, and after that we got all the power we needed.

The trouble all started when a skinny little runt come up the trail one day and seemed surprised to see Maw take the washing out in the yard. I trailed along, interested like.

"Right nice day," Maw said. "Want a drink, stranger?"

He said he didn't mind if'n he did, so I got him a dipperful, and after he had drunk the corn he took a few gasping breaths and said, thanks, no, he didn't want any more just then or ever. He said he could cut his throat cheaper, and get the same effect.

"Just moved in here?" he asked.

Maw said yes, we had, and Lemuel was a relative. The feller looked at Lemuel, sitting on the porch with his eyes shut, and said, "You mean he's alive?"

"Shore is," Maw said. "Alive and kicking, so to speak."

"We thought he'd been dead for years," the man said. "That's why we never bothered about collecting the poll tax for him. I guess you'd better pay yours, too, now that you've moved in. How many of you are there?"

"'Bout six," Maw said.

"All of age?"

"There's Paw and Saunk and the baby—"

"How old?"

"The baby's about four hundred now, ain't he, Maw?" I asked, but she clouted me 'longside the haid and said I should shet up. The man pointed at me and said he'd meant how old was I. Heck, I couldn't tell him. I lost track round about Cromwell's time. Finally he said we'd all have to pay a poll tax except the baby.

"Not that it matters," he said, writing in a little book. "You have to vote the right way in this town. The Machine's in to stay. There's only one boss in Piperville, and his name's Eli Gandy. Twenty dollars that'll be."

Maw told me to git some money, so I went searchin'. Grandpaw didn't have anything except something he said was a denarius, and that was his lucky piece anyhow; he said he'd swiped it from a feller named Julius up in Gaul. Paw was daid drunk. The baby had three dollars. I went and looked through Lemuel's pockets but didn't find nothing but an old oriole's nest with two eggs in it.

When I told Maw, she scratched her haid, so I said, "We can make some by tomorrow, Maw. You'll take gold, won't you, Mister?"

Maw clouted me. The man looked kind of funny and said sure, he'd take gold. Then he went away through the woods passing a coon that was carrying a bundle of twigs fer firewood, and I figgered Lemuel was getting hungry. The man started to walk faster.

I started looking fer some old iron I could change into gold.

The next day we got carted off to jail.

We knew about it in advance, of course, but there wasn't much we could do. It's allus been our idea to keep our haids down and not attract no special attention. That's what Grandpaw told us to do now. We all went up to the attic—all but the baby and Lemuel, who never stirred—and I kept looking at a spiderweb up in one corner, so I wouldn't have to look at Grandpaw. He hurts my eyes.

"Out upon them for stinkard knaves," Grandpaw said. "'Tis best that we go to their gaol; the days of the Inquisition are over. 'Twill be safe enough."

"Cain't we hide that thar gadget we made?" I asked him.

Maw clouted me fer speaking before my elders. "That won't do no good," she said. "Them spies from Piperville was up here this morning and seen it."

Grandpaw said, "Have you hollowed a cavern under this house? Good. Hide me and the baby there. The rest of you—" He relapsed into old-fashioned language. "'Tis pity if we were to live thus long and be found out by these black-avised dullards. 'Twere better their weasands were slit. Nay, Saunk—I spoke in jest. We would not call attention to ourselves. We will find a way."

That was the way it was. We all got toted off, all but Grandpaw and the baby, who were down in the cave by that time. We got carried off to Piperville and put in the hoosegow. Lemuel never woke up. They drug him off by the heels.

As fer Paw, he stayed drunk. He's got a trick he knows. He can drink corn, and then, as I understand it, the alcohol goes in his blood and gets changed into sugar or something. Magic, I guess. He tried to explain it to me, but it made oncommon bad sense. Likker goes into your stummick; how kin it go up inside your skull and turn into sugar? Plumb silly. Or conjure, anyhow. But what I was going to say, Paw says he's trained some friends of his named Enzymes—furriners, by the name—so they change the sugar right back to alcohol, and he kin stay drunk as long as he wants. Still, he likes fresh corn if he can get it. Me, I don't like them conjure tricks; they make me skittery.

I was took into a room with people in it and told to sit down in a chair. They asked me questions. I played dumb. I said I didn't know nothing.

"It's impossible!" somebody said. "They couldn't have built it themselves—illiterate hillbillies! But, unmistakably, there's a uranium pile in their henhouse!"

Shucks.

I kept on playing dumb. After a while they took me back to my cell. There was bedbugs. I made a sort of ray come out of my eyes and killed 'em off, much to the surprise of a seedy little feller with pink whiskers who was asleep in the upper bunk, and who I didn't notice was awake till it was too late.

"I have been in some strange prisons in my time," said the seedy little feller, blinking rapid, "and I have had some unusual cellmates, but never yet have I encountered one whom I suspected to be the devil. My name is Armbruster, Stinky Armbruster, and I'm up for vagrancy. What's the charge against you, my friend? Buying souls over the ceiling price?"

I said I was pleased to meet him. I had to admire his language. He had eddication something fearful.

"Mr. Armbruster," I said, "I got no idea why I'm here. They just carted me off—Paw and Maw and Lemuel. Lemuel's asleep, though, and Paw's drunk."

"I would like to be drunk," Mr. Armbruster told me. "Then I wouldn't be so surprised to see you floating two feet off the floor."

That kind of embarrassed me. Nobody likes to be caught doing things like that. It was just that I was absent-minded, but I felt foolish. I said I was sorry.

"It doesn't matter," Mr. Armbruster said, rolling over and scratching his whiskers. "I've been expecting this for years. I've had a pleasant life, all in all. And this is a delightful way to go crazy. Why did you say they arrested you?"

"They said we had a uranium pile," I told him. "I bet we ain't. We got a woodpile, I know, 'cause I chopped the wood. But I know I never chopped no uranium."

"You'd remember it if you had," he said. "It's probably some political gambit. Election's a week off. There's a reform party starting, and old Gandy's smashing it before it can start."

"Well, we ought to be getting home," I said.

"Where do you live?"

I told him, and he thought that over. "I wonder. You're on the river, aren't you—the creek, I mean? Big Bear?"

"It ain't even a creek," I said.

Mr. Armbruster laughed. "Gandy called it the Big Bear River. That was before he got the Gandy Dam built, down below your place. There hasn't been any water in that creek for fifty years, but old Gandy put through an appropriation for I don't know how much money, about ten years ago. He got the dam built by calling the creek a river."

"What did he want to do that for?" I asked.

"Do you know how much crooked money you can make out of building a dam?" Mr. Armbruster asked me. "But Gandy's in to stay, I guess. When a man owns the newspapers, he can write his own ticket. Oh-oh. Here comes somebody."

A man come with keys and took Mr. Armbruster away. After quite awhile somebody else come and let me out. I was took into another room full of lights. Mr. Armbruster was there, and Maw and Paw and Lemuel, and some big fellers with guns. There was a little skinny wizened man with a bald head and snaky eyes, and everybody done what he told 'em. They called him Mr. Gandy.

"This boy's an ordinary hillbilly," Mr. Armbruster said, when I come in. "If he's got into trouble, it must be by accident."

They told him to keep quiet and banged him one. So he kept quiet. That Mr. Gandy sat off in a corner and sort of nodded, looking mean. He had a bad eye. "Listen, boy," he said to me. "Who are you shielding? Who built that uranium pile in your woodshed? You'd better tell me the truth or you'll get hurt."

I just looked at him, so somebody hit me on top of the haid. Shucks. You can't hurt a Hogben by hitting him on the haid. I recollect the time the feuding Adamses cotched me and banged me on the haid till they was plumb wore out and couldn't even squeal when I dumped 'em down a cistern.

Mr. Armbruster made noises.

"Listen, Mr. Gandy," he said. "I know it'll make a big story if you find out who built that uranium pile, but you'll get re-elected without it. Maybe it isn't a uranium pile anyway."

"I know who built it," Mr. Gandy said. "Renegade scientists. Or escaped Nazi war criminals. And I intend to find them!"

"Oh-oh," said Mr. Armbruster. "Now I get the idea. A story like that would be nationwide, wouldn't it? You could run for Governor or the Senate or—or write your own ticket."

"What did that boy tell you?" Mr. Gandy asked. But Mr. Armbruster said I hadn't told him nothing.

Then they started to whup Lemuel.

It was tiresome. Nobody can't wake up Lemuel when he's sot on a nap, and I never seen nobody so sot just then. They give him up fer daid after a time. He might as well of been. Lemuel is so bone lazy that when he's sleeping hard he don't even trouble to breathe.

Paw was working magic with them Enzyme friends of his'n, and he was remarkable drunk. It sort of tickled him to get whupped. Every time they whammed him with a length of hose he giggled kind of foolish. I was ashamed.

Nobody tried to whup Maw. When anybody got close enough to hit her, he'd go all over white as a goose wing and start busting out with sweat and shaking. Once we knowed a perfesser feller who said Maw could emit a tight-beam subsonic. He was a liar. She just made a noise nobody could hear and aimed it wherever she wanted. All them high-falutin words! Simple as firing a squirrel rifle. I can do it myself.

Mr. Gandy said to take us back to where we was, and he'd see us later. So they drug out Lemuel, and we all went back to our cells. Mr. Armbruster had a lump on his haid the size of a duck egg. He lay down on his bunk moaning, and I sot in a corner looking at his haid, and sort of shooting a light out of my eyes, only nobody couldn't see the light. What it did was—shucks, I ain't eddicated. It worked like a poultice, anyhow. After a while the bump on Mr. Armbruster's haid went away, and he stopped groaning.

"You're in trouble, Saunk," he said—I had told him my name by then. "Gandy's got big ideas now. And he's got the people of Piperville hypnotized. What he wants is to hypnotize the state, or even the nation. He wants to be a national figure. The right sort of news story could do that for him. Besides, it would ensure his re-election next week—not that he needs insurance. He's got the city in his pocket. *Was* that a uranium pile?"

I just looked at him.

"Gandy seems certain," he went on. "He sent up some physicists, and they said it was apparently Two-thirty-five with the graphite dampers. Saunk, I heard them talking. For your own good, you'd better not shield anyone. They're going to use a truth drug on you—sodium pentathol or scopolamine."

"You better go to sleep," I said, because I heard Grandpaw calling me, inside my haid. I shet my eyes and listened. 'Twarn't simple, because Paw kept tuning in. Oh, my, he was drunk!

"Have a drink," Paw said, cheerful, only without talking, if you understand.

"Beshrew thee for a warrantable louse," Grandpaw said, much less cheerful. "Get thy dullard mind away from here. Saunk!"

"Yes, Grandpaw," I said, silent-like.

"We must make a plan—"

Paw said, "Have a drink, Saunk."

"Now, Paw, do shet up," I told him. "Have some respect fer your elders. I mean Grandpaw. Besides, how can I have a drink? You're 'way off in some other cell."

"I got me a pipeline," Paw said. "I can give you a what-you-call-it, a transfusion. Teleportation, that's what it is. I just short-circuit space between your blood stream and mine and I can pump alcohol from my veins into your'n. Look, this is how I do it." He showed me how, in a sort of picture inside my haid. It looked easy enough. For a Hogben, I mean.

I got mad. "Paw," I said, "don't make your loving son disrespect you more than natcheral, you runty old wood-shoat, you. I know you ain't got no book-larnin'. You're just picking them four-bit words out of somebody's skull."

"Have a drink," Paw said, and then yelled. I heard Grandpaw chuckle.

"Stealing the wisdom from men's minds, eh?" he said. "I, too, can do that. I have just rapidly cultured a migraine virus in my blood stream and teleported it to your brain—you gorbellied knave! A plague upon the varlet! Hearken to me, Saunk. Thy rascally sire will not trouble us bewhiles."

"Yes, Grandpaw," I said. "Are you fit?"

"Aye."

"And the baby?"

"Aye. But you must act. 'Tis your task, Saunk. The trouble lies in that—what is the word? That uranium pile."

"So that's what it is," I said.

"Who would have thought anyone in the world could recognize it? My own grandsire told me how to make it; they existed in his time. Indeed, 'twas through such things that we Hogbens became mutants. Faith, I must pick a brain myself to make this clear. There are men in the town where you are, Saunk, who know the words I need—let me see."

He sort of shuffled through a few brains. Then he went on.

"When my grandsire lived, men had begun to split the atom. There were—um—secondary radiations. They affected the genes and chromosomes of some men and women—a dominant mutation, with us Hogbens. So we are mutants."

"That's what Roger Bacon said, wasn't it?" I asked.

"Aye. But he was friendly and kept silence. Had men known our powers in those days, we'd have been burned. Even today, it would not be safe for us to reveal ourselves. Eventually—you know what we plan eventually, Saunk."

"Yes, Grandpaw," I said, for I did know.

"Well, here's the rub. It seems that men have split the atom again. Thus they were able to recognize this uranium pile. We must destroy it; we do not want men's eyes upon us. Yet we need power. Not much, but some. The uranium pile was the easiest way to get it, but we cannot use it now. Saunk, here is what you must do— so that enough energy will be supplied for the baby and for me."

He told me what to do.

Then I went and done it.

When I sort of shift my eyes, I can see real purty things. Like them bars on the window, I mean. They get busted up into teeny-weeny little bits, all rushing around like they was crazy. I hear tell them is atoms. My, they look cheerful—all bustling like they was hurrying to git to meeting on a Sunday. 'Course it's easy to juggle 'em like blocks. You look real hard and make something come out of your eyes, and more teeny little fellers come busting out of your eyes and they all get together and it's mighty amusing. I made a mistake the first time and changed them iron bars into gold. Missed an atom, I expect. But after that I got it right and turned the bars into nothing much. I clomb out and turned 'em back into iron. First I'd made sure Mr. Armbruster was asleep. That was easy.

We was seven stories up above the street, in a big building that was part the city hall and part jail. It was nighttime, so nobody noticed me. I flew away. Once an owl came past, figgering I couldn't see in the dark, and I spit on him. Hit him, too.

I fixed that there uranium pile. There was guards around it with lights, but I hung up in the sky where they couldn't see me and got busy. First I hotted the thing up so the stuff Mr. Armbruster had called graphite turned into nothing and blew away. Then it was safe to handle the rest of the junk—Two-thirty-five, is it?—so I did, and I turned that into lead. The real crumbly kind. I made it so fearful crumbly it started to blow away. Soon there wasn't nothing left.

Then I flew away up the crick. There was only a dollop of water in it, and Grandpaw said he needed more than that. I got way up in the mountains, but didn't have no luck. Grandpaw started to talk to me. He said the baby was crying. I guess I shouldn't have tore up the uranium pile till I'd made plumb certain of getting more power.

Only thing to do was to make it rain.

There are several ways to do that, but I friz a cloud, sort of. Had to land and build a gadget fast and then fly way up where there was clouds; it took time, but pretty soon there was a thunderstorm coming up, and then it rained. But the water didn't go down the crick. I searched for a while, till I found a place where the whole crick bottom had fell out. Seems like there was caves underneath. I did some rapid plugging. No wonder there hadn't been no water to speak of in the crick for so long. I fixed that.

Grandpaw wanted a steady supply, though, and I smelled around till I located some big springs. I opened them up. By that time it was raining oncommon rapid. I went back to see Grandpaw.

Them men who was on guard had gone home, I guess. Grandpaw said the baby had plumb upset them when he started crying. They all stuck their fingers in their ears and screamed and run off. I looked over the water wheel, like Grandpaw told me, and done a few repairs. There warn't much needed. They built purty good a hundred years ago—and the wood had got seasoned, too. I admired that wheel, turning and turning as the water piled up in the crick—crick, nothing! It was a river now.

But Grandpaw said I oughta of seen the Appian Way when it was being set up.

I fixed him and the baby up nice and comfortable, and then I flew back to Piperville. It was coming on dawn, and I didn't want nobody to see me flying. This time I spit on a pigeon.

There was a rumpus going on in the city hall. Seems like Maw and Paw and Lemuel had plumb vanished. There was people running around remarkable upset, and there was great confusion. I knowed what had happened, though. Maw spoke to me, in my haid, and told me to come up to the cell at the end of the block, which was spacious. They was all there. Invisible, though.

I fergot to say I'd made myself invisible too, after I'd snuck in, seen Mr. Armbruster was still asleep, and noticed the excitement.

"Grandpaw told me what was happening," Maw said. "I figgered we'd better stay out'n the way for a while. Raining hard, ain't it?"

"Shore is," I said. "What's everybody so excited about?"

"They cain't figger out what become of us," Maw told me. "Soon as the ruckus quiets down, we'll all go home. You fixed it, I guess."

"I done what Grandpaw said," I explained, and then there was sudden yells from down the corridor. A little old fat coon come trundling in, carrying a bundle of sticks. He come right along till he got to the bars in front of where we was. Then he sot himself down and begun arranging the sticks to make a fire. He had that dazed look in his eyes, so I knew Lemuel must of hypnotized him.

People came crowding around outside. They couldn't see us, natcherally, but they were watching that there little old coon. I watched too, on account of I never was able to figger out how Lemuel could get the critter skun. I seen them build fires before—Lemuel could make 'em do that—but I just never happened to be around when one of his coons stripped down and skun hisself. That I wanted to see.

Just before the coon got started, though, a policeman put him in a bag and took him away, so I never did know. It was light by then. I kept hearing bellers from somewheres, and once I heard a voice I knew sing out.

"Maw," I said, "that sounds like Mr. Armbruster. I better go see what they're doing to the pore little guy."

"Time we was going home," she said. "We got to dig up Grandpaw and the baby. You say the water wheel's turning?"

"Yes, Maw," I said. "There's plenty electric power now."

She reached around till she found Paw and whammed him. "Wake up," she said.

"Have a drink," Paw said.

But she roused him up and said we was going home. Ain't nobody can wake up Lemuel, though. Finally Maw and Paw took Lemuel between them and flew out through the window, after I fixed the bars so they could get through. They stayed invisible, on account of there was a crowd down below. It was still raining, but Maw said they warn't made of sugar nor salt, and I'd better come along or I'd get my britches tanned.

"Yes, Maw," I said, but I wasn't going to. I stayed behind. I was going to find out what they were doing to Mr. Armbruster.

They had him in that big room with the lights on. Mr. Gandy was standing by the window, looking real mean, and they had Mr. Armbruster's sleeve rolled up and was going to stick a sort of glass needle into his hide. Well! Right away I made myself get visible again.

"You better not do that," I said.

"It's the Hogben kid!" somebody yelled. "Grab him!"

They grabbed me. I let 'em. Pretty soon I was sitting in a chair with my sleeve rolled up, and Mr. Gandy was grinning at me like a wolf.

"Use the truth serum on him," he said. "No need to ask that tramp questions now."

Kind of dazed, Mr. Armbruster kept saying, "I don't know what happened to Saunk! I wouldn't tell you if I knew—"

They whammed him.

Mr. Gandy stuck his face right into mine.

"We'll get the truth about that uranium pile now," he told me. "One shot of this and you'll answer our questions. Understand?"

So they stuck the needle in my arm and squirted the stuff into me. It tickled.

Then they asked me questions. I said I didn't know nothing. Mr. Gandy said to give me another shot. They done it.

It tickled worse than ever.

Right then somebody ran into the room and started yelling.

"The dam's busted!" he bellered. "The Gandy Dam!
It's flooded out half the farms in the south valley!"

Mr. Gandy rared back and squalled. "You're crazy!"
he told everybody. "It's impossible! There's been no
water in Big Bear River for a hundred years!"

Then they all got together and started whispering.
Something about samples. And a big mob downstairs.

"You've got to calm 'em down," somebody told Mr.
Gandy. "They're boiling mad. All the crops ruined—"

"I'll calm 'em down," Mr. Gandy said. "There's no
proof. And only a week before election!"

He rushed out of the room and everybody ran out
after him. I got up out of my chair and scratched. That
stuff they pumped into me itched fearful inside my
skin. I was kind of mad at Mr. Gandy.

"Quick!" Mr. Armbruster said. "Let's sneak out.
Now's our chance."

We snuck out the back way. It was easy. We circled
around to the front, and there was a big mob standing there in the rain. Up on the court-house steps was
Mr. Gandy, mean as ever, facing a big, husky feller who
was waving a chunk of rock.

"Every dam has its breaking point," Mr. Gandy
said, but the big feller roared and shook the rock over
his haid.

"I know good concrete from bad!" he bellered. "This
stuff's all sand. That dam won't hold a gallon of water
backed up behind it!"

Mr. Gandy shook his head.

"Outrageous!" he said. "I'm just as shocked as you
are. Of course we gave out the contracts in all good
faith. If the Ajax Construction Company used shoddy
material, we'll certainly sue them."

At that point I got so tired of itching that I decided
to do something about it. So I did.

The husky feller stepped back a pace and pointed

his finger at Mr. Gandy. "Listen," he said. "There's a
rumor around that you own the Ajax Construction
Company. Do you?"

Mr. Gandy opened his mouth and closed it. He
shivered a little.

"Yes," he said. "Yes, I own it."

You should of heard the roar that went up from that
mob.

The big feller sort of gasped.

"You admit it? Maybe you'll admit that you knew
the dam was no good, too, huh? How much did you
make out of the deal?"

"Eleven thousand dollars," Mr. Gandy said. "That
was net, after I'd paid off the sheriff, the aldermen,
and—"

But at that point the crowd sort of moved up the
steps, and there wasn't no more heard from Mr. Gandy.

"Well, well," said Mr. Armbruster. "Now I've seen
everything. Know what this means, Saunk? Gandy's
gone crazy. He must have. But the reform administra-
tion will go in, they'll throw out all the crooks, and I
will have a pleasant life in Piperville once more. Until
I move south, that is. Come winter, I always move
south. By a strange happenstance, I find I have a few
coins in my pocket. Will you join me in a drink,
Saunk?"

"No, thanks," I said. "Maw'll be wondering where
I got to. Won't there be no more trouble, Mr. Armbruster?"

"Eventually," he said. "But not for quite awhile.
They're carrying old Gandy into the jail, see? For his
own protection, probably. I must celebrate this, Saunk.
Sure you won't—Saunk! Where are you?"

But I had went invisible.

Well, that was all there was to it. I didn't itch no
more, so I flew back home and helped rig up the

electric current from the water wheel. After a time the flood had died down, but we got a steady flow down the crick thereafter, because of the way I'd arranged things upstream. We settled down to the sort of quiet life we Hogbens like. It's safest, for us.

Grandpaw said it was quite a flood. It reminded him of something his Grandpaw had told him. Seems like when Grandpaw's Grandpaw was alive, they had uranium piles and a lot more, and pretty soon the things got out of hand and they had a real flood. Grandpaw's Grandpaw had to move out of the country right fast. Ain't nothing been heard of the place from that day to this. I gather everybody in Atlantis got drowned daid. But they was only furriners.

Mr. Gandy went to jail. Nobody ever knew what made him confess the way he did; maybe he got an attack of conscience. I don't suppose it could have been because of me. 'Tain't likely. Still—

Remember that trick Paw showed me about making a short-circuit in space and pumping the corn likker from his blood into mine? Well, I got tired of itching where I couldn't scratch it, so I used that trick myself. That stuff they'd squirted into me was making me itch, whatever it was. I just twisted space around a mite and pumped it right into Mr. Gandy's blood, up where he was standing on them court-house steps. After that I stopped itching, but Mr. Gandy must have been itching real bad. Served him right, though.

Wonder if it could have plump itched him into telling the truth?

See You Later

Old Yancey was just about the meanest man in the world. I never seen a feller so downright, sot-in-his-ways, shortsighted, plain, ornery mean. What happened to him reminded me of what another feller told me oncet, quite a spell ago. Fergit exactly who it was—name of Louis, maybe, or could be Tamerlane—but one time he said he wished the whole world had only one haid, so's he could chop it off.

Trouble with Yancey, he got to the point where he figgered everybody in the world was again' him, and blamed if he warn't right. That was a real spell of trouble, even for us Hogbens.

Oh, Yancey was a regular stinker, all right. The whole Tarbell family was bad-eyed, but Yancey made even them plumb disgusted. He lived up in a little one-room shanty back of the Tarbell place, and wouldn't let nobody near, except to push vittles through the cut-out moon in the door.

Seems like some ten years back there was a new survey or something and the way it worked out, through some funny legal business, Yancey had to prove he'd got squatter's rights on his land. He had to prove it by living there for a year or something. 'Bout then he had an argument with his wife and moved out to the little shack, which was across the property line, and said he was a-gonna let the land go right back to the government, for all he cared, and that'd show the whole family. He knew his wife sot store by her turnip patch and was afraid the government would take it away.

The way it turned out, nobody wanted the land anyhow. It was all up and down and had too many rocks in it, but Yancey's wife kept on worriting and begging Yancey to come back, which he was just too mean to do.

Yancey Tarbell couldn't have been oncommon comfortable up in that little shack, but he was short-sighted as he was mean. After a spell Mrs. Tarbell died of being hit on the haid with a stone she was throwing up the slope at the shack, and it bounced back at her. So that left only the eight Tarbell boys and Yancey. He stayed right where he was, though.

He might have stayed there till he shriveled up and went to glory, except the Tarbells started feuding with us. We stood it as long as we could, on account of they couldn't hurt us. Uncle Les, who was visiting us, got skittery, though, and said he was tired of flying up like a quail, two or three miles in the air, every time a gun went off behind a bush. The holes in his hide closed up easy enough, but he said it made him dizzy, on account of the air being thinned out that high up.

This went on for a while, leastwise, and nobody got hurt, which seemed to rile the eight Tarbell boys. So one night they all come over in a bunch with their

shooting irons and busted their way in. We didn't want
no trouble.

Uncle Lem—who's Uncle Les's twin except they was
born quite a spell apart—he was asleep for the winter, off in a holler tree somewheres, so he was out of
it. But the baby, bless his heart, is gitting kind of
awkward to shift around, being as how he's four
hunnerd years old and big for his age—'bout three
hunnerd pounds, I guess.

We could of all hid out or gone down to Piperville
in the valley for a mite, but then there was Grandpaw
in the attic, and I'd got sort of fond of the little
Perfesser feller we keep in a bottle. Didn't want to
leave him on account of the bottle might of got
smashed in the ruckus, if the eight Tarbell boys was
likkered up enough.

The Perfesser's cute—even though he never did have
much sense. Used to say we was mutants, whatever
they are, and kept shooting off his mouth about some
people he knowed called chromosomes. Seems like they
got mixed up with what the Perfesser called hard
radiations and had some young 'uns which was either
dominant mutations or Hogbens, but I allus got it
mixed up with the Roundhead plot, back when we was
living in the old country. 'Course I don't mean the real
old country. That got sunk.

So, seeing as how Grandpaw told us to lay low, we
waited till the eight Tarbell boys busted down the door,
and then we all went invisible, including the baby. Then
we waited for the thing to blow over, only it didn't.

After stomping around and ripping up things a lot,
the eight Tarbell boys come down in the cellar. Now,
that was kind of bad, because we was caught by surprise. The baby had gone invisible, like I say, and so
had the tank we keep him in, but the tank couldn't
move around fast like we could.

One of the eight Tarbell boys went and banged into it and hit hisself a smart crack on the shank bone. How he cussed! It was shameful for a growing boy to hear, except Grandpaw kin outcuss anybody I ever heard, so I didn't larn nothing.

Well—he cussed a lot, jumped around, and all of a sudden his squirrel rifle went off. Must have had a hair trigger. That woke up the baby, who got scared and let out a yell. It was the blamedest yell I'd ever heard out of the baby yet, and I've seen men go all white and shaky when he bellers. Our Perfesser feller told us oncet the baby emitted a subsonic. Imagine!

Anyhow, seven of the eight Tarbell boys dropped daid, all in a heap, without even time to squeal. The eighth one was up at the haid of the cellar steps, and he got all quivery and turned around and ran. I guess he was so dizzy he didn't know where he was heading. 'Fore he knowed it, he was up in the attic, where he stepped right square on Grandpaw.

Now, the fool thing was this: Grandpaw was so busy telling us what to do he'd entirely fergot to go invisible hisself. And I guess one look at Grandpaw just plumb finished the eighth Tarbell boy. He fell right down, daid as a skun coon. Cain't imagine why, though I got to admit Grandpaw wasn't looking his best that week. He'd been sick.

"You all right, Grandpaw?" I asked, sort of shaking him out. He cussed me.

" 'Twarn't my fault," I told him.

" 'Sblood!" he said, mad-like. "What rabble of canting jolt-heads have I sired? Put me down, you young scoundrel." So I put him back on the gunny sack and he turned around a couple of times and shut his eyes. After that, he said he was going to take a nap and not to wake him up for nothing, bar Judgment Day. He meant it, too.

So we had to figger out for ourselves what was best to do. Maw said it warn't our fault, and all we could do was pile the eight Tarbell boys in a wheelbarrow and take 'em back home, which I done. Only I got to feeling kind of shy on the way, on account of I couldn't figger out no real polite way to mention what had happened. Besides, Maw had told me to break the news gentle. "Even a polecat's got feelings," she said.

So I left the wheelbarrow with the eight Tarbell boys in it behind some scrub brush, and I went on up the slope to where I could see Yancey sitting, airing hisself out in the sun and reading a book. I still hadn't studied out what to say. I just traipsed along slow-like, whistling "Yankee Doodle." Yancey didn't pay me no mind for a while.

He's a little, mean, dirty man with chin whiskers. Couldn't be much more'n five feet high. There was tobacco juice on his whiskers, but I might have done old Yancey wrong in figgering he was only sloppy. I heard he used to spit in his beard to draw flies, so's he could ketch 'em and pull off their wings.

Without looking, he picked up a stone, and flang it past my head. "Shet up an' go way," he said.

"Just as you say, Mr. Yancey," I told him, mighty relieved, and started to. But then I remembered Maw would probably whup me if I didn't mind her orders, so I sort of moved around quiet till I was in back of Yancey and looking over his shoulder at what he was reading. It looked like a book. Then I moved around a mite more till I was upwind of him.

He started cackling in his whiskers.

"That's a real purty picture, Mr. Yancey," I said.

He was giggling so hard it must of cheered him up.

"Ain't it, though!" he said, banging his fist on his skinny old rump. "My, my! Makes me feel full o' ginger just to look at it."

It wasn't a book, though. It was a magazine, the kind they sell down at the village, and it was opened at a picture. The feller that made it could draw real good. Not as good as an artist I knowed once, over in England. He went by the name of Crookshank or Crookback or something like that, unless I'm mistook.

Anyway, this here that Yancey was looking at was quite a picture. It showed a lot of fellers, all exactly alike, coming out of a big machine which I could tell right off wouldn't work. But all these fellers was as like as peas in a pod. Then there was a red critter with bugged-out eyes grabbing a girl, I dunno why. It was sure purty.

"Wisht something like that could really happen," Yancey said.

"It ain't so hard," I told him. "Only that gadget's all wrong. All you need is a washbasin and some old scrap iron."

"Hey?"

"That thing there," I said. "The jigger that looks like it's making one feller into a whole lot of fellers. It ain't built right."

"I s'pose you could do it better?" he snapped, sort of mad.

"We did, once," I said. "I forget what Paw had on his mind, but he owed a man name of Cadmus a little favor. Cadmus wanted a lot of fighting men in a real hurry, so Paw fixed it so's Cadmus could split hisself up into a passel of soldiers. Shucks. I could do it myself."

"What are you blabbering about?" Yancey asked. "You ain't looking at the right thing. This here red critter's what I mean. See what he's a-gonna do? Gonna chaw that there purty gal's haid off, looks like. See the tusks on him? Heh, heh, heh. I wisht I was a critter like that. I'd chaw up plenty of people."

"You wouldn't chaw up your own kin, though, I bet," I said, seeing a way to break the news gentle.

"'Tain't right to bet," he told me. "Allus pay your debts, fear no man, and don't lay no wagers. Gambling's a sin. I never made no bets and I allus paid my debts." He stopped, scratched his whiskers, and sort of sighed. "All except one," he added, frowning.

"What was that?"

"Oh, I owed a feller something. Only I never could locate him afterward. Must be nigh on thutty years ago. Seems like I got likkered up and got on a train. Guess I robbed somebody, too, 'cause I had a roll big enough to choke a hoss. Never tried that, come to think of it. You keep hosses?"

"No, sir," I said. "We was talking about your kin."

"Shet up," old Yancey said. "Well, now, I had myself quite a time." He licked his whiskers. "Ever heard tell of a place called New York? In some furrin country, I guess. Can't understand a word nobody says. Anyway, that's where I met up with this feller. I often wisht I could find him again. An honest man like me hates to think of dying without paying his lawful debts."

"Did your eight boys owe any debts?" I asked.

He squinted at me, slapped his skinny leg, and nodded.

"Now I know," he said. "Ain't you the Hogben boy?"

"That's me. Saunk Hogben."

"I heard tell 'bout you Hogbens. All witches, ain't you?"

"No, sir."

"I heard what I heard. Whole neighborhood's buzzing. Hexers, that's what. You get outa here, go on, git!"

"I'm a-going," I said. "I just come by to say it's real unfortunate you couldn't chaw up your own kin if'n you was a critter like in that there picture."

"Ain't nobody big enough to stop me!"

"Maybe not," I said, "but they've all gone to glory."

When he heard this, old Yancey started to cackle. Finally, when he got his breath back, he said, "Not them! Them varmints have gone plumb smack to perdition, right where they belong. How'd it happen?"

"It was sort of an accident," I said. "The baby done kilt seven of them and Grandpaw kilt the other, in a way of speaking. No harm intended."

"No harm done," Yancey said, cackling again.

"Maw sent her apologies, and what do you want done with the remains? I got to take the wheelbarrow back home."

"Take 'em away. I don't want 'em. Good riddance to bad rubbish," old Yancey said, so I said all right and started off. But then he yelled out and told me he'd changed his mind. Told me to dump 'em where they was. From what I could make out, which wasn't much because he was laughing so hard, he wanted to come down and kick 'em.

So I done like he said and then went back home and told Maw, over a mess of catfish and beans and pot-likker. She made some hush puppies, too. They was good. I sat back, figgering I'd earned a rest, and thunk a mite, feeling warm and nice around the middle. I was trying to figger what a bean would feel like, down in my tummy. But it didn't seem to have no feelings.

It couldn't of been more than half an hour later when the pig yelled outside like he was getting kicked, and then somebody knocked on the door. It was Yancey. Minute he come in, he pulled a bandanna out of his britches and started sniffling. I looked at Maw, wide-eyed. I couldn't tell her nothing.

Paw and Uncle Les was drinking corn in a corner, and giggling a mite. I could tell they was feeling good because of the way the table kept rocking, the one between them. It wasn't touching neither one, but it kept jiggling, trying to step fust on Paw's toes and then on Uncle Les's. They was doing it inside their haids, trying to ketch the other one off guard.

It was up to Maw, and she invited old Yancey to set down a spell and have some beans. He just sobbed.

"Something wrong, neighbor?" Maw asked, polite.

"It sure is," Yancey said, sniffling. "I'm a real old man."

"You surely are," Maw told him. "Mebbe not as old as Saunk here, but you look awful old."

"Hey?" Yancey said, staring at her. "Saunk? Saunk ain't more'n seventeen, big as he is."

Maw near looked embarrassed. "Did I say Saunk?" she covered up, quick-like. "I meant this Saunk's grandpaw. His name's Saunk too." It wasn't; even Grandpaw don't remember what his name was first, it's been so long. But in his time he's used a lot of names like Elijah and so forth. I ain't even sure they had names in Atlantis, where Grandpaw come from in the first place. Numbers or something. It don't signify, anyhow.

Well, seems like old Yancey kept snuffling and groaning and moaning, and made out like we'd kilt his eight boys and he was all alone in the world. He hadn't cared a mite half an hour ago, though, and I said so. But he pointed out he hadn't rightly understood what I was talking about then, and for me to shet up.

"Ought to had a bigger family," he said. "They used to be two more boys, Zeb and Robbie, but I shot 'em one time. Didn't like the way they was looking ory-eyed at me. The point is, you Hogbens ain't got no right to kill my boys."

"We didn't go for to do it," Maw said. "It was more or less an accident. We'd be right happy to make it up to you, one way or another."

"That's what I was counting on," old Yancey said.

"It seems like the least you could do, after acting up like you done. It don't matter whether the baby kilt my boys, like Saunk says and he's a liar. The idea is that I figger all you Hogbens are responsible. But I guess we could call it square if'n you did me a little favor. It ain't really right for neighbors to hold bad feelings."

"Any favor you name," Maw said, "if it ain't out of line."

" 'Tain't much," old Yancey said. "I just want you to split me up into a rabble, sort of temporary."

"Hey, you been listening to Medea?" Paw said, being drunk enough not to know no better. "Don't you believe her. That was purely a prank she played on Pelias. After he got chopped up he stayed daid; he didn't git young like she said he would."

"Hey?" Yancey said. He pulled that old magazine out of his pocket and it fell open right to that purty picture. "This here," he said. "Saunk tells me you kin do it. And everybody round here knows you Hogbens are witches. Saunk said you done it once with a feller named of Messy."

"Guess he means Cadmus," I said.

Yancey waved the magazine. I saw he had a queer kind of gleam in his eye.

"It shows right here," he said, wild-like. "A feller steps inside this here gimmick and then he keeps coming out of it, dozens of him, over and over. Witch-craft. Well, I know about you Hogbens. You may fool the city folk, but you don't fool me none. You're all witches."

"We ain't," Paw said from the corner. "Not no more."

"You are so," Yancey said. "I heard stories. I even seen him"—he pointed right at Uncle Les—"I seen him flying around in the air. And if that ain't witchcraft I don't know what is."

"Don't you, honest?" I asked. "That's easy. It's when you get some—"

But Maw told me to shet up.

"Saunk told me you kin do it," he said. "An' I been sitting and studying and looking over this here magazine. I got me a fine idea. Now, it stands to reason, everybody knows a witch kin be in two places at the same time. Couldn't a witch mebbe git to be in three places at the same time?"

"Three's as good as two," Maw said. "Only there ain't no witches. It's like this here science you hear tell about. People make it up out of their haids. It ain't natcheral."

"Well, then," Yancey said, putting the magazine down. "Two or three or a whole passel. How many people are there in the world, anyway?"

"Two billion, two hunnerd fifty million, nine hunnerd and fifty-nine thousand, nine hunnerd and nineteen," I said.

"Then—"

"Hold on a minute," I said. "Now it's two hunnerd fifty million, nine hunnerd and fifty-nine thousand, nine hunnerd and twenty. Cute little tyke, too."

"Boy or girl?" Maw asked.

"Boy," I told her.

"Then why can't you make me be in two billion whatever it was places at the same time? Mebbe for just a half a minute or so. I ain't greedy. That'd be long enough, anyhow."

"Long enough for what?" Maw asked.

Yancey give me a sly look. "I got me a problem," he said. "I want to find a feller. Trouble is, I dunno if I kin find him now. It's been a awful long time. But I got to, somehow or other. I ain't a-gonna rest easy in my grave unless I done paid all my debts, and for thutty years I been owing this feller something. It lays heavy on my conscience."

"That's right honorable of you, neighbor," Maw said.

Yancey snuffled and wiped his nose on his sleeve.

"It's a-gonna be a hard job," he said. "I put it off mebbe a mite too long. The thing is, I was figgering on sending my eight boys out to look for this feller sometime, so you kin see why it's busted me all up, the way them no-good varmints up and got kilt without no warning. How am I gonna find that feller I want now?"

Maw looked troubled and passed Yancey the jug.

"Whoosh!" he said, after a snort. "Tastes like real hellfire for certain. Whoosh!" Then he took another swig, sucked in some air, and scowled at Maw.

"If'n a man plans on sawing down a tree and his neighbor busts the saw, seems to me that neighbor ought to lend his own saw. Ain't that right?"

"Sure is," Maw said. "Only we ain't got eight boys to lend you."

"You got something better," Yancey said. "Black, wicked magic, that's what. I ain't saying yea or nay 'bout that. It's your own affair. But seeing as how you kilt off them wuthless young 'uns of mine, so's I can't do like I was intending—why, then it looks like you ought to be willing to help me in some other way. Long as I kin locate that feller and pay him what I owe him, I'm satisfied. Now, ain't it the gospel truth that you kin split me up into a passel of me-critters?"

"Why, I guess we kin do that, I s'pose," Maw said.

"An' ain't it gospel that you kin fix it so's every dang one of them me-critters will travel real fast and see everybody in the whole, entire world?"

"That's easy," I said.

"If'n I kin git to do that," Yancey said, "it'd be easy for me to spot that feller and give him what he's got coming to him." He snuffled. "I allus been honest. I'm skeered of dying unless I pay all my debts fust. Danged if'n I want to burn through all eternity like you sinful Hogbens are a-gonna."

"Shucks," Maw said, "I guess we kin help out, neighbor, being as how you feel so het up about it. Yes, sir, we'll do like you want."

Yancey brightened up considerable.

"Promise?" he asked. "Swear it, on your word an' honor?"

Maw looked kind of funny, but Yancey pulled out his bandanna again, so she busted down and made her solemn promise. Right away Yancey cheered up.

"How long will the spell take?" he asked.

"There ain't no spell," I said. "Like I told you, all I need is some scrap iron and a washbasin. 'Twon't take long."

"I'll be back real soon," Yancey said, sort of cackling, and run out, laughing his haid off. Going through the yard, he kicked out at a chicken, missed, and laughed some more. Guess he was feeling purty good.

"You better go on and make that gadget so's it'll be ready," Maw told me. "Git going."

"Yes, Maw," I said, but I sat there for a second or two, studying. She picked up the broomstick.

"You know, Maw—"

"Well?"

"Nothing," I said, and dodged the broomstick. I went on out, trying to git clear what was troubling me. Something was, only I couldn't tell what. I felt kind of unwilling to make that there gadget, which didn't make right good sense, since there didn't seem to be nothing really wrong.

I went out behind the woodshed, though, and got busy. Took me 'bout ten minutes, but I didn't hurry much. Then I come back to the house with the gadget and said I was done. Paw told me to shet up.

Well, I sat there and looked at the gimmick and still felt trouble on my mind. Had to do with Yancey, some-how or other. Finally I noticed he'd left his old maga-zine behind, so I picked it up and started reading the story right under that picture, trying to make sense out of it. Durned if I could.

It was all about some crazy hillbillies who could fly. Well, that ain't no trick but what I couldn't figger out was whether the feller that writ it was trying to be funny or not. Seems to me people are funny enough anyhow, without trying to make 'em funnier.

Besides, serious things ought to be treated serious, and from what our Perfesser feller told me once, there's an awful lot of people what really believe in science and take it tremendous serious. He allus got a holy light in his eye when he talked about it. The only good thing about that story, it didn't have no girls in it. Girls make me feel funny.

I didn't seem to be gitting nowheres, so I went down to the cellar and played with the baby. He's kind of big for his tank these days. He was glad to see me. Winked all four of his eyes at me, one after the other. Real cute.

But all the time there was something about that magazine that kept nagging at me. I felt itchy inside, like when before they had that big fire in London, some while ago. Quite a spell of sickness they had then, too.

It reminded me of something Grandpaw had told me once, that he'd got the same sort of skitters just before Atlantis foundered. 'Course, Grandpaw kin sort of look into the future—which ain't much good, really, on account of it keeps changing around. I cain't do that myself yet. I ain't growed up enough. But I had a kind of hunch that something real bad was around, only it hadn't happened quite yet.

I almost decided to wake up Grandpaw, I felt so troubled. But around then I heard tromping upstairs, so I clomb up to the kitchen, and there was Yancey, swigging down some corn Maw'd give him. Minute I looked at the old coot, I got that feeling again.

Yancey said, "Whoosh," put down the jug, and wanted to know if we was ready. So I pointed at the gadget I'd fixed up and said that was it, all right, and what did he think about it?

"That little thing?" Yancey asked. "Ain't you a-gonna call up Old Scratch?"

"Ain't no need," Uncle Les said. "Not with you here, you little water moccasin, you."

Yancey looked right pleased. "That's me," he said. "Mean as a moccasin, and fulla pizen. How does it work?"

"Well," I said, "it sort of splits you up into a lot of Yanceys, is all."

Paw had been setting quiet, but he must of tuned in inside the haid of some perfesser somewheres, on account of he started talking foolish. He don't know any four-bit words hisself.

I wouldn't care to know 'em myself, being as how they only mix up what's simple as cleaning a trout.

"Each human organism," Paw said, showing off like crazy, "is an electromagnetic machine, emitting a pattern of radiations, both from brain and body. By reversing polarity, each unity of you, Yancey, will be automatically attracted to each already existent human unit, since unlikes attract. But first you will step on Saunk's device and your body will be broken down—"

"Hey!" Yancey yelped.

Paw went right on, proud as a peacock.

"—into a basic electronic matrix, which can then be duplicated to the point of infinity, just as a type face may print millions of identical copies of itself in reverse—negative instead of positive.

"Since space is no factor where electronic wave-patterns are concerned, each copy will be instantly attracted to the space occupied by every other person in the world," Paw was going on, till I like to bust. "But since two objects cannot occupy the same space-time, there will be an automatic spacial displacement, and each Yancey-copy will be repelled to approximately two feet away from each human being."

"You forgot to draw a pentagram," Yancey said, looking around nervous-like. "That's the awfullest durn spell I ever heard in all my born days. I thought you said you wasn't gonna call up Old Scratch?"

Maybe it was on account of Yancey was looking oncommon like Old Scratch hisself just then, but I just couldn't stand it no longer—having this funny feeling inside me. So I woke up Grandpaw. I did it inside my haid, the baby helping, so's nobody noticed. Right away there was a stirring in the attic, and Grandpaw heaved hisself around a little and woke up. Next thing I knew he was cussing a blue streak.

Well, the whole family heard that, even though Yancey couldn't. Paw stopped showing off and shet up.

"Dullards!" Grandpaw said, real mad. "Rapscallions! Certes, y-wist it was no wonder I was having bad dreams. Saunk, you've put your foot in it now. Have you no sense of process? Didn't you realize what this caitiff schmo was planning, the stinkard? Get in the groove, Saunk, ere manhood's state shall find thee unprepared." Then he added something in Sanskrit. Living as long as Grandpaw has, he gits mixed up in his talk sometimes.

"Now, Grandpaw," Maw thunk, "what's Saunk been and done?"

"You've all done it!" Grandpaw yelled. "Couldn't you add cause and effect? Saunk, what of the picture y-wrought in Yancey's pulp mag? Wherefore hys sodien change of herte, when obviously the stinkard hath no more honor than a lounge lizard? Do you want the world depopulated before its time? Ask Yancey what he's got in his britches pocket, dang you!"

"Mr. Yancey," I said, "what have you got in your britches pocket?"

"Hey?" he said, reaching down and hauling out a big, rusty monkey wrench. "You mean this? I picked it up back of the shed." He was looking real sly.

"What you aiming to do with that?" Maw asked, quick.

Yancey give us all a mean look. "Ain't no harm telling you," he said. "I aim to hit everybody, every durn soul in the whole, entire world, right smack on top of the haid, and you promised to help me do it."

"Lawks a-mercy," Maw said.

"Yes, siree," Yancey giggled. "When you hex me, I'm a-gonna be in every place everybody else is, standing right behind 'em. I'll whang 'em good. Thataway, I kin be sure I'll git even. One of them people is just bound to be the feller I want, and he'll git what I been owing him for thutty years."

"What feller?" I said. "You mean the one you met up with in New York you was telling me about? I figgered you just owed him some money."

"Never said no sech thing," Yancey snapped. "A debt's a debt, be it money or a bust in the haid. Ain't nobody a-gonna step on my corn and git away with it, thutty years or no thutty years."

"He stepped on your corn?" Paw asked. "That's all he done?"

"Yup. I was likkered up at the time, but I recollect

I went down some stairs to where a lot of trains was rushing around under the ground."

"You was drunk."

"I sure was," Yancey said. "Couldn't be no sech thing—trains running underground! But I sure as shooting wasn't dreaming 'bout the feller what stepped on my corn. Why, I kin still feel it. I got mad. It was so crowded I couldn't even move for a mite, and I never even got a good look at the feller what stepped on me.

"By the time I hit out with my stick, he must of got away. Never knew what he looked like. Might have been a female, but that don't signify. I just ain't a-gonna die till I pay my debts and git even with everybody what ever done me dirt. I allus got even with every dang soul what done me wrong, and most everybody I ever met did."

Riled up a whole lot was Yancey Tarbell. He went right on from there:

"So I figgered, since I never found out just who this feller was what stepped on my corn, I better make downright sure and take a lick at everybody, man, woman, and child."

"Now you hold your hosses," I said. "Ain't no children could have been alive thutty years ago, an' you know it."

"Makes no difference," Yancey snapped. "I was a-thinking, and I got an awful idea: suppose that feller went and died. Thutty years is a long time. But then I figgered, even if he did up and die, chances are he got married and had kids fust. If'n I can't git even with him, I kin get even with his children. The sins of the father—that's Scripture. If'n I hit everybody in the world, I can't go fur wrong."

"You ain't hitting no Hogbens," Maw said. "None of

us been in New York since afore you was born. I mean, we ain't never been there. So you kin just leave us out of it. How'd you like to git a million dollars instead? Or maybe you want to git young again or something like that? We kin fix that for you instead, if you'll give up this here wicked idea."

"I ain't a-gonna," Yancey said, stubborn. "You give your gospel word to help me."

"Well, we ain't bound to keep a promise like that," Maw said, but then Grandpaw chimed in from the attic.

"The Hogben word is sacred," he told us. "It's our bond. We must keep our promise to this booby. But, having kept it, we are not bound further."

"Oh?" I said, sort of gitting a thought. "That being the case—Mr. Yancey, just what did we promise, exact?"

He waved the monkey wrench at me.

"I'm a-gonna git split up into as many people as they are people in the world, and I'm a-gonna be standing right beside all of 'em. You give your word to help me do that. Don't you try to wiggle out of it."

"I ain't wiggling," I said. "Only we better git it clear, so's you'll be satisfied and won't have no kick coming. One thing, though. You got to be the same size as everybody you visit."

"Hey?"

"I kin fix it easy. When you step on this here gadget, there'll be two billion, two hunnerd fifty million, nine hunnerd and fifty-nine thousand, nine hunnerd and twenty Yanceys all over the world. S'posin', now, one of these here Yanceys finds himself standing next to a big feller seven feet tall. That wouldn't be so good, would it?"

"I want to be eight feet high," Yancey said.

"No, sir. The Yancey who goes to visit a feller that high is a-gonna be just that high hisself, exactly. And the one who visits a baby only two feet high is a-gonna be only two feet high hisself. What's fair's fair. You agree to that, or it's all off. Only other thing, you'll be just exactly as strong as the feller you're up again'."

I guess he seen I was firm. He hefted the monkey wrench.

"How'll I git back?" he asked.

"We'll take care of that," I said. "I'll give you five seconds. That's long enough to swing a monkey wrench, ain't it?"

"It ain't very long."

"If'n you stay longer, somebody might hit back."

"So they might," he said, turning pale under the dirt. "Five seconds is plenty."

"Then if'n we do just that, you'll be satisfied? You won't have no kick coming?"

He swung the monkey wrench and laughed.

"Suits me fine and dandy," he said. "I'll bust their haids good. Heh, heh, heh."

"Then you step right on here," I said, showing him. "Wait a mite, though. I better try it fust, to make sure it works right."

I picked up a stick of firewood from the box by the stone and winked at Yancey. "You git set," I said. "The minute I git back, you step right on here."

Maw started to say something, but all of a sudden Grandpaw started laughing in the attic. I guess he was looking into the future again.

I stepped on the gadget, and it worked slick as anything. Afore I could blink, I was split up into two billion, two hunnerd and fifty million, nine hunnerd and fifty-nine thousand, nine hunnerd and nineteen Saunk Hogbens.

There was one short, o' course, on account of I left out Yancey, and o' course the Hogbens ain't listed in no census. But here I was, standing right in front of everybody in the whole entire world except the Hogben fam'ly and Yancey hisself. It was plumb onreasonable.

Never did I know there was so many faces in this world! They was all colors, some with whiskers, some without, some with clothes on, some naked as needles, some awful big and some real short, and half of them was in daylight and half was in the nighttime. I got downright dizzy.

For just a flash, I thought I could make out some of the people I knowed down in Piperville, including the Sheriff, but he got mixed up with a lady in a string of beads who was casing a kangaroo-critter, and she turned into a man dressed up fit to kill who was speechifyin' in a big room somewheres.

My, I was dizzy.

I got ahold of myself and it was about time, too, for just about then near everybody in the whole world noticed me. 'Course, it must have looked like I'd popped out of thin air, right in front of them, real sudden, and—well, you ever had near two billion, two hunnerd and fifty million, nine hunnerd and fifty-nine thousand, nine hunnerd and nineteen people looking you right square in the eye? It's just awful. I forgot what I'd been intending. Only I sort of heard Grandpaw's voice telling me to hurry up.

So I pushed that stick of firewood I was holding, only now it was two billion, two hunnerd and fifty million, nine hunnerd and fifty-nine thousand, nine hunnerd and nineteen sticks, into just about the same number of hands and let go. Some of the people let go too, but most of 'em held on to it. Then I tried to remember the speech I was a-gonna make, telling 'em to git in the fust lick at Yancey afore he could swing that monkey wrench.

But I was too confounded. It was funny. Having all

them people looking right at me made me so down-right shy, I couldn't even open my mouth. What made it worse was that Grandpaw yelled I had only one second left, so there wasn't even time to make a speech. In just one second, I was a-gonna flash back to our kitchen, and then old Yancey was all ready to jump in the gadget and swing that monkey wrench. And I hadn't warned nobody. All I'd done was give every-body a little old stick of firewood.

My, how they stared! I felt plumb naked. Their eyes bugged right out. And just as I started to thin out around the edges like a biscuit, I—well, I don't know what came over me. I guess it was feeling so oncommon shy. Maybe I shouldn't of done it, but—

I done it!

Then I was back in the kitchen. Grandpaw was laughing fit to kill in the attic. The old gentleman's got a funny kind of sense of humor, I guess. I didn't have no time for him then, though, for Yancey jumped past me and into the gadget. And he disappeared into thin air, the way I had. Split up, like I'd been, into as many people as there was in the world, and standing right in front of 'em.

Maw and Paw and Uncle Les was looking at me real hard. I sort of shuffled.

"I fixed it," I said. "Seems like a man who's mean enough to hit little babies over the haid deserves what he's"—I stopped and looked at the gadget—"what he's been and got," I finished, on account of Yancey had tumbled out of thin air, and a more whupped-up old rattlesnake I never seen. My!

Well, I guess purty near everybody in the whole world had took a whang at Mr. Yancey. He never even had a chance to swing that monkey wrench. The whole world had got in the fust lick.

Yes, siree. Mr. Yancey looked plumb ruined.

But he could still yell. You could of heard him a mile off. He kept screaming that he'd been cheated. He wanted another chance, and this time he was taking his shooting iron and a bowie knife. Finally Maw got disgusted, took him by the collar, and shook him up till his teeth rattled.

"Quoting Scripture!" she said, madlike. "You little dried-up scraggle of downright pizen! The Good Book says an eye for an eye, don't it? We kept our word, and there ain't nobody kin say different."

"That's the truth, certes," Grandpaw chimed in from the attic.

"You better go home and git some arnicy," Maw said, shaking Yancey some more. "And don't you come round here no more, never again, or we'll set the baby on you."

"But I didn't git even!" Yancey squalled.

"I guess you ain't a-gonna, ever," I said. "You just cain't live long enough to git even with everybody in the whole world, Mr. Yancey."

By and by, that seemed to strike Yancey all in a heap. He turned a rich color like beet soup, made a quacking noise, and started cussing. Uncle Les reached for the poker, but there wasn't no need.

"The whole dang world done me wrong!" Yancey squealed, and clapped his hands to his haid. "I been flummoxed! Why in tarnation did they hit me fust? There's something funny about—"

"Hush up," I said, all of a sudden realizing the trouble wasn't over, like I'd thought. "Listen, anybody hear anything from the village?"

Even Yancey shet up whilst we listened. "Don't hear a thing," Maw said.

"Saunk's right," Grandpaw put in. "That's what's wrong."

Then everybody got it—that is, everybody except

Yancey. Because about now there ought to of been quite a rumpus down at Piperville. Don't fergit me and Yancey went visiting the whole world, which includes Piperville, and people don't take a thing like that quiet. There ought to of been some yelling going on, at least.

"What are you all standing round dumb as mutes for?" Yancey busted out. "You got to help me git even!"

I didn't pay him no mind. I sat down and studied the gadget. After a minute I seen what it was I'd done wrong. I guess Grandpaw seen it about as quick as I did. You oughta heard him laugh. I hope it done the old gentleman good. He has a right peculiar sense of humor sometimes.

"I sort of made a mistake in this gadget, Maw," I said. "That's why it's so quiet down in Piperville."

"Aye, by my troth," Grandpaw said, still laughing. "Saunk had best seek cover. Twenty-three skiddoo, kid."

"You done something you shouldn't, Saunk?" Maw said.

"Blabber, blabber, blabber!" Yancey yelled. "I want my rights! I want to know what it was Saunk done that made everybody in the world hit me over the haid! He must of done something. I never had no time to—"

"Now you leave the boy alone, Mr. Yancey," Maw said. "We done what we promised, and that's enough. You git outa here and simmer down afore you say something you regret."

Paw winked at Uncle Les, and before Yancey could yell back at Maw the table sort of bent its legs down like they had knees in 'em and snuck up behind Yancey real quiet. Then Paw said to Uncle Les, "All together now, let 'er go," and the table straightened up its legs and give Yancey a terrible bunt that sent him flying out the door.

The last we heard of Yancey was the whoops he

kept letting out whenever he hit the ground all the way down the hill. He rolled half the way to Piperville, I found out later. And when he got there he started hitting people over the haid with his monkey wrench.

I guess he figgered he might as well make a start the hard way.

They put him in jail for a spell to cool off, and I guess he did, 'cause afterward he went back to that little shack of his'n. I hear he don't do nothing but set around with his lips moving, trying to figger a way to git even with the hull world. I don't calc'late he'll ever hit on it, though.

At that time, I wasn't paying him much mind. I had my own troubles. As soon as Paw and Uncle Les got the table back in place, Maw lit into me again.

"Tell me what happened, Saunk," she said. "I'm a-feared you done something wrong when you was in that gadget. Remember you're a Hogben, son. You got to behave right when the whole world's looking at you. You didn't go and disgrace us in front of the entire human race, did you, Saunk?"

Grandpaw laughed again. "Not yet, he hasn't," he said. Then down in the basement I heard the baby give a kind of gurgle and I knowed he could see it too. That's surprising, kinda. We never know for sure about the baby. I guess he really kin see a little bit into the future too.

"I just made a little mistake, Maw," I said. "Could happen to anybody. It seems the way I fixed that gadget up, it split me into a lot of Saunks, all right, but it sent me ahead into next week too. That's why there ain't no ruckus yet down in Piperville."

"My land!" Maw said. "Child, you do things so careless!"

"I'm sorry, Maw," I said. "Trouble is, too many people in Piperville know me. I'd better light out for the woods and pick me a nice holler tree. I'll be needing it, come next week."

"Saunk," Maw said, "you been up to something. Sooner or later I'll find out, so you might as well tell me now."

Well, shucks, I knowed she was right. So I told her, and I might as well tell you, too. You'll find out anyhow, come next week. It just showed you can't be too careful. This day next week, everybody in the whole world is a-gonna be mighty surprised when I show up out of thin air, hand 'em a stick of firewood, and then r'ar back and spit right smack in their eye.

I s'pose that there two billion, two hunnerd and fifty million, nine hunnerd and fifty-nine thousand, nine hunnerd and nineteen includes everybody on earth.

Everybody!

Sometime next week, I figger.

See you later.

Cold War

1. Last of the Pughs

I'll never have a cold in the haid again without I think of little Junior Pugh. Now there was a repulsive brat if ever I saw one. Built like a little gorilla, he was. Fat, pasty face, mean look, eyes so close together you could poke 'em both out at once with one finger. His paw thought the world of him though. Maybe that was natural, seeing as how little Junior was the image of his pappy.

"The last of the Pughs," the old man used to say, stickin' his chest out and beamin' down at the little gorilla. "Finest little lad that ever stepped."

It made my blood run cold sometimes to look at the two of 'em together. Kinda sad, now, to think back to those happy days when I didn't know either of 'em. You may not believe it but them two Pughs, father and son, between 'em came within that much of conquerin' the world.

Us Hogbens is quiet folks. We like to keep our heads down and lead quiet lives in our own little valley, where nobody comes near withouten we say so. Our neighbors and the folks in the village are used to us by now. They know we try hard not to act conspicuous. They make allowances.

If Paw gets drunk, like last week, and flies down the middle of Main Street in his red underwear, most people make out they don't notice, so's not to embarrass Maw. They know he'd walk like a decent Christian if he was sober.

The thing that druv Paw to drink that time was Little Sam, which is our baby we keep in a tank downcellar, startin' in to teethe again. First time since the War Between the States. We'd figgered he was through teething, but with Little Sam you never can tell. He was mighty restless, too.

A perfesser we keep in a bottle told us once Little Sam e-mitted sub-sonic somethings when he yells but that's just his way of talking. Don't mean a thing. It makes your nerves twiddle, that's all. Paw can't stand it. This time it even woke up Grandpaw in the attic and he hadn't stirred since Christmas. First thing after he got his eyes open he bust out madder'n a wet hen at Paw.

"I see ye, wittold knave that ye are!" he howled. "Flying again, is it? Oh, sic a reowfule sigte! I'll ground ye, ywis!" There was a far-away thump.

"You made me fall a good ten feet!" Paw hollered from away down the valley. "It ain't fair. I could of busted something!"

"Ye'll bust us all, with your dronken carelessness," Grandpaw said. "Flying in full sight of the neighbors! People get burned at the stake for less. You want mankind to find out all about us? Now shut up and let me tend to Baby."

Grandpaw can always quiet the baby if nobody else can. This time he sung him a little song in Sanskrit and after a bit they was snoring a duet.

I was fixing up a dingus for Maw to sour up some cream for sour-cream biscuits. I didn't have much to work with but an old sled and some pieces of wire but I didn't need much. I was trying to point the top end of the wire north-northeast when I seen a pair of checked pants rush by in the woods.

It was Uncle Lem. I could hear him thinking. "It *ain't* me!" he was saying, real loud, inside his haid. "Git back to yer work, Saunk. I ain't within a mile of you. Yer Uncle Lem's a fine old feller and never tells lies. Think I'd fool ye, Saunkie boy?"

"You shore would," I thunk back. "If you could. What's up, Uncle Lem?"

At that he slowed down and started to saunter back in a wide circle.

"Oh, I just had an idy yer Maw might like a mess of blackberries," he thunk, kicking a pebble very non-chalant. "If anybody asks you say you ain't seen me. It's no lie. You ain't."

"Uncle Lem," I thunk, real loud, "I gave Maw my bounden word I wouldn't let you out of range without me along, account of the last time you got away—"

"Now, now, my boy," Uncle Lem thunk fast. "Let bygones be bygones."

"You just can't say no to a friend, Uncle Lem," I reminded him, taking a last turn of the wire around the runner. "So you wait a shake till I get this cream soured and we'll both go together, wherever it is you have in mind."

I saw the checked pants among the bushes and he come out in the open and give me a guilty smile. Uncle Lem's a fat little feller. He means well, I guess, but he can be talked into most anything by most anybody, which is why we have to keep a close eye on him.

"How you gonna do it?" he asked me, looking at the creamjug. "Make the little critters work faster?"

"Uncle Lem!" I said. "You know better'n that. Cruelty to dumb animals is something I can't abide. Them there little critters work hard enough souring milk the way it is. They're such teentsy-weentsy fellers I kinda feel sorry for 'em. Why, you can't even see 'em without you go kinda crosseyed when you look. Paw says they're enzymes. But they can't be. They're too teeny."

"Teeny is as teeny does," Uncle Lem said. "How you gonna do it, then?"

"This here gadget," I told him, kinda proud, "will send Maw's creamjug ahead into next week some time. This weather, don't take cream more'n a couple of days but I'm giving it plenty of time. When I bring it back—bingo, it's sour." I set the jug on the sled.

"I never seen such a do-lass brat," Uncle Lem said, stepping forward and bending a wire crosswise. "You better do it thataway, on account of the thunderstorm next Tuesday. All right now, shoot her off."

So I shot her off. When she come back, sure enough, the cream was sour enough to walk a mouse. Crawling up the can there was a hornet from next week, which I squashed. Now that was a mistake. I knowed it the minute I touched the jug. Dang Uncle Lem, anyhow.

He jumped back into the underbrush, squealing real happy.

"Fooled you that time, you young stinker," he yelled back. "Let's see you get your thumb outa the middle of next week!"

It was the time-lag done it. I mighta knowed. When he crossed that wire he didn't have no thunderstorm in mind at all. Took me nigh onto ten minutes to work myself loose, account of some feller called Inertia, who mixes in if you ain't careful when you fiddle around with time. I don't understand much about it myself. I ain't got my growth yet. Uncle Lem says he's already forgot more'n I'll ever know.

With that head start I almost lost him. Didn't even have time to change into my store-bought clothes and I knowed by the way he was all dressed up fit to kill he was headed for somewheres fancy.

He was worried, too. I kept running into little stray worrisome thoughts he'd left behind him, hanging like teeny little mites of clouds on the bushes. Couldn't make out much on account of they was shredding away by the time I got there but he'd shore done something he shouldn't. That much *anybody* coulda told. They went something like this:

"Worry, worry—wish I hadn't done it—oh, heaven help me if Grandpaw ever finds out—oh, them nasty Pughs, how could I a-been such a fool? Worry, worry— pore ole feller, such a good soul, too, never done nobody no harm and look at me now.

"That Saunk, too big for his britches, teach him a thing or two, ha-ha. Oh, worry, worry—never mind, brace up, you good ole boy, everything's bound to turn out right in the end. You deserve the best, bless you, Lemuel. Grandpaw'll never find out."

Well, I seen his checkered britches high-tailing through the woods after a bit but I didn't catch up to him until he was down the hill, across the picnic grounds at the edge of town and pounding on the sill of the ticket-window at the railroad station with a Spanish dubloon he snitched from Paw's sea-chest.

It didn't surprise me none to hear him asking for a ticket to State Center. I let him think I hadn't caught up. He argued something turrible with the man behind the window but finally he dug down in his britches and fetched up a silver dollar, and the man calmed down.

The train was already puffing up smoke behind the station when Uncle Lem darted around the corner. Didn't leave me much time but I made it too—just. I had to fly a little over the last half-dozen yards but I don't think anybody noticed.

Once when I was just a little shaver there was a Great Plague in London, where we were living at the time, and all us Hogbens had to clear out. I remember the hullabaloo in the city but looking back now it don't seem a patch on the hullabaloo in State Center station when the train pulled in. Times have changed, I guess.

Whistles blowing, horns honking, radios yelling bloody murder—seems like every invention in the last two hundred years has been noisier than the one before it. Made my head ache until I fixed up something Paw once called a raised decibel threshold, which was pure showing-off.

Uncle Lem didn't know I was anywhere around. I took care to think real quiet but he was so wrapped up in his worries he wasn't paying no mind to nothing. I followed him through the crowds in the station and out onto a wide street full of traffic. It was a relief to get away from the trains.

I always hate to think what's going on inside the boiler, with all the little bitty critters so small you can't hardly see 'em, pore things, flying around all hot and excited and bashing their heads together. It seems plumb pitiable.

Of course, it just don't do to think what's happening inside the automobiles that go by.

Uncle Lem knowed right where he was headed. He took off down the street so fast I had to keep reminding myself not to fly, trying to keep up. I kept thinking I ought to get in touch with the folks at home, in case this turned into something I couldn't handle, but I was plumb stopped everywhere I turned. Maw was at the church sociable that afternoon and she whopped me the last time I spoke to her outa thin air right in front of the Reverend Jones. He ain't used to us Hogbens yet.

Paw was daid drunk. No good trying to wake him up. And I was scared to death I would wake the baby if I tried to call on Grandpaw.

Uncle Lem scuttled right along, his checkered legs a-twinkling. He was worrying at the top of his mind, too. He'd caught sight of a crowd in a side-street gathered around a big truck, looking up at a man standing on it and waving bottles in both hands.

He seemed to be making a speech about headaches. I could hear him all the way to the corner. There was big banners tacked along the sides of the truck that said, PUGH HEADACHE CURE.

"Oh, worry, worry!" Uncle Lem thunk. "Oh, bless my toes, what *am* I going to do? I never *dreamed* anybody'd marry Lily Lou Mutz. Oh, worry!"

Well, I reckon we'd all been surprised when Lily Lou Mutz up and got herself a husband awhile back— around ten years ago, I figgered. But what it had to do with Uncle Lem I couldn't think. Lily Lou was just about the ugliest female that ever walked. Ugly ain't no word for her, pore gal.

Grandpaw said once she put him in mind of a family name of Gorgon he used to know. Not that she wasn't a good-hearted critter. Being so ugly, she put up with a lot in the way of rough acting-up from the folks in the village—the riff-raff lot, I mean.

She lived by herself in a little shack up the mountain and she musta been close onto forty when some feller from the other side of the river come along one day and rocked the whole valley right back on its heels

by asking her to marry up with him. Never saw the
feller myself but I heard tell he wasn't no beauty-prize
winner neither.

Come to think of it, I told myself right then, looking at the truck—come to think of it, feller's name was
Pugh.

2. A Fine Old Feller

Next thing I knowed, Uncle Lem had spotted somebody under a lamp-post on the sidewalk, at the edge
of the crowd. He trotted over. It seemed to be a big
gorilla and a little gorilla, standing there watching the
feller on the truck selling bottles with both hands.

"Come and get it," he was yelling. "Come and get
your bottle of Pugh's Old Reliable Headache Cure
while they last!"

"Well, Pugh, here I am," Uncle Lem said, looking
up at the big gorilla. "Hello, Junior," he said right
afterward, glancing down at the little gorilla. I seen him
shudder a little.

You shore couldn't blame him for that. Two nastier
specimens of the human race I never did see in all my
born days. If they hadn't been *quite* so pasty-faced or
just the least mite slimmer, maybe they wouldn't have
put me so much in mind of two well-fed slugs, one
growed-up and one baby-sized. The paw was all dressed
up in a Sunday-meeting suit with a big gold watch-
chain across his front and the way he strutted you'd
a thought he'd never had a good look in a mirror.

"Howdy, Lem," he said, casual-like. "Right on time,
I see. Junior, say howdy to Mister Lem Hogben. You
owe Mister Hogben a lot, sonny." And he laughed a
mighty nasty laugh.

Junior paid him no mind. He had his beady little eyes fixed on the crowd across the street. He looked about seven years old and mean as they come.

"Shall I do it now, paw?" he asked in a squeaky voice. "Can I let 'em have it now, paw? Huh, paw?" From the tone he used, I looked to see if he'd got a machine-gun handy. I didn't see none but if looks was ever mean enough to kill Junior Pugh could of mowed the crowd right down.

"Manly little feller, ain't he, Lem?" Paw Pugh said, real smug. "I tell you, I'm mighty proud of this youngster. Wish his dear old grandpaw coulda lived to see him. A fine old family line, the Pughs is. Nothing like it anywhere. Only trouble is, Junior's the last of his race. You see why I got in touch with you, Lem."

Uncle Lem shuddered again. "Yep," he said. "I see, all right. But you're wasting your breath, Pugh. I ain't a-gonna do it."

Young Pugh spun around in his tracks.

"Shall I let him have it, paw?" he squeaked, real eager. "Shall I, paw? Now, paw? Huh?"

"Shaddup, sonny," the big feller said and he whammed the little feller across the side of the haid. Pugh's hands was like hams. He shore was built like a gorilla.

The way his great big arms swung down from them big hunched shoulders, you'd of thought the kid would go flying across the street when his paw whopped him one. But he was a burly little feller. He just staggered a mite and then shook his haid and went red in the face.

He yelled out, loud and squeaky, "Paw, I warned you! The last time you whammed me I warned you! Now I'm gonna let you have it!"

He drew a deep breath and his two little teeny eyes got so bright I coulda sworn they was gonna touch each other across the middle of his nose. His pasty face got bright red.

"Okay, Junior," Paw Pugh said, real hasty. "The crowd's ready for you. Don't waste your strength on me, sonny. Let the crowd have it!"

Now all this time I was standing at the edge of the crowd, listening and watching Uncle Lem. But just then somebody jiggled my arm and a thin kinda voice said to me, real polite, "Excuse me, but may I ask a question?"

I looked down. It was a skinny man with a kind-hearted face. He had a notebook in his hand.

"It's all right with me," I told him, polite. "Ask away, mister."

"I just wondered how you feel, that's all," the skinny man said, holding his pencil over the notebook ready to write down something.

"Why, peart," I said. "Right kind of you to inquire. Hope you're feeling well too, mister."

He shook his head, kind of dazed. "That's the trouble," he said. "I just don't understand it. I feel fine."

"Why not?" I asked. "Fine day."

"Everybody here feels fine," he went right on, just like I hadn't spoke. "Barring normal odds, everybody's in average good health in this crowd. But in about five minutes or less, as I figure it—" He looked at his wristwatch.

Just then somebody hit me right on top of the haid with a red-hot sledge-hammer.

Now you shore can't hurt a Hogben by hitting him on the haid. Anybody's a fool to try. I felt my knees buckle a little but I was all right in a couple of seconds and I looked around to see who'd whammed me.

Wasn't a soul there. But oh my, the moaning and groaning that was going up from that there crowd! People was a-clutching at their foreheads and a-staggering around the street, clawing at each other to get to that truck where the man was handing out the bottles of headache cure as fast as he could take in the dollar bills.

The skinny man with the kind face rolled up his eyes like a duck in thunder.

"Oh, my head!" he groaned. "What did I tell you? Oh, my head!" Then he sort of tottered away, fishing in his pocket for money.

Well, the family always did say I was slow-witted but you'd have to be downright feeble-minded if you didn't know there was something mighty peculiar going on around here. I'm no ninny, no matter what Maw says. I turned around and looked for Junior Pugh.

There he stood, the fat-faced little varmint, red as a turkey-gobbler, all swole up and his mean little eyes just a-flashing at the crowd.

"It's a hex," I thought to myself, perfectly calm. "I'd never have believed it but it's a real hex. Now how in the world—"

Then I remembered Lily Lou Mutz and what Uncle Lem had been thinking to himself. And I began to see the light.

The crowd had gone plumb crazy, fighting to get at the headache cure. I purty near had to bash my way over towards Uncle Lem. I figgered it was past time I took a hand, on account of him being so soft in the heart and likewise just about as soft in the haid.

"Nosirree," he was saying, firm-like. "I won't do it. Not by no manner of means I won't."

"Uncle Lem," I said.

I bet he jumped a yard into the air.

"Saunk!" he squeaked. He flushed up and grinned sheepish and then he looked mad, but I could tell he was kinda relieved, too. "I told you not to foller me," he said.

"Maw told me not to let you out of my sight," I said. "I promised Maw and us Hogbens never break a promise. What's going on here, Uncle Lem?"

"Oh, Saunk, everything's gone dead wrong!" Uncle Lem wailed out. "Here I am with a heart of gold and I'd just as soon be dead! Meet Mister Ed Pugh, Saunk. He's trying to get me kilt."

"Now Lem," Ed Pugh said. "You know that ain't so. I just want my rights, that's all. Pleased to meet you, young fellow. Another Hogben, I take it. Maybe you can talk your uncle into—"

"Excuse me for interrupting, Mister Pugh," I said, real polite. "But maybe you'd better explain. All this is purely a mystery to me."

He cleared his throat and threw his chest out, important-like. I could tell this was something he liked to talk about. Made him feel pretty big, I could see.

"I don't know if you was acquainted with my dear departed wife, Lily Lou Mutz that was," he said. "This here's our little child, Junior. A fine little lad he is too. What a pity we didn't have eight or ten more just like him." He sighed real deep.

"Well, that's life. I'd hoped to marry young and be blessed with a whole passel of younguns, being as how I'm the last of a fine old line. I don't mean to let it die out, neither." Here he gave Uncle Lem a mean look. Uncle Lem sorta whimpered.

"I ain't a-gonna do it," he said. "You can't make me do it."

"We'll see about that," Ed Pugh said, threatening. "Maybe your young relative here will be more reasonable. I'll have you know I'm getting to be a power in this state and what I says goes."

"Paw," little Junior squeaked out just then, "Paw, they're kinda slowing down. Kin I give it to 'em double-strength this time, Paw? Betcha I could kill a few if I let myself go. Hey, Paw—"

Ed Pugh made as if he was gonna clonk the little varmint again, but I guess he thought better of it.

"Don't interrupt your elders, sonny," he said. "Paw's busy. Just tend to your job and shut up." He glanced out over the moaning crowd. "Give that bunch over beyond the truck a little more treatment," he said. "They ain't buying fast enough. But no double-strength, Junior. You gotta save your energy. You're a growing boy."

He turned back to me. "Junior's a talented child," he said, very proud. "As you can see. He inherited it from his dear dead-and-gone mother, Lily Lou. I was telling you about Lily Lou. It was my hope to marry young, like I said, but the way things worked out, somehow I just didn't get around to wifin' till I got well along into the prime of life."

He blew out his chest like a toadfrog, looking down admiring. I never did see a man that thought better of himself. "Never found a woman who'd look at—I mean, never found the right woman," he went on, "till the day I met Lily Lou Mutz."

"I know what you mean," I said, polite. I did, too. He musta searched a long, long ways before he found somebody ugly enough herself to look twice at him. Even Lily Lou, pore soul, musta thunk a long time before she said yes.

"And that," Ed Pugh went on, "is where your Uncle Lem comes in. It seems like he'd give Lily Lou a bewitchment quite some while back."

"I never!" Uncle Lem squealed. "And anyway, how'd I know she'd get married and pass it on to her child? Who'd ever think Lily Lou would—"

"He gave her a bewitchment," Ed Pugh went right on talking. "Only she never told me till she was a-layin' on her death-bed a year ago. Lordy, I sure woulda whopped her good if I'd knowed how she held out on me all them years! It was the hex Lemuel gave her and she inherited it on to her little child."

"I only done it to protect her," Uncle Lem said, right quick. "You know I'm speaking the truth, Saunk boy. Pore Lily Lou was so pizon ugly people used to up and heave a clod at her now and then afore they could help themselves. Just automatic-like. Couldn't blame 'em. I often fought down the impulse myself.

"But pore Lily Lou, I shore felt sorry for her. You'll never know how long I fought down my good impulses, Saunk. But my heart of gold does get me into messes. One day I felt so sorry for the pore hideous critter I gave her the hexpower. Anybody'd have done the same, Saunk."

"How'd you do it?" I asked, real interested, thinking it might come in handy someday to know. I'm young yet, and I got lots to learn.

Well, he started to tell me and it was kinda mixed up. Right at first I got a notion some furrin feller named Gene Chromosome had done it for him and after I got straight on that part he'd gone cantering off into a rigamarole about the alpha waves of the brain.

Shucks, I knowed that much my own self. Everybody musta noticed the way them little waves go a-sweeping over the tops of people's haids when they're thinking. I've watched Grandpaw sometimes when he had as many as six hundred different thoughts follering each other up and down them little paths where his brain is. Hurts my eyes to look too close when Grandpaw's thinking.

"So that's how it is, Saunk," Uncle Lem wound up. "And this here little rattlesnake's inherited the whole shebang."

"Well, why don't you get this here Gene Chromosome

feller to unscramble Junior and put him back the way other people are?" I asked. "I can see how easy you could do it. Look here, Uncle Lem." I focused down real sharp on Junior and made my eyes go funny the way you have to when you want to look inside a person.

Sure enough, I seen just what Uncle Lem meant. There was teensy-weensy little chains of fellers, all hanging on to each other for dear life, and skinny little rods jiggling around inside them awful teensy cells everybody's made of—except maybe for Little Sam, our baby.

"Look here, Uncle Lem," I said. "All you did when you give Lily Lou the hex was to twitch these here little rods over *thataway* and patch 'em onto them little chains that wiggle so fast. Now why can't you switch 'em back again and make Junior behave himself. It oughta be easy."

"It would be easy," Uncle Lem kinda sighed at me. "Saunk, you're a scatterbrain. You wasn't listening to what I said. I can't switch 'em back without I kill Junior."

"The world would be a better place," I said.

"I know it would. But you know what we promised Grandpaw? No more killings."

"But Uncle Lem!" I bust out. "This is turrible! You mean this nasty little rattlesnake's gonna go on all his life hexing people?"

"Worse than that, Saunk," pore Uncle Lem said, almost crying. "He's gonna pass the power on to his descendants, just like Lily Lou passed it on to him."

For a minute it sure did look like a dark prospect for the human race. Then I laughed.

"Cheer up, Uncle Lem," I said. "Nothing to worry about. Look at the little toad. There's ain't a female critter alive who'd come within a mile of him. Already he's as repulsive as his daddy. And remember, he's Lily Lou Mutz's child, too. Maybe he'll get even horribler as he grows up. One thing's sure—he ain't never gonna get married."

"Now there's where you're wrong," Ed Pugh busted in, talking real loud. He was red in the face and he looked mad. "Don't think I ain't been listening," he said. "And don't think I'm gonna forget what you said about my child. I told you I was getting to be a power in this town. Junior and me can go a long way, using his talent to help us.

"Already I've got on to the board of aldermen here and there's gonna be a vacancy in the state senate come next week—unless the old coot I have in mind's a lot tougher than he looks. So I'm warning you, young Hogben, you and your family's gonna pay for them insults."

"Nobody oughta get mad when he hears the gospel truth about himself," I said. "Junior is a repulsive specimen."

"He just takes getting used to," his paw said. "All us Pughs is hard to understand. Deep, I guess. But we got our pride. And I'm gonna make sure the family line never dies out. Never, do you hear that, Lemuel?"

Uncle Lem just shut his eyes up tight and shook his head fast. "No-sirree," he said. "I'll never do it. Never, never, never, never—"

"Lemuel," Ed Pugh said, real sinister. "Lemuel, do you want me to set Junior on you?"

"Oh, there ain't no use in that," I said. "You seen him try to hex me along with the crowd, didn't you? No manner of use, Mister Pugh. Can't hex a Hogben."

"Well—" He looked around, searching his mind. "Hm-m. I'll think of something. I'll—soft-hearted, aren't you? Promised your Grandpappy you wouldn't kill nobody, hey? Lemuel, open your eyes and look over there across the street. See that sweet old lady walking with the cane? How'd you like it if I had Junior drop her dead in her tracks?"

Uncle Lemuel just squeezed his eyes tighter shut.

"I won't look. I don't know the sweet old thing. If she's that old, she ain't got much longer anyhow. Maybe she'd be better off dead. Probably got rheumatiz something fierce."

"All right, then, how about that purty young girl with the baby in her arms? Look, Lemuel. Mighty sweet-looking little baby. Pink ribbon in its bonnet, see? Look at them dimples. Junior, get ready to blight them where they stand. Bubonic plague to start with maybe. And after that—"

"Uncle Lem," I said, feeling uneasy. "I dunno what Grandpaw would say to this. Maybe—"

Uncle Lem popped his eyes wide open for just a second. He glared at me, frantic.

"I can't help it if I've got a heart of gold," he said. "I'm a fine old feller and everybody picks on me. Well, I won't stand for it. You can push me just so far. Now I don't care if Ed Pugh kills off the whole human race. I don't care if Grandpaw *does* find out what I done. I don't care a hoot about nothing no more." He gave a kind of wild laugh.

"I'm gonna get out from under. I won't know nothing about nothing. I'm gonna snatch me a few winks, Saunk."

And with that he went rigid all over and fell flat on his face on the sidewalk, stiff as a poker.

3. Over a Barrel

Well, worried as I was, I had to smile. Uncle Lem's kinda cute sometimes. I knowed he'd put hisself to sleep again, the way he always does when trouble catches up with him. Paw says it's catalepsy but cats sleep a lot lighter than that.

Uncle Lem hit the sidewalk flat and kinda bounced a little. Junior gave a howl of joy. I guess maybe he figgered he'd had something to do with Uncle Lem falling over. Anyhow, seeing somebody down and helpless, Junior naturally rushed over and pulled his foot back and kicked Uncle Lem in the side of the haid.

Well, like I said, us Hogbens have got pretty tough haids. Junior let out a howl. He started dancing around nursing his foot in both hands.

"I'll hex you good!" he yelled at Uncle Lem. "I'll hex you good, you—you ole Hogben, you!" He drew a deep breath and turned purple in the face and—

And then it happened.

It was like a flash of lightning. I don't take no stock in hexes, and I had a fair idea of what was happening, but it took me by surprise. Paw tried to explain to me later how it worked and he said it just stimulated the latent toxins inherent in the organism. It made Junior into a catalytoxic agent on account of the way the rearrangement of the desoxyribonucleic acid his genes was made of worked on the kappa waves of his nasty little brain, stepping them up as much as thirty microvolts. But shucks, you know Paw. He's too lazy to figger the thing out in English. He just steals them fool words out of other folks' brains when he needs 'em.

What really happened was that all the pizon that little varmint had bottled up in him, ready to let go on the crowd, somehow seemed to r'ar back and smack Uncle Lem right in the face. I never seen such a hex. And the awful part was—it worked.

Because Uncle Lem wasn't resisting a mite now he was asleep. Red-hot pokers wouldn't have waked him up and I wouldn't put red-hot pokers past little Junior Pugh. But he didn't need 'em this time. The hex hit Uncle Lem like a thunderbolt.

He turned pale green right before our eyes.

Somehow it seemed to me a turrible silence fell as Uncle Lem went green. I looked up, surprised. Then I realized what was happening. All that pitiful moaning and groaning from the crowd had stopped.

People was swigging away at their bottles of headache cure, rubbing their foreheads and kinda laughing weak-like with relief. Junior's whole complete hex had gone into Uncle Lem and the crowd's headaches had naturally stopped right off.

"What's happened here?" somebody called out in a kinda familiar voice. "Has that man fainted? Why don't you help him? Here, let me by—I'm a doctor."

It was the skinny man with the kind-looking face. He was still drinking out of the headache bottle as he pushed his way through the crowd toward us but he'd put his notebook away. When he saw Ed Pugh he flushed up angry-like.

"So it's you, is it, Alderman Pugh?" he said. "How is it you're always around when trouble starts? What did you do to this poor man, anyhow? Maybe this time you've gone too far."

"I didn't do a thing," Ed Pugh said. "Never touched him. You watch your tongue, Dr. Brown, or you'll regret it. I'm a powerful man in this here town."

"Look at that!" Dr. Brown yells, his voice going kinda squeaky as he stares down at Uncle Lem. "The man's dying! Call an ambulance, somebody, quick!"

Uncle Lem was changing color again. I had to laugh a little, inside my haid. I knowed what was happening and it was kinda funny. Everybody's got a whole herd of germs and viruses and suchlike critters swarming through them all the time, of course.

When Junior's hex hit Uncle Lem it stimulated the entire herd something turrible, and a flock of little bitty critters Paw calls antibodies had to get to work pronto. They ain't really as sick as they look, being white by nature.

Whenever a pizon starts chawing on you these pale little fellers grab up their shooting-irons and run like crazy to the battlefield in your insides. Such fighting and yelling and swearing you never seen. It's a regular Bull Run.

That was going on right then inside Uncle Lem. Only us Hogbens have got a special militia of our own inside us. And they got called up real fast.

They was swearing and kicking and whopping the enemy so hard Uncle Lem had gone from pale green to a sort of purplish color, and big yeller and blue spots was beginning to bug out all over him where it showed. He looked oncommon sick. Course it didn't do him no real harm. The Hogbens militia can lick any germ that breathes.

But he sure looked revolting.

The skinny doctor crouched down beside Uncle Lem and felt his pulse.

"Now you've done it," he said, looking up at Ed Pugh. "I don't know how you've worked this, but for once you've gone too far. This man seems to have bubonic plague. I'll see you're put under control this time and that young Kallikak of yours, too."

Ed Pugh just laughed a little. But I could see he was mad.

"Don't you worry about me, Dr. Brown," he said, mean. "When I get to be governor—and I got my plans all made—that there hospital you're so proud of ain't gonna operate on state funds no more. A fine thing!

"Folks laying around in hospitals eating their fool

heads off! Make 'em get out and plough, that's what I say. Us Pughs never gets sick. I got lots of better uses for state money than paying folks to lay around in bed when I'm governor."

All the doctor said was, "Where's that ambulance?"

"If you mean that big long car making such a noise," I said, "it's about three miles off but coming fast. Uncle Lem don't need no help, though. He's just having an attack. We get 'em in the family all the time. It don't mean nothing."

"Good heavens!" the doc said, staring down at Uncle Lem. "You mean he's had this before and lived?" Then he looked up at me and smiled all of a sudden. "Oh, I see," he said. "Afraid of hospitals, are you? Well, don't worry. We won't hurt him."

That surprised me some. He was a smart man. I'd fibbed a little for just that reason. Hospitals is no place for Hogbens. People in hospitals are too danged nosy. So I called Uncle Lem real loud, inside my head.

"Uncle Lem," I hollered, only thinking it, not out loud. "Uncle Lem, wake up quick! Grandpaw'll nail your hide to the barn door if'n you let yourself get took to a hospital. You want 'em to find out about them two hearts you got in your chest? And the way your bones are fixed and the shape of your gizzard? Uncle Lem! Wake up!"

It wasn't no manner of use. He never even twitched.

Right then I began to get really scared. Uncle Lem had sure landed me in the soup. There I was with all that responsibility on my shoulders and I didn't have the least idea how to handle it. I'm just a young feller after all. I can hardly remember much farther back than the great fire of London, when Charles II was king, with all them long curls a-hanging on his shoulders. On him, though, they looked good.

"Mister Pugh," I said, "you've got to call off Junior.

I can't let Uncle Lem get took to the hospital. You know I can't."

"Junior, pour it on," Mister Pugh said, grinning real nasty. "I want a little talk with young Hogben here." The doctor looked up, puzzled, and Ed Pugh said, "Step over here a mite, Hogben. I want a private word with you. Junior, bear down!"

Uncle Lem's yellow and blue spots got green rings around their outside edges. The doctor sorta gasped and Ed Pugh took my arm and pulled me back. When we was out of earshot he said to me, confidential, fixing me with his tiny little eyes:

"I reckon you know what I want, Hogben. Lem never did say he *couldn't*, he only said he wouldn't, so I know you folks can do it for me."

"Just exactly what is it you want, Mister Pugh?" I asked him.

"You know. I want to make sure our fine old family line goes on. I want there should always be Pughs. I had so much trouble getting married off myself and I know Junior ain't going to be easy to wife. Women don't have no taste nowadays.

"Since Lily Lou went to glory there hasn't been a woman on earth ugly enough to marry a Pugh and I'm skeered Junior'll be the last of a great line. With his talent I can't bear the thought. You just fix it so our family won't never die out and I'll have Junior take the hex off Lemuel."

"If I fixed it so your line didn't die out," I said, "I'd be fixing it so everybody else's line *would* die out, just as soon as there was enough Pughs around."

"What's wrong with that?" Ed Pugh asked, grinning. "Way I see it we're good strong stock." He flexed his gorilla arms. He was taller than me, even. "No harm in populatin' the world with good stock, is there? I figger given time enough us Pughs could conquer the whole danged world. And you're gonna help us do it, young Hogben."

"Oh, no," I said. "Oh, no! Even if I knowed how—"

There was a turrible noise at the end of the street and the crowd scattered to make way for the ambulance, which drawed up at the curb beside Uncle Lem. A couple of fellers in white coats jumped out with a sort of pallet on sticks. Dr. Brown stood up, looking real relieved.

"Thought you'd never get here," he said. "This man's a quarantine case, I think. Heaven knows what kind of results we'll find when we start running tests on him. Hand me my bag out of the back there, will you? I want my stethoscope. There's something funny about this man's heart."

Well, *my* heart sunk right down into my boots. We was goners and I knowed it—the whole Hogben tribe. Once them doctors and scientists find out about us we'll never know a moment's peace again as long as we live. We won't have no more privacy than a corncob.

Ed Pugh was watching me with a nasty grin on his pasty face.

"Worried, huh?" he said. "You gotta right to be worried. I know about you Hogbens. All witches. Once they get Lem in the hospital, no telling what they'll find out. Against the law to be witches, probably. You've got about half a minute to make up your mind, young Hogben. What do you say?"

Well, what could I say? I couldn't give him a promise like he was asking, could I? Not and let the whole world be overrun by hexing Pughs. Us Hogbens live a long time. We've got some pretty important plans for the future when the rest of the world begins to catch up with us. But if by that time the rest of the world is all Pughs, it won't hardly seem worth while, some-how. I couldn't say yes.

But if I said no Uncle Lem was a goner. Us Hogbens was doomed either way, it seemed to me.

Looked like there was only one thing to do. I took a deep breath, shut my eyes, and let out a desperate yell inside my head.

"Grandpaw!" I hollered.

"Yes, my boy?" said a big deep voice in the middle of my brain. You'd athought he'd been right alongside me all the time, just waiting to be called. He was a hundred-odd miles off, and sound asleep. But when a Hogben calls in the tone of voice I called in he's got a right to expect an answer—quick. I got it.

Mostly Grandpaw woulda dithered around for fif-teen minutes, asking cross questions and not listening to the answers, and talking in all kinds of queer old-fashioned dialects, like Sanskrit, he's picked up through the years. But this time he seen it was serious.

"Yes, my boy?" was all he said.

I flapped my mind wide open like a school-book in front of him. There wasn't no time for questions and answers. The doc was getting out his dingus to listen to Uncle Lem's two hearts beating out of tune and once he heard that the jig would be up for us Hogbens.

"Unless you let me kill 'em, Grandpaw," I added. Because by that time I knowed he'd read the whole situation from start to finish in one fast glance.

It seemed to me he was quiet an awful long time after that. The doc had got the dingus out and he was fitting its little black arms into his ears. Ed Pugh was watching me like a hawk. Junior stood there all swole up with pizon, blinking his mean little eyes around for somebody to shoot it at. I was half hoping he'd pick on me. I'd worked out a way to make it bounce back in his face and there was a chance it might even kill him.

I heard Grandpaw give a sorta sigh in my mind.

"They've got us over a barrel, Saunk," he said. I remember being a little surprised he could speak right plain English when he wanted to. "Tell Pugh we'll do it."

"But Grandpaw—" I said.

"*Do as I say!*" It gave me a headache, he spoke so firm. "Quick, Saunk! Tell Pugh we'll give him what he wants."

Well, I didn't dare disobey. But this once I really came close to defying Grandpaw.

It stands to reason even a Hogben has got to get senile someday, and I thought maybe old age had finally set in with Grandpaw at last.

What I thunk at him was, "All right, if you say so, but I sure hate to do it. Seems like if they've got us going and coming, the least we can do is take our medicine like Hogbens and keep all that pizon bottled up in Junior stead of spreading it around the world." But out loud I spoke to Mister Pugh.

"All right, Mister Pugh," I said, real humble. "You win. Only, call off your hex. Quick, before it's too late."

4. Pughs A-Coming

Mister Pugh had a great big yellow automobile, low-slung, without no top. It went awful fast. And it was sure awful noisy. Once I'm pretty sure we run over a small boy in the road but Mister Pugh paid him no mind and I didn't dare say nothing. Like Grandpaw said, the Pughs had us over a barrel.

It took quite a lot of palaver before I convinced 'em they'd have to come back to the homestead with me. That was part of Grandpaw's orders.

"How do I know you won't murder us in cold blood once you get us out there in the wilderness?" Mister Pugh asked.

"I could kill you right here if I wanted," I told him. "I would too but Grandpaw says no. You're safe if Grandpaw says so, Mister Pugh. The word of a Hogben ain't never been broken yet."

So he agreed, mostly because I said we couldn't work the necessary spells except on home territory. We loaded Uncle Lem into the back of the car and took off for the hills. Had quite an argument with the doc, of course. Uncle Lem sure was stubborn.

He wouldn't wake up nohow but once Junior took the hex off Uncle Lem faded out fast to a good healthy color again. The doc just didn't believe it coulda happened, even when he saw it. Mister Pugh had to threaten quite a lot before we got away. We left the doc sitting on the curb, muttering to himself and rubbing his haid dazedlike.

I could feel Grandpaw a-studying the Pughs through my mind all the way home. He seemed to be sighing and kinda shaking his hair—such as it is—and working out problems that didn't make no manner of sense to me.

When we drawed up in front of the house there wasn't a soul in sight. I could hear Grandpaw stirring and muttering on his gunnysack in the attic but Paw seemed to have went invisible and he was too drunk to tell me where he was when I asked. The baby was asleep. Maw was still at the church sociable and Grandpaw said to leave her be.

"We can work this out together, Saunk," he said as soon as I got outa the car. "I've been thinking. You know that sled you fixed up to sour your Maw's cream this morning? Drag it out, son. Drag it out."

I seen in a flash what he had in mind. "Oh, no, Grandpaw!" I said, right out loud.

"Who you talking to?" Ed Pugh asked, lumbering down outa the car. "I don't see nobody. This your homestead? Ratty old dump, ain't it? Stay close to me, Junior. I don't trust these folks any farther'n I can see 'em."

"Get the sled, Saunk," Grandpaw said, very firm. "I got it all worked out. We gonna send these two gorillas right back through time, to a place they'll really fit."

"But Grandpaw!" I hollered, only inside my head this time. "Let's talk this over. Lemme get Maw in on it anyhow. Paw's right smart when he's sober. Why not wait till he wakes up? I think we oughta get the Baby in on it too. I don't think sending 'em back through time's a good idea at all, Grandpaw."

"The Baby's asleep," Grandpaw said. "You leave him be. He read himself to sleep over his Einstein, bless his little soul."

I think the thing that worried me most was the way Grandpaw was talking plain English. He never does when he's feeling normal. I thought maybe his old age had all caught up with him at one bank, and knocked all the sense outa his—so to speak—haid.

"Grandpaw," I said, trying to keep calm. "Don't you see? If we send 'em back through time and give 'em what we promised it'll make everything a million times worse than before. You gonna strand 'em back there in the year one and break your promise to 'em?"

"Saunk!" Grandpaw said.

"I know. If we promised we'd make sure the Pugh line won't die out, then we gotta make sure. but if we send 'em back to the year one that'll mean all the time between then and now they'll spend spreading out and spreading out. More Pughs every generation.

"Grandpaw, five seconds after they hit the year one, I'm liable to feel my two eyes rush together in my haid and my face go all fat and pasty like Junior. Grandpaw, everybody in the world may be Pughs if we give 'em that much time to spread out in!"

"Cease they chirming, thou chilce dolt," Grandpaw hollered. "Do my bidding, young fool!"

That made me feel a little better but not much. I went and dragged out the sled. Mister Pugh put up quite an argument about that.

"I ain't rid on a sled since I was so high," he said. "Why should I git on one now? This is some trick. I won't do it."

Junior tried to bite me.

"Now Mister Pugh," I said, "you gotta cooperate or we won't get nowheres. I know what I'm doing. Just step up here and set down. Junior, there's room for you in front. That's fine."

If he hadn't seen how worried I was I don't think he'd a-done it. But I couldn't hide how I was feeling.

"Where's your Grandpaw?" he asked, uneasy. "You're not going to do this whole trick by yourself, are you? Young ignorant feller like you? I don't like it. Suppose you made a mistake?"

"We give our word," I reminded him. "Now just kindly shut up and let me concentrate. Or maybe you don't want the Pugh line to last forever?"

"That was the promise," he says, settling himself down. "You gotta do it. Lemme know when you commence."

"All right, Saunk," Grandpaw says from the attic, right brisk. "Now you watch. Maybe you'll learn a thing or two. Look sharp. Focus your eyes down and pick out a gene. Any gene."

Bad as I felt about the whole thing I couldn't help

being interested. When Grandpaw does a thing he does it up brown. Genes are mighty slippery little critters, spindle-shaped and awful teensy. They're partners with some skinny guys called chromosomes, and the two of 'em show up everywhere you look, once you've got your eyes focused just right.

"A good dose of ultraviolet ought to do the trick," Grandpaw muttered. "Saunk, you're closer."

I said, "All right, Grandpaw," and sort of twiddled the light as it sifted down through the pines above the Pughs. Ultraviolet's the color at the *other* end of the line, where the colors stop having names for most people.

Grandpaw said, "Thanks, son. Hold it for a minute."

The genes began to twiddle right in time with the light-waves. Junior said, "Paw, something's tickling me."

Ed Pugh said, "Shut up."

Grandpaw was muttering to himself. I'm pretty sure he stole the words from that perfesser we keep in the bottle, but you can't tell, with Grandpaw. Maybe he was the first person to make 'em up in the beginning.

"The euchromatin," he kept muttering. "That ought to fix it. Ultraviolet gives us hereditary mutation and the euchromatin contains the genes that transmit heredity. Now that other stuff's heterochromatin and *that* produces evolutionary change of the cataclysmic variety.

"Very good, very good. We can always use a new species. Hum-m-m. About six bursts of hetero-chromatinic activity ought to do it." He was quiet for a minute. Then he said, "Ich am eldre and ek magti! Okay, Saunk, take it away!"

I let the ultraviolet go back where it came from.

"The year one, Grandpaw?" I asked, very doubtful.

"That's close enough," he said. "Wite thou the way?"

"Oh yes, Grandpaw," I said. And I bent over and give them the necessary push.

The last thing I heard was Mister Pugh's howl.

"What's that you're doin'?" he hollered at me. "What's the idee? Look out, there, young Hogben or— what's this? Where we goin'? Young Saunk, I warn you, if this is some trick I'll set Junior on you! I'll send you such a hex as even you-u . . ."

Then the howl got real thin and small and far away until it wasn't no more than the noise a mosquito makes. After that it was mighty quiet in the dooryard.

I stood there all braced, ready to stop myself from turning into a Pugh if I could. Them little genes is tricky fellers.

I knowed Grandpaw had made a turrible mistake.

The minute them Pughs hit the year one and started to bounce back through time toward now I knowed what would happen.

I ain't sure how long ago the year one was, but there was plenty of time for the Pughs to populate the whole planet. I put two fingers against my nose to keep my eyes from banging each other when they started to rush together in the middle like all us Pughs' eyes do—

"You ain't a Pugh yet, son," Grandpaw said, chuckling. "Kin ye see 'em?"

"No," I said. "What's happening?"

"The sled's starting to slow down," he said. "Now it's stopped. Yep, it's the year one, all right. Look at all them men and women flockin' outa the caves to greet their new company! My, my, what great big shoulders the men have got. Bigger even than Paw Pugh's.

"An' ugh—just look at the women! I declare, little Junior's positively handsome alongside them folks! He won't have no trouble finding a wife when the time comes."

"But Grandpaw, that's turrible!" I said.

"Don't sass your elders, Saunk," Grandpaw chuckled. "Looka there now. Junior's just pulled a hex. Another little child fell over flat on his ugly face. Now the little child's mother is knocking Junior endwise. Now his pappy's sailing into Paw Pugh. Look at that fight! Just look at it! Oh, I guess the Pugh family's well took care of, Saunk."

"But what about our family?" I said, almost wailing.

"Don't you worry," Grandpaw said. "Time'll take care of that. Wait a minute, let me watch. Hm-m. A generation don't take long when you know how to look. My, my, what ugly little critters the ten baby Pughs was! They was just like their pappy and their grandpappy.

"I wish Lily Lou Mutz could see her grandbabies, I shorely do. Well, now, ain't that cute? Every one of them babies growed up in a flash, seems like, and each of 'em has got ten babies of their own. I like to see my promises working out, Saunk. I said I'd do this, and I done it."

I just moaned.

"All right," Grandpaw said. "Let's jump ahead a couple of centuries. Yep, still there and spreading like crazy. Family likeness is still strong, too. Hum-m. Another thousand years and—well, I declare! If it ain't Ancient Greece! Hasn't changed a bit, neither. What do you know, Saunk?" He cackled right out, tickled pink.

"Remember what I said once about Lily Lou putting me in mind of an old friend of mine named Gorgon? No wonder! Perfectly natural. You ought to see Lily Lou's great-great-great-grandbabies! No, on second thought, it's lucky you can't. Well, well, this is shore interesting."

✦   ✦   ✦

He was still about three minutes. Then I heard him laugh.

"Bang," he said. "First heterochromatinic burst. Now the changes start."

"What changes, Grandpaw?" I asked, feeling pretty miserable.

"The changes," he said, "that show your old Grandpaw ain't such a fool as you thought. I know what I'm doing. They go fast, once they start. Look there now, that's the second change. Look at them little genes mutate!"

"You mean," I said, "I ain't gonna turn into a Pugh after all? But Grandpaw, I thought we'd promised the Pughs their line wouldn't die out."

"I'm keeping my promise," Grandpaw said, dignified. "The genes will carry the Pugh likeness right on to the toot of the judgment horn, just like I said. And the hex power goes right along with it."

Then he laughed.

"You better brace yourself, Saunk," he said. "When Paw Pugh went sailing off into the year one seems like he uttered a hex threat, didn't he? Well, he wasn't fooling. It's a-coming at you right now."

"Oh, Lordy!" I said. "There'll be a million of 'em by the time they get here! Grandpaw! What'll I do?"

"Just brace yourself," Grandpaw said, real unsympathetic. "A million, you think? Oh, no, lots more than a million."

"How many?" I asked him.

He started in to tell me. You may not believe it but he's *still* telling me. It takes that long. There's that many of 'em.

You see, it was like with that there Jukes family that lived down south of here. The bad ones was always a mite worse than their children and the same dang thing happened to Gene Chromosome and his kin, so to speak. The Pughs stayed Pughs and they kept the hex power—and I guess you might say the Pughs conquered the whole world, after all.

But it could of been worse. The Pughs could of stayed the same size down through the generations. Instead they got smaller—a whole lot smaller. When I knowed 'em they was bigger than most folks—Paw Pugh, anyhow.

But by the time they'd done filtering the generations from the year one, they'd shrunk so much them little pale fellers in the blood was about their size. And many a knock-down drag-out fight they have with 'em, too.

Them Pugh genes took such a beating from the heterochromatinic bursts Grandpaw told me about that they got whopped all outa their proper form. You might call 'em a virus now—and of course a virus is exactly the same thing as a gene, except the virus is friskier. But heavens above, that's like saying the Jukes boys is exactly the same as George Washington!

The hex hit me—hard.

I sneezed something turrible. Then I heard Uncle Lem sneezing in his sleep, lying back there in the yeller car. Grandpaw was still droning on about how many Pughs was a-coming at me right that minute, so there wasn't no use asking questions. I fixed my eyes different and looked right down into the middle of that sneeze to see what had tickled me—

Well, you never seen so many Junior Pughs in all your born days! It was the hex, all right. Likewise, them Pughs is still busy, hexing everybody on earth, off and on. They'll do it for quite a time, too, since the Pugh line has got to go on forever, account of Grandpaw's promise.

They tell me even the microscopes ain't never yet got a good look at certain viruses. The scientists are sure in for a surprise someday when they focus down real close and see all them pasty-faced little devils, ugly as sin, with their eyes set real close together, wiggling around hexing everybody in sight.

It took a long time—since the year one, that is— but Gene Chromosome fixed it up, with Grandpaw's help. So Junior Pugh ain't a pain in the neck no more, so to speak.

But I got to admit he's an awful cold in the haid.

OLD NATHAN

David Drake

DEDICATION

To my late friend
Manly Wade Hampton Wellman

ACKNOWLEDGMENTS

Among the people who made this book possible are my wife, Jo; my parents, Earle and Maxine Drake; Janet Morris; and Manly himself. My thanks to all of them.

The Bull

The cat slunk in the door with angry grace and snarled to Old Nathan, "Somebody's coming, and he's bringing a great blond bitch-dog with 'im." Then he sprang up the wall, using a chink in the logs at the height of a man's head to boost himself the last of the way to the roof trestle.

"She comes close t' me, I'll claw'er eyes out," muttered the hunching cat. "See if I don't."

"Just keep your britches on," snapped Old Nathan as he rose from the table at which he breakfasted on milk and mush.

Despite the chill of the morning, he wore only trousers tucked into his boot-tops and held up by galluses. The hair of his head and bare chest was white with a yellow tinge, but his raggedly cropped beard was so black that he could pass for a man of thirty when he wore a slouch hat against the sun.

There was nothing greatly unusual about an old man's

beard growing in dark; but because he was Old Nathan
the Cunning Man—the man who claimed the Devil was
loose in the world but that he was the Devil's master—
that, too, was a matter for fear and whispering.

Even as Nathan stepped to the door, he heard the
clop of shod hooves carefully negotiating his trail. The
cat hadn't mentioned the visitor was mounted; but the
cat made nothing of the difference between someone
on foot who hoped to barter for knowledge, and a
horseman in whose purse might jingle silver.

Spanish King smelled the visitors and snorted in the
pasture behind Old Nathan's cabin. A man or a dog
was beneath the notice of the huge bull, save on those
days when the motion of even a sparrow was sufficient
to draw his fury. A horse, though, was of a size to be
considered a potential challenger. King wasn't afraid
of challenge, or of anything walking the earth. The blat
of sound from his nostrils simply staked his claim to
lordship over all who heard him.

The horse, a well-groomed bay gelding, stutter-
stepped sideways, almost unseating his rider, and
whickered, "No, I'm not goin' close to that. D'ye hear
how mean he is?"

"Damn ye, Virgil!" shouted the rider as he hauled
on the reins. The gelding's head came around, but his
body continued to slide away from the cabin.

"Now jist calm down!" Nathan snapped as he
stepped onto the porch. "That bull, he's fenced, and
he wouldn't trifle with you noways if he got a look. Set
quiet and I might could find a handful uv oats t' feed
you."

"Hmph!" snorted the horse. "And what'd you know?"
But he settled enough to let his rider dismount and
loop the reins around the hitching rail pegged to the
porch supports.

"I find speakin' with 'em helps the beasts behave,

sometimes," said Old Nathan, truthfully enough, to the man who watched him in some puzzlement and more pure fear. He didn't know the fellow, not truly, but from his store-bought clothes and the lines of his smooth-shaven face he had to be kin to Newt Boardman. "Reckon you're a Boardman?" the cunning man prompted.

"There's a cat here, too," said the shaggy, blond-haired dog who had ambled out of the woods to intersect with the more deliberate horse at the porch rail. The dog sniffed the edge of the puncheon step to the porch and wagged her tail.

"I'm John Boardman, that's a fact," said the visitor with a hardening of his face muscles that made him look even younger. "But I'm here on my own account, not my daddy's."

Old Nathan knelt and held out the clenched knuckles of his right hand for the dog to sniff. "You leave the cat alone and we'll be fine, hear me?" he said to the bitch firmly.

"Sure, they're not the fun uv squirrels t' chase nohow," the dog agreed.

The old man stared at the visitor. Boardman's ramrod stiffness gilded the fear it tried to conceal.

"Scared to death, that one," said the dog and licked the offered knuckles.

"Come in and set, then, John Boardman," Old Nathan said with enough of a pause that his visitor could see there had been one. "I got coffee."

The coffee boiled on the coals in an enameled iron pot. Old Nathan had roasted the green beans in his frying pan the night before and had ground them at dawn when he rose. He lifted the pot's wire handle with a billet of lightwood while the dog padded in quickly to snuffle the interior of the cabin and the Boardman boy followed more gingerly.

"I will claw yer eyes out!" shrieked the cat from the roofbeam, reaching down with one hooked paw in a pantomime of intention.

"Bag it, now, damn ye!" snarled Old Nathan from the chimney alcove, twisting to face the cat and add the weight of his glare to his tone, as savage as that of the animal itself.

The cat subsided, muttering. Boardman's bitch slurped water from the tub in the corner of the single room and curled herself beside the rocking chair.

Five china cups with a blue pattern about the rim rested upside down on the mantlepiece. Boardman got a hold of himself enough to fetch two of the cups down so that the older man did not have to straighten to get them. They were neither chipped nor cracked, and the visitor said approvingly, "Fine as we have at home," as he watched Old Nathan pour.

"Fine as your daddy has," Old Nathan corrected. He gestured Boardman toward the straight chair, near the table which still held the remains of breakfast. He himself took the rocker and reached down absently to stroke the dog's fur with his long knobby fingers.

Boardman seated himself on the front of the chair like a child preparing for an interrogation with a whipping at the end of it. "I thought you didn't like dogs," he ventured with a doubtful glance at his bitch, lifting to nuzzle the hand that rumpled her fur. "I'd heard that."

"Don't doubt ye heard worse damned nonsense 'n that about me," Old Nathan replied, his green eyes slitting and the coffee cup frozen an inch short of his lips. "I don't choose t' eat red meat nor keep it in the house. That 'un"—he lifted his black beard to the cat, now licking his belly fur on the beam with all his foreclaws extended—"fetches his own, as a dog would not . . . so I don't keep a dog."

All that was the truth, and it concealed the greater truth that Old Nathan would no more have hunted down the animals he talked with than he would have waylaid human travellers and butchered them for his larder. There were fish in good plenty, with milk, grains, and his garden. Enough for him, enough for any man, though others could go their own way and the cat— the cat would go the way of his kind, in grinning slaughter as natural as the fall of rain from heaven.

"Hit may be," the old man continued as he sipped his coffee, hot and bitter and textured with floating grounds, "thet ye've come fer yer curiosity and no business uv mine. In sich case, boy, you'll take yerself off now before the toe t' my boot helps ye."

"I have business with ye," Boardman said, setting his cup on the table so sharply that the fluid sloshed over the rim. "You may hev heard I'm fixin' to be married?"

"I may and I may not," said Old Nathan, rocking slowly. He wasn't as much a part of the casual gossip of the community as most of those settled hereabouts, but when folk came to consult him he heard things from their hearts which a spouse of forty years would never learn. He recalled being told that Sally Ann Hewitt, the storekeeper's daughter from Advance, was being courted by rich Newt Boardman's boy among others. "Say on, say on."

"Sally Ann wouldn't have a piece from my daddy's cleared land," said the boy, confirming the name of the girl—and also confirming the intelligence and strength of character Old Nathan had heard ascribed to Hewitt's daughter. "So I set out to clear newground, the forty acres in Big Bone Valley, and I did that."

"Hired that done," said Old Nathan, rocking and sipping and scratching the dog.

"Hired Bully Ransden and his yoke uv oxen to help

me," retorted Boardman, "fer ten good silver dollars—and where's the sin uv thet?"

"Honest pay fer honest work," agreed Old Nathan, turning his hand to knuckle the dog's fur. Ridges of callus bulged at the base of each finger and in the web of his palm. "No sin at all."

"So I fixed to plant a crop afore raisin' the cabin, and in the Fall we'd be wed," the boy continued. "Only my horses, they wouldn't plow. Stood in the traces and shivered, thin they'd bolt."

Boardman tried a sip of his coffee and grimaced unconsciously.

"There's milk," his host offered with a nod toward the pitcher on the table beside the bowl of mush. "If ye need sweetnin', I might could find a comb uv honey."

"This here's fine," the boy lied and swallowed a mouthful of the coffee. He blinked. "Well," he continued, "I hired Bully Ransden t' break the ground, seein's he'd cleared it off. But his oxen, they didn't plow but half a furrow without they wouldn't move neither, lash'em though he did. So he told me he wouldn't draw the plow himself, and best I get another plot uv ground, for what his team wouldn't do there was no other on this earth thet could."

"Did he say thet, now?" said the cunning man softly. "Well, go on, boy. Hev you done thet? Bought another track uv land?"

"Sally Ann told me," said Boardman miserably to his coffee cup, "thet if I wasn't man enough to plow thet forty acres, I wasn't man enough t' marry her. And so I thought I'd come see you, old man, that mayhap there was a curse on the track as you could lift."

Old Nathan said nothing for so long that his visitor finally raised his eyes to see if the cunning man were even listening. Old Nathan wore neither a smile nor a frown, but there was nothing in his sharp green eyes to suggest that he was less than fully alert.

"Well?" Boardman said, flexing back his shoulders.

"There's a dippin' gourd there by the tub," said Old Nathan, nodding toward that corner. "Fetch it back to me full from the stream and I'll see what I kin do."

"There's water in the tub already," said Boardman, glancing from the container to his host.

"Fetch me living water from the stream, boy," the older man snapped, "or find yer own way out uv yer troubles."

"Yessir," said Boardman—Boardman's son—as he came bolt upright off the chair and scurried to the dipper. It was thonged to a peg on the wall. When the boy snatched hastily, the leather caught and jerked the gourd back out of his hand the first time.

The cunning man said nothing further until his visitor had disappeared through the back door of the cabin. The cat gave a long glower at the bitch, absorbed in licking her own paws, before leaping to the floor and out the swinging door himself.

"Hope the boy's got better sense'n to cut through Spanish King's pasture," Old Nathan muttered.

"Oh, he's not so bad for feeding," said the dog, giving a self-satisfied lick at her own plump side.

"You were there at the newground, weren't ye, when the plow team balked?" asked the old man. He twisted to look down at the bitch and meet her heavy-browed eyes directly.

"Where the bull is, you mean?" the dog queried in turn.

"Bull? There's a bull in thet valley?"

"Oh, you won't catch me coming in hornsweep uv that 'un," said the dog as she got up and ambled to the water tub again. "Mean hain't in it, and fast. . . ." Anything further the dog might have said was interrupted by the sloppy enthusiasm with which she drank.

"Well, thet might be," thought the cunning man aloud as he stood, feeling the ache in the small of his back and in every joint that he moved. Wet mornings. . . . "Thet might well be."

Old Nathan set his coffee cup, empty save for the grounds, on the table for later cleaning. He frowned for a moment at the mush and milk remaining in his bowl, then set it down on the floor. "Here," he said to the bitch. "It's for you."

"Well, don't mind if I do," the animal replied, padding over to the food as Old Nathan himself walked to the fireboard.

The soup plate there had the same pattern as the five cups. The cunning man took it down and carried it with him out the back door.

Boardman was trudging up the slope from the creek, a hundred yards from the cabin. His boots were slipping, and he held the dipper out at arm's length to keep from sloshing his coat and trousers further. Old Nathan's plowland was across the creek; on the cabin side he pastured his two cows and Spanish King, the three of them now watching their master over the rail fence as their jaws ratcheted sideways and back to grind their food.

"Not so bad a day, King," said Old Nathan to his bull while his eyes followed the approach of his stumbling, swearing visitor.

"No rain in it, at least," the bull replied. He watched both Boardman and the cunning man, his jaws working and his hump giving him the look of being ready to crash through the hickory rails. The fence wouldn't hold King in a real rage. Most likely the log walls of the cabin would stop him, but even that was a matter of likelihood rather than certainty.

"Any chance we might be goin' out, thin?" Spanish King added in a rumble.

"Maybe some, maybe," Old Nathan admitted.

"Good," said the bull.

He wheeled away from the fence, appearing to move lightly until his splayed forehooves struck the ground again and the soil shook with the impact. King stretched his legs out until his deep chest rubbed the meadow while his tail waved like a flagstaff above his raised haunches. His bellow drove the cows together in skittish concern and made Boardman glance up in terror that almost dumped the gourdful of water a few steps from delivering it.

"You hevn't a ring in thet bull's nose," said the visitor when he had recovered himself and handed the gourd—still half full—over to Old Nathan. "D'ye trust him so far?"

"I trust him t' go on with what he's about," said the cunning man, "though I twisted the bridge out'n his nose t' stop it. Some folk er ruled more by pain thin others are."

"Some bulls, you mean," said Boardman.

"Thet too," Old Nathan agreed as he emptied the gourd into the soup plate and handed the dipper back to his visitor. "Now, John Boardman, you carry this back to its peg, and then go set on the porch fer a time. I reckon yer horse is latherin' hisself fer nervousness with the noise." A quick nod indicated Spanish King. The bull had begun rubbing the sides of his horns, one and then the other, on the ground while he snorted.

"Well, but what's yer answer?" Boardman pressed.

"Ye'll git my answer when I come out and give it to you, boy," said the cunning man, peevish at being questioned. Some folk 'ud grouse if they wuz hanged with a golden rope. "Now, go mind yer affairs whilst I mind mine."

❖   ❖   ❖

Nathan's cat reappeared from the brushplot to the west of the cabin, grinning and licking his lips. The old man walked over to the pasture fence, spinning the water gently to the rim of the shallow bowl to keep it from spilling, and the cat leaped to a post. "He thinks he's tough," said the cat, ears back as he watched King's antics.

"Now, don't come on all high 'n mighty and git yerself hurt," the cunning man said. "Never did know a tomcat with the sense t' know when to stop provoking things as could swaller'em down in a gulp."

He paused at the fence and closed his eyes with his right hand open in front of him. For a moment he merely stood there, visualizing a pocketknife. It was a moderate-sized one with two blades, light-colored scales of jigged bone, and bolsters of German silver. Old Nathan had bought it from a peddler and the knife, unlike the clock purchased at the same time, had proven to be as fine a tool as a man could wish.

As the cunning man pictured the knife in his mind, his empty hand curled and he reached forward. He saw his fingers closing over the warm bone and cooler metal mountings . . . and when after a moment he felt the knife in his hand also, he withdrew it and opened his eyes. There the knife was, just as it should be.

Old Nathan let out the breath he had been holding unconsciously and set down the soup plate so that he could open the smaller blade. There was a spot of rust on it, which he polished off on his trousers. No help for that: good steel rusted, there were no two ways about it.

"King!" the old man called. "Come over here!"

The bull twisted his forequarters with the speed and grace of a cat taking a mockingbird from the air. "Says who?" he snorted.

"Mind this, damn ye, or we'll go nowhere!" the man retorted in exasperation. As bad as the Boardman boy. Nobody'd let Old Nathan get along with his business without an argument.

Grumbling threats that were directed as much against the world as they were the cunning man specifically, King strode deliberately to the fence and his master. Flies glittered against his hide, many of them clumped in chitinous rosettes instead of scattering evenly over the whole expanse. There was a matting of sweat on the bull's withers from anticipation rather than present exercise, and his tail lashed to emphasize the swagger of his hindquarters.

"Three hairs from your poll," said Old Nathan, reaching deliberately between the horns of the big animal whose muzzle bathed him in a hot sweet breath of clover. He kept a wire edge on the knife's shorter blade, and it severed three of the coarse hairs of King's with no more drag than a razor would have made on so many whiskers.

"And a drop of blood from me," the cunning man continued, stepping back and grimacing at the three long hairs before he chose his location—the back of his left index finger, not the calloused pad—and pricked himself with the point of the blade.

While the blood welled slowly, Old Nathan wiped the steel clean on his trousers and closed the knife. Closing his eyes again, he mimed putting the knife away on an invisible shelf. He saw it there, saw his fingers releasing it—and they did release it, so that when he withdrew his hand and opened his eyes, the well-kept tool was nowhere to be seen.

There was enough blood now on the back of the finger which pressed the bull hairs against his thumb. Sighing, Old Nathan settled himself on his haunches in front of the bowl he had placed on the ground. One of his splayed knees touched the lowest rail of the fence, giving him a little help in balancing when his mind had to be elsewhere.

Spanish King made a gurgling sound in his throat as he watched over the fence, and his breath ruffled the surface of the water. That would be beneficial to the process, if it made any difference at all. Old Nathan was never sure how the things he did came about. Some things—techniques—felt right at a given time but the results did not always seem to require the same words and movements.

The cunning man dipped the tips of his left index finger and thumb in the shallow basin and whisked the bull hairs through the water. The blood on the back of his finger trailed off in a curve like a sickle blade, dispersing into a mist too thin to have color.

Old Nathan closed his eyes, visualizing the soup plate in which now drifted the blood and the hairs he had released. The water in his mind clouded abruptly—first red as blood, then red as fire, and finally as white as the sun frozen in a desert sky.

The white flare did not clear but rather coalesced like curds forming in cultured milk. The color shrank and gained density, becoming a great piebald bull that romped in a valley cleared so recently that smoke still curled from heaped brush. Tree stumps stood like grave markers for the forest which had covered the ground for millennia.

The bull's hide was white with a freckling, especially on the face and forequarters, of black and russet spots. Its horns curved sharply forward from above the beast's eyes, long and sharp and as black as the Devil's heart. The bull raised its short, powerful neck and bellowed to the sky while its hooves spaded clods from the loam.

The vision shattered. Spanish King was bellowing in fury, rattling the shakes with which the cabin was roofed. Old Nathan shivered back to present awareness, flinging out his arms to save him from toppling backward.

For an instant, the real soup plate trembling on the ground seemed as full of blood as the one which the cunning man had imagined.

King stamped through a narrow circle, feinting toward invisible foes. His own horns flared more broadly from his head than did those of the piebald giant in the vision, but Old Nathan would not have sworn that King's weapons were really longer from base to point.

The bull calmed, though with the restive calm of a high-mettled horse prepared to race. He paced back to the fence, raising his hooves high at each step, and demanded, "Where is he? Where is that one?"

Old Nathan stood, aiding himself with one hand on the nearest fencepost. Before answering, he stooped to pick up the soup plate and sluice the hairs and water from it. There was no trace of blood, only one drop spread through a pint. The cat had vanished again also, whether through whim, King's antics, or what he had seen Old Nathan conjure in the water.

"What in damnation!" shouted John Boardman as he burst through the back doorway of the cabin. His dog loped ahead of him and yapped, "A fight, is there a fight?"

"I don't know we want any truck with this, big feller," said the cunning man to his bull. Memory of the beast glimpsed on the newground was blurring already, but though the details faded, they left a core of brutal power that could not be forgotten.

"What in damn-nation are ye about?" the visitor repeated as he paused just outside the cabin. "I never in all my born days heard a bellerin' like thet!"

"Why, old man, I'll knock this poor farm t' flinders

ifen you cross me!" roared Spanish King, and suited
action to his words with a sweep of his head. Old
Nathan jerked his hand away just in time. A horn struck
the stout cedar fencepost and skewed it so badly from
its socket in the soil that the top rails fell to the ground.

"God'n blazes!" cried the Boardman boy as he
hopped back within the sturdy cabin.

"King, damn ye!" Old Nathan shouted as he slapped
the bull hard on his flaring nostrils. "Did I say we'd
not go? D'ye think I care ifen yer neck's broke fer yer
foolishness?"

"Hmph!" snorted the bull as he calmed again. "See
thet you're straight with me, old man." He walked away
from the bedraggled fence, throwing his head back
once over his powerful shoulder to repeat, "See thet
you are."

No lack of damn fools in the world, thought the
cunning man as he trudged back to the house and his
visitor. Human damn fools and otherwise.

"Oh, there'll be a fight!" yelped the bitch in cheerful anticipation of carnage. She jumped up against Old
Nathan from behind, the mud on her paws icy against
the bare skin above his waistband. He swatted her
away awkwardly, because the dog was to his left and
he did not want to break the plate he carried in that
hand. The bitch ran back to her master and smudged
his fawn-colored waistcoat as he too tried to thrust
her off.

"Here, damn ye, here," said Old Nathan to the dog
in a coaxing voice as he knelt, embarrassed to have lost
his temper with the animal. She sprang back to him,
calming somewhat as he kneaded the fur over her
shoulders and prevented her from jumping further.

Boardman walked forward again. "Well?" he said,
fluffing back the tails of his coat with his hands behind
him. The gold chain of his watch stood out in the

sunlight, as did the muddy pawprints on his vest. "Well, what am I t' do?"

"Now hush," Old Nathan said firmly to the bitch. He rose to his full height, topping his visitor's average frame by a full hand's breadth.

"I kin make it so's ye kin plow yer newground," the cunning man went on. "If thet's what ye want. And the cost of it to you is a hundred minted dollars."

"What?" the younger man blurted, stepping back as if his bitch had leaped up in his face. "Why, I paid Bully Ransden only ten to clear it, and he thought himself paid well."

"I ain't sellin' ye forty acres, John Boardman," the cunning man replied with his jaw and black beard thrust out. "What I hev to offer is Sally Ann Hewitt, and whether er no she's a hundred dollars value is a question ye'll answer yerself."

"You think I cain't pay thet," the younger man said in flat anger, meeting Old Nathan's eyes.

"I think yer daddy kin," said the cunning man. "But it makes no matter to me, yea 'r nay."

"Then ye'll hev yer silver money," said his visitor. "Though I reckon you're humbug, and we'll hev that money back outen yer hide if ye fail us."

" 'Us,' " Old Nathan repeated with a sneer. "Oh, aye, you'd do wonders, boy. But I'll not fail."

In the pasture behind him, Spanish King bawled a challenge to the world.

When Old Nathan saw him, Bully Ransden was plowing on a hilltop a furlong from the road. Unlike horses, bulls have no certain gait between ambling and a panic rush, so the younger man easily had time to outspan his plow oxen and trot down the hill. He met Old Nathan and King in front of the cabin Ransden shared with a black-haired woman. The homeplace,

where Ransden's mother still lived, was a quarter mile
away on the far side of the acreage.

"So-o-o . . ." said Bully Ransden, arms akimbo and
his legs spread to put one boot just within each of the
road's single pair of wagon ruts. "Where d'ye think you
wuz goin', old man?"

"You know me, Cullen Ransden," Old Nathan replied.
He laid an arm over the neck of Spanish King and
murmured, "Whoa, now, old friend, we'll have us t' drink
and a bit uv rest here."

He was a fine figure to look at, was Bully Ransden.
He stood as tall as Old Nathan and supported with his
broad shoulders a bulk of muscle that the older man
could never have matched at the height of his physical powers long decades before.

Ransden's long hair was bright blond, the sole legacy
he had received from the father who had beaten the
boy and the boy's mother indiscriminately . . . until the
night the eleven-year-old Cullen proved that fury and
an axe handle made him a better man than his father.
The elder Ransden had bolted into the night, streaming
blood and supplications, never to be seen since in the
county.

Cullen Ransden had now spent a decade reinforc-
ing the lesson he had taught himself that night: that
his will and his strength would gain him aught in the
world that he wanted. All the county knew him as
Bully, but no one as yet had shown that wisdom of his
to be false.

"Oh, I know the humbug what skins fools worse'n
a Yankee peddler," Ransden said in mock agreement.

He took a step forward and Old Nathan stepped
also, halving the distance between them to little more
than the reach of a fist. It was a dangerous choice,
putting his back to the horns of Spanish King. If he
did not step forward, however, it would look as though

he were trying to shelter in the bull's strength—a challenge that Ransden would likely meet with a blow of his ox-driving whip to King's nose.

Besides, Old Nathan was as little willing to crouch away from trouble as the bull was, or Bully Ransden.

"Well, where's the water, then?" King grumbled as he sidled to the hitching post before Ransden's door and began rubbing his black hide on it.

"I'd thank'ee fer a bucket uv water, as the day's a hot'un," said the cunning man. His shirt of homespun wool, gray where it was dry, was black with sweat in the middle of the back and beneath his armpits. As he stood, he lifted his hat and fanned himself with it, smelling nervousness and anger in his own perspiration.

"Cull, what—" called a clear voice.

As both men turned to look over the back of Spanish King, a woman appeared at the open door of the cabin. She wore a gingham dress over a shift, and the body beneath was so youthfully taut that it had shape despite the loose garments. Her hair was black and might have fallen to her ankles had it not been caught up with pins and combs. Amazingly, it was clean and shone like strands of burnished metal when the sunlight past the edge of the porch touched it.

"Well," she continued, "what do we hev?"

"We got the liar as says he'll plow Boardman's newground when I couldn't," said Bully Ransden. He glanced back at the cunning man with the eye of a butcher for a hog squealing in the chute. "It's what he does, milk old women and boys with no more balls 'n old women."

"Ransden, leave this be afore—" Old Nathan began, his mind white with the fear of the thing Bully was about to say and what would come when he replied.

"Ye know, Ellie," Bully Ransden continued, still

astraddle the center of the path, "his own balls, they wuz shot off by the Redcoats at New Or-leens."

"Did your mother tell you that, Cullen Ransden?" Old Nathan said softly. His skin formed layers, hot and prickly on the outside while the inner surface froze against his flesh as hard as the ice on which Satan shivered in Hell. "And did she tell ye besides how thet came t' be her business?"

The younger man could have been blasted by a thunderbolt without the hair prickling up more sharply on his head and arms. He struck with the suddenness of reflex and the skill of long years' practice with the blacksnake whip in his hand.

It was a measure of what lay at Ransden's core that the target his instinct chose was the ton of muscle that was Spanish King rather than the sparse old man who looked unable to stand the very wind of a blow.

The whip, long enough to drive a team of four span, curled out and around Old Nathan as if it were really the snake its braided leather mimicked. Ransden could flick a fly from an oxen's ear without touching the beast itself, but this time he aimed to cut. The crackling end of the whip touched Spanish King at the base of the tail, where the hair gave way to the bare skin of the bull's anus.

Rather than bolting like a startled cow or an ox broken to the whip and yoke, Spanish King reacted as a predator might have. The bull spun, questing for the presumed horsefly with a clop of his square incisors. Old Nathan ducked and lurched sideways to avoid the bull's sweeping horns. The four-inch hickory hitching post that Spanish King swatted in the other direction with his haunches broke off even with the ground and clubbed Ellie on its way to thudding against the cabin's log forewall.

King danced back, hooves splaying, as his eyes

searched for the horsefly which had escaped him at
the first attempt. "When I find her!" the bull bellowed,
referring to the horsefly. "When I find her!" His tail
lashed. Blood welling from the whip-cut began to
dribble along the appendage in dark red streaks.

As the old man and the woman sprawled, Bully
Ransden dropped his whip. He lunged for the porch
but had to back hastily away as Spanish King stepped
between, tossing his head over either of his shoulders
in turn.

The cunning man took a pinch of dust between his
right thumb and forefinger as he lay on his opposite
hand and hip. "Ransden!" he called.

The younger man glanced instinctively toward his
name. Old Nathan blew the dust at his face, though
at four yards distance none could actually have reached
the Bully. He sprang back anyway and fell, clutching
his eyes and shouting, "I'm blind, damn ye!"

The cunning man scrambled to his feet, sweeping
up the hat he had dropped in dodging. His bull was
pacing smartly down the road, striding at a rate half
again that of his normal walk. He kept switching his
tail and looking behind him, searching for the horsefly he was still convinced had stabbed him.

Old Nathan followed the bull at a rate just enough
short of a trot to save his dignity. Ransden was up on
his feet, thrusting his arms out before him as he
stumbled in the direction of his cabin.

"Ellie?" he called, his voice rising in fear on the
second syllable. He would regain his sight within
minutes, perhaps less, but all he could know for the
moment was that his eyes felt as if they had been
plucked out and their sockets filled with sand.

Ransden's black-haired woman was gripping the
doorjamb with one hand to help pull herself upright,

while the other hand clamped against her side where
the hickory post had struck. Under other circumstances,
Old Nathan might have helped her—but under other
circumstances, King wouldn't have bolted, and the
cunning man had no wish to be present when Bully
Ransden found he could see again.

For that matter, there were men not so touchy as
the Bully who would sooner see their woman die than
watch another man lay hands on her. The couple would
do well enough without the cunning man's ministra-
tions, and Old Nathan himself would do far better by
getting out of the way.

The road curved, skirting the base of the hill which
Ransden had been plowing, so by the time Old Nathan
caught up with his bull they were out of sight of the
cabin. A creek, nameless and at present shallow,
notched the road and Spanish King stood there fetlock-
deep in the water, drinking. He ignored the cunning
man's approach.

There was no ford proper, since the stream could
be stepped across at any point save when it was in
spate—and then it became uncrossable for its full
length. The steep banks were a barrier to most beasts
and all vehicles, so here, where the road crossed, they
had been trampled down by use with little intention
toward the road's long-term improvement.

Rather than squelch through the mud into which the
main path had been churned, Old Nathan gripped the
stem of one of the mimosas which grew as thick as a
man's arm. He lowered himself cautiously down the
bank to the smooth-washed stones of the streambed.
Only then did King look up at him and grunt, "Well?"
from lips that still slobbered the water he had been
drinking.

There was neither anger nor skittishness in the bull's
tone. He had forgotten the whip-cut or filed it at the

almost instinctual level which warned that horseflies bit like coals from the floor of Hell.

Bully Ransden would likely be less forgetful about the incident, but not even hindsight offered the cunning man a view of a more desirable resolution. Ransden could be a bad enemy, if he chose; but so could Old Nathan, the Devil's Master. Perhaps the boy would let bygones be bygones.

"Come on, thin, big feller," said the cunning man, embracing the bull's humped shoulders before readjusting the slung panniers holding a day's food for both of them. "Savin' ye'd rather go back home thin go on with all this?"

"Humph!" Spanish King snorted. He gathered himself and sprang lightfootedly out of the stream, his forehooves planted solidly on the bank top and his hind legs crossing them neatly in the same motion, like the feet of a horse at a gallop. "I'll fight that one. Sure as the sun rises."

And he bellowed a challenge that silenced for a fearful moment the birds whose chattering made the woods a living place.

"I misdoubted you," said John Boardman. His saddle blanket was folded as a pad at the base of an oak tree, but he had been pacing restively for some time before King and Old Nathan appeared around the bend in the road. "It's late in the day, and I thought ye might not come."

"Said I would," Old Nathan replied, wrinkling his nose in disgust at a man who was surprised when another man kept his word. "Long about evenin', I said." He waggled his beard toward the west, where the sun would have been visible near the horizon were it not for the forest that stretched in all directions from the winding road.

"Well, I thought—" temporized Boardman as he tried to find some useful way to continue the sentence. One of his hands held the heavy saddlebag he had carried even as he paced alone on the road. His free hand played with the butt of the six-barreled pistol thrust between his belt and waistband instead of loose in his pocket. His gelding tugged its reins to browse more leaves from the sapling to which it was tethered.

"Well, I brought the money," Boardman began again, hefting the leather bag, "but you'll not have it till ye've done as ye claim. Laid the curse."

Old Nathan snorted. He and Spanish King had continued to saunter forward as the men talked. The bull's cleft hooves spread under his weight at every step, and he placed them with greater care than would a horse shod against the stones which rain and traffic had brought to the surface of the narrow road. Despite his size, King's step was so quiet that his approach had gone unremarked by Boardman who had been awaiting it desperately.

"Oh, I guess ye'll pay for the work I do ye," the cunning man said. He paused, his arm across the back of Spanish King whose tail-tip flicked like a pendulum. "I don't guess yer sech a fool as ye'd face the powers I'd bring onto yer head ifen ye played me false."

That was more bluster than not. Mere money was unlikely to be worth the trouble it would take to bring a major sending onto a man as well protected as the wealth and servants of Boardman's father made the boy. Nonetheless, the threat was useful . . . and not wholly empty. Old Nathan flew hot frequently, and the anger puffed away like flame from thistledown. But he was capable of cold rages also; and they, like glaciers, ground inexorably to a conclusion.

"Well," said Boardman, "I'll take ye into the valley."

He began to resaddle the gelding. It was a comment on his focus and nervousness that he tried to spread the saddle blanket with one hand for some moments before he thought to set down the satchel with the money. Old Nathan waited, his strong, knobby fingers massaging the bull's hide while Spanish King rumbled in pleasure and anticipation.

The track to Big Bone Valley meandered a quarter mile from the public road, through forest which had remained unaffected by white settlement of the region. Custom and Boardman's deed both gave him the right to lay out a fifteen-foot cartway through the intervening land, the waterless side of a tilted rockshelf. Instead, someone—perhaps Bully Ransden—had hacked down so straight a path through the sparse undergrowth that Old Nathan only with difficulty could walk abreast of his bull.

The work of clearing the newground had not been skimped, however.

The track debouched on the valley head and a scene of devastation which suggested natural disaster rather than human agency. There was still a tang of smoke in the air, though the fires that devoured the piled cuttings had been cold a month. Rain had beaten down the ashes and carved long gouges through the red clay beneath. Though the spring-fed stream in the valley's heart had cleared, the moss and crevices of its bed were stained by heavier particles of clay that would not wash away until another storm renewed them.

Ransden and his oxen had dragged the tree boles together at the far end of the valley, but the stumps would remain until rot and termites dissolved their roots enough that a team could tug them free. There was no evident reason the shallow valley should not have been plowed despite the stumps, but the one straggling attempt at a furrow was shorter than the rain-cut gulleys it intersected.

The sun was by now beneath the horizon and the sky, though bright, cast a diffuse illumination which softened the scene. Nonetheless, the valley's starkness was so evident that John Boardman muttered, "Sally Ann would have this and not forty acres uv bottom as good as any land in the county. And we'd hev lived at the homeplace till our first crop was in the store, besides."

The cunning man looked at the boy who had hired him and said, "Sally Ann Hewitt may be able t' carve ye into a man yit, but I don't know I think much of what yer daddy's left her t' work with."

"He ain't here, now," said Spanish King, striding deliberately down the slope with his nose high and his tail vertical. "But he's been here, yes, he's been here."

"I said I didn't like this place!" interjected the gelding on a note that rose close to panic. The horse curvetted with a violence which took his rider unaware.

"Virgil!" cried Boardman, glad enough for an excuse to ignore the insult he had just received. He sawed the gelding's reins and pounded his boot heel into the outer flank of the rotating horse. "Virgil, I'll flay the hide offen ye!"

"Steady, ye fool horse," Old Nathan put in, understood but just as likely as Boardman to be ignored. With animals as with humans, being heard was a far cry from being listened to. "Settle yerself and ye'll be out uv here in no time, seein's it flusters ye so much."

For whatever reason, the gelding calmed enough for Boardman to dismount and lash his reins to a dead-fall too heavy for the horse to drag. Panting with exertion, the young man followed Old Nathan on foot as the cunning man walked slowly into the newground. The shadows thrown eastward by the taller stumps were beginning to merge and drain the color from the soil.

Old Nathan tapped a stump with his toe-tip when Boardman had caught up with him. "Eight inches," he said. "Not so very big fer a pine. This track's been cut over before, thin?"

"Vance Satterfield held it all on a Spanish patent," the younger man said, holding his arms tight and crossed on his chest as if he feared something would poke him in the ribs. Down near the creek, Spanish King's black hide was almost lost in the gathering darkness. The bull's white horns danced like fairy wands, tossing and sweeping through the empty air while the beast explored the newground.

"Could be," the younger man continued with a shudder at something in his imagination, "that Satterfield er kin t' him cleared the valley forty years back er so. Reckon somebody found bones, thet they give it the name they did."

"Reckon they didn't settle long neither, thin," said the cunning man grimly.

Though to look at, it was a tolerable tract or even better. Well watered, and though the valley was aligned east and west, it was shallow enough that the north slope would get enough sun to bring corn to fruition.

"Hit's good land," Boardman said with a frustrated whine in his voice. "It must be there's an Injun curse on it." His tone became one of potentous certainty. "I reckon that's hit, all right. Injuns."

Spanish King was trotting up toward the two men. His hooves clopped like splitting mauls when they struck on stumps or unburnt timber.

"Stick to yer own affairs, boy," Old Nathan gibed. "That is, effen ye hev sich. There's no curse onto this valley, not Injun nor white neither."

"You say that now thet the sun's down," responded

Boardman without, for a wonder, either bluster or whimpering. "Come back by daylight'n tell me then there's no curse on my newground."

"I'll tear 'im up!" bellowed Spanish King, making the younger man jump. "I'll gore and I'll stomp 'im!"

"Tain't a curse, fer all thet," the cunning man explained. "This track, this's been forest fer a long time. Onct, though, it wuz in grass. When ye cut the timber off 'n sun got t' the ground agin, ye brought back somethin' as wuz here aforetimes."

Old Nathan hacked and spat into the darkness before he concluded, "Hain't a curse yer lookin at, John Boardman. Hit's a ghost. And we figger t' stay here till we lays it, King 'n me."

"Tear 'im and toss 'im and gouge 'im t' tatters!" rumbled the black bull, and the night trembled.

The shadows thrown down the valley by the morning sun were sharper than those of evening, and the unshadowed clay was red as blood.

Old Nathan stood slowly and faced the sun. His shirt bosom and his hat were wet with dew, but the night had not chilled him because he had slept against the flank of Spanish King. His joints ached, but that was as much a fact of life in his own cabin as here on Boardman's newground.

King snorted to his feet, hunching his downside—right-side—legs before he rolled left and stood. The whole maneuver was as smooth and as complex as the workings of a fine clock. He looked toward the dawn sky and said, flicking his ears, "Well, shan't be long."

Turning, the black bull stepped toward the nearby creek, carrying his head high. He seemed disinterested in the sparse browse, even though he had finished the grain from his panniers.

A mockingbird flew past on the left. Spanish King drowned its cries with a challenge to the world.

"Hit ain't here," said Old Nathan, placing a hand on the bull's rib cage so that the distracted animal did not turn suddenly and crush him by accident.

"He'll come to me," rumbled Spanish King. "Er I'll go t' him. Hit makes no nevermind." He stepped deliberately into the creek and lowered his head to drink.

"There's blood in the water," said the cunning man, feeling his soul freeze within him.

"No, hit's the red sun," replied Spanish King, but his muzzle paused a hand's breadth from the surface. His tongue sucked back within his lips without touching the water.

"Runnin' with blood," said the cunning man, aware of his words as he would have been aware of words spoken by another whom he could not control. "Heart's-blood pourin' out like spring water."

"There's blood red clay in this stream," said the bull. "That's what you're seein'." But he backed out of the creek, two short steps and a hop that brought his shoulder even with Old Nathan as the man stood transfixed beside him.

Another bull bellowed from the foot of the valley, where the sun would just be touching the spring that fed the creek through a fissure in the limestone.

"Well," said Spanish King quietly, and then he bawled back, "There's none my like on this earth!"

The black bull began to stride along the stream, his broadly spreading horns winking with the ruddy light of dawn.

The waste that was Boardman's newground was three furlongs in length, valley head to valley foot. Old Nathan, tramping beside King, could see the other bull before they had covered a quarter of that distance. It was the piebald brute he had scryed in the plate of water, pacing toward them as they approached him.

"Big 'un," muttered Spanish King. "Well, we'll show 'im."

"Run, little one!" roared the strange bull. "I've crushed your like into the stone beneath this clay!"

The piebald bull was a match in size for King, but they were not twins. The stranger was higher at the shoulder than the black bull, and the difference was in the length of his legs as well as his pronounced hump. His horns thrust forward where King's spread widely, and they were as black and wicked as the creature's eyes.

"Well, reckon I kin take 'im," Spanish King murmured.

He paused a hundred feet short of the piebald stranger and lashed his tail vertical, then down again as sharply as a railroad semaphore. "You walk on my earth!" bellowed Spanish King, and he launched himself toward his rival at a trot that snatched him away from the supportive touch of Old Nathan.

The stranger's roar and the hammer of his hooves shook the sunstruck clay. The bulls met head to head, with no more finesse than icebergs grinding together in the swell of Ocean. Both of them recoiled onto their haunches, the thud of their foreheads overlaid by the sharper clack of the horns striking against one another.

The piebald bull, the aurochs, bellowed with the wild fury of which the Biblical prophets had spoken. He shook himself and got his hindquarters solidly beneath him again by pivoting to his left around his firmly planted forelegs. He snorted angrily, tossed his head, and lunged again at his rival.

Spanish King's hooves shoveled deep into the clay with his effort, but nonetheless he was marginally slower than the piebald beast—and a battle of this sort had narrow margins. King twisted to face the aurochs, but he did not have his hind legs anchored when their horns clashed again. He went down, his left flank skidding on the ground.

The piebald bull trumpeted victory and surged forward, very nearly losing the battle in that moment.

When Spanish King went down, he and the aurochs pivoted around their locked horns. King's left horn was so long that it touched the piebald bull between his shoulder and the base of his neck. When the stranger advanced, it was by impaling himself on the cruel point.

Blatting in shock and pain, the aurochs stumbled backward. The black bull scrambled up and followed, snorting deep breaths through nostrils which were already flared to their widest extent. Six inches of the left horn were blood-smeared, and the blood dripping down the aurochs' right shoulder was richer and brighter than the orange clay on King's black flank.

"Mine!" snorted Spanish King, and he strode toward his rival with a deliberation that seemed gentle until the two of them again crashed head to head.

Both bulls had learned caution and a respect for the present rival as for no other in their experience. They locked horns, and all obvious motion stopped.

Old Nathan found the stump of a beech forty inches in diameter, a survivor of the valley's first clearing, and settled himself on it regardless of the layer of soot from brush burned nearby. He was not a participant in this battle, though he had made it possible. The aurochs would not have had sufficient material form in this world—and Spanish King would not have had form in the valley the aurochs trod in life—save for the rent between their existences which the cunning man had opened with his scrying glass.

Even without Old Nathan's intervention, animals

would have known of the presence of the great piebald bull. Smaller ones, like Boardman's bitch and the rabbits who would come to crop flowers springing from the newground, would skulk and remain beneath notice— even as their kin had done during the aurochs' proper life. Perhaps even deer would browse in the waste which would become meadow and then forest again, as it had done in the past.

But no animal large enough to drag a plow through roots and half-burnt saplings could coexist with the aurochs' fury. Horses and oxen would panic at the challenge and the glowering phantom of the piebald bull, even if it were no more than a memory in the soil itself. . . .

The aurochs was no phantasm now. He and Spanish King both pawed forward without moving, as if they were trying to pull stoneboats too heavy for even their huge muscles. Clay heaped behind each of the bulls' forehooves as the thrust which could not drive the beasts forward began to force the ground back.

King's tail lashed in a circular motion, rising to the top slowly and then cutting through the remainder of the arc with a snap like that of the whip which had cut him the day before. The aurochs' brushier tail was almost still, but his ears popped repeatedly against the base of his horns as if to add even their weight to the force mustered against Spanish King.

The bulls' first contact had been like the lightning, a cataract of sudden power that would slay or fail but could not last. This second struggle mimicked the thunder in its rumbling omnipresence, shaking the world without changing it; but not even thunder rolls forever.

The rivals sprang apart as if by concert, each of them pivoting their hindquarters left and keeping their heads low to face a renewed attack by the other. When they had backed till twenty yards separated them, each began to sidle toward the creek. The blood which would otherwise have matted the fur of the aurochs' right shoulder had been washed away by sweat.

Old Nathan got up and followed his bull to the nearby stream. He kept a wary eye on the aurochs, splay-legged and already slurping water. Though the cunning man knew that he could neither affect nor be affected by the phantom, the piebald bull had a savage reality which penetrated to grosser planes of existence. Big Bone Valley would not become plowland so long as the aurochs' ghost walked it.

And that mattered not a whit to Old Nathan now.

The cunning man stepped down into the shallow creek and laid a hand on the shoulder of Spanish King. The black bull was shuddering as his muscles strove to throw off fatigue poisons accumulated in the nearly motionless struggle, and the air reeked with hormones saturating the sweat which foamed across his torso as far back as the last ribs. King's deep exhalations roiled the surface of the creek in counterpoint with his slobbering gulps of water.

"Ye've whipped 'im, boy," said Old Nathan earnestly, trying to keep the fear out of his voice. "Hain't another bull on this earth could've done what you did. Now, let's ussens go off and leave him t' his business. Hit ain't no affair of ours if some triflin' daddy's boy lays in a stand uv corn here er no."

"Ain't finished, old man," said the bull as he paused in drinking and got his breath enough under control that he could rumble out the words. "You know thet." The creek curled around his fetlocks, and his black hide steamed with sweat.

"What call do we hev t' stay here, damn ye?" the cunning man demanded.

The piebald bull pranced out of the stream, his tail

lifted so that the center of it curved higher than his rump though the brush of long black hairs still hung down. Mud his hooves had stirred upstream began to drift past Old Nathan's boots.

"Come away," the man cried.

"And give him best?" murmured Spanish King. "Don't reckon so." He poised himself. "Watch yerself, old man," he warned, and he launched himself from the creek to charge his rival.

"Blood and dust!" thundered the aurochs as he pounded with his head high toward the black bull.

"King, he's hook—" cried Old Nathan, but the warning would have been too late even if it could have been heard over the competing bellows of the bulls.

The aurochs ducked so low that he seemed almost to have stumbled, his lower jaw sweeping dust from the clay. Neither the feint nor the piebald bull's attempt to hook him low took Spanish King by surprise, but his reflexes played him false for all that.

King twisted to block the thrust of a long-horned bull like himself, and the aurochs' right horn stabbed over King's guard and deep into his throat.

The black bull grunted in shock, and his legs stiffened as if the blow had been to the cortex of his brain. The aurochs rumbled in triumph and backed a step to give his rival time to die. Beads of arterial blood stained the right horn like rubies in black onyx.

Spanish King strode forward as the piebald bull stepped away. Their horns met and locked again with the sound of lightning striking a tall tree, and the aurochs gave back a further pace with surprise that the struggle had not ended. Blood rolled down King's black chest, and the stream lifted from the fur around the wound every time his heart beat.

Old Nathan fell to his knees in the dirt beside the trampling bulls, his hands clasped as if for prayer . . . but it was too late to pray, even if he had not forsworn the god, the God, of his father long years before. The blood that trailed from King's deep chest splashed on the clay like molten metal.

The aurochs kicked out against his black rival. When he kicked again with the other foreleg, Old Nathan realized that the piebald bull was lifting his forequarters from the ground in order to avoid being thrown down by the turning force King was applying through their locked horns.

"No!" the aurochs said. "No, you can't—" he thundered, and his forehooves lashed out together. They waggled short of Spanish King, though they splashed in the bloodstream as the piebald bull twisted to the right despite himself.

The crack of the aurochs' spine was as sharp as a pistol shot, but it was far too loud for that.

The piebald bull did not sprawl limp with his tongue thrusting in a vain effort to drive out sounds that his lungs no longer knew to power. Instead he vanished, uncanny only in the moment of his end.

Spanish King stumbled to the ground when the aurochs disappeared. His forelegs folded under him, and the gouting neck wound rubbed the furrow his lower jaw gouged in the dirt.

Old Nathan thought the black bull had died in the moment of victory, but when he ran to the beast, cursing the Devil in whom he believed as he could not God, King wallowed up from the side on which he had fallen. The bull got his forelegs beneath him, but instead of trying to rise he let his haunches down as well so that he lay on the ground in a parody of relaxation.

The cunning man knelt beside the black bull and pressed his right hand to the wound, muttering the words by which he marshalled the forces within himself to staunch the blood. It wasn't any good. On the lids of his closed eyes he could see the form of Spanish King wasting away like a salt carving in water, and his palm burned as if he held it in a stream of liquid rock.

"No, let it go, old man," the bull said in a voice gentler than any his master had ever heard come from his throat.

"Damn ye!" Old Nathan snarled, his eyes pressed closed because the tears would wash down even harder if he opened the lids. "You hold hard er I'll crack yer neck fer ye!"

"A big 'un," said Spanish King slowly. "But we showed 'im, old man. We showed that 'un who rules here."

"There was never yer like, big feller," murmured Old Nathan with his face pressed against the steaming neck of the bull. "There'll never be yer like, not till the sun goes cold."

The great black head lowered to the ground. "... showed 'im," whispered Spanish King as he died.

John Boardman rode his bay gelding slowly through the newground, coming from the west end as the piebald bull had done earlier that morning. His bitch gamboled about the man and horse, rushing from stump to charred brush pile, yapping enthusiastically at the small birds he put up. When the blond dog noticed Old Nathan, she trotted over to him a hundred yards in advance of her master. Her head was thrown back and her tail held high, giving the impression that she was already in flight after a rebuff.

"G'day t' ye," said the bitch, well back from the arc Old Nathan could sweep with the knife he wielded. She could smell his mood, and she had no way of telling that it was not directed at her or the world of which she was one of the nearer parts.

"I've knowed better," said the cunning man. He

wiped the knife's longer blade on the bull's hide to clean the steel, then cocked up the sole of his left boot and stropped the edge on it, two strokes to a side with a metronome's precision. He paused and added with the same lack of anything but a desire to be precise, "And worse, I reckon. Maybe worse."

"Chased off t'other bull, did he?" the bitch remarked, stretching her muzzle out to snuffle Spanish King. Her right forepaw began a cautious step forward as she continued, "Wouldn't hev believed it, but he's gone sure 'nuff. Mean 'un, thet. Too mean t' live nor die, seemed t' me."

"Whoa, Virgil!" John Boardman called to his gelding, who had stopped twenty feet from the carcase anyway. The odors of blood and death threw the horse into a shivering panic not far short of driving him off in a mad stampede back up the way he had come. The gelding calmed somewhat when his rider dismounted, knotted the reins on an upturned tree root, and stepped between him and the scene of slaughter.

"Well, I reckon ye did it," said Boardman as he approached Old Nathan as cautiously as his dog had done a moment before. The landowner could not scent fiery rage in the cunning man's sweat, but he could watch and wonder at the knife and the sinewed, capable hands flaying a strip of hide from the bull's back.

"I rode all the way from the west boundary cut t' here," the younger man continued—standing out of knife range. "And Virgil shied nary onct but when a pigeon flapped up in 'is face. Couldn't hev rid 'im here this time yestiddy."

"Said I'd do it," Old Nathan muttered, then wrinkled his face in embarrassment. This boy couldn't know it, but success had never been more doubtful than in the moment it came . . . and the cunning man had no heart

now for bluster, when his hands were red to the elbows
with the blood of Spanish King.

Old Nathan did not stand up or even uncross his
legs, but he paused in what he was doing to give
Boardman his attention and a full answer. "What wuz
here," he said, "hit's gone and won't be back. Ye kin
plow here er pasture, whatever you please."

The cunning man resumed his work. He had already
removed a hand's breadth of hide from Spanish King's
nose to his croup. The horns were included by a strip
of the poll.

"There's a thing I wonder, though," said Boardman,
squatting down on his haunches with care not to let
the tails of his frock coat brush the bloody soil. "The
spring, ye see, it's closed up. The rock's cracked down
all around it, and hain't no water come out at all."

He pointed toward the creek, as if Old Nathan
would not already have noticed. The slime of finely
divided clay particles gleamed between stones where
it was still damp. Higher up on the rocks, the mud was
cracking and lifting its edges toward the naked sun.

The cunning man ignored him, making the final cuts
at the base of the dead bull's tail.

"Well," continued Boardman, disconcerted both by
the older man's activity and his lack of response to the
implied question, "I reckon thet's no affair of yourn.
I'll hire Bully Ransden en his team t' grub out the
landslip and get the spring t' flowing agin."

Old Nathan stood up slowly, lifting with his left hand
the strop he had just cut and still holding in his right
the knife which the coating of blood joined to his flesh.
"He kin grub t' Hell, I reckon," the cunning man said,
"and he'll not strike water there. What lived through
the flow uv that spring, it's gone now and the water
besides."

Boardman overbalanced as he tried to stand up and

had to brace his right fingertips on the ground. His face had a queasy expression as he straightened, and he neither looked at that hand nor allowed the splayed fingers to touch one another for some moments.

"I see," he said in a voice that made it clear he understood nothing of what he had just been told. "Well, I reckon the Bully'll grub till he fetches water somehow."

The cunning man began to coil the bloody strap he held, starting from the back but letting the tail stick out to one side because it was too stiff to roll. The fresh hide made a fat bundle as well as a heavy one.

The younger man waited for Old Nathan to add something further, until it became evident that he had said all he cared to say. "Well," began Boardman. He paused to clear his throat, starting to shield the cough with his right hand. Then he thrust the member with its charnel slime back down at his side, a safe distance from his pants leg.

"Rub it in clean earth," said Old Nathan unexpectedly. His hands were occupied, but he twisted his neck so that his beard gestured up the slope where the ground was loose and dry. "Better'n water t' clean thet, evens if there wuz water."

"Well," said Boardman. "Well, thank . . ." He trudged a few steps away, scuffing his boots to find suitable soil and clear it of ash and soot. "Oh," he added as if by afterthought as he turned. "Reckon we might pay you yer price . . . though I don't know we ought to"—his gaze glinted away from Old Nathan's hard green eyes like lamp oil dripping from ice—"seeins as we don't want it put about that we wuz sacrificin' bulls 'r any sich heathen thing."

He did not realize that Old Nathan still held the open jackknife until the cunning man carefully set the roll of hide back on the ground. The horns, connected by a strip of skin but removed from their bony cores, flopped loose.

"Don't you dare t' threaten me!" the younger man bleated. He scuttled backward two steps with his hands out in prohibition toward Old Nathan, then tumbled over a stump in mewling panic.

"What's that?" his dog barked, leaping to her feet and baring her teeth. "Don't touch him now, don't touch him!"

Old Nathan raised the knife beside his ear and flicked the blade closed with his thumb. The blood on it and his forearm were already black. He made a motion that young Boardman's eyes could not follow, and the weapon vanished somewhere.

"Boy," the cunning man whispered, "we hev a bargain you and me, and ye'll keep yer part of it as I did mine."

He paused. Though Old Nathan's face was shaded by the brim of his hat, it seemed to Boardman, looking up from his sprawl, that the old man's eyes spit green sparks like pinches of copper salts thrown in a lamp flame.

"But . . ." continued the cunning man in the same whisper which carried as if his lips were an inch from the hearer's ear, "if I ever hear you've told anyone thet I killed a friend fer you, who hain't enough man t' hev rubbed the scale from 'is hoofs. . . . Ifen I ever hear thet, John Boardman, I'll cut a strop offen you as I done with him, and ye'll scream while I do it."

Old Nathan snapped his fingers above his head . . . but the sound was loud as a thunderclap, and Boardman thought he saw looming behind the cunning man the shape of a great black bull.

The Gold

"Might save a few fer the rest of us," squawked the mockingbird as Old Nathan dropped another blackberry into his poplar-bark basket.

Old Nathan looked up from what he was doing and snagged his hand in the thorns. "Go 'way, bird," the cunning man grumbled as he detached himself from the brambles. "Ye don't look ill-fed—and if ye did starve, the world 'd be a better place without your screechin'."

He eased a half step farther. The blackberry vines grew out from the margin of the woods into his oats. They'd need to be cut back before Old Nathan cradled the grain—but first he'd have berries.

"Tsk!" said the bird. "Now thet's a lie if ever I heard one! Why"—he half-spread his black-and-white barred wings to examine the interlocking edges of the flight feathers—"ifen I wish to, there's no prettier tune in all the world 'n mine."

Old Nathan grunted and collected three more of the ripe black fruit. The fingertips of his right hand were stained purple.

The strap supporting the basket over Old Nathan's left shoulder was cloth, gray linsey-woosey worn soft as soft from the days it was a shirt. Though the fabric didn't bite flesh the way a bail of split white oak would have done, there was nigh a gallon of blackberries in the bucket already. That, plus the weight of the long rifle in the cunning man's left hand, had about convinced him that it was time to traipse back to the cabin.

He reached out once more. The mockingbird got to the berry first and twisted his neck quickly to pluck it.

"Git on with you!" the cunning man said in irritation. He prodded with his rifle muzzle. The bird flew to the top branches of a dogwood growing up beside the cleared field.

Old Nathan scowled, mostly at himself. He hadn't needed the berry . . . and the bird was right, his best call was as pretty as anything on earth. Finer 'n a nightingale, said the English beau who'd heard both.

Purple juice squirted from both sides of the mockingbird's beak. It lifted its throat and swallowed, keeping one sharp black eye on Old Nathan.

"Tsk!" the bird repeated. "Don't know why you carry thet old smoke-pole anyhow. You don't hunt."

Old Nathan found a ripe berry and twisted it off the vine. He popped it into his mouth instead of the bucket. Sweet and tart together, and gritty from the tiny seeds. Better 'n the all-sweet of honey, lessen you had a perticular notion for sweet.

"Don't eat meat," the cunning man corrected. "Thet don't mean I choose t' find a bear in my own patch and hev nothin' to go on but a bear's good natur'."

The mockingbird trilled merrily at the ridiculous

notion of a bear having a good nature. "Tain't no bears hereabouts," the bird sang. "There's a couple folk up t' your cabin though, waitin' you. People's worse nor bears, most times."

Old Nathan glanced north reflexively, in the direction of his cabin. There was nothing to be seen through the heads of his grain and the swell of the ground. Even if he'd been in a treetop like the bird, he didn't guess he'd have been able to tell much. His old eyes were sharp enough still, at a distance; but he wasn't a mockingbird for vision, no more than he was a bull for strength.

"Reckon I better go see 'em, thin," the cunning man muttered. "Reckon they've come t' consult me, not t' raise trouble."

But he checked the priming of his long rifle first; because what the mockingbird had said about humans and bears was pretty much Old Nathan's opinion too.

When the cunning man came up to the back door of his cabin, past the greetings of his two cows and the mule, the visitors were standing, but they hadn't been on their feet long. The cane-bottom rocker still tapped back and forth, and the straight chair had been moved to a corner where a man sitting in it could face out with solid logs behind him.

The man who'd gotten up from the rocker was Bascom Hardy. Hardy might not be the richest man in the county as he claimed, but he was right enough the richest man who'd made his money here.

"Earned his money" was another matter. Hardy dealt in loans and land—and in the law, to enforce those dealings.

Old Nathan couldn't put a name to the other man, but the type was frequent enough. The fellow had smallpox scars on the left side of his face and a knife-track trailing from below his right ear across his nose. From his hair and features, he was a half-breed.

No sin in that. White women had been mighty thin on the ground when Europeans settled the Tennessee Territory. Old Nathan himself had Cherokee blood. There was good and bad in any race, though, and the scarred man standing in the corner didn't appear to have been fortunate in the mixture he'd gotten from his parents.

The half-breed wouldn't meet Old Nathan's eyes, but his fingers played with the stock of his short-barreled caplock musket while he looked sidelong at the cunning man. Old Nathan figured the weapon was loaded with buck and ball, several heavy shot wadded down on top of a ball the size of the barrel's diameter. A wasteful load for hunting.

Unless you were hunting men.

Another time, the cunning man would have pulled the charge from his flintlock as soon as he came in the door. This time he did not, and he leaned the long rifle against the wall instead of hanging it over the chimney board where it would be closer to the half-breed than to its owner across the room.

Not that he figured there'd be that sort of trouble.

"Hope you don't mind me waiting for you here," said Bascom Hardy, saying and not asking, and talking as if the half-breed didn't exist at all. "I reckon you know who I am."

Old Nathan dipped a gourd of water from the barrel on the back porch. He drank some and splashed the rest over his face and neck. The cool liquid soaked the front of his shirt and dripped onto the puncheon floor with the irritated sound of frying grease.

"You're a man needs my he'p," the cunning man said. "Thet's why you're here."

He kneaded his face with strong, sinewy fingers. Another time he'd have gotten a dipper of buttermilk from the jug cooling in the creek; but that would mean offering some to his visitors, and just now he didn't care t' do so.

Bascom Hardy's face stiffened. "I don't need no man," he said sharply. "You'd best remember thet."

Hardy was a tall, hollow-cheeked man, near as tall as Old Nathan himself. He wore good store-bought clothes, but he seemed to have wizened up after the garments were fitted; now they hung loose. A gold chain with several gold seals swung across Hardy's narrow chest to a pocket of his waistcoat.

Old Nathan looked his visitor up and down. There were those who accused the cunning man of hating all mankind; but there were sure-God some folk easier t' hate than others.

"Thin I guess," Old Nathan said, "thet you kin leave, for I druther have your space thin your presence."

The cat sauntered in, licking cobwebs from his fur. He'd hidden under the cabin when the strangers arrived, showing that he didn't care any more for the folk than his master did.

"Wouldn't mind a bowl of milk," the cat yowled. "Seein's as you won't fetch me a dollop of good bloody meat."

Old Nathan bent sideways to scratch the ears of the big yellow tom. He kept his eyes on the human visitors and didn't answer the animal.

For a moment, the two men were all stillness and silence. Then Bascom Hardy shook the tension loose with a laugh and said, "Didn't mean to start off on the wrong foot. My name's Bascom Hardy, and I've come t' make a business offer t' you. Ned"—he didn't look around at the half-breed—"whyn't you set on the porch while me 'n Mister Nathan, here, we talk business."

"No more juice to either of 'em thin woods rats," the cat remarked scornfully. "Though they might be fun t' kill, specially"—he eyed the half-breed slouching onto the porch as ordered—"the squatty one."

"Set, then," the cunning man said grudgingly. He gestured his visitor to the straight-backed chair and sat in the rocker himself. "What is it you come t' see me for?"

Hardy lifted the offered chair closer to the table in the center of the single room. He glanced around with a false smile as he seated himself.

The cabin had few amenities, though they were all the owner required. Two chairs—the rocker to set in, and the straight chair by the table for when he ate, wrote, or did figures. Chests along one sidewall with stored clothing and a handful of personal items—nothing that would tempt a thief. On the table, an alcohol lamp; and on the chimney board above the walk-in fireplace, five fine porcelain cups, a plate, and a few knickknacks of less obvious purpose.

Hardy focused again on the cunning man's hot green eyes. "Waal," he said, "I guess you're a man wouldn't be feared of a spook, now, would ye?"

He thought nothing of the sort. His voice cajoled, encouraging Old Nathan to create a fearless self-image which would agree to do whatever the rich man wanted done—but feared to do himself.

"Say yer piece," Old Nathan said flatly. The chair rocked minutely beneath him, scritch-scritch; the high pine back moving no more than an inch at a stroke.

A pair of titmice, blue-gray with a black tip to their crests, flew in the cabin's open front door and perched for a moment—one on the underside of a roof pole and the other on the muzzle of the cunning man's rifle.

"My brother Bynum died over t' Maury County nigh

three months ago," Bascom Hardy said. "A day past the new moon. He was a rich man, rich as rich."

"Tsk! There's a cat here," chirped one of the titmice as it fluttered from the gun to the roof, then out the back door in concert with its companion. "Tsk! But he can't ketch us!"

"Like you are yerse'f," Old Nathan stated flatly. He knuckled his beard, black despite his age, with his knobby right hand.

The cat's head turned to watch the birds. His tail beat twice. The second time it made a soft thump against the puncheon floor. The big tom got up from beside the rocker and walked toward the visitor's chair with an evil look in his eyes.

"That's true, I am," Bascom Hardy said. His tone was half between irritation at being interrupted and pride at what he took for flattery. "But that's not a speck t' do with my brother, and my brother Bynum's the reason I'm here."

He glanced around again, unable or unwilling to keep his lip from lifting in a sneer.

The cat rubbed firmly against the visitor's ankles, leaving a track of hair against the fabric of the black trousers. Hardy squawked, jerking his legs aside as though his boots had slid him into a cesspool.

"Cat!" Old Nathan snapped, coming up off the rocker. "You git back from there!"

The cat lifted his nose. "Hmpf," he said. "That un don't half hate cats, don't he?"

The cunning man's left index finger pointed. A spark of static popped in the air between Old Nathan and the animal.

"All right, all right," the cat grumped. "Keep yer britches on." He padded across the floor, then disappeared out the back door in a single fluid bound.

Bascom Hardy settled himself again in his chair.

"That's better," he growled. He indicated the roof poles with a lift of his clean-shaven chin. "If thet dirty beast comes up t' me again, I'll kick him right through yer shakes."

Old Nathan remained standing. "Did you hear thet I don't eat meat, Bascom Hardy?" he asked.

Hardy raised an eyebrow. "I heard thet," he said. "I don't see how it signifies."

"But," the cunning man rasped, "ye never heerd I was a Quaker as wouldn't larrup a man to an inch of his life ifen he kicked my cat in my home. Did ye now?"

He grinned at his visitor. His eyes flashed like sparks of burning copper.

"I beg your pardon," said Bascom Hardy. His voice was sincere, at least in its undertone of fear.

Old Nathan relaxed and walked again to the water barrel. "Tell yer tale, Mister Hardy," he said. "Tell yer tale."

"I reckon Bynum knew his time or purty close to it," Bascom Hardy resumed. "For nigh a month, he'd been sellin' his notes and his land holdins—at a discount to shift 'em fast, like he'd gone out of his head!"

Hardy's voice lowered from its tone of shrill disbelief. He bent forward and added, "But he turned it into gold, all his paper and land into gold; and there must 've been a mort of it, rich as Bynum was!"

Old Nathan felt his skin tingling. There was nothing he could put a name to, no image or echo from the words his visitor had spoken; but there was something here waiting, and mayhap waiting for the cunning man himself. . . .

Old Nathan saw the image of gold coins tumbling across the surface of the rich man's mind, as though the brown eyes were windows to Hardy's thoughts. "Go on," he said. "Tell yer tale, Bascom Hardy."

The rocker still nodded from the vehemence with which the old man had risen from it; back and forth, a skritch and a squeal against the wear-polished pine floor.

Hardy blinked and returned to the present moment, but his voice was husky with memory as he said, "Bynum 'n me, we didn't git on, never had from childhood. We split Pappy's holdings when he died, and I don't mind tellin' ye that Bynum would hev cheated me on the settlement—but I was too sharp fer him!"

"You were full blood kin, you and your brother?" Old Nathan asked suddenly.

Bascom Hardy blinked again. "Eh?" he said. "The same mother, you mean? Thet's so, but I don't see how it sig . . ."

His voice trailed off as he heard it echoing previous words.

Old Nathan reached into the air above and behind his head. His eyes were open but fixed somewhere far beyond the solid log walls of his cabin. He felt . . . and it was there, his fingers closing on the bone-scaled jackknife as they always did when he twisted them just right.

He wasn't sure where the knife was or how he found it; but he did find it, this time and each time before, and perhaps the next time as well.

His visitor's eyes narrowed. Hardy was sure that the knife had come from Old Nathan's sleeve, or perhaps had been hidden all the time by the cunning man's long knobby fingers . . . but it looked as though—

Old Nathan handed the knife to Hardy and said, "Take it, take it. There's no magic t' this."

No more was there; but wherever the knife had been was cooler than the late-August air of the cabin.

Bascom Hardy frowned as he took the knife. It was an ordinary two-blade jackknife, with German-silver

bolsters and scales of jigged bone. The shield in the
center of one yellow scale was the only thing to dif-
ferentiate it from thousands of other knives brought
into the territory in peddlers' packs. The inset was true
silver, which Old Nathan himself had hammered from
a section of ten-cent piece and fixed to the knife by
a silver rivet.

"Rub the silver plate with yer thumb 'n hand it back
to me," the cunning man directed. Hardy obeyed, but
he frowned both at the brusque tone of the command
and his inability to tell what the older man had in mind.

"Tell your tale, Bascom Hardy," Old Nathan repeated
quietly. He held the knife with the shield facing him.
When he whispered a few words under his breath, the
silver became a clouded gray.

"When I heard the discounts Bynum was takin', I
rid right over to him," Hardy said. "Fust time I'd seen
him since we settled Pappy's estate, but blood's thicker
'n water."

"And gold's thicker nor both," the cunning man
muttered, his eyes on the shield.

"Lived in a little scrape-hole cabin not so big as
this," Bascom Hardy said scornfully. "Bynum never
knew thet if money was power, then power was money
too. You got to put out to bring in, the way I do. He
was the elder by a year, but I'm the one who got the
sense."

"Some families," said Old Nathan, "the one child's
as big a durned fool as the next." If he had glanced
up as he spoke, the comment would have been pointed,
but the cunning man continued staring at the knife in
his hand.

"He'd took to his bed," Hardy continued. "He knowed
he was failin', thet was sure. Didn't own a thing no more
but the cabin and a few sticks o' furniture—" The
visitor's eyes danced around the room in which he sat.

"And gold. He'd sold all thet land and all them notes-of-hand for gold. And he wouldn't tell me where it was he kept the gold."

A figure formed, on the silver shield or in Old Nathan's mind; he couldn't be sure, nor did it matter. A crab-faced man, his skin stained yellow by the lingering death of his liver, lying on a corn-shuck mattress with a threadbare blanket pulled up to his throat. The man was bald and aged by sickness, so that he might as easily have been Bascom Hardy's father as brother.

"He warn't able t' care for that gold!" Bascom Hardy added bitterly. "He warn't able t' care fer nothin, him a-layin' there on the bed and not a servant in the house. Couldn't get up to fetch a dipper of water, Bynum couldn't't!"

"Hadn't any neighbors in t' he'p him, then?" Old Nathan asked.

Bascom's voice had caught when he mentioned the dipper of water. The cunning man did not need his arts to imagine the hale brother at the bedside, tempting the sick man with sight of a cool drink that could be his if only he spoke where his wealth was hidden. . . .

"Bynum didn't hold with neighbors pokin' their noses in his business," Bascom Hardy said sharply.

Old Nathan smiled at the silver. "No more do you," he said.

"Thet's as may be!" his visitor snapped. "I told you once, it's not me thet's your affair, d'ye hear?"

"Say on, Bascom Hardy," the cunning man said.

Hardy settled back in his chair, though he couldn't have been said to relax. "He said he'd come back and tell me of the gold whin the moon was new again," Bascom said.

On or through the knife's silver window, Bynum's jaundiced image mimed the words Bascom spoke aloud.

"'Come back here', that was how he put it," Bascom continued, "and then he died." Hardy frowned at the memory. "Didn't even ask fer a drink, though I had the dipper right there."

He looked up, his brown eyes full of purpose and as hard as polished chert. "I want you t' set up in Bynum's old cabin when the moon goes in, three nights from now. You listen t' what he says and you won't be the loser fer it, you hear me?"

Old Nathan was in a dream state where all knowledge was bounded by the blurry walls of the tunnel which linked him to the shield on the knife scale. It was broad daylight in the world of the cabin, but formless gray in his mind.

Bascom Hardy's voice penetrated with difficulty to the cunning man's consciousness. The cries of birds and animals going about the business of their lives were lost in the shadows.

"Hit's been nigh three months since your brother died," Old Nathan said. The face on the silver was changing to that of a hard, square man of middle age. His front teeth were missing. "Who did ye put t' setting up afore me?"

"I don't see it signifies," Bascom Hardy grumbled. His host's blurred consciousness disturbed him, though he had no idea of what was going on behind Old Nathan's hooded eyes.

After a moment, Hardy said, "Gray Jack it was. I have enemies, you kin see thet. He looked out fer me, the way Ned does now. I figgered when the new moon come again, Jack could spend a night in the cabin. If anybody come by t' speak—waal, he was a brave man, so he told me."

Old Nathan's lips twisted into an expression that could have been a smile or a sneer, whichever way a man wanted to read it. "You didn't say to him thet it

was your dead brother would come t' speak, did ye?"
he said. His voice echoed from the gray tunnel of his
mind.

"How did I know it was?" the rich man blazed in
defensive anger. "Anyhow, Jack didn't ask me, did he?
And there's an all-fired mess of gold thet my brother
hid somewhur, a mess of gold, I tell ye!"

"There's a well in front of yer brother's cabin," Old
Nathan said as images streamed across the silver and
through his mind.

"There's nothin' to the well but water 'n a rock
floor," Bascom Hardy said dismissively. "D'ye think I
didn't try thet the first thing out whin Bynum died?"

"Sompin come out of the well," the cunning man
said. "What I cain't tell, because my mirror's silver and
there's things silver won't show . . . but I reckon it was
yer brother."

"Gray Jack said nobody come," Bascom said harshly.
"I knowed he was lying. Shook like an aspen, he did,
whin he tole me in the morning. I figger he run away
soon as he seen Bynum."

"You figger wrong," Old Nathan said, too flat to be
an argument. "The cabin has one door only, and Bynum
was to thet door afore yer man heard him. He'd hev
run if he could, but he hid under the bed. And yer
brother, he et the supper and went out t' the well
again."

"There's nothing in thet well, I tell you!" Bascom
shouted. "Nor in the cabin neither! I warrant I searched
it like no cabin been searched afore."

He swallowed, then continued more calmly, "Bynum,
he's buried t' the back of the plot, not the front. I'd
hev put him in the churchyard down t' Ridley, but the
Baptists wouldn't hev him. I reckon they figgered I
oughta pay them—but how was I t' do thet, I ask you,
whin I haven't found airy cent of Bynum's money?"

Old Nathan smiled again. "Don't guess money was the problem, them not wanting yer t' bury yer brother," he said. The distance from which he spoke took the edge off the words. "What happened t' Jack, Bascom Hardy?"

The rich man looked up at the roof poles. A strip of bullhide dangled from them, the horns at the top and the coarse hairs of the bull's tail-tip brushing the floor. "I reckon," he lied, "Jack went off on his own."

"He hung hisself," said the cunning man.

"And what if he did?" Bascom Hardy shouted. "Hit was his own choice, warn't it? Just like the poor folk, they don't hoe their crop 'n thin they blame me when I buy their land at the sheriff's sale!"

"Was a woman the next time," said Old Nathan as the images in his silver-washed mind changed. "Old Mamie Fergusson from Battle Branch down Columbia way."

Bascom Hardy had come to Old Nathan because of the cunning man's reputation, but he squirmed none-theless at proof of the reality behind that reputation. "Guess hit might hev been. She come t' me. I reckon she thought she'd find the gold herse'f, but what she said was she'd sit up fer me."

"Calls herse'f a witch," Old Nathan said quietly. "There's other folks as call her worse."

"What's thet to me?" his visitor demanded. "Anyhow, who're you to speak?"

"The Devil's loose in the world, Bascom Hardy," Old Nathan said without emotion, staring into the silver pool. "But I'm the Devil's master, depend on it."

Hardy grimaced, upset by the thought and the turn of conversation. "Don't signify," he muttered. "Anyhow, she didn't he'p neither. Guess she run off too."

"Guess she would hev chose to," said Old Nathan, "but she didn't get thet pick. Hit was at the door, and she hid in an old chest while hit et her supper. Your brother Bynum did."

"Warn't nothing in thet chest worth hauling off," Bascom Hardy said uncomfortably. "Nor the chest itself, neither."

Forestalling the next question, he added, "The old woman, she went off with her daughter. I reckon they'll put her in the State Farm if she don't quit shoutin' and carryin' on, but thet's not my business neither!"

Layers of thick gray felt peeled back one by one from around the cunning man. Sunlight streamed into his consciousness, but for a moment he could only shiver despite its warming impact. The knife trembled in his hand, but he didn't trust his control to put it away just yet.

Birds chirped in fear and anger. One of Old Nathan's heifers complained loudly at a rabbit which had hopped across the meadow and startled her.

"What's the matter with you?" Hardy demanded. He was concerned not with his host's condition, but that the condition might somehow threaten him.

Old Nathan shook himself. He gripped the back of the rocking chair. The solid contact was all that had kept him upright for a moment. "You mind yerself," he muttered. "Nothin's the matter with me."

The yellow tomcat stepped into the cabin again with his head high. There was a titmouse in his jaws. It peeped and fluttered one wing minusculy.

"Whyn't you set up fer your brother yerse'f, Bascom Hardy?" the cunning man asked.

His visitor looked away from the probing green eyes. "Bynum 'n me, we didn't git along when he was alive," Hardy said. "Don't guess him bein' dead ud change thet fer the better now—ifen it is him comin' back, the way he said he would."

Hardy lost the aura of discomfort which had momentarily

softened his angular body. "Look here," he said. "Thet gold's mine now, not some dead man's. Mine by law and mine by right. I mean t' have it!"

He leaned forward again. "Now, you know about spooks, I reckon. Nothing there t' skeer you. You set up in Bynum's cabin when the moon's dark these three nights from now, and I'll see you right of it. D'ye hear me?"

I hear more 'n you think you're sayin', Bascom Hardy, the cunning man thought as he looked down at the other man. Aloud he said, "Reckon I kin git a neighbor t' milk the cows fer a few days."

When he smiled, as now, Old Nathan's mouth looked like an axe-cut in a block of walnut heartwood. "I don't know thet I'd claim t' hev friends hereabouts. But airy soul knows I pay my debts . . . and there's none so sure of hisse'f thet he don't think he might need what I could do fer him one day."

Bascom Hardy stood up. "Waal," he said, though the words were flummery, "I'm a businessman and I like t' see another businessman. Will ye come with me now t' Bynum's cabin?"

"I reckon I kin find it myse'f," Old Nathan said. "I'll be there afore the new moon."

"I'll look for ye," Hardy said in false joviality.

He opened the front door wider to leave. The motion pulled a breeze that scattered a slush of gray pinfeathers across the cabin floor. It was always amazing to see how many feathers a bird had, even a small bird.

"He had his say," muttered the cat past a mouthful of titmouse, " 'n I had mine."

Old Nathan scowled—at the cat's ruthlessness, and at the image of that same set of mind which he knew was within his own soul.

❖   ❖   ❖

"Thur's horses waitin' up around the next bend," said the mule as his shoes click-clicked down the loose stones of the sloping trail. "Thur's men with 'em too, I reckon."

"Thankee," said Old Nathan.

He shifted his flintlock so that it lay crossways to the saddle horn, not slanting forward. The undergrowth springing from this rocky clay soil was open enough that the long barrel wouldn't catch; and it was neither polite nor safe to offer a stranger his first view of you over a rifle's muzzle.

"Thet mean we're goin' t' set a piece, thin?" the mule asked.

"I reckon it does," the cunning man agreed.

The mule blew its lips out. "'Bout damn time," it muttered.

It was a good beast. Always grumbling, but no worse than any other mule; and always willing to do its job, though never happy about it.

Bascom Hardy scrambled to his feet when he saw Old Nathan mounted on the mule. His bodyguard Ned was a step slower, but that was because the half-breed's first thought was to point the musket toward the sudden sound. Ned had a hard man's instincts, but he warn't sharp enough nor quick enough t' be a problem if he decided to try conclusions at the small end of a rifle.

Folk hereabouts hed got soft. Back in the days when he followed Colonel Sevier to King's Mountain, then men were men.

The hillside had never been cut for planting. Bynum Hardy's cabin was just out of sight among pines and the dogwoods which had grown up where the narrow clearing let in the sun. Old Nathan knew the building was there, though, because he'd seen it in the silver shield of his knife. The well that he'd seen also, just downslope of the dwelling, set right there next the trail where Bascom Hardy and his man waited.

Hardy tugged out his watch, gold like the chain on which it hung, and flipped up the cover of its hunter case. "I figgered I'd come t' make sure you kept your bargain," he said irritably. "I'd come t' misdoubt thet you would."

"You keep yer britches on," snapped the cunning man. A feller who used a watch t' tell time in broad daylight spent too much of his life with money in tight-hedged rooms. . . . "I said I'd be here, 'n here I am—"

He looked pointedly up at the sky. The sun was below the pine-fringed rim of the notch, but the visible heavens were still bright blue "—well afore time."

"Could use a drink," the mule grumbled. It kept walking on, toward the well. There wasn't a true spring house, but the well had a curb of mud-chinked field-stones and a shelter roof from which half the shingles had blown or broken.

"Us too," whickered Bascom Hardy's walking horse, tied by his reins to a trailside alder. He jerked his head and made the alder sway. "Didn't neither of 'em water us whin we got here, 'n thet was three hours past."

"Lead yer horses t' me," Old Nathan grunted as he swung off the mule. "I'll water the beasts like a decent man ought."

The curb's chinking was riddled with wasp burrows. The well rope had seen better days, but it was sound enough and the wooden bucket was near new. The old one must uv rotted clean away, for a man as tight as Bynum Hardy to replace it.

Old Nathan looked down into the well.

"There's nothing there, I tell ye," Hardy said. A tinge of color in his voice suggested the rich man wasn't fully sure he spoke the truth—and that it might be more than callous disregard for his horse which kept him away from the well.

"There's water," said Old Nathan. He leaned his rifle carefully against the well curb and released the brake to lower the bucket.

The same two poles that held up the shelter roof supported a pivot log as thick as one of the cunning man's shanks. The crank and take-up spool, also wooden, were clamped to the well curb. The pivot log squealed loudly as it turned, but it kept the rope from rubbing as badly as it would have done against a fixed bar.

"Ned, take our horses over," Hardy ordered abruptly.

The well was square dug and faced with rock. When the bucket splashed against the water a dozen feet below ground level, the sky's bright reflection through missing shingles shattered into a thousand jeweled fragments. The white-oak bucket bobbed for a moment before it tipped sideways and filled for Old Nathan to crank upward again.

He took a mouthful of water before tipping the rest of the bucket into the pine trough beside the well curb. It tasted clean, without a hint of death or brimstone . . . or of gold, which had as much of Satan in it as the other two together, thet was no more 'n the truth.

"You wait yer turn," the mule demanded as Hardy's horse tried to force its head into the trough first. "Lessen you want a couple prints the size uv my hind shoes on yer purty hide."

"Well!" the horse said. "There's room for all I'd say— ifen all were gentlemen." But he backed off, and the mule made a point of letting the bodyguard's nondescript mare drink before shifting himself out of the walking horse's way at about the time Old Nathan spilled the third bucketful into the trough.

Old Nathan looked up to the cabin, dug into the backslope sixty feet up from the well. It squatted there, solid and ugly and grim. The door in the front was low, and the side windows were no bigger than a man's arm could reach through.

The cabin's roof was built bear-proof. Axe-squared logs were set edge to edge from the walls to the heavy ridgepole, with shingles laid down the seams t' keep out the rain. The whole thing was more like a hog barn thin a cabin; but it warn't hogs nor people neither that the sturdy walls pertected, hit was gold. . . .

"Well, ye coming in with me?" Old Nathan said in challenge.

"I bin there," Bascom Hardy said without meeting the cunning man's eyes. "Don't guess there's much call I should do thet again, what with it gettin' so late."

Hardy's hand twitched toward his watch pocket again, but he caught himself before he dipped out the gold hunter. "I reckon I'll be going," he said, tugging the reins of his horse away from the water trough. "I'll be by come sun-up t' see thet you've kept yer bargain, though."

The rich man and his bodyguard mounted together. If Ned had been the man he was hired t' be, he'd hev waited so they weren't the both of 'em hanging with their hands gripping saddles and each a leg dangling in the air.

Bascom Hardy settled himself. "I warn ye not t' try foolin' me," he called. "I kin see as far into a millstone as the next man."

"Hmpf," grunted Old Nathan. He took his rifle in one hand and the mule's reins in the other. "Come along, thin, mule," he said as he started walking toward the cabin. No point in climbin' into the saddle t' ride sixty feet.

"Ye'd think," he muttered, "thet if they trust me not

t' hie off in the night with the gold, they oughtn't worry I'd come where I said I'd come."

The mule clucked in amusement. "Whur ye goin' t' run?" it asked. "Past them, settlin' a few furlongs up the road, er straight inter the trees like a squirrel? The trail don't go no further thin we come."

The cunning man looked over his shoulder in surprise. The two horsemen had disappeared for now; but, as the mule said, they wouldn't go far. Just far enough to be safe from whatever came visiting the cabin.

And Bynum Hardy's cabin really was the end of the trail that led to it. "Broad as the trail was beat, I reckoned there was more cabins 'n the one along hit," Old Nathan muttered.

Gold had beaten the trail. Need for money had brought folk to Bynum Hardy's door, even back here in a hollow too steep-sided to be cleared while there was better land still to be had. A cheap tract, where a cheap man could settle and sow the crop he knew, gold instead of corn.

And when the loans sprouted, they brought folk back a dozen times more. People bent with the effort of raising the payments until they broke—and Bynum Hardy took their land and changed it in good time to more gold.

"You'll feed me now, I reckon," the mule said at the door of the cabin.

Much of the clay chinking had dropped out from between the logs. It lay as a reddish smear at the base of the walls. The cabin was still solid, but it had deteriorated badly since the day it was built for want of care.

Old Nathan looked upward. The sky was visibly darker than it had been when he met Bascom Hardy. "I figger," he said, "I'll get a fire going whilst there's daylight. Like as not I'll need t' cut wood, and I only packed a hand-axe along."

"Reckon you'll feed me now," the mule repeated. "Thur's no stable hereabouts, and I don't guess yer fool enough to think the reins 'll hold me ifen I'm hungry."

The cunning man leaned his rifle against the wall, then turned to uncinch the saddle. Most of the load in the saddlebags was grain and fodder for the mule. He hadn't expected to find pasture around the dead miser's cabin. . . .

"You're nigh as stubborn as a man, ye know thet?" he said to the mule.

The beast snorted with pleasure at the flattery. "What is it ye need t' do here?" it asked.

Old Nathan lifted off the saddle with the bags still attached to it. "Set till somebody comes by," he said. "Listen t' what they say."

The mule snorted again. "Easy 'nuff work," it said. "Beats draggin' a plow all holler."

"Easy enough t' say," Old Nathan said grimly as he unbuckled one of the bags. "How easy hit is t' do, thet we'll know come morning."

There were no clouds in the sky, but the blue had already richened to deep indigo.

The soil round about the cabin had been dug up like a potato field, and the fireplace within was in worse shape yet. All the stones of the hearth had been levered out of their mud grouting and cast into a corner.

Somebody since, Gray Jack or the witchwoman Mamie Fergusson, had set a fire on the torn clay beneath the flue. Recently cut wood lay near the fireplace where the bodyguard tumbled it the day he watched and waited—for Bynum Hardy, though he didn't know that at the time.

Old Nathan got to work promptly, notching feathers

from the edge of a split log with his hand-axe. He made a fireset of punk and dry leaves to catch the sparks he struck from a fire steel with a spare rifle flint, then fed the tiny flames with a blob of pine pitch before adding the wood. When that log had well and truly caught, he added others with care.

The process was barely complete before the hollow's early dark covered the cabin. The cunning man stepped back, breathing through nostrils flared by the mental strain of his race with the light. There were other ways Old Nathan could have ignited a fire . . . but though some of those ways looked as easy as a snap of the fingers, they had hidden costs. It was better to struggle long in the dark with flint and steel than to use those other ways.

The orange flames illuminated but did not brighten the interior of the cabin. The single room was bleak and as dank as a cave. The furnishings were slight and broken down—but most likely as good as they had been while Bynum Hardy lived in this fortified hovel. There was a flimsy table and a sawn section of tree bole, a foot in diameter, to act as a stool.

The bed frame was covered with a corn-shuck mattress and a blanket so tattered that Bascom Hardy had abandoned it after his brother's death. The cunning man remembered the image of Gray Jack cowering beneath the low bed, hopelessly slight cover but all there was . . . and sufficient, because the one/thing who entered the cabin the night of the new moon wasn't interested in looking for whoever might be hiding.

The leather hinges had rotted off the chest by the sidewall. The lid hung askew to display a few scrappy bits of clothing. Gray Jack was too big to fit into the chest, but it had been just the right size for Mistress Fergusson.

Neither of Bascom Hardy's two watchers had escaped, not in the end. One hanged and one raving; and a third, Old Nathan, waiting for his fire to burn down so that he could make ash cakes with the coals.

The cunning man sighed. He'd been afraid before, plenty of times; but he'd never been so fearful that he didn't stand up to it. If there was a thing on earth he was sure of, it was that running didn't make fear less, and standing couldn't make it greater.

But that didn't mean the thing you feared and faced wouldn't eat you alive. There were false fears; but some were true enough, and there was nothing false about whatever came to this cabin for the bodyguard and the witch a month ago, and a month before that.

Old Nathan added more wood to the fire, then began a task to keep his hands full and his mind calm. As he worked, he clucked his tongue against the roof of his mouth and called softly, "Hey there! Anybody t' home?"

"Who's thet you're speakin' to, then?" the mule demanded from the other side of the closed door. Like everything else about the cabin, the door panel was crude but massively strong. It had wrought iron hinges and crossed straps of iron on the outer face.

"I reckon there might be somebody as could tell me about Bynum Hardy," Old Nathan answered. "A squirrel, maybe, er a mouse."

The mule snorted. "Naught here t' bring airy soul," the beast said. " 'Cept a man, I reckon, 'n they ain't got the sense God gave a rock."

Old Nathan opened his mouth to snarl a reply; but when he thought through the mule's comment, it was all true enough. No food, and shelter worse nor a log rotted holler. . . .

He went on with his task.

"Whut is hit you're doin' in thur, then?" the mule asked.

It occurred to the cunning man that his animal was uneasy, though there was little chance of a bear or a painter hereabouts. Bynum Hardy's cabin was strengthened against human enemies, not beasts. . . .

"I'm pulling the charge from my rifle gun," Old Nathan said. He tipped down the flintlock's muzzle. The powder charge dribbled along the bore and out onto a square of hard-finished leather. From there he would transfer the powder back to the polished cowhorn whose wooden stopper measured the charge proper to this weapon.

"Whutever possessed ye t' do sich a durn-fool thing as that?" the mule demanded in outrage. "Whut sort uv place d'ye think this is, anyhow?"

On the table before Old Nathan lay the ball and the patch lubricated with a mixture of butter and beeswax. He would not use tallow, anymore than he would eat meat; from a bird, a beast, or a human, it was all the same in his mind.

"Ifen I leave the charge in the bore overnight," he said softly, more to himself than the mule, "hit'll draw water 'n rust. And besides . . ."

Firelight winked from fresh, unoxidized lead where the screw in the back of the cunning man's ramrod had dug in to withdraw the ball. When he returned home, Old Nathan would recast the bullet; but—needs must and the Devil drove—he could use the ball as it was. Seated with the screw gouge down against the powder, it would fly true enough for the purpose.

"And besides," the old man said, "I don't reckon whativer comes 'll be much fazed by a rifle ball, so mebbe hit's best I don't put temptation in my way."

The mule grunted, but it said nothing more.

Old Nathan set the empty flintlock in a corner beside the door, away from the smoke and sparks of the fire. There weren't any pegs to hang a rifle up properly, though he didn't guess a man as rich and fearful as Bynum Hardy had done his business without a gun to hand.

He set the cloth-wrapped paste of corn meal on the hearth and raked coals over it to cook the batter into ash cakes. It wasn't so very late, but it felt late.

The Devil himse'f knew it felt late.

The sauce pan was full of leather-britches beans boiled with hot peppers. Old Nathan set the container on the table, then stepped back to the fireplace to fetch the ash cakes.

"Hey!" the mule snorted. "Ye've comp'ny comin', old man!"

Old Nathan poised for a moment, hunched over the hearth with his eyes closed. Well, he hadn't come all this way not t' meet Bynum Hardy. He straightened and walked to the door, opening it wide.

Something—somebody—was climbing out of the well. The figure was almost over the curb, but Old Nathan had time Gray Jack and the witchwoman didn't have. Time to run . . . except there was never a good time to run.

The mule snorted restively. The beast was a warm presence, but Old Nathan could see nothing of it beyond the glint of starlight on one wide, staring eyeball.

Bynum Hardy wore a suit of rusty black with a collarless shirt. The soles of his ankle boots were patched with patterned cowhide. He and his garments were as clear as though a living man stood in broad daylight, but whatever illuminated the figure cast no glow on the solid objects around it.

"I'm not so durned a fool thet I'll wait here!" the mule muttered as it moved off at a shambling trot. The animal's course was marked by occasional sparks from its shoes on quartz and the crash of undergrowth at the edge of the clearing.

Bynum Hardy began walking up the short trail to the cabin.

Old Nathan went back inside. He left the door open. His fire had burned down, but its orange flames had a cheerful character that he hadn't imagined in them until after he saw the cold gray light dripping onto the surface of the figure from the well.

He recollected how much afraid he'd been at King's Mountain—after the bullet hit him. His buckskin breeches wet with hot blood, and him unwilling to look down to see what the bullet had done. Though he knew where the bullet passed—and what it passed through on its way.

Old Nathan spilled the layers of ash and burned-out coals from the cloth over his cakes. Before he placed the ash cakes on the table, however, he added a fresh log to the fire.

When he turned with the cakes, Bynum Hardy was at the door.

"Howdy do," Old Nathan said in a voice as gruff and clear as that with which he'd greet any benighted traveller. He put the hot corn cakes down on a slab of bark and peeled the cloth off the top of them. "How ye gettin' on?"

"All right, I guess," said Bynum Hardy. He sounded as though he were still calling up out of the well, but it might be he always sounded that way—alive as well as now that he was dead.

He looked at the cunning man and added, "I hope you're well?"

"About like common," Old Nathan said. He flicked his bearded chin to indicate the food on the table. "Set 'n eat with me, won't ye? Hain't much, but it's hot."

"No thankee," said the cabin's dead owner. He walked around the table to the hearth. His feet did not sound on the puncheon floor. "Reckon I'll jist warm myse'f at yer fire, ifen ye don't mind."

Old Nathan stared at the dead man's back. "Suit yerse'f," he said; and sat on the sawn round of treebole; and began to eat.

The food had no taste in his mouth, for all the pepper in the beans and a touch of onion in the ash-cake batter.

When the cunning man finished his meal, using his hands and the spoon from his budget, he looked at Bynum Hardy again. Mostly the fellow held his palms out to the fire, but occasionally he turned his hands to warm the backs. His body appeared solid as a living man's, but the cold internal glow defined parts which should have been in shadow.

Old Nathan took another swig from his water bottle. The last bite of ash cake hed like t' stuck in his throat. . . .

He got up and stepped to the hearth, carrying the slab of poplar bark he'd cut for a plate. Bynum Hardy moved aside in a mannerly fashion, making room for the living man. His figure had no temperature Old Nathan could feel, neither as warm as life, nor cold like a corpse buried three months in the wet clay.

The fire had sunk to a few sawteeth of flame and coals reflecting back from white ash. The cunning man tossed the bark in and watched it flare into bright popping yellow. Bynum Hardy folded his arms, but he did not back away.

"If ye like," Old Nathan said, "I'd throw another stick er two on the fire fer ye."

No response. "Er you kin fix it the way ye choose, I reckon."

The bark burned away to a twisted black scrap. The

room seemed darker than before the quick flames had lighted it.

Bynum Hardy turned and said, "Thankee, but I reckon this'll do me. You jist go about yer business."

Old Nathan met the dead man's eyes. "Myse'f," he said, "I figger I'll turn in. Hit's been a long day."

He opened his blanket roll, took off his boots, and settled down against a sidewall, away from both the fire and the rotten scraps of Bynum Hardy's bed.

He didn't guess he'd be able to sleep. Bedding down was the best way to keep from showing the fear that would otherwise consume him.

But sleep the cunning man did, looking back toward the settling fire and the crisply illuminated figure standing in front of it.

Old Nathan awoke.

It was nigh about midnight from the fire's state. The hearth cast a patch of warmth into the air, but only the faintest glow suggested coals were still alive.

Bynum Hardy was walking toward the door, and his boots made no sound.

"Howdy," the cunning man said.

The ghost image turned and looked at him. "Reckon I'll go off, now," he said in hollow tones. "Thankee fer the fire. I been mighty cold the past while."

Hardy took another step toward the open door.

"I thought there was maybe a message ye wanted t' speak," Old Nathan said, supporting his torso with one arm. "Fer yer brother, it might be."

Bynum Hardy turned again. "Not here," he said. "You foller me t' home, then I'll give you a word t' take t' Bascom."

"I understood this t' be yer cabin," Old Nathan said. He fetched his left boot forward in the dark and began to draw it onto his foot.

"Hain't mine now," said Bynum Hardy. "You foller me, and ye'll git the word ye come fer."

He went out the door. The cunning man hopped after him, pulling on his right boot.

It wasn't a surprise, not really, to see Bynum Hardy disappear back into the well.

Old Nathan paused at the curb. He gripped the well rope, wishing he were younger; wishing—

No. He was where he chose to be, and he was the man he chose to be. He wouldn't have it otherwise.

Hand over hand, Old Nathan climbed down into darkness.

Old Nathan's head dropped below the level of the well curb. The world above him became a handful of gray blotches cast on greater blackness: patches where shingles missing from the shelter roof showed the sky. Some hint of light must remain to the heavens, though there had been no sign of it when the cunning man looked up before grasping the well rope.

He waited for the splash that meant Bynum Hardy had reached the surface of the water. He heard nothing but his own breath wheezing in the square stone confines of the well shaft.

He waited for his boots to touch the water. Wondered what he would do then, go on like a blame fool till he was soaked and cold, or haul up again and tell Bascom Hardy that he'd failed. . . .

He didn't come to a conclusion. The choices kept walking through his mind as his strong old hands lowered him further—until he realized that if this rope led anywhere, it was not to the water from which Old Nathan drank and drew for the horses.

The cunning man's mouth worked, but he said nothing aloud. He'd not been able to pray since King's Mountain; and this was no place for a man to curse.

His arms ached. He sweated with the effort of the descent, but the droplets runneling down the troughs beside his spine were cold by the time they soaked the waistband of his trousers.

Abruptly, Old Nathan began to laugh. He wheezed from exhaustion, but the humor was real enough. It wasn't every durn fool who had time to see what an all-mighty durn fool he'd been for the last time in his life!

There was Zeb Frawley, who thought he could call down lightning, which was maybe right—and thought he could direct that lightning's path, which was wrong as wrong, and his bloated body to prove it the next morning. There was John Wesley Ives who'd witched Leesha Tazewell into his bed—and forgot that while Rufe Tazewell didn't know a lick of magic, he could shoot out a squirrel's eye at thirty paces; or shoot through the bridge of John Wesley Ives' nose at a hundred, as it turned out.

Then there was—

The weight came off the cunning man's arms. The distant echo of his laughter rumbled back to him, as if from the walls of an immense cavern. He felt nothing under his feet to support him, but neither was he falling.

The air around the cunning man was not black but gray, a gray so dense that he could not see his own hands when he raised them to his face. His calloused palms felt rough and loose from the pull of the rope.

"Bynum Hardy!" he called. "I've come t' ye. Now show yerself!"

He didn't know what he expected; only that he was no longer afraid. He'd faced this one till he beat the part of it that was in him; and for the rest, well, every man had his time, and if this was his time—so be it.

The gray cleared like fog streaming in a windstorm. A long tunnel with a figure at the end of it, then up close enough to touch: Bynum Hardy, twisting like a pat of butter across a hot skillet, and nowhere to go however it turns.

"I played yer games," Old Nathan said harshly. "Now I'll hev my side of the bargain. Give me the word t' take t' your brother."

"D'ye know where I am, wizard?" Bynum Hardy said. He spoke through tight-clenched lips, like a man tensing against the pain of a gunshot—knowing that his blood and life ran out regardless.

"Thet makes no matter t' me," Old Nathan replied harshly. "Hit's between you 'n whoever it was put ye here. Just answer me where yer brother's gold is at."

"The gold's in the pivot log of the well," Hardy said. "But it hain't Bascom's gold."

Vague figures reached up from behind the dead man, or they may have been wisps of fog. Something constrained and tortured Bynum Hardy, but there was no sign of it to the cunning man's eyes.

"Tain't your'n anyways," Old Nathan snapped. His conscious mind had only loathing for the tortured figure, but the skin of the cunning man's arms pricked up in goosebumps from the sight. It warn't fright; only the way his body was contending.

But the righteous truth was, he wanted no more part of this wherever place.

"I've told you what Bascom wants t' hear," Bynum Hardy said, twitching and grimacing between the words. "Now I'll tell ye what he must hear. He's t' take thet gold and give it t' them poor folk I wronged when I was alive. Tell him!"

"If bein' poor meant bein' virtuous," Old Nathan said in sudden anger, "thin there'd be a sight less wickedness in the world. D'ye think scatt'ring money on good folk 'n bad alike is going t' buy you out uv this here place?"

"Don't you be a greater fool 'n God made ye, Nathan Ridgeway," said the dead man, speaking a name Old Nathan thought there wasn't a soul in the county to remember or care.

Bynum Hardy leaned forward, against the pull of invisible, flamingly-cold bonds. He gasped with pain, then went on, "Hit don't signify what they were, good men nor bad. Hit's what I did thet put me here. I squeezed, 'n whin they cried out I squeezed the harder, fer thet meant they were weak. Bascom's to give the gold t' them as I took it from, their crops 'n their land . . . and if I could, the very clothes they wore."

The skin of Bynum Hardy's cheeks drew out to either side, as though men with tongs had gripped him. He sobbed wordlessly with his eyes closed for a moment. "All the gold, all the prayers on earth, wizard . . ." Hardy managed to whisper.

His eyes opened, filled with pain, as he continued, "None of it's airy good t' me now. Hit's all too late. I never done a speck uv good t' airy soul while I was alive—but I'll do this now fer my brother Bascom, ifen he'll only listen. Tell him t' give my gold away, and maybe he'll find a better place whin he follows me."

A spasm of something unendurable dragged a scream from the dead man's throat. "Tell him thet . . ." he rasped, and the smoke-gray emptiness swept over Old Nathan again.

The cunning man felt movement, but he could not tell how or whither. There were moans, but they might have been the blood soughing in his ears—

And the clammy fingers that twice plucked Old Nathan's garments could have come from his imagination alone. . . .

❖   ❖   ❖

"Thur's a couple horses comin' down the trail," called the mule. "Reckon thur's men with 'em too."

It was dawn, thought barely. Old Nathan was wrapped in his blanket, but he felt as stiff and cold as if he'd spent the night in the rain on a barn roof.

He threw his cover back. His feet were bare, and his boots stood upright at the foot of the blanket.

The mule stuck its head in the cabin's open door. "Wouldn't turn down some breakfast," it said. "Say, whur was it ye went last night?"

Old Nathan drew his boots on. "Don't know thet I did," he said as he stood up.

The mule snorted and backed away to allow the cunning man to pass him. "Don't give me thet," the beast said. "What d'ye take me fer, a horse? I watched fum the trees whilst you went down the well with thet feller. Didn't see ye come back, though."

Old Nathan kneaded the mane and neck muscles of his mule. The beast butted him and muttered contrarily, "Naow, thur's no cause fer this." It was happy for the attention nonetheless.

"If I was down thet place . . ." the cunning man said. He looked toward the well, but he thought about somewhere far more distant. "Thin I'm right glad I did come back, however thet was."

He strode toward the well.

"Hoy!" called the mule. "Ye forgit my breakfast!"

"I forgit nothing!" Old Nathan growled without turning around. "Ifen you come down here, yer majesty, I'll pull ye some water, though."

He had the third bucketful in the trough and the mule was drinking, when Bascom Hardy and his half-breed companion came around the bend in the trail. The bodyguard led. When Hardy saw that the cunning man was up and about, he pushed his horse past his servant's and trotted the short distance to the well.

"Waal, what did ye see, old man?" Bascom Hardy demanded.

He wore the same clothes he'd wore yesterday, and he'd slept in them. There was a wild look in his eyes that reminded Old Nathan of Hardy's brother Bynum; and reminded him also that there was more than hot iron as could torture a man.

"I seen yer brother," the cunning man said simply. "He's in a right bad place—"

"Told ye he tried t' cheat me of Pappy's prope'ty, didn't I?" the rich man crowed. He swung out of the saddle. "But where's the gold, thin, tell me thet?"

Hardy's horse, with a patch of mud on its side that hadn't been curried off, would have bumped Old Nathan on the way to the water if the cunning man hadn't stepped back. The mule raised its huge, bony head from the trough and said, "Tsk! Watch it, purty boy, er they'll find yer ribs in the middle uv next week."

"But I'm parched!" the horse whinnied.

"Let the poor feller drink, mule," the cunning man said. "He's jist the way he was born. Hain't nothin' he kin help."

"What's thet?" demanded Bascom Hardy. "What's thet you say?"

"Hit don't signify," Old Nathan said tiredly.

He rubbed his eyes, then met the rich man's nervous glare. Hardy shifted from one leg to the other, ready to bust with frustration.

"Bynum said where the gold was," the cunning man continued, "and ye'll hev thet in a moment, so don't git yer bowels in an uproar. But he said you're t' pay the money out t' all the folk he took it from. You would've took his papers off first thing whin he died, so I reckon you kin find a few of them folks, anyways."

Bascom Hardy's mouth gawped open and let out something between a snort and a hoot of laughter.

"Bynum was a fool airy day he lived," the rich man said. "But he warn't no sich fool as thet!"

His face hardened into fury. "What I figger," Hardy rasped, "is thet you reckon t' keep the gold fer yerse'f, old man. Well—"

He lifted his left hand and snapped his fingers. The half-breed cocked the hammer of his musket, though he kept the muzzle pointed down on the far side of his mare. Hardy's own walking horse skittered sideways in panic at the metallic warning.

"Oh, yer a fine brave crew," Old Nathan whispered. His voice sounded like a file setting up sawteeth. "Ye want the gold, d'ye? Well, I reckon you kin hev it."

Anger sluiced the stiffness out of the old man's joints. He stepped onto the well curb, then gripped the pivot log with both hands as he shouldered the nearer of the support poles aside.

"What's thet you're doin'?" Hardy demanded.

The pole gave enough for Old Nathan to spring the turned-down end of the pivot from the auger hole in the support. He pulled the log free, letting the well rope tumble down the shaft.

The pivot log was red oak. A heavy wood in all truth, but this was far heavier than wood.

The cunning man turned. Ned swung his musket over the mare's neck to half-point in the old man's direction.

"You do thet, boy," Old Nathan said. "And you better be quick with the way you use it."

"Ned," said Bascom Hardy. "There's no call . . ."

But the bodyguard had already hidden the weapon again, behind his body and the horse's.

Old Nathan reached over his head. His fingers touched, gripped . . . came out into open air with the bone-scaled case knife. He stood on the stone curb, smiling coldly and staring at Ned. The half-breed refused to meet his eyes.

The cunning man used the knife's larger blade to pry at the faint seam in the end of the pivot log. The plug dropped. The cavity within was the diameter of a man's fist. Bascom Hardy's breath drew in.

Old Nathan tilted the log and slid out the long leather poke that filled the hollow. It was so heavy that it clanked with a sound more like a smithy than a banker's till.

Hardy snatched the sack from the trampled dirt. "Ned," he gabbled in a high-pitched voice as he trotted up to the cabin, "you watch the door, ye hear me?"

The cunning man tossed the empty oak cylinder away and stepped to the ground. He didn't reckon Bascom Hardy meant him to follow to see what was in the poke; but—he smiled grimly at Ned, who twisted his face away to avoid the hard green eyes—he didn't reckon there'd be anyone try to stop him, neither.

He folded the blade and put his knife away.

The rich man trotted up the trail, but the sack's weight slowed him. Anyhow, Old Nathan's long legs had covered more miles in their time than Bascom Hardy had rode over. The two men reached the cabin together.

Hardy reached to close the door. The cunning man held the panel open with an arm as thin and hard as a hickory pole.

"Reckon you'll want light," Old Nathan said. "Lessen ye brung a tallow dip?"

The fury left the rich man's face. "No," he said. "I reckon the door kin stay."

The poke was folded three times at the neck, but it had no drawstring tie. Hardy opened the end and gently fed its contents onto the table like a farmer squeezing milk from a cow's udder.

The contents were gold, all gold but for one thin Spanish dollar.

"Oh . . ." the rich man sighed as he laid a glittering worm of coins across the surface of the rickety table.

There were twenty-dollar double eagles and every manner of other gold coins of the United States, but that was no more than half the assemblage. British guineas gleamed beside broad coins bearing the image of Maria Theresa, and the gold of a score of other nations and dynasties spilled across the table with them.

The folk who settled central Tennessee came from every part of Europe and from the world beyond. Those who had wealth brought it with them; and a part of that wealth had stuck to the fingers of Bynum Hardy. . . .

Old Nathan looked at the gold and looked at the face of Bascom Hardy; and began to pack his traps.

The rich man's fingers moved with the precision of a clock's escapement as he ordered the mingled coins into stacks and rows. Old Nathan rolled and tied his blanket, then gathered loose items and packed them in his budget.

He saved the sauce pan out. He'd scour that with water and sandy clay when he reached the well.

Gold chinked and whispered across the tabletop. Bascom Hardy did not look up.

"There's the matter uv my pay," the cunning man said.

Hardy started upward. For the first instant, his face bore the snarl of a fox surprised in a henhouse; but that passed as quickly as a lightning flash, leaving behind the stony haughtiness of a banker in his lair.

"Your pay, old feller?" Hardy said. "Show me the writing! I s'pect you know there's no contract between us, not so's any court 'ud find."

Old Nathan said nothing; only stared.

Bascom Hardy met the cunning man's eyes, then looked away.

"I'm a generous man," the rich man said. His fingers played across his stacks of gold, touching them as lightly as wisps of spidersilk trailing from the grass. "I wouldn't hev it said I didn't treat a man better thin the law requires."

He glanced up, meeting Old Nathan's eyes briefly, then looking down again. On the table before Hardy were eleven guineas in stacks of five and five and one. His sallow index finger touched the lone piece, then raised again to hover above the sheen of pale African gold.

With a convulsive movement, Bascom Hardy slid the Spanish dollar instead across the table toward the cunning man.

"There," the rich man said. "Take it 'n thankee. I'll tell all I come to thet you're a clever man. Thet'll be money in yer pocket so long as ye live."

Old Nathan took the eight-real coin between two fingers and turned it over. He set the silver piece back on the table.

"I tell ye!" Hardy said, his voice rising. "There's no contract! You cain't force me t' pay you airy a cent!"

Old Nathan picked up his saddlebags and pan in one hand, then paused in the doorway to take his rifle from where he'd leaned it.

"Hain't loaded," he said with a tiny smile. "Don't guess there's ought I'll meet t' worry me on the road back."

He walked out of the cabin. Hardy's bodyguard had dismounted by the cabin. He watched the cunning man sidelong, nervously lipping his moustache.

"Wait!" Bascom Hardy called from the doorway. "Take your pay. It's good silver!"

Old Nathan turned and looked at the rich man. "I reckon," the cunning man said, "hit may take a heap of money fer ye to get where ye desarve t' be. I wouldn't want ye to come up short."

As Old Nathan walked toward his mule, he whistled the air of a grim old ballad between his smiling teeth.

The Bullhead

"That don't half stink," grumbled the mule as Old Nathan came out of the shed with the saddle over his left arm and a bucket of bait in his right hand.

"Nobody asked you t' like it," the cunning man replied sharply. "Nor me neither, ifen it comes t' thet. It brings catfish like it's manna from hivven, and I do like a bit of smoked catfish fer supper."

"Waal, then," said the mule, "you go off t' yer fish and I'll mommick up some more oats while yer gone. Then we're both hap—"

The beast's big head turned toward the cabin and its ears cocked forward. "Whut's thet coming?" it demanded.

Old Nathan set the bucket down and hung the saddle over a fence rail. He'd been raised in a time when the Tennessee Territory was wilderness and the few folk you met liable to be wilder yet—the Whites worse than the Indians.

But that was long decades ago. He'd gotten out of the habit of always keeping his rifle close by and loaded. But a time like this, when somebody crept up so you didn't hear his horse on the trail—

Then you remembered that your rifle was in the cabin, fifty feet away, and that a man of seventy didn't move so quick as the boy of eighteen who'd aimed that same rifle at King's Mountain.

"Halloo the house?" called the visitor, and Old Nathan's world slipped back to this time of settlement and civilization. The voice was a woman's, not that of an ambusher who'd hitched his horse to a sapling back along the trail so as to shoot the cunning man unawares.

"We're out the back!" Old Nathan called. "Come through the cabin, or I'll come in t' ye."

It wasn't that he had enemies, exactly; but there were plenty folks around afraid of what the cunning man did—or what they thought he did. Fear had pulled as many triggers as hatred over the years, he guessed.

"T'morry's a good time t' traipse down t' the river," the mule said complacently as it thrust its head over the snake-rail fence to chop a tuft of grass just within its stretch. "Or never a'tall, that's better yet."

"We're goin' t' check my trot line t'day, sooner er later!" Old Nathan said over his shoulder. "Depend on it!"

Both doors of the one-room cabin were open. Old Nathan liked the ventilation, though the morning was cool. His visitor came out onto the back porch where the water barrel stood and said, "Oh, I didn't mean t' take ye away from business. You jest go ahead 'n I'll be on my way."

Her name was Ellie. Ellie Ransden, he reckoned, since she'd been living these three years past with Bully Ransden, though it wasn't certain they'd had a preacher

marry them. Lot of folks figured these old half-lettered
stump-hole preachers hereabouts, they weren't much
call to come between a couple of young people and
God no-ways.

Though she still must lack a year of twenty, Ellie
Ransden had a woman's full breasts and hips. Her hair,
black as thunder, was her glory. It was piled now on
top of her head with pins and combs, but if she shook
it out, it would be long enough to fall to the ground.

The combs were the only bit of fancy about the
woman. She wore a gingham dress and went barefoot,
with calluses to show that was usual for her till the
snow fell. Bully Ransden wasn't a lazy man, but he had
a hard way about him that put folk off, and he'd started
from less than nothing. . . .

If there was a prettier woman in the county than Ellie
Ransden, Old Nathan hadn't met her.

"Set yerse'f," Old Nathan grunted, nodding her back
into the cabin. "I'll warm some grounds."

"Hit don't signify," Ellie said. She looked up toward
a corner of the porch overhang where two sparrows
argued about which had stolen the thistle seed from
the other. "I jest figgered I'd drop by t' be neighborly,
but if you've got affairs . . . ?"

"The fish'll wait," said the cunning man, dipping a
gourd of water from the barrel. He'd drunk the coffee in the pot nigh down to the grounds already. "I
was jest talkin' t' my mule."

Ellie's explanation of what she was doing here was
a lie for at least several reasons. First, Bully Ransden
was no friend to the cunning man. Second, the two
cabins, Old Nathan's and Ransden's back some miles
on the main road, were close enough to be neighbors
in parts as ill-settled as these—but in the three years
past, Ellie hadn't felt the need to come down this way.

The last reason was the swollen redness at the

corners of the young woman's eyes. Mis'ry was what
brought folks most times t' see the cunning man, t' see
Old Nathan the Witch. Mis'ry and anger. . . .

Old Nathan poured water into the iron coffeepot on
the table of his one-room cabin. Some of last night's
coffee grounds, the beans bought green and roasted
in the fireplace, floated on the inch of liquid remaining. They'd have enough strength left for another
heating.

"Lots of folks, they talk t' their animals," he added
defensively as he hung the refilled pot on the swinging bar and pivoted it back over the fire. Not so many
thet hear what the beasts answer back, but thet was
nobody's affair save his own.

"Cullen ain't a bad man, ye know," Ellie Ransden
said in a falsely idle voice as she examined one of the
cabin's pair of glazed sash-windows.

Old Nathan set a knot of pitchy lightwood in the
coals to heat the fire up quickly. She was likely the only
soul in the county called Bully Ransden by his bap-
tized name. "Thet's for them t' say as knows him better
'n I do," he said aloud. "Or care t' know him."

"He was raised hard, thet's all," Ellie said to the
rectangles of window glass. "I reckon—"

She turned around and her voice rose in challenge,
though she probably didn't realize what was happening. "—thet you're afeerd t' cross him, same as airy
soul hereabouts?"

Old Nathan snorted. "I cain't remember the time
I met a man who skeerd me," he said. "Seeins as I've
got this old, I don't figger I'll meet one hereafter
neither."

He smiled, amused at the way he'd reacted to the
girl's—the woman's—obvious ploy. "Set," he offered,
gesturing her to the rocking chair.

Ellie moved toward the chair, then angled off in a

flutter of gingham like a butterfly unwilling to light for
nervousness. She stood near the fireplace, staring in
the direction of the five cups of blue-rimmed porcelain on the fireboard above the hearth. Her hands
twisted together instinctively as if she were attempting to strangle a snake.

"Reckon you heerd about thet Modom Taliaferro
down t' Oak Hill," she said.

Old Nathan seated himself in the rocker. There was
the straight chair beside the table if Ellie wanted it.
Now that he'd heard the problem, he didn't guess she
was going to settle.

"Might uv heard the name," the cunning man agreed.
"Lady from New Orleens, bought 'Siah Chesson's house
from his brother back in March after thet dead limb hit
'Siah."

Oak Hill, the nearest settlement, wasn't much, but
its dozen dwellings were mostly of saw-cut boards.
There was a store, a tavern, and several artisans who
supplemented their trade with farm plots behind the
houses.

Not a place where a wealthy, pretty lady from New
Orleans was likely to be found; but it might be that
Madame Francine Taliaferro didn't choose to be found
by some of those looking for her.

Ellie turned and glared at Old Nathan. "She's a
whore!" she blazed, deliberately holding his eyes.

Pitch popped loudly in the hearth. Old Nathan
rubbed his beard. "I ain't heard," he said mildly, "thet
the lady's sellin' merchandise of any sort."

"Then she's a witch," Ellie said, as firm as a treetrunk
bent the last finger's breadth before it snaps.

"Thet's a hard word," the cunning man replied. "Not
one t' spread where it mayn't suit."

He had no desire to hurt his visitor, but he wasn't
the man to tell a lie willingly; and he wasn't sure that

right now, a comforting lie wouldn't be the worse hurt.

"Myse'f," the cunning man continued, "I don't reckon she's any such a thing. I reckon she's a purty woman with money and big-city ways, and thet's all."

Ellie threw her hands to her face. "She's old!" the girl blubbered as she turned her back. "She mus' be thutty!"

Old Nathan got up from the rocker with the caution of age. "Yes ma'm," he agreed dryly. "I reckon thet's rightly so."

He looked at the fire to avoid staring at the back of the woman, shaking with sobs. "I reckon the coffee's biled," he said. "I like a cup t' steady myse'f in the mornings."

Ellie tugged a kerchief from her sleeve. She wiped her eyes, then blew her nose violently before she turned again.

"Why look et the time!" she said brightly. "Why, I need t' be runnin' off right now. Hit's my day t' bake light-bread fer Cullen, ye know."

Ellie's false, fierce smile was so broad that it squeezed another tear from the corner of her eye. She brushed the drop away with a knuckle, as though it had been a gnat about to bite.

"He's powerful picky about his vittles, my Cull is," she went on. "He all'us praises my cookin', though."

Ellie might have intended to say more, but her eyes scrunched down and her upper lip began to quiver with the start of another sob. She turned and scampered out the front door in a flurry of check-patterned skirt. "Thankee fer yer time!" she called as she ran up the trail.

Old Nathan sighed. He swung the bar off the fire, but he didn't feel any need for coffee himself just now. He looked out the door toward the empty trail.

And after a time, he walked to the pasture to resume saddling the mule.

The catfish was so large that its tail and barbel-fringed head both poked over the top of the oak-split saddle basket. "It ain't so easy, y'know," the mule complained as it hunched up the slope where the track from the river joined the main road, "when the load's unbalanced like that."

Old Nathan sniffed. "Ifen ye like," he said, "I'll put a ten-pound rock in t'other side t' give ye balance."

The mule lurched up onto the road. "Hey, watch it, ye old fool!" shouted a horseman, reining up from a canter. Yellow grit sprayed from beneath the horse's hooves.

Old Nathan cursed beneath his breath and dragged the mule's head around. There was no call fer a body t' be ridin' so blame fast where a road was all twists 'n tree roots—

But there was no call fer a blamed old fool t' drive his mule acrost thet road, without he looked first t' see what might be a'comin'.

"You damned old hazard!" the horseman shouted. His horse blew and stepped high in place, lifting its hooves as the dust settled. "I ought t' stand you on yer haid 'n drive you right straight int' the dirt like a tint-peg!"

"No, ye hadn't ought t' do thet, Bully Ransden," the cunning man replied. "And ye hadn't ought t' try, neither."

He muttered beneath his breath, then waved his left hand down through the air in an arc. A trail of colored light followed his fingertips, greens and blues and yellows, flickering and then gone. Only the gloom of late afternoon among the overhanging branches made such pale colors visible.

"But I'll tell ye I'm sorry I rid out in front of ye," Old Nathan added. "Thet ye do hev a right to."

He was breathing heavily with the effort of casting the lights. He could have fought Bully Ransden and not be any more exhausted—but he would have lost the fight. The display, trivial though it was in fact, set the younger man back in his saddle.

"Howdy, mule," said Ransden's horse. "How're things goin' down yer ways?"

"I guess ye think I'm skeered of yer tricks!" Ransden said. He patted the neck of his horse with his right hand, though just now the animal was calmer than the rider.

" 'Bout like common, I reckon," the mule replied. "Work, work, work, an' fer whut?"

"If yer not," Old Nathan replied in a cold bluster, "thin yer a fool, Ransden. And thet's as may be."

He raised his left hand again, though he had no intention of doing anything with it.

Now that Old Nathan had time to look, his eyes narrowed at the younger man's appearance. Ransden carried a fishing pole in his left hand. The ten-foot length of cane was an awkward burden for a horseman hereabouts—where even the main road was a pair of ruts, and branches met overhead most places.

Despite the pole, Bully Ransden wasn't dressed for fishing. He wore a green velvet frock coat some sizes too small for his broad shoulders, and black storebought trousers as well. His shirt alone was homespun, but clean and new. The garment was open well down the front so that the hair on Ransden's chest curled out in a vee against the gray-white fabric.

"Right now," the mule continued morosely, "we been off loadin' fish. Whutiver good was a fish t' airy soul, I ask ye?"

"Waal," Ransden said, "I take yer 'pology. See thet ye watch yerse'f the nixt time."

"I'm headed inter the sittlement," said the horse in satisfaction. "I allus git me a feed uv oats there, I do."

"Goin' into the settlement, thin?" Old Nathan asked, as if it were no more than idle talk between two men who'd met on the road.

The cunning man and Bully Ransden had too much history between them to be no more than that, though. Each man was unique in the county—known by everyone and respected, but feared as well.

Old Nathan's art set him apart from others. Bully Ransden had beaten his brutal father out of the cabin when he was eleven. Since that time, fists and knotted muscles had been the Bully's instant reply to any slight or gibe directed at the poverty from which he had barely raised himself—or the fact he was the son of a man hated and despised by all in a land where few angels had settled.

Old Nathan's mouth quirked in a smile. He and Ransden were stiff-necked men, as well, who both claimed they didn't care what others thought so long as they weren't interfered with. There was some truth to the claim as well. . . .

"I reckon I might head down thet way," Ransden said, as though there was ought else in the direction he was heading. "Might git me some supper t' Shorty's er somewhere."

He took notice of the mule's saddle baskets and added, "Say, old man—thet's a fine catfish ye hev there."

"Thet's right," Old Nathan agreed. "I figger t' fry me a steak t'night 'n smoke the rest."

"Hmph," the mule snorted, looking sidelong up at the cunning man. "Wish thut some of us iver got oats t' eat."

"I might buy thet fish offen ye," Ransden said. "I've got a notion t' take some fish back fer supper t'morry. How much 'ud ye take fer him?"

"Hain't intersted in sellin'," Old Nathan said, his eyes narrowing again. "Didn't figger airy soul as knew Shorty 'ud et his food—or drink the pizen he calls whiskey. I'd uv figgered ye'd stay t' home t'night. Hain't nothin' so good as slab uv hot bread slathered with butter."

Bully Ransden flushed, and the tendons of his bull neck stood out like cords. "You been messin' about my Ellie, old man?" he asked.

The words were almost unintelligible. Emotion choked Ransden's voice the way ice did streams during the spring freshets.

Old Nathan was careful not to raise his hand. A threat that might forestall violence at a lower emotional temperature would precipitate it with the younger man in his current state. Nothing would stop Bully Ransden now if he chose to attack; nothing but a bullet in the brain, and that might not stop him soon enough to save his would-be victim.

"I know," the cunning man said calmly, "what I know. D'ye doubt thet, Bully Ransden?"

The horse stretched out his neck to browse leaves from a sweet-gum sapling which had sprouted at the edge of the road. Ransden jerked his mount back reflexively, but the movement took the danger out of a situation cocked and primed to explode.

Ransden looked away. "Aw, hit's no use t' talk to an old fool like you," he muttered. "I'll pick up a mess uv bullheads down t' the sittlement. Gee-up, horse!"

He spurred his mount needlessly hard. As the horse sprang down the road with a startled complaint, Ransden shouted over his shoulder, "I'm a grown man! Hit's no affair of yourn where I spend my time—nor Ellie's affair neither!"

Old Nathan watched the young man go. He was still staring down the road some moments after Ransden had disappeared. The mule said in a disgusted voice, "I wouldn't mind t' get back to a pail of oats, old man."

"Git along, thin," the cunning man said. "Fust time I ever knowed ye t' be willing t' do airy durn thing."

But his heart wasn't in the retort.

The cat came in, licking his muzzle both with relish and for the purpose of cleanliness. "Found the fish guts in the mulch pile," he said. "Found the head too. Thankee."

"Thought ye might like hit," said Old Nathan as he knelt, adding sticks of green hickory to his fire. "Ifen ye didn't, the corn will next Spring."

The big catfish, cleaned and split open, lay on the smokeshelf just below the throat of the fireplace. Most folk, they had separate smokehouses—vented or chinked tight, that was a matter of taste. Even so, the fireplace smokeshelf was useful for bits of meat that weren't worth stoking up a smoker meant for whole hogs and deer carcases.

As for Old Nathan—he wasn't going to smoke and eat a hog any more than he was going to smoke and eat a human being . . . though there were plenty hogs he'd met whose personalities would improve once their throats were slit.

Same was true of the humans, often enough.

Smoke sprouted from the underside of the hickory billet and hissed up in a sheet. Trapped water cracked its way to the surface with a sound like that of a percussion cap firing.

"Don't reckon there's an uglier sight in the world 'n a catfish head," said the cat as he complacently groomed his right forepaw. He spread the toes and extended the white, hooked claws, each of them needle sharp. "A passel uv good meat to it, though."

"Don't matter what a thing looks like," Old Nathan said, "so long's it tastes right." He sneezed violently, backed away from his fire, and sneezed again.

"Thought I might go off fer a bit," he added to no one in particular.

The cat chuckled and began to work on the other paw. "Chasin' after thet bit uv cunt come by here this mornin', are ye? Give it up, ole man. You're no good t' the split-tails."

"Ye think thet's all there is, thin?" the cunning man demanded. "Ifen I don't give her thet one help, there's no he'p thet matters a'tall?"

"Thet's right," the cat said simply. He began licking his genitals with his hind legs spread wide apart. His belly fur was white, while the rest of his body was yellow to tigerishly orange.

Old Nathan sighed. "I used t' think thet way myse'f," he admitted as he carried his tin wash basin out to the back porch. Bout time t' fill the durn water barrel from the creek; but thet 'ud wait. . . .

"Used t' think?" the tomcat repeated. "Used t' know, ye mean. Afore ye got yer knackers shot away."

"I knowed a girl a sight like Ellie Ransden back thin . . ." Old Nathan muttered.

The reflection in the water barrel was brown, the underside of the shakes covering the porch. Old Nathan bent to dip a basinful with the gourd scoop. He saw his own face, craggy and hard. His beard was still black, though he wouldn't see seventy again.

Then, though he hadn't wished it—he thought—and he hadn't said the words—aloud—there was a woman's face, young and full-lipped and framed in hair as long and black as the years since last he'd seen her, the eve of marching off with Colonel Sevier to what ended at King's Mountain. . . .

"Jes' turn 'n let me see ye move, Slowly," Old

Nathan whispered to his memories. "There's nairy a thing so purty in all the world."

The reflection shattered. The grip of the cunning man's right hand had snapped the neck of the gourd. The hollowed body fell into the barrel.

Old Nathan straightened, wiping his eyes and forehead with the back of his hand. He tossed the gourd neck off the porch. "Niver knew why her folks, they named her thet, Slowly," he muttered. "Ifen it was them 'n not a name she'd picked herse'f."

The cat hopped up onto the cane seat of the rocking chair. He poised there for a moment, allowing the rockers to return to balance before he settled himself.

"I'll tell ye a thing, though, cat," the cunning man said forcefully. "Afore King's Mountain, I couldn't no more talk t' you an' t' other animals thin I could talk t' this hearth rock."

The tomcat curled his full tail over his face, then flicked it barely aside.

"Afore ye got yer knackers blowed off, ye mean?" the cat said. The discussion wasn't of great concern to him, but he demanded precise language nonetheless.

"Aye," Old Nathan said, glaring at the animal. "Thet's what I mean."

The cat snorted into his tail fur. "Thin you made a durned bad bargain, old man," he said.

Old Nathan tore his eyes away from the cat. The tin basin was still in his left hand. He sighed and hung it up unused.

"Aye," he muttered. "I reckon I did, cat."

He went out to saddle the mule again.

Ransden's cabin had a single door, in the front. It was open, but there was no sign of life within.

Old Nathan dismounted and wrapped the reins around the porch rail.

"Goin' t' water me?" the mule snorted.

"In my own sweet time, I reckon," the cunning man snapped back.

"Cull?" Ellie Ransden called from the cabin. "Cullen?" she repeated as she swept to the door. Her eyes were swollen and tear-blurred; they told her only that the figure at the front of her cabin wasn't her man. She ducked back inside—and reappeared behind a long flintlock rifle much like the one which hung on pegs over Old Nathan's fireboard.

"Howdy," said the cunning man. "Didn't mean t' startle ye, Miz Ransden."

Old Nathan spoke as calmly as though it were an everyday thing for him to look down the small end of a rifle. It wasn't. It hadn't been for many years, and that was a thing he didn't regret in the least about the passing of the old days.

"Oh!" she said, coloring in embarrassment. "Oh, do please come in. I got coffee, ifen hit ain't biled dry by now."

She lifted the rifle's muzzle before she lowered the hammer. The trigger dogs made a muted double click in releasing the mainspring's tension.

Ellie bustled quickly inside, fully a housewife again. "Oh, law!" she chirped as she set the rifle back on its pegs. "Here the fust time we git visitors in I don't know, and everything's all sixes 'n sevens!"

The cabin was neat as a pin, all but the bed where the eagle-patterned quilt was disarrayed. It didn't take art to see that Ellie had flung herself there crying, then jumped up in the hope her man had come home.

Bully Ransden must have knocked the furniture together himself. Not fancy, but it was all solid work, pinned with trenails rather than iron. There were two chairs, a table, and the bed. Three chests held clothes and acted as additional seats—though from what Ellie had blurted, the couple had few visitors, which was no surprise with Bully Ransden's reputation.

The windows in each end wall had shutters but no glazing. Curtains, made from sacking and embroidered with bright pink roses, set off their frames.

The rich odor of fresh bread filled the tiny room.

"Oh, law, what hev I done?" Ellie moaned as she looked at the fireplace.

The dutch oven sat on coals raked to the front of the hearth. They'd burned down, and the hotter coals pilled onto the cast iron lid were now a mass of fluffy white ash. Ellie grabbed fireplace tongs and lifted the lid away.

"Oh, hit's ruint!" the girl said.

Old Nathan reached into the oven and cracked the bread loose from the surface of the cast iron. The loaf had contracted slightly as it cooled. It felt light, more like biscuit than bread, and the crust was a brown as deep as a walnut plank.

"Don't look ruint t' me," he said as he lifted the loaf to one of the two pewter plates sitting ready on the table. "Looks right good. I'd admire t' try a piece."

Ellie Ransden picked up a knife with a well-worn blade. Unexpectedly, she crumpled into sobs. The knife dropped. It stuck in the cabin floor between the woman's bare feet, unnoticed as she bawled into her hands.

Old Nathan stepped around the table and touched Ellie's shoulders to back her away. Judging from how the light played, the butcher knife had an edge that would slice to the bone if she kicked it. The way the gal carried on, she might not notice the cut—and she might not care if she did.

"I'm ugly!" Ellie cried as she wrapped her arms

around Old Nathan. "I cain't blame him, I've got t' be an old frumpy thing 'n he don't love me no more!"

For the moment, she didn't know who she held, just that he was warm and solid. She could talk at the cunning man, whether he listened or not.

"Tain't thet," Old Nathan muttered, feeling awkward as a hog on ice. One of the high-backed tortoiseshell combs that held and ornamented Ellie's hair tickled his beard. "Hit's jest the newness. Not thet he don't love ye. . . ."

He spoke the words because they were handy; but as he heard them come out, he guessed they were pretty much the truth. "Cullen ain't a bad man," the girl had said, back to the cunning man's cabin. No worse 'n most men, the cunning man thought, and thet's a durned poor lot.

"Don't reckon there's a purtier girl in the county," Old Nathan said aloud. "Likely there's not in the whole blame state."

Ellie squeezed him firmly, this time a conscious action, and stepped back. She reached into her sleeve for her handkerchief, then saw it crumpled on the quilt where she'd been lying. She snatched up the square of linen, turned aside, and blew her nose firmly.

"You're a right good man," Ellie mumbled before she looked around again.

She raised her chin and said, pretending that her face was not flushed and tear-streaked, "Ifen it ain't me, hit's thet bitch down t' the sittlement. Fer a month hit's been Francine this 'n Francine that an' him spendin' the ev'nins out an' thin—"

Ellie's upper lip trembled as she tumbled out her recent history. The cunning man bent to tug the butcher knife from the floor and hide his face from the woman's.

"She witched him, sir!" Ellie burst out. "I heerd what

you said up t' yer cabin, but I tell ye, she witched my Cull. He ain't like this!"

Old Nathan rose. He set the knife down, precisely parallel to the edge of the table, and met the woman's eyes. "Yer Cull ain't the fust man t' go where his pecker led," he said, harshly to be able to get the words out of his own throat. "Tain't witch'ry, hit's jest human natur. An' don't be carryin' on, 'cause he'll be back— sure as the leaves turn."

Ellie wrung her hands together. The handkerchief was a tiny ball in one of them. "Oh, d' ye think he will, sir?" she whispered. "Oh, sir, could ye give me a charm t' bring him back? I'd be iver so grateful. . . ."

She looked down at her hands. Her lips pressed tightly together while silent tears dripped again from her eyes.

Old Nathan broke eye contact. He shook his head slightly and said, "No, I won't do thet."

"But ye could?" Ellie said sharply. The complex of emotions flowing across her face hardened into anger and determination. The woman who was wife to Bully Ransden could either be soft as bread dough or as strong and supple as a hickory pole. There was nothing in between—

And there was nothing soft about Ellie Ransden.

"I reckon ye think I couldn't pay ye," she said. "Waal, ye reckon wrong. There's my combs—"

She tossed her head; the three combs of translucent tortoiseshell, decorative but necessary as well to hold a mass of hair like Ellie's, quivered as they caught the light.

"Rance Holden, he'd buy thim back fer stock, I reckon. Mebbe thet Modom Francine—" the viciousness Ellie concentrated in the words would have suited a mother wren watching a blacksnake near her chicks "—'ud want thim fer her hair. And there's my Pappy's watch, too, thet Cullen wears now. Hit'll fetch somethin', I reckon, the case, hit's true gold."

She swallowed, chin regally high—but looking so young and vulnerable that Old Nathan wished the world were a different place than he knew it was and always would be.

"So, Mister Cunning Man," Ellie said. "I reckon I kin raise ten silver dollars. Thet's good pay fer some li'l old charm what won't take you nothin' t' make."

"I don't need yer money," Old Nathan said gruffly. "Hain't thet. I'm tellin' ye, hit's wrong t' twist folks around thet way. Ifen ye got yer Cullen back like thet, ye wouldn't like what it was ye hed. An' I ain't about t' do thet thing!"

"Thin you better go on off," Ellie said. "I'm no sort uv comp'ny t'day."

She flung herself onto the bed, burying her face in the quilt. She was sobbing.

Old Nathan bit his lower lip as he stepped out of the cabin. "Hit warn't the world I made, hit's jest the one I live in."

"Leastways when ye go fishin'," the mule grumbled from the porch rail, "thur's leaves t' browse."

Wouldn't hurt him t' go see Madame Taliaferro with his own eyes, he reckoned.

Inside the cabin the girl cried, "Oh why cain't I jes' die, I'm so miser'ble!"

For as little good as he'd done, Old Nathan guessed he might better have stayed to home and saved himself and his mule a ride back in the dark.

The sky was pale from the recently set sun, but the road was in shadows. They would be deeper yet by the time the cunning man reached the head of the track to his cabin. The mule muttered a curse every time it clipped a hoof in a rut, but it didn't decide to balk.

The bats began their everlasting refrain, "Dilly, dilly, come and be killed," as they quartered the air above the road. Thet peepin' nonsense was enough t' drive a feller t' distraction—er worse!

Just as well the mule kept walking. This night, Old Nathan was in a mood to speak phrases that would blast the bones right out of the durned old beast.

Somebody was coming down the road from Oak Hill, singing merrily. It took a moment to catch actual phrases of the song, " . . . went a-courtin', he did ride . . ." and a moment further to identify the voice as Bully Ransden's.

" . . . an' pistol by his side, uh-huh!"

Ransden came around the next bend in the trail, carrying not the bottle Old Nathan expected in his free hand but rather a stringer of bullheads. He'd left the long cane pole behind somewhere during the events of the evening.

"Hullo, mule," Ransden's horse whinnied. "Reckon I ate better'n you did t'night."

"Hmph," grunted the mule. "Leastways my master ain't half-shaved an' goin' t' ride me slap inter a ditch 'fore long."

"Howdy, feller," Bully Ransden caroled. "Ain't it a fine ev'nin'?"

Ransden wasn't drunk, maybe, but he sure-hell didn't sound like the man he'd been since he grew up—which was about age eleven, when he beat his father out of the cabin with an ax handle.

"Better fer some thin others, I reckon," Old Nathan replied. He clucked the mule to the side, giving the horseman the room he looked like he might need.

Ransden's manner changed as soon as he heard the cunning man's voice. "So hit's you, is it, old man?" he said.

He tugged hard on his reins, twisting his mount

across the road in front of Old Nathan. "Hey, easy on!" the horse complained. "No call fer thet!"

"D'ye figger t' spy on me, feller?" Ransden demanded, turned crossways in his saddle. He shrugged his shoulders, straining the velvet jacket dangerously. "Or—"

Bully Ransden didn't carry a gun, but there was a long knife in his belt. Not that he'd need it. Ransden was young and strong enough to break a fence rail with his bare hands, come to that. He'd do the same with Old Nathan, for all that the cunning man had won his share of fights in his youth—

And later. It was a hard land still, though statehood had come thirty years past.

"I'm ridin' on home, Cullen Ransden," Old Nathan said. "Reckon ye'd do well t' do the same."

"By God," said Ransden. "By God! Where you been to, old man? Hev you been sniffin' round my Ellie? By God, if she's been—"

The words echoed in Old Nathan's mind, where he heard them an instant before they were spoken.

The power that poured into the cunning man was nothing that he had summoned. It wore him like a cloak, responding to the threat Bully Ransden was about to voice.

"—slippin' around on me, I'll wring the bitch's—"

Old Nathan raised both hands. Thunder crashed in the clear sky, then rumbled away in diminishing chords.

The power was nothing to do with the cunning man, but he shaped it as a potter shapes clay on his wheel. He spread his fingers. The tree trunks and roadway glowed with a light as faint as foxfire. It was just enough to throw each rut and bark ridge into relief, as though they were reflecting the pale sky.

"Great God Almighty!" muttered Bully Ransden. His mouth fell open. The string of small fish in his left hand trembled slightly.

"Ye'll do what to thet pore little gal, Bully Ransden?" the cunning man asked in a harsh, cracked voice.

Ransden touched his lips with his tongue. He tossed his head as if to clear it. "Reckon I misspoke," he said; not loud but clearly, and he met Old Nathan's eyes as he said the words.

"Brag's a good dog, Ransden," Old Nathan said. "But Hold-fast is better."

He lowered his arms. The vague light and the last trembling of thunder had already vanished.

The mule turned and stared back at its rider with one bulging eye. "Whut in tar-nation was that?" it asked.

Bully Ransden clucked to his hose. He pressed with the side, not the spur, of his right boot to swing the beast back in line with the road. "Don't you think I'm afeerd t' meet you, old man," he called; a little louder than necessary, and at a slightly higher pitch than intended.

Ransden was afraid; but that wouldn't keep him from facing the cunning man, needs must—

As surely as Old Nathan would have faced the Bully's fists and hobnailed boots some moments earlier.

The rushing, all-mastering power was gone now, leaving Old Nathan shaken and as weak as a man wracked with a three-days flux. "Jest go yer way, Ransden," he muttered, "and I'll go mine. I don't wish fer any truck with you."

He heeled the mule's haunches and added, "Git on with ye, thin, mule."

The mule didn't budge. "I don't want no part uv these doins," it protested. "Felt like hit was a dad-blame thunderbolt sittin' astride me, hit did."

Ransden walked his nervous horse abreast of the cunning man. "I don't know why I got riled no-how," he said, partly for challenge but mostly just in the brutal banter natural to the Bully's personality. "Hain't as though you're a man, now, is it?"

He spurred his horse off down the darkened trail, laughing merrily.

Old Nathan trembled, gripping the saddle horn with both hands. "Git on, mule," he muttered. "I hain't got the strength t' fight with ye."

Faintly down the road drifted the words, "Froggie wint a-courtin', he did ride . . ."

Bright midday sun dappled the white-painted boards of the Isiah Chesson house. It was a big place for this end of the country, with two rooms below and a loft. In addition, there was a stable and servant's quarters at the back of the lot. How big it seemed to Madame Francine Taliaferro, late of New Orleans, was another matter.

"Whoa-up, mule," Old Nathan muttered as he peered at the dwelling. It sat a musket shot down the road and around a bend from the next house of the Oak Hill settlement. The front door was closed, and there was no sign of life behind the curtains added to the windows since the new tenant moved in.

Likely just as well. The cunning man wanted to observe Madame Taliaferro, but barging up to her door and knocking didn't seem a useful way to make her introduction.

Still. . . .

In front of the house was a well-manicured lawn. A pair of gray squirrels, plump and clothed in fur grown sleekly full at the approach of Fall, hopped across the lawn—and over the low board fence which had protected Chesson's sauce garden, now grown up in vines.

"Hoy, squirrel!" Old Nathan called. "Is the lady what lives here t' home?"

The nearer squirrel hopped up on his hind legs, looking in all directions. "What's thet? What's thet I heard?" he chirped.

"Yer wastin' yer time," the mule said. "Hain't a squirrel been born yet whut's got brain enough t' tell whether hit's rainin'."

"He's talkin' t' ye," the other squirrel said as she continued to snuffle across the short grass of the lawn. "He says, is the lady home t' the house?"

The male squirrel blinked. "Huh?" he said to his mate. "What would I be doin' in a house?" He resumed a tail-high patrol which seemed to ignore the occasional hickory nuts lying in the grass.

"Told ye so," the mule commented.

Old Nathan scowled. Boards laid edgewise set off a path from the front door to the road. A pile of dog droppings marked the gravel.

"Squirrel," the cunning man said. "Is there a little dog t' home, now?"

"What?" the male squirrel demanded. "Whur is it? Thet nasty little monster's come back!"

"Now, don't ye git yerse'f all stirred up!" his mate said. "Hit's all right, hit's gone off down the road already."

"Thankee, squirrels," Old Nathan said. "Git on, mule."

"Ifen thet dog's not here, thin whyiver did he say it was?" the male squirrel complained loudly.

"We could uv done thet a'ready, ye know," the mule said as he ambled on toward the main part of town. "Er we could uv stayed t' home."

"Thet's right," Old Nathan said grimly. "We could."

He knew he was on a fool's errand, because only a durned fool would think Francine Taliaferro might be using some charm or other on the Ransden boy. He didn't need a mule to tell him.

Rance Holden's store was the center of Oak Hill,

unless you preferred to measure from Shorty Hitchcock's tavern across the one dirt street. Holden's building was gable-end to the road. The store filled the larger square room, while Rance and his wife lived in the low rectangular space beneath the eaves overhanging to the left.

The family's space had been tight when the Holdens had children at home. The five boys and the girl who survived were all moved off on their own by now.

"Don't you tie me t' the rail thur," the mule said. "Somebody 'll spit t'baccy at me sure."

"Thin they'll answer t' me," the cunning man said. "But seeins as there's nobody on the porch, I don't figger ye need worry."

Four horses, one with a side-saddle, were hitched to the rail. Usually there were several men sitting on the board porch among barrels of bulk merchandise, chewing tobacco and whittling; but today they were all inside. That was good evidence that Madame Francine Taliaferro was inside as well. . . .

The interior of Holden's store was twelve foot by twelve foot. Not spacious by any standard, it was now packed with seven adults—

And a pug dog who tried to fill as much space as the humans.

"Hey, you old bastard!" the dog snapped as the cunning man stepped through the open door. "I'm going to bite you till you bleed, and there's nothing you can do about it!"

"Howdy Miz Holden, Rance," Old Nathan said. "Thompson—" a nod to the saddler, a cadaverous man with a full beard but no hair above the level of his ears "—Bart—" another nod, this time to the settlement's miller, Bart Alpers—

"I'm going to bite you!" the little dog yapped as it lunged forward and dodged back. "I'll do just that, and you don't dare to stop me!"

Nods, murmured howdies/yer keepin' well from the folk who crowded the store.

"—'n Mister M'Donald," the cunning man said with a nod for the third white man, a husky, hard-handed man who'd made a good thing of a tract ten miles out from the settlement. M'Donald looked even sillier in an ill-fitting blue tailcoat than Bully Ransden had done in his finery the evening before.

Madame Taliaferro's black servant, on the other hand, wore his swallowtail coat, ruffed shirt, and orange breeches with an air of authority. He stood behind his mistress, with his eyes focused on infinity and his hands crossed behind his back.

"Now, Cesar," the woman who was the center of the store's attention murmured to her dog. She looked at Old Nathan with an unexpected degree of appraisal. "Baby be good for ma-ma."

"Said I'm going to bite you!" insisted the dog. "Here goes!"

Old Nathan whispered inaudible words with his teeth in a tight smile. The little dog did jump forward to bite his pants leg, sure as the Devil was loose in the world.

The dog froze.

"Mum," Old Nathan said as he reached down and scooped the dog up in his hand. The beast's mouth was open. Sudden terror filled its nasty little eyes.

Francine Taliaferro had lustrous dark hair—not a patch on Ellie's, but groomed in a fashion the younger woman's could never be. Her face was pouty-pretty, heavily powdered and rouged, and the skirt of her blue organdy dress flared out in a fashion that made everyone else in the store stand around like the numbers on a clock dial with her the hub.

But that's what it would have been anyway; only perhaps with the others pressing in yet closer.

Old Nathan handed the stiffened dog to Madame Taliaferro. "Hain't he the cutest li'l thing?" the cunning man said.

The woman's red lips opened in shock, but by reflex her gloved hands accepted the petrified animal that was thrust toward her. As soon as Old Nathan's fingers no longer touched the animal's fur, the dog resumed where it had stopped. Its teeth snapped into its mistress's white shoulder.

Three of the men shouted. Madame Taliaferro screamed in outrage and flung Cesar up into the roof shakes. The dog bounced down into a shelf of yard goods, then ran out the door. It was yapping unintelligibly.

Old Nathan smiled. "Jest cute as a button."

There was no more magic in this woman than there was truth in a politician's heart. If Ellie had a complaint, it was against whatever fate had led a woman— a lady—so sophisticated to Oak Hill.

And complaint agin Bully Ransden, fer bein' a durned fool; but folks were, men 'n women both. . . .

"By God!" M'Donald snarled. "I oughter break ye in two fer thet!"

He lurched toward the cunning man but collided with Alpers, who cried, "I won't let ye fall!" as he tried to grab the woman. Rance Holden tried to crawl out from behind the counter while his wife glared, and Thompson blathered as though somebody had just fallen into a mill saw.

"Everyone stop this at once!" Madame Taliaferro cried with her right index finger held upright. Her voice was as clear and piercing as a well-tuned bell.

Everyone did stop. All eyes turned toward the woman; which was no doubt as things normally were in Madame Taliaferro's presence.

"I'll fetch yer dog," blurted Bart Alpers.

"Non!" Taliaferro said. "Cesar must have had a little cramp. He will stay outside till he is better."

"Warn't no cramp, Francine, honey," M'Donald growled. "Hit war this sonuvabitch here what done it!" He pushed Alpers aside.

"What d'ye reckon happint t' Cesar, M'Donald?" Old Nathan said. The farmer was younger by thirty years and strong, but he hadn't the personality to make a threat frightening even when he spoke the flat truth. "D'ye want t' touch me 'n larn?"

M'Donald stumbled backward from the bluff—for it was all bluff, what Old Nathan had done to the dog had wrung him out bad as lifting a quarter of beef. But the words had this much truth in them: those who struck the cunning man would pay for the blow, in one way or another; and pay in coin they could ill afford.

"I don't believe we've been introduced," said the woman. She held out her hand. The appraisal was back in her eyes. "I'm Francine Taliaferro, but do call me Francine. I'm—en vacance in your charming community."

"He ain't no good t' ye," M'Donald muttered bitterly, his face turned to a display of buttons on a piece of card.

The cunning man took Taliaferro's hand, though he wasn't rightly sure what she expected him to do with it. There were things he knew, plenty of things and important ones; but right just now, he understood why other men reacted as they did to Francine Taliaferro.

"M' name's Nathan. I live down the road a piece, Columbia ways."

Even a man with a woman like Ellie waiting at home for him.

"I reckon this gen'lman come here t' do business,

Rance," said Mrs. Holden to her husband in a poison-
ous tone of voice. "Don't ye reckon ye ought t' he'p
him?"

"I'll he'p him, Maude," Holden muttered, trying—
and he knew he would fail—to interrupt the rest of
the diatribe. He was a large, soft man, and his hair had
been white for years. "Now, how kin—"

"Ye are a storekeeper, ain't ye?" Mrs. Holden
shrilled. "Not some spavined ole fool thinks spring has
come again!"

Holden rested his hands on the counter. His eyes
were downcast. One of the other men chuckled. "Now,
Nathan," the storekeeper resumed. "Reckon you're here
fer more coffee?"

The cunning man opened his mouth to say he'd take
a peck of coffee and another of baking soda. He didn't
need either just now, but he'd use them both and they'd
serve as an excuse for him to have come into Oak Hill.

"Ye've got an iv'ry comb," he said. The words he
spoke weren't the ones he'd had in mind at all. "Reckon
I'll hev thet and call us quits fer me clearin' the rats
outen yer barn last fall."

Everyone in the store except Holden himself stared
at Old Nathan. The storekeeper winced and, with his
eyes still on his hands, said, "I reckon thet comb, hit
must hev been sold. I'd like t' he'p ye."

"Whoiver bought thet thing!" cried the storekeeper's
wife in amazement. She turned to the niche on the wall
behind the counter, where items of special value were
flanked to either side by racks of yard goods. The two crystal
goblets remained, but they had been moved inward to
cover the space where the ornate ivory comb once stood.

Mrs. Holden's eyes narrowed. "Rance Holden, you
go look through all the drawers this minute. Nobody
bought thet comb and you know it!"

"Waal, mebbe hit was stole," Holden muttered. He

half-heartedly pulled out one of the drawers behind the counter and poked with his fingers at the hairpins and brooches within.

The cunning man smiled grimly. "Reckon I kin he'p ye," he said.

He reached over the counter and took one of the pins, ivory like the comb for which he was searching. The pin's blunt end was flattened and drilled into a filigree for decoration. He held the design between the tips of his index fingers, pressing just hard enough to keep the pin pointed out horizontally.

"What is this that you are doing, then?" Francine Taliaferro asked in puzzlement.

The other folk in the store knew Old Nathan. Their faces were set in gradations between fear and interest, depending on the varied fashions in which they viewed the cunning man's arts.

Old Nathan swept the pin over the counter. Midway it dipped, then rose again.

"Check the drawers there," the cunning man directed. He moved the hairpin back until it pointed straight down. "Reckon hit's in the bottom one."

"Why, whut would that iv'ry pin be doin' down there with the women's shoes?" Mrs. Holden demanded.

"Look, I tell ye, I'll pay ye cash fer what ye did with the rats," the storekeeper said desperately. "How much 'ud ye take? Jest name—"

He was standing in front of the drawer Old Nathan had indicated. His wife jerked it open violently, banging it against Holden's instep twice and a third time until he hopped away, wincing.

Mrs. Holden straightened, holding a packet wrapped with tissue paper and blue ribbon. It was of a size to contain the comb.

She started to undo the ribbon. Her face was red with fury.

Old Nathan put his hand out. "Reckon I'll take it the way i'tis," he said.

"How d'ye guess the comb happint t' be all purtied up 'n hid like thet, Rance?" Bart Alpers said loudly. "Look to me like hit were a present fer som'body, if ye could git her alone."

Francine Taliaferro raised her chin. "I know nothing of this," she said coldly.

Rance Holden took the packet from his wife's hands and gave it to Old Nathan. "I figger this makes us quits fer the rats," he said in a dull voice. He was slumped like a man who'd been fed his breakfast at the small end of a rifle.

"Thankee," Old Nathan said. "I reckon thet does."

The shouting behind him started before the cunning man had unhitched his mule. The timbre of Mrs. Holden's voice was as sharp and cutting as that of Francine Taliaferro's lapdog.

Taking the comb didn't make a lick of sense, except that it showed the world what a blamed fool God had made of Rance Holden.

Old Nathan rode along, muttering to himself. It would have been awkward to carry the packet in his hand, but once he'd set the fancy bit of frippery down into a saddle basket, that didn't seem right either.

Might best that he sank the durn thing in the branch, because there wasn't ought he could do with the comb that wouldn't make him out to be a worse fool than Rance. . . .

The mule was following its head onto the cabin trail. Suddenly its ears cocked forward and its leading foot hesitated a step. Through the woods came, "Froggie wint a-courtin', he did ride. . . ."

"Hey, thur!" called the mule.

"Oh, hit's you come back, is it?" Bully Ransden's horse whinnied in reply. "I jest been down yer way."

Horse and mule came nose to nose around a bend fringed by dogwood and alders. The riders watched one another: Old Nathan stiff and ready for trouble, but the younger man as cheerful as a cat with a mouse for a toy.

"Glad t' see ye, Nathan old feller," Bully Ransden said.

He kneed his mount forward to bring himself alongside the cunning man, left knee to left knee. The two men were much of a height, but the horse stood taller than the mule and increased the impression of Ransden's far greater bulk. "I jest dropped by in a neighborly way," he continued, "t' warn ye there's been prowlers up t' my place. Ye might want t' stick close about yer own."

He grinned. His teeth were square and evenly set. They had taken the nose off a drover who'd wrongly thought he was a tougher man than Bully Ransden.

This afternoon Ransden wore canvas breeches and a loose-hanging shirt of gray homespun. The garment's cut had the effect of emphasizing Bully's muscular build, whereas the undersized frock coat had merely made him look constrained.

"I thankee," Old Nathan said stiffly. He wished Bully Ransden would stop glancing toward the saddle basket, where he might notice the ribbon-tied packet. "Reckon I kin deal with sech folk as sneak by whin I'm gone."

He wished he were forty years younger, and even then he'd be a lucky man to avoid being crippled in a rough and tumble with Bully Ransden. This one was cat-quick, had shoulders like an ox . . . and once the fight started, Bully Ransden didn't quit so long as the other fellow still could move.

Ransden's horse eyed Old Nathan, then said to the mule, "Yer feller ain't goin' t' do whativer hit was he did last night, is he? I cain't much say I liked thet."

"Didn't much like hit myse'f," the mule agreed morosely. "He ain't a bad old feller most ways, though."

"Like I said," Ransden grinned. "Jest a neighborly warnin'. Y' see, I been leavin' my rifle-gun t' home most times whin I'm out 'n about . . . but I don't figger t' do thet fer a while. I reckon if I ketch someb'dy hangin' round my cabin, I'll shoot him same's I would a dog chasin' my hens."

Old Nathan looked up to meet the younger man's eyes. "Mebbe," he said deliberately, "you're goin' t' stay home 'n till yer own plot fer a time?"

"Oh, land!" whickered the horse, reacting to the sudden tension. "Now it'll come sure!"

For a moment, Old Nathan thought the same thing . . . and thought the result was going to be very bad. Sometimes you couldn't help being afraid, but that was a reason itself to act as fear warned you not to.

Ransden shook his head violently, as if he were a horse trying to brush away a gadfly. His hair was shoulder length and the color of sourwood honey. The locks tossed in a shimmering dance.

Suddenly, unexpectedly, the mood changed. Bully Ransden began to laugh. "Ye know," he said good-humoredly, "ifen you were a man, I might take unkindly t' words like thet. Seeins as yer a poor womanly critter, though, I don't reckon I will."

He kicked his horse a step onward, then reined up again as if to prove his mastery. The animal nickered in complaint.

"Another li'l warning, old man," Ransden called playfully over his shoulder. "Ye hadn't ought t' smoke meat on too hot uv a fire. You might shrink hit right up."

Ransden spurred his mount forward, jerking the left

rein at the same time. The horse's flank jolted solidly
against the mule's hindquarters, knocking the lighter
animal against an oak sapling.

"Hey thur, you!" the mule brayed angrily.

"Sword 'n pistol by his side!" Bully Ransden caroled
as he trotted his horse down the trail.

"Waal," said the mule as he resumed his measured
pace toward the cabin, "I'm glad that's ended."

"D'ye think it is, mule?" the cunning man asked
softly. "From the way the Bully was talkin', I reckon
he jest managed t' start it fer real."

The two cows were placidly chewing their cud in
the railed paddock behind the cabin. "Thar's been
another feller come by here," the red heifer offered
between rhythmic, sideways strokes of her jaws.

"Wouldn't milk us, though," the black heifer added.
" 'Bout time somebody does, ifen ye ask me."

"Don't recall askin' ye any blame thing," Old Nathan
muttered.

He dismounted and uncinched the saddle. "Don't
'spect ye noticed what the feller might be doin' whilst
he was here, did ye?" he asked as if idly.

"Ye goin' t' strip us now?" the black demanded. "My
udder's full as full, it is."

"He wint down t' the crik," the red offered. "Carried a fish down t' the crik."

Old Nathan dropped two gate bars and led the mule
into the enclosure with the cows. His face was set.

"Criks is whur fish belong," the black heifer said.
"Only I wish they didn't nibble at my teats whin I'm
standing thur, cooling myse'f."

"This fish don't nibble airy soul," the red heifer
explained in a superior tone. "This fish were dead 'n
dry."

Old Nathan removed the mule's bridle and patted
the beast on the haunch. "Git some hay," he said. "I'll

give ye a handful uv oats presently. I reckon afore long you 'n me goin' t' take another ride, though."

"Whyever do a durn fool thing like that?" the mule complained. "Ye kin ride a cow the next time. I'm plumb tuckered out."

" 'Bout time," the black heifer repeated with emphasis, "thet you milk us!"

The cunning man paused, halfway to his back porch, and turned. "I'll be with ye presently," he said. "I ain't in a mood t' be pushed, so I'd advise ye as a friend thet y'all not push me."

The cows heard the tone and looked away, as though they were studying the movements of a late-season butterfly across the paddock. The mule muttered, "Waal, I reckon I wouldn't mind a bit uv a walk, come t' thet."

The cat sauntered through the front door of the cabin as Old Nathan entered by the back. "Howdy, old man," the cat said. "I wouldn't turn down a bite of somp'in if it was goin'."

"I'll hev ye a cup uv milk if ye'll wait fer it," the cunning man said as he knelt to look at the smoke shelf of his fireplace. The greenwood fire had burnt well down, but there was no longer any reason to build it higher.

The large catfish was gone, as Old Nathan had expected. In its place was a bullhead less than six inches long; one of those Ransden had bought in town the day before, though he could scarcely have thought that Ellie believed he'd spent the evening fishing.

"What's thet?" the cat asked curiously.

Old Nathan removed the bullhead from the shelf. "Somethin' a feller left me," he said.

The bullhead hadn't been a prepossessing creature even before it spent a day out of water. Now its smooth skin had begun to shrivel and its eyes were

sunken in; the eight barbels lay like a knot of des-
iccated worms.

"He took the fish was there and tossed hit in the
branch, I reckon," he added in a dreamy voice, holding the bullhead and thinking of a time to come shortly.
"He warn't a thief, he jest wanted t' make his point
with me."

"Hain't been cleaned 'n it's gittin' good 'n ripe," the
cat noted, licking his lips. "Don't figger you want it,
but you better believe I do."

"Sorry, cat," the cunning man said absently. He set
the bullhead on the fireboard to wait while he got
together the other traps he would need. Ellie Ransden
would have a hand mirror, so he needn't take his
own. . . .

"Need t' milk the durn cows, too," he muttered
aloud.

The cat stretched up the wall beside the hearth. He
was not really threatening to snatch the bullhead, but
he wasn't far away in case the cunning man walked out
of the cabin and left the fish behind. "Whativer do you
figger t' do with thet ole thing?" he complained.

"Feller used hit t' make a point with me," Old
Nathan repeated. His voice was distant and very hard.
"I reckon I might hev a point t' make myse'f."

"Hallo the house!" Old Nathan called as he dismounted in front of Ransden's cabin.

He'd covered more miles on muleback recently than
his muscles approved. Just now he didn't feel stiff,
because his blood was heated with what he planned
to do—and what was likely to come of it.

He'd pay for that in the morning, he supposed; and
he supposed he'd be alive in the morning to pay. He'd
do what he came for regardless.

The cabin door banged open. Ellie Ransden wore

a loose dress she'd sewn long ago of English cloth, blue in so far as the sun and repeated washings had left it color. Her eyes were puffy from crying, but the expression of her face was compounded of concern and horror.

"Oh sir, Mister Nathan, ye mustn't come by here!" she gasped. "Cullen, he'll shoot ye sure! I niver seen him so mad as whin he asked hed you been by. An' my Cull. . . ."

The words "my Cull" rang beneath the surface of the girl's mind. Her face crumpled. Her hands pawed out blindly. One touched a porch support. She gripped it and collapsed against the cedar pole, blubbering her heart out.

Old Nathan stepped up onto the porch and put his arms around her. Decent folk didn't leave an animal in pain, and that's what this girl was now, something alive that hurt like to die. . . .

The mule snorted and began to sidle away. There hadn't been time to loop his reins over the porch railing.

Old Nathan pointed an index finger at the beast. "Ifen you stray," he snarled, "hit's best thet ye find yerse'f another hide. I'll hev thet off ye, sure as the Divil's in Hell."

"Fine master you are," the mule grumbled in a subdued voice.

Though the words had not been directed at Ellie, Old Nathan's tone returned the girl to present circumstances as effectively as a bucket of cold water could have done. She stepped back and straightened.

"Oh, law," she murmured, dabbing at her face with her dress's full sleeves. "But Mister Nathan, ye mustn't stay. I won't hev ye kilt over me, nor—"

She eyed him quickly, noting the absence of an obvious weapon but finding that less reassuring than she would have wished. "Nor aught t' happen to my Cull neither. He—" she started to lose control over her voice and finished in a tremolo "—ain't a bad man!"

"Huh," the cunning man said. He turned to fetch his traps from the mule's panniers. He was about as embarrassed as Ellie, and he guessed he had as much reason.

"I ain't goin' t' hurt Bully Ransden," he said, then added what was more than half a lie, "And better men thin him hev thought they'd fix my flint."

Ellie Ransden tossed her head. "Waal," she said, "I reckon ye know yer own business, sir. Won't ye come in and set a spell? I don't mind sayin' I'm glad fer the comp'ny."

Her face hardened into an expression that Old Nathan might have noticed on occasion if he looked into mirrors more often. "I've coffee, an' there's a jug uv good wildcat . . . but ifen ye want fancy French wines all the way from New Or-leens, I guess ye'll hev t' go elsewheres."

With most of his supplies in one hand and the fish wrapped in a scrap of bark in his left, Old Nathan followed the woman into her cabin. "I'd take some coffee now," he said. "And mebbe when we've finished, I'd sip a mite of whiskey."

Ellie Ransden took the coffee pot a step toward the bucket in the corner, half full with well water. Without looking at the cunning man, she said, "Thin you might do me up a charm after all?"

"I will not," Old Nathan said flatly. "But fer what I will do, ye'll hev to he'p."

He set his gear on the table. The bark unwrapped. The bullhead's scaleless skin was black, and the fish had a noticeable odor.

Ellie filled the pot and dropped in an additional pinch of beans, roasted and cracked rather than ground.

"Reckon I'll he'p, thin," she said bitterly. "All I been doin', keepin' house 'n fixin' vittles, thet don't count fer nothing the way some people figgers."

"I'll need thet oil lamp," the cunning man said, "but don't light it. And a plug t' fit the chimley end; reckon a cob 'll suit thet fine. And a pair of Bully Ransden's britches. Best they be a pair thet ain't been washed since he wore thim."

"Reckon I kin find thet for ye," the woman said. She hung the coffee over the fire, then lifted a pair of canvas trousers folded on top of a chest with a home-spun shirt. They were the garments Bully Ransden wore when Old Nathan met him earlier in the day. "Cull allus changes 'fore he goes off in the ev'nin' nowadays. Even whin he pretends he's fishin'."

She swallowed a tear. "An' don't he look a sight in thet jacket he had off Neen Tobler fer doin' his plowing last spring? Like a durned ole greenbelly fly, thet's how he looks!"

"Reckon ye got a mirror," Old Nathan said as he unfolded the trousers on the table beside the items he had brought from his own cabin. "If ye'll fetch it out, thin we can watch; but hit don't signify ifen ye don't."

"I've a hand glass fine as iver ye'll see," Ellie Ransden said with cold pride. She stepped toward a chest, then stopped and met the cunning man's eyes. "You won't hurt him, will ye?" she asked. "I—"

She covered her face with her hands. "I druther," she whispered, "thet she hev him thin thet he be hurt."

"Won't hurt him none," Old Nathan said. "I jest figger t' teach the Bully a lesson he's been beggin' t' larn, thet's all."

The young woman was on the verge of tears again. "Fetch the mirror," Old Nathan said gruffly. That gave her an excuse to turn away and compose herself as he proceeded with the preparations.

The words that the cunning man murmured under his breath were no more the spell than soaking yeast in water made a cake; but, like the other, these words were necessary preliminaries.

By its nature, the bullhead's wrinkling corpse brought the flies he needed. The pair that paused momentarily to copulate may have been brought to the act by nature alone or nature aided by art. The cause didn't matter so long as the necessary event occurred.

Old Nathan swept his right hand forward, skimming above the bullhead to grasp the mating pair unharmed within the hollow of his fingers. He looked sidelong to see whether the girl had noticed the quickness and coordination of his movement: he was an old man, right enough, but that didn't mean he was ready for the knacker's yard. . . .

He realized what he was doing and compressed his lips over a sneer of self-loathing. Durned old fool!

The flies blurred within the cunning man's fingers like a pair of gossamer hearts beating. He positioned his fist over the lamp chimney, then released his captives carefully within the glass. For a moment he continued to keep the top end of the chimney covered with his palm; then Ellie slid a corncob under the cunning man's hand to close the opening.

The flies buzzed for some seconds within the thin glass before they resumed their courtship.

The woman's eyes narrowed as she saw what Old Nathan was doing with the bullhead, but she did not comment. He arranged the other items to suit his need before he looked up.

"I'll be sayin' some words, now," he said. "Hit wouldn't do ye airy good t' hear thim, and hit might serve ye ill ifen ye said thim after me, mebbe by chance."

Ellie Ransden's mouth tightened at the reminder of

the forces being brought to bear on the man she loved.
"I reckon you know best," she said. "I'll stand off till
ye call me."

She stepped toward the cabin's only door, then
paused and looked again at Old Nathan. "These words
you're a-speakin'—ye found thim writ in books?"

He shook his head. "They're things I know," he
explained, "the way I know . . ."

His voice trailed off. He'd been about to say, "—yer
red hen's pleased as pleased with the worm she jest
grubbed up from the leaves," but that wasn't something
he rightly wanted to speak, even to this girl.

"Anyhow, I just know hit," he finished lamely.

Ellie nodded and walked out onto the porch of her
cabin. "I'll water yer mule," she called. "Reckon he
could use thet."

The beast wheezed its enthusiastic agreement.

Old Nathan sang and gestured his way through the
next stage of the preliminaries. His voice cracked and
he couldn't hold a key, but that didn't seem to matter.

The cunning man wasn't sure what did matter. When
he worked, it was as if he walked into a familiar room
in the dead dark of night. Occasionally he would
stumble, but not badly; and he would always feel his
way to the goal that he could not see.

He laid the bullhead inside the crotch of Ransden's
trousers.

In between snatches of verse—not English, and not
any language to which he could have put a name—Old
Nathan whistled. He thought of boys whistling as they
passed through a churchyard; chuckled bitterly; and
resumed whistling, snatches from Mossy Groves that
a fiddler would have had trouble recognizing.

> "How would ye like, my Mossy Groves,
>   T' spend one night with me?"

✧   ✧   ✧

Most of the life had by now crackled out of the extra stick of lightwood Ellie had tossed on the fire. Beyond the cabin walls, the night was drawing in.

The pair of trousers shifted on the table, though the air was still.

A familiar task; but, like bear hunting, familiarity didn't remove all the danger. This wasn't for Ellie, for some slip of a girl who loved a fool of a man. This was because Bully Ransden had issued a challenge, and because Old Nathan knew the worst that could happen to a man was to let fear cow him into a living death—

And maybe it was a bit for Ellie.

> The ver' first blow the king gave him,
> Moss' Groves, he struck no more. . . .

Life had risks. Old Nathan murmured his spells.

He was breathing hard when he stepped back, but he knew he'd been successful. Though the lines of congruence were invisible, they stretched their complex web among the objects on the table and across the forest to the house on the outskirts of Oak Hill. The lines were as real and stronger than the hard steel of a knife edge. The rest was up to Bully Ransden. . . .

Old Nathan began to chuckle.

Ellie stood beside him. She had moved back to the doorway when the murmur of the cunning man's voice ceased, but she didn't venture to speak.

Old Nathan grinned at her. "Reckon I'd take a swig uv yer popskull, now," he said. His throat was dry as a summer cornfield.

"Hit's done, thin?" the girl asked in a distant tone. She hefted a brown-glazed jug out from the corner by the bed and handed it to the cunning man, then turned again to toss another pine knot on the fire. The coffee pot, forgotten, still hung from the pivot bar.

Old Nathan pulled the stopper from the jug and swigged the whiskey. It was a harsh, artless run, though it had kick enough for two. Bully Ransden's taste in liquor was similar to Madame Taliaferro's taste in the men of these parts. . . .

"My part's done," the cunning man said. He shot the stopper home again. "Fer the rest, I reckon we'll jest watch."

He set the jug down against the wall. "Pick up the mirror," he explained. "Thet's what we'll look in."

Gingerly, Ellie raised the mirror from the table where it lay among the other paraphernalia. The frame and handle were curly maple finished with beeswax, locally fitted though of the highest craftsmanship. The bevel-edged four-inch glass was old and European in provenance. Lights glinted like jewels on its flawless surface.

Ellie gasped. The lights were not reflections from the cabin's hearth. They shone through the curtained windows of Francine Taliaferro's house.

"Won't hurt ye," Old Nathan said. "Hain't airy thing in all this thet could hurt you."

When he saw the sudden fear in her eyes, he added gruffly, "Not yer man neither. I done told ye thet!"

Ellie brought the mirror close to her face to get a better view of the miniature image. When she realized that she was blocking the cunning man's view, she colored and held the glass out to him.

Old Nathan shook his head with a grim smile. "You watch," he said. "I reckon ye earned thet from settin' up alone the past while."

Bully Ransden's horse stood in the paddock beside the Taliaferro house. Madame Taliaferro's black servant, now wearing loose garments instead of his livery, held the animal by a halter and curried it with smooth, flowing strokes.

"He's singin'," the woman said in wonder. She looked over at the cunning man. "I kin hear thet nigger a-singin'!"

"Reckon ye might," Old Nathan agreed.

Ellie pressed her face close to the mirror's surface again. Her expression hardened. Lamplight within the Chesson house threw bars of shadow across the curtains as a breeze caressed them.

"She's laughin'," Ellie whispered. "She's laughin', an' she's callin' him on."

"Hain't nothin' ye didn't know about," Old Nathan said. "Jest watch an' wait."

The cunning man's face was as stark as the killer he had been; one time and another, in one fashion or other. It was a hard world, and he was not the man to smooth its corners away with lies.

The screams were so loud that the mule heard them outside and snorted in surprise. Francine Taliaferro's voice cut the night like a glass-edged saw, but Bully Ransden's tenor bellows were louder yet.

The servant dropped his curry comb and ran for the house. Before he reached it, the front door burst open. Bully Ransden lurched out onto the porch, pulling his breeches up with both hands.

The black tried to stop him or perhaps just failed to get out of the way in time. Ransden knocked the servant over the porch rail with a sideways swipe of one powerful arm.

"What's hap'nin?" Ellie cried. Firelight gleamed on her fear-widened eyes. "What is hit?"

Old Nathan lifted the lamp chimney and shook it, spilling the flies unharmed from their glass prison. Mating complete for their lifetimes, they buzzed from the cabin on separate paths.

The trousers on the table quivered again. The tip of a barbel peeked from the waistband.

"Hain't airy thing hap'nin' now," the cunning man said. "I figgered thet's how you'd choose hit t' be."

Bully Ransden leaped into the paddock and mounted his horse bareback. He kicked at the gate bars, knocking them from their supports.

Madame Taliaferro appeared at the door, breathing in great gasps. The peignoir she wore was so diaphanous that with the lamplight behind her she appeared to be clothed in fog. She stared in horror at Bully Ransden.

Riding with nothing but his knees and a rope halter, Ransden jumped his horse over the remaining gate bars and galloped out of the mirror's field. Taliaferro and her black servant watched him go.

"I'll be off, now," Old Nathan said. There was nothing of what he'd brought to Ransden's cabin that he needed to take back. "I don't choose t' meet Bully on the road, though I reckon he'll hev things on his mind besides tryin' conclusions with me."

He was shivering so violently that his tongue and lips had difficulty forming the words.

"But what's the matter with Cull?" Ellie Ransden begged.

"Hain't nothin' the matter!" Old Nathan gasped.

He put a hand on the doorframe to steady himself, then stepped out into the night. Had it been an ague, he could have dosed himself, but the cunning man was shaking in reaction to the powers he had summoned and channeled . . . successfully, though at a price.

Ellie followed him out of the cabin. She gripped Old Nathan's arm as he fumbled in one of the mule's panniers. "Sir," she said fiercely, "I've a right to know."

"Here," the cunning man said, thrusting a tissue-wrapped package into her hands. "Yer Cull, hit niver was he didn't love ye. This is sompin' he put back t' hev Rance Holden wrap up purty-like. I told Rance I'd bring it out t' ye."

The girl's fingers tugged reflexively at the ribbon, but she paused with the packet only half untied. The moon was still beneath the trees, so there was no illumination except the faint glow of firelight from the cabin's doorway. She caressed the lines of the ivory comb through the tissue.

"I reckon," Ellie said deliberately, "Cullen fergot 'cause of all the fishin' he's been after this past while." She tilted up her face and kissed Old Nathan's bearded cheek, then stepped away.

The cunning man mounted his mule and cast the reins loose from the rail. He was no longer shivering.

"Yer Cull, he give me a bullhead this forenoon," he said.

"We goin' home t' get some rest, naow?" the mule asked.

"Git up, mule," Old Nathan said, turning the beast's head. To Ellie he went on, "T'night, I give thet fish back t' him; an fer a while, I put hit where he didn't figger t' find sech a thing."

As the mule clopped down the road at a comfortable pace, Old Nathan called over his shoulder, "Sure hell thet warn't whut Francine Taliaferro figgered t' see there!"

The Fool

"Now jest ignore him," said the buck to the doe as Old Nathan turned in the furrow he was hoeing twenty yards ahead of them.

"But he's looking at us," whispered the doe from the side of her mouth. She stood frozen, but a rapidly pulsing artery made shadows quiver across her throat in the evening sun.

"G'wan away!" called Old Nathan, but his voice sounded half-hearted even in his own ears. He lifted the hoe and shook it. A hot afternoon cultivating was the best medicine the cunning man knew for his aches . . . but the work did not become less tiring because it did him good. "Git, deer!"

"See, it's all right," said the buck as he lowered his head for another mouthful of turnip greens.

Old Nathan stooped for a clod to hurl at them. As he straightened with it the deer turned in unison and fled in great floating bounds, their heads thrust forward.

"Consarn it," muttered the cunning man, crumbling the clod between his long, knobby fingers as he watched the animals disappear into the woods beyond his plowland.

"Hi, there," called a voice from behind him, beside his cabin back across the creek.

Old Nathan turned, brushing his hand against his pants leg of coarse homespun. His distance sight was as good as it ever had been, so even at the length of a decent rifleshot he had no trouble in identifying his visitor as Eldon Bowsmith. Simp Bowsmith, they called the boy down to the settlement . . . and they had reason, though the boy was more an innocent than a natural in the usual sense.

"Hi!" Bowsmith repeated, waving with one hand while the other shaded his eyes from the low sun. "There wuz two deer in the field jist now!"

They had reason, that was sure as the sunrise.

"Hold there," Old Nathan called as the boy started down the path to the creek and the field beyond. "I'm headed back myself." Shouldering his hoe, he suited his action to his words.

Bowsmith nodded and plucked a long grass stem. He began to chew on the soft white base of it while he leaned on the fence of the pasture which had once held a bull and two milk cows . . . and now held the cows alone. The animals, startled at first into watchfulness, returned to chewing their cud when they realized that the stranger's personality was at least as placid as their own.

Old Nathan crossed the creek on the puncheon that served as a bridge—a log of red oak, adzed flat on the top side. A fancier structure would have been pointless, because spring freshets were sure to carry any practicable bridge downstream once or twice a year. The simplest form of crossing was both easily replaced and adequate to the cunning man's needs.

As he climbed the sloping path to his cabin with long, slow strides, Old Nathan studied his visitor. Bowsmith was tall, as tall as the cunning man himself, and perhaps as gangling. Age had shrunk Old Nathan's flesh over its framework of bone and sinew to accentuate angles, but there was little real difference in build between the two men save for the visitor's greater juiciness.

Bowsmith's most distinguishing characteristic—the factor that permitted Old Nathan to recognize him from 200 yards away—was his hair. It was a nondescript brown in color, but the way it stood out in patches of varying length was unmistakable; the boy had cut it himself, using a knife.

The cunning man realized he must have been staring when Bowsmith said with an apologetic grin, "There hain't a mirror et my place, ye see. I do what I kin with a bucket uv water."

"Makes no matter with me," Old Nathan muttered. Nor should it have, and he was embarrassed that his thoughts were so transparent. He'd been late to the line hisself when they gave out good looks. "Come in 'n set, and you kin tell me what brought ye here."

Bowsmith tossed to the ground his grass stem— chewed all the way to the harsh green blades—and hesitated as if to pluck another before entering the cabin. " 'Bliged t'ye," he said and, in the event, followed Old Nathan without anything to occupy his hands.

The doors, front and back, of the four-square cabin were open when the visitor arrived, but he had walked around instead of through the structure on his way to find the cunning man. Now he stared at the interior, his look of anticipation giving way to disappointment at the lack of exotic trappings.

There were two chairs, a stool, and a table, all solidly

fitted but shaped by a broadaxe and spokeshave rather than a lathe. The bed was of similar workmanship, with a rope frame and corn-shuck mattress. The quilted coverlet was decorated with a Tree-of-Life applique of exceptional quality, but there were women in the county who could at least brag that they could stitch its equal.

A shelf set into the wall above the bed held six books, and two chests flanked the fireplace. The chests, covered in age-blackened leather and iron-bound, could bear dark imaginings—but they surely did not require such. Five china cups and a plate stood on the fireboard where every cabin but the poorest displayed similar knick-knacks; and the rifle pegged to the wall above them would have been unusual only by its absence.

"Well . . ." Bowsmith murmured, turning his head slowly in his survey. He had expected to feel awe, and lacking that, he did not, his tongue did not know quite how to proceed. Then, on the wall facing the fireplace, he finally found something worthy of amazed comment. "Well . . ." he said, pointing to the strop of black bullhide. The bull's tail touched the floor, while the nose lifted far past the rafters to brush the roof peak. "What en tarnation's thet?"

"Bull I onct hed," Old Nathan said gruffly, answering the boy as he might not have done with anyone who was less obviously an open-eyed innocent.

"Well," the boy repeated, this time in a tone of agreement. But his brow furrowed again and he asked, "But how come ye keep hit?"

Old Nathan grimaced and, seating himself in the rocker, pointed Bowsmith to the upright chair. "Set," he ordered.

But there was no harm in the lad, so the older man explained, "I could bring him back, I could. Don't choose to, is all, cuz hit'd cost too much. There's a price for ever'thing, and I reckon that 'un's more thin the gain."

"Well," said the boy, beaming now that he was sure Old Nathan wasn't angry with him after all.

He sat down on the chair as directed and ran a hand through his hair while he paused to collect his thoughts. Bowsmith must be twenty-five or near it, but the cunning man was sure that he would halve his visitor's age if he had nothing to go by except voice and diction.

"Ma used t' barber me 'fore she passed on last year," the boy said in embarrassment renewed by the touch of his ragged scalp. "Mar' Beth Neill, she tried the onct, but hit wuz worser'n what I done."

He smiled wanly at the memory, tracing his fingers down the center of his scalp. "Cut me bare, right along here," he said. "Land but people laughed. She hed t' laugh herself."

"Yer land lies hard by the Neill clan's, I b'lieve?" the cunning man said with his eyes narrowing.

"Thet's so," agreed Bowsmith, bobbing his head happily. "We're great friends, thim en me, since Ma passed on." He looked down at the floor, grinning fiercely, and combed the fingers of both hands through his hair as if to shield the memories that were dancing through his skull. "Specially Mar' Beth, I reckon."

"First I heard," said Old Nathan, "thet any uv Baron Neill's clan wuz a friend to ary soul but kin by blood er by marriage . . . and I'd heard they kept marriage pretty much in the clan besides."

Bowsmith looked up expectantly, though he said nothing. Perhaps he hadn't understood the cunning man's words, though they'd been blunt enough in all truth.

Old Nathan sighed and leaned back in his rocker.

"No matter, boy, no matter," he said. "Tell me what it is ez brings ye here."

The younger man grimaced and blinked as he considered the request, which he apparently expected to be confusing. His brow cleared again in beaming delight and he said, "Why, I'm missin' my plowhorse, and I heard ye could find sich things. Horses what strayed."

Lives next to the Neill clan and thinks his horse strayed, the cunning man thought. Strayed right through the wall of a locked barn, no doubt. He frowned like thunder as he considered the ramifications, for the boy and for himself, if he provided the help requested.

"The Bar'n tried t' hep me find Jen," volunteered Bowsmith. "Thet's my horse. He knows about findin' and sichlike, too, from old books. . . ." He turned, uncomfortably, to glance at the volumes on the shelf there.

"I'd heard thet about the Baron," said Old Nathan grimly.

"But it wuzn't no good," the boy continued. "He says, the Bar'n does, must hev been a painter et Jen." He shrugged and scrunched his face up under pressure of an emotion the cunning man could not identify from the expression alone. "So I reckon thet's so . . . but she wuz a good ol' horse, Jen wuz, and it don't seem right somehows t' leave her bones out in the woods thet way. I thought maybe . . . ?"

Well, by God if there was one, and by Satan who was as surely loose in the world as the Neill clan— and the Neills good evidence for the Devil—Old Nathan wasn't going to pass this by. Though finding the horse would be dangerous, and there was no need for that. . . .

"All right, boy," said the cunning man as he stood up. The motion of his muscles helped him find the right words, sometimes, so he walked toward the fire-place alcove. "Don't ye be buryin' yer Jen till she's dead, now. I reckon I kin bring her home fer ye."

A pot of vegetables had been stewing all afternoon on the banked fire. Old Nathan pivoted to the side of the prong holding the pot and set a knot of pitchy lightwood on the coals. "Now," he continued, stepping away from the fire so that when the pine knot flared up its sparks would not spatter him, "you fetch me hair from Jen, her mane and her tail partikalarly. Ye kin find thet, cain't ye, clingin' in yer barn and yer fences?"

Bowsmith leaped up happily, "Why, sure I kin," he said. "Thet's all ye need?"

His face darkened. "There's one thing, though," he said, then swallowed to prime his voice for what he had to admit next. "I've a right strong back, and I reckon there hain't much ye kin put me to around yer fields here ez I cain't do fer ye. But I hain't got money t' pay ye, and since Ma passed on—" he swallowed again "—seems like ever' durn thing we owned, I cain't find whur I put it. So effen my labor's not enough fer ye, I don't know what I could give."

The boy met Old Nathan's eyes squarely and there weren't many folk who would do that, for fear that the cunning man would draw out the very secrets of their hearts. Well, Simp Bowsmith didn't seem to have any secrets; and perhaps there were worse ways to be.

"Don't trouble yerself with thet," said Old Nathan aloud, "until we fetch yer horse back."

The cunning man watched the boy tramping cheer-fully back up the trail, unconcerned by the darkness and without even a stick against the threat of bears and cougars which would keep his neighbors from travel-ling at night. Hard to believe, sometimes, that the same world held that boy and the Neill clan besides.

A thought struck him. "Hoy!" he called, striding to

the edge of his porch to shout up the trail. "Eldon Bowsmith!"

"Sir?" wound the boy's reply from the dark. He must already be to the top of the knob, among the old beeches that were its crown.

"Ye bring me a nail from a shoe Jen's cast besides," Old Nathan called back. "D'ye hear me?"

"Yessir."

"Still, we'll make a fetch from the hair first, and thet hed ought t'do the job," the cunning man muttered; but his brow was furrowing as he considered consequences, things that would happen despite him and things that he—needs must—would initiate.

"I brung ye what ye called fer," said Bowsmith, sweating and cheerful from his midday hike. His whistling had announced him as soon as he topped the knob, the happiest rendition of "Bonny Barbry Allen" Old Nathan had heard in all his born days.

The boy held out a gob of gray-white horsehair in one hand and a tapered horseshoe nail in the other. Then his eyes lighted on movement in a corner of the room, the cat slinking under the bedstead.

"Oh!" said Bowsmith, kneeling and setting the nail on the floor to be able to extend his right hand toward the animal. "Ye've a cat. Here, pretty boy. Here, handsome." He clucked his tongue.

"Hain't much fer strangers, that 'un," said Old Nathan, and the cat promptly made a liar of him by flowing back from cover and flopping down in front of Bowsmith to have his belly rubbed.

"Oh," said the cat, "he's all right, ain't he," as he gripped the boy's wrist with his forepaws and tugged it down to his jaws.

"Watch—" the cunning man said in irritation to one or the other, he wasn't sure which. The pair of them ignored him, the cat purring in delight and closing his jaws so that the four long canines dimpled the boy's skin but did not threaten to puncture it.

Bowsmith looked up in sudden horror.

"Don't stop, damn ye!" growled the cat and kicked a knuckle with a hind paw.

"Is he . . . ?" the boy asked. "I mean, I thought he wuz a cat, but . . . ?"

"He's a cat, sure ez I'm a man—" Old Nathan snapped. He had started to add "—and you're a durn fool," but that was too close to the truth, and there was no reason to throw it in Bowsmith's face because he made up to Old Nathan's cat better than the cunning man himself generally did.

"Spilesport," grumbled the cat as he rolled to his feet and stalked out the door.

"Oh, well," said the boy, rising and then remembering to pick up the horseshoe nail. "I wouldn't want, you know, t' trifle with yer familiars, coo."

"Don't hold with sich," the cunning man retorted. Then a thought occurred to him and he added, "Who is it been tellin' ye about familiar spirits and sechlike things?"

"Well," admitted the boy, and "admit" was the right word for there was embarrassment in his voice, "I reckon the Bar'n might could hev said somethin'. He knows about thet sort uv thing."

"Well, ye brung the horsehair," said Old Nathan softly, his green eyes slitted over the thoughts behind them. He took the material from the boy's hand and carried it with him to the table.

The first task was to sort the horsehair—long white strands from the tail; shorter but equally coarse bits of mane; and combings from the hide itself, matted together and gray-hued. The wad was more of a blur to his eyes than it was even in kinky reality. Sighing,

the old man started up to get his spectacles from one
of the chests.

Then, pausing, he had a better idea. He turned and
gestured Bowsmith to the straight chair at the table.
"Set there and sort the pieces fer length," he said
gruffly.

The cunning man was harsh because he was angry
at the signs that he was aging; angry that the boy was
too great a fool to see how he was being preyed upon;
and angry that he, Old Nathan the Devil's Master,
should care about the fate of one fool more in a world
that already had a right plenty of such.

"Yessir," said the boy, jumping to obey with such
clumsy alacrity that his thigh bumped the table and
slid the solid piece several inches along the floor. "And
thin what do we do?"

Bowsmith's fingers were deft enough, thought Old
Nathan as he stepped back a pace to watch. "No we
about it, boy," said the cunning man. "You spin it to
a bridle whilst I mebbe say some words t' help."

Long hairs from the tail to form the reins; wispy
headbands and throat latch bent from the mane, and
the whole felted together at each junction by tufts of
gray hair from the hide.

"And I want ye t' think uv yer Jen as ye do thet,
boy," Old Nathan said aloud while visions of the coming
operation drifted through his mind. "Jest ez t'night ye'll
think uv her as ye set in her stall, down on four legs
like a beast yerself, and ye wear this bridle you're
makin'. And ye'll call her home, so ye will, and thet'll
end the matter, I reckon."

" 'Bliged t' ye, sir," said Eldon Bowsmith, glancing
up as he neared the end of the sorting. There was no
more doubt in his eyes than a more sophisticated visitor
would have expressed at the promise the sun would
rise.

Old Nathan wished he were as confident. He especially wished that he were confident the Neill clan would let matters rest when their neighbor had his horse back.

Old Nathan was tossing the dirt with which he had just scoured his cookware off the side of the porch the next evening when he saw Bowsmith trudging back down the trail. The boy was not whistling, and his head was bent despondently.

His right hand was clenched. Old Nathan knew, as surely as if he could see it, that Bowsmith was bringing back the fetch bridle.

"Come and set," the cunning man called, rising and flexing the muscles of his back as if in preparation to shoulder a burden.

"Well," the boy said, glumly but without the reproach Old Nathan had expected, "I reckon I'm in a right pickle now," as he mounted the pair of steps to the porch.

The two men entered the cabin; Old Nathan laid another stick of lightwood on the fire. It was late afternoon in the flatlands, but here in the forested hills the sun had set and the glow of the sky was dim even outdoors.

"I tried t' do what ye said," Bowsmith said, fingering his scalp with his free hand, "but someways I must hev gone wrong like usual."

The cat, alerted by voices, dropped from the rafters to the floor with a loud thump. "Good t' see ye agin," the animal said as he curled, tail high, around the boots of the younger man. Even though Bowsmith could not understand the words as such, he knelt and began kneading the cat's fur while much of the frustrated distress left his face.

"Jen didn't fetch t' yer summons, thin?" the cunning man prodded. Durn fool, durn cat, durn nonsense.

He set down the pot he carried with a clank, not bothering at present to rinse it with a gourdful of water.

"Worsen thet," the boy explained. "I brung the ol' mule from Neills', and wuzn't they mad ez hops." He looked up at the cunning man. "The Bar'n wuz right ready t' hev the sheriff on me fer horse stealin', even though he's a great good friend t' me."

The boy's brow clouded with misery, then cleared into the same beatific, full-face smile Old Nathan had seen cross it before. "Mar' Beth, though, she quietened him. She told him I hadn't meant t' take their mule, and thet I'd clear off the track uv newground they been meanin' t' plant down on Cane Creek."

"You figger t' do thet?" the cunning man asked sharply. "Clear canebrake fer the Neill clan, whin there's ten uv thim and none willin' t' break his back with sich a chore?"

"Why I reckon hit's the least I could do," Bowsmith answered in surprise. "Why, I took their mule, didn't I?"

Old Nathan swallowed his retort, but the taste of the words soured his mouth. "Let's see the fetch bridle," he said instead, reaching out his hand.

The cunning man knelt close by the spluttering fire to examine the bridle while his visitor continued to play with the cat in mutual delight. The bridle was well made, as good a job as Old Nathan himself could have done with his spectacles on.

It was a far more polished piece than the bridle Eldon Bowsmith had carried off the day before, and the hairs from which it was hand-spun were brown and black.

"Where'd ye stop yestiddy, on yer way t' home?" Old Nathan demanded.

Bowsmith popped upright, startling the cat out the door with an angry curse. "Now, how did you know thet?" he said in amazement, and in delight at being amazed.

"Boy, boy," the cunning man said, shaking his head. He was too astounded at such innocence even to snarl in frustration. "Where'd ye stop?"

"Well, I reckon I might uv met Mary Beth Neill," Bowsmith said, tousling his hair like a dog scratching his head with a forepaw. "They're right friendly folk, the Neills, so's they hed me stay t' supper."

"Where you told thim all about the fetch bridle, didn't ye?" Old Nathan snapped, angry at last.

"Did I?" said the boy in open-eyed wonder. "Why, not so's I kin recolleck, sir . . . but I reckon ef you say I did, thin—"

Old Nathan waved the younger man to silence. Bowsmith might have blurted the plan to the Neills and not remember doing so. Equally, a mind less subtle than Baron Neill's might have drawn the whole story from a mere glimpse of the bridle woven of Jen's hair. That the Neill patriarch had been able to counter in the way he had done suggested he was deeper into the lore than Old Nathan would have otherwise believed.

"Well, what's done is done," said the cunning man as he stepped to the fireboard. "Means we need go a way I'd not hev gone fer choice."

He took the horseshoe nail from where he had lodged it, beside the last in line of his five china cups. He wouldn't have asked the boy to bring the nail if he hadn't expected—or at least feared—such a pass. If Baron Neill chose to raise the stakes, then that's what the stakes would be.

Old Nathan set the nail back, for the nonce. There was a proper bed of coals banked against the wall of the fireplace now during the day. The cunning man chose two splits of hickory and set them sharp-edge down on the ashes and bark-sides close together. When

the clinging wood fibers ignited, the flames and the
blazing gases they drove out would be channeled up
between the flats to lick the air above the log in blue
lambency. For present purposes, that would be sufficient.

"Well, come on, thin, boy," the cunning man said
to his visitor. "We'll git a rock fer en anvil from the
crik and some other truck, and thin we'll forge ye a
pinter t' pint out yer horse. Wheriver she be."

Old Nathan had chosen for the anvil an egg of
sandstone almost the size of a man's chest. It was an
easy location to lift, standing clear of the streambed
on a pedestal of limestone blocks from which all the
sand and lesser gravel had been sluiced away since the
water was speeded by constriction.

For all that the rock's placement was a good one,
Old Nathan had thought that its weight might be too
much for Bowsmith to carry up to the cabin. The boy
had not hesitated, however, to wade into the stream
running to mid-thigh and raise the egg with the
strength of his arms and shoulders alone.

Bowsmith walked back out of the stream, feeling
cautiously for his footing but with no other sign of
the considerable weight he balanced over his head.
He paused a moment on the low bank, where mud
squelched from between his bare toes. Then he
resumed his steady stride, pacing up the path.

Old Nathan had watched to make sure the boy could
handle the task set him. As a result, he had to rush
to complete his own part of the business in time to
reach the cabin when Bowsmith did.

A flattened pebble, fist-sized and hand-filling, would
do nicely for the hammer. It was a smaller bit of the
same dense sandstone that the cunning man had chosen
for the anvil. He tossed it down beside a clump of

alders and paused with his eyes closed. His fingers crooked, groping for the knife he kept in a place he could "see" only within his skull.

It was there where it should be, a jackknife with two blades of steel good enough to accept a razor edge—which was how Old Nathan kept the shorter one. His fingers closed on the yellow bone handle and drew the knife out into the world that he and others watched with their eyes.

The cunning man had never been sure where it was that he put his knife. Nor, for that matter, would he have bet more than he could afford to lose that the little tool would be there the next time he sought it. Thus far, it always had been. That was all he knew.

He opened the longer blade, the one sharpened to a 301 degree angle, and held the edge against a smooth-barked alder stem that was of about the same diameter as his thumb. Old Nathan's free hand gripped the alder above the intended cut, and a single firm stroke of the knife severed the stem at a slant across the tough fibers.

Whistling himself—"The Twa Corbies," in contrast to Bowsmith's rendition of "Bonny Barbry Allen" on the path ahead—Old Nathan strode back to the cabin. The split hickory should be burning to just the right extent by now.

"And I'll set down on his white neck bone," the cunning man sang aloud as he trimmed the alder's branches away, "T' pluck his eyes out one and one."

The Neill clan had made their bed. Now they could sleep in it with the sheriff.

"Gittin' right hot," said Bowsmith as he squatted and squinted at the nail he had placed on the splits according to the cunning man's direction. "Reckon the little teensie end's so hot hit's nigh yaller t' look et."

Old Nathan gripped the trimmed stem with both hands and twisted as he folded it, so that the alder doubled at the notch he had cut in the middle. What had been a yard-long wand was now a pair of tongs with which the cunning man bent to grip the heated nail by its square head.

"Ready now," he directed. "Remember thet you're drawin' out the iron druther thin bangin' hit flat."

"Wisht we hed a proper sledge," the boy said. He slammed the smaller stone accurately onto the glowing nail the instant Old Nathan's tongs laid it on the anvil stone.

Sparks hissed from the nail in red anger, though the sound of the blow was a clock! rather than a ringing crash. A dimple near the tip of the nail brightened to orange. Before it had faded, the boy struck again. Old Nathan turned the workpiece 90° on its axis, and the hand-stone hit it a third time.

While the makeshift hammer was striking, the iron did not appear to change. When the cunning man's tongs laid it back in the blue sheet of hickory flame, however, the workpiece was noticeably longer than the smith had forged it originally.

Old Nathan had been muttering under his breath as the boy hammered. They were forging the scale on the face of the nail into the fabric of the pointer, amalgamating the proteins of Jen's hoof with the hot iron. Old Nathan murmured, "As least is to great," each time the hammer struck. Now, as the nail heated again, the gases seemed to flow by it in the pattern of a horse's mane.

"Cain't use an iron sledge, boy" the cunning man said aloud. "Not fer this, not though the nail be iron hitself."

He lifted out the workpiece again. "Strike on," he said. "And the tip this time, so's hit's pinted like an awl."

The stone clopped like a horse's hoof and clicked like a horse's teeth, while beside them in the chimney corner the fire settled itself with a burbling whicker.

As least is to great . . .

Eldon Bowsmith's face was sooty from the fire and flushed where runnels of sweat had washed the soot away, but there was a triumphant gleam in his eyes as he prepared to leave Old Nathan's cabin that evening. He held the iron pointer upright in one hand and his opposite index finger raised in balance. The tip of his left ring finger was bandaged with a bit of tow and spiderweb to cover a puncture. The cunning man had drawn three drops of the boy's blood to color the water in which they quenched the iron after its last heating.

"I cain't say how much I figger I'm 'bliged t' ye fer this," said Bowsmith, gazing at the pointer with a fondness inexplicable to anyone who did not know what had gone in to creating the instrument.

The bit of iron had been hammered out to the length of a man's third finger. It looked like a scrap of bent wire, curved and recurved by blows from stone onto stone, each surface having a rounded face. The final point had been rolled onto it between the stones, with the boy showing a remarkable delicacy and ability to coordinate his motions with those of the cunning man who held the tongs.

"Don't thank me till ye've got yer Jen back in her stall," said Old Nathan. His mind added, "And not thin, effen the Neills burn ye out and string ye to en oak limb." Aloud he said, "Anyways, ye did the heavy part yerself."

That was true only when limited to the physical portion of what had gone on that afternoon. Were the hammering of primary importance, then every blacksmith would have been a wizard. Old Nathan, too, was panting and worn from exertion; but like Bowsmith, the success he felt at what had been accomplished made the effort worthwhile. He had seen the plowhorse pacing in her narrow stall when steam rose as the iron was quenched.

The boy cocked his head aside and started to comb his fingers through his hair in what Old Nathan had learned was a gesture of embarrassment. He looked from the pointer to his bandaged finger, then began to rub his scalp with the heel of his right hand. "Well . . ." he said. "I want ye t' know thet I . . ."

Bowsmith grimaced and looked up to meet the eyes of the cunning man squarely. "Lot uv folk," he said, "they wouldn't hev let me hep. They call me Simp, right t' my face they do thet. . . . En, en I reckon there's no harm t' thet, but . . . sir, ye treated me like Ma used to. You air ez good a friend ez I've got in the world, 'ceptin' the Neills."

"So good a friend ez thet?" said the cunning man drily. He had an uncomfortable urge to turn his own face away and comb fingers through his hair.

"Well," he said instead and cleared his throat in order to go on. "Well. Ye remember what I told ye. Ye don't speak uv this t' ary soul. En by the grace uv yer Ma in heaven whur she watches ye—"

Old Nathan gripped the boy by both shoulders, and the importance of what he had to get across made emotionally believable words that were not part of the world's truth as the cunning man knew it "—don't call t' Jen and foller the pinter to her without ye've the sheriff et yer side. Aye, en ef he wants t' bring half the settlement along t' boot, thin I reckon thet might be a wise notion."

"Ain't goin' t' fail ye this time, sir," promised the boy brightly. "Hit'll all be jist like you say."

He was whistling again as he strode up the hill into

the dusk. Old Nathan imagined a cabin burning and a lanky form dangling from a tree beside it.

He spat to avoid the omen.

Old Nathan sat morosely in the chimney corner, reading with his back to the fire, when his cat came in the next night.

"Caught a rabbit nigh on up t' the road," the cat volunteered cheerfully. "Land sakes didn't it squeal and thrash."

He threw himself down on the puncheon floor, using Old Nathan's booted foot as a brace while he licked his belly and genitals. "Let it go more times thin I kin count," the cat went on. "When it wouldn't run no more, thin I killed it en et it down t' the head en hide."

"I reckon ye did," said the cunning man. To say otherwise to the cat would be as empty as railing against the sky for what it struck with its thunderbolts. He carefully folded his reading glasses and set them in the crease of his book so that he could stroke the animal's fur.

"Hev ye seen thet young feller what wuz here t'other day?" the cat asked, pawing his master's hand but not—for a wonder—hooking in his claws.

"I hev not," Old Nathan replied flatly. He had ways by which he could have followed Bowsmith's situation or even anticipated it. It was more than the price such sources of information came with that stayed him; they graved an otherwise fluid future on the stone of reality. He would enter that world of knowledge for others whose perceived need was great enough, but he would not enter it for himself. Old Nathan had experienced no greater horror in his seventy years of life than the certain knowledge of a disaster he could not change.

"Well," said the cat, "reckon ye'll hev a chanct to

purty quick, now. Turned down yer trail, he did, 'bout time I licked off them rabbit guts en come home myself."

"Halloo the house!" called Eldon Bowsmith from beyond the front door, and the cat bit Old Nathan's forearm solidly as the cunning man tried to rise from the rocking chair.

"Bless en save ye, cat!" roared the old man, gripping the animal before the hind legs, feeling the warm distended belly squishing with rabbit meat. "Come in, boy," he cried, "come in en set," and he surged upright with the open book in one hand and the cat cursing in the other.

Bowsmith wore a look of such dejection that he scarcely brightened with surprise at the cunning man's incongruous appearance. A black iron pointer dangled from the boy's right hand, and the scrap of bandage had fallen from his left ring finger without being replaced.

"Ev'nin' t' ye, sir," he said to Old Nathan. "Wisht I could say I'd done ez ye told me, but I don't reckon I kin."

When the cat released Old Nathan's forearm, the cunning man let him jump to the floor. The animal promptly began to insinuate himself between Bowsmith's feet and rub the boy's knees with his tailtip, muttering, "Good t' see ye, good thet ye've come."

"Well, you're alive," said Old Nathan, "en you're here, which ain't a bad start fer fixin' sich ez needs t' be fixed. Set yerself en we'll talk about it."

Bowsmith obeyed his host's gesture and seated himself in the rocker, still warm and clicking with the motion of the cunning man rising from it. He held out the pointer but did not look at his host as he explained, "I wint to the settlemint, and I told the sheriff what ye said. He gathered up mebbe half a dozen uv the men thereabouts, all totin' their guns like they wuz en army. En I named Jen, like you said, and this nail, hit like t' pull outen my hand it wuz so fierce t' find her."

Old Nathan examined by firelight the pointer he had taken from the boy. He was frowning, and when he measured the iron against his finger the frown became a thundercloud in which the cunning man's eyes were flashes of green lightning. The pointer was a quarter inch longer than the one that had left his cabin the morning before.

"En would ye b'lieve it, but hit took us straight ez straight t' the Neill place?" continued the boy with genuine wonderment in his voice. He shook his head. "I told the sheriff I reckoned there wuz a mistake, but mebbe the Bar'n had found Jen en he wuz keepin' her t' give me whin I next come by."

Bowsmith shook his head again. He laced his fingers together on his lap and stared glumly at them as he concluded, "But I be hanged ef thet same ol' spavined mule warn't tied t' the door uv the barn, and the pinter wouldn't leave afore it touched hit's hoof." He sucked in his lips in frustration.

"Here, I'd admire ef you sleeked my fur," purred the cat, and he leaped into the boy's lap. Bowsmith's hands obeyed as aptly as if he could have understood the words of the request.

"What is it happened thin, boy?" Old Nathan asked in a voice as soft as the whisper of powder being poured down the barrel of a musket.

"Well, I'm feared to guess what might hev happened," explained Bowsmith, "effen the Baron hisself hedn't come out the cabin and say hit made no matter."

He began to nod in agreement with the words in his memory, saying, "The Bar'n, he told the sheriff I wuzn't right in the head sometimes, en he give thim all a swig outen his jug uv wildcat so's they wouldn't hammer me fer runnin' thim off through the woods like a durned fool. They wuz laughin' like fiends whin they left, the sheriff and the folk from the settlement."

Bowsmith's hands paused. The cat waited a moment, then rose and battered his chin against the boy's chest until the stroking resumed.

"Reckon I am a durn fool," the boy said morosely. "Thet en worse."

"How long did ye stop over t' the Neills after ye left here yestiddy?" Old Nathan asked in the same soft voice.

"Coo," said Bowsmith, meeting the cunning man's eyes as wonder drove the gloom from his face. "Well, I niver . . . Wuzn't goin' t' tell ye thet, seein's ez ye'd said I oughtn't t' stop. But Mar' Beth, she seed me on the road en hollered me up t' the cabin t' set fer a spell. Don't guess I was there too long, though. The Baron asked me whin I was going t' clear his newground. And then whin he went out, me en the boys, we passed the jug a time er two."

He frowned. "Reckon hit might uv been longer thin I'd recollected."

"Hit wuz dark by the time ye passed the Neills, warn't it?" Old Nathan said. "How'd Mary Beth see down t' the road?"

"Why, I be," replied the boy. "Why—" His face brightened. "D'ye reckon she wuz waiting on me t' come back by? She's powerful sweet on me, ye know, though I say thet who oughtn't."

"Reckon hit might be she wuz waitin'," said the cunning man, his voice leaden and implacable. He lifted his eyes from Bowsmith to the end wall opposite the fireplace. The strop that was all the material remains of Spanish King shivered in a breeze that neither man could feel.

"Pinter must hev lost all hit's virtue whin I went back on what ye told me," the boy said miserably. "You bin so good t' me, en I step on my dick ever' time I turn around. Reckon I'll git back t' my place afore I cause more trouble."

"Set, boy," said Old Nathan. "Ye'll go whin I say go . . . and ye'll do this time what I say ye'll do."

"Yessir," replied Bowsmith, taken aback. When he tried instinctively to straighten his shoulders, the chair rocked beneath him. He lurched to his feet in response. Instead of spilling the cat, he used the animal as a balancer and then clutched him back to his chest.

"Yessir," he repeated, standing upright and looking confused but not frightened. And not, somehow, ridiculous, for all his ragged spray of hair and the grumbling tomcat in his arms.

Old Nathan set the book he held down on the table, his spectacles still marking his place against the stiff binding which struggled to close the volume. With both hands free, he gripped the table itself and walked over to the fireplace alcove.

Bowsmith poured the cat back onto the floor as soon as he understood what his host was about, but he paused on realizing that his help was not needed. The tabletop was forty inches to a side, sawn from thick planks and set on an equally solid framework—all of oak. The cunning man shifted the table without concern for its weight and awkwardness. He had never been a giant for strength, but even now he was no one to trifle with either.

"Ye kin fetch the straight chair to it," he said over his shoulder while he fumbled with the lock of one of the chests flanking the fireplace. "I'll need the light t' copy out the words ye'll need."

"Sir, I cain't read," the boy said in a voice of pale, peeping despair.

"Hit don't signify," replied the cunning man. The lid of the chest creaked open. "Fetch the chair."

Old Nathan set a bundle of turkey quills onto the table, then a pot of ink stoppered with a cork. The ink moved sluggishly and could have used a dram of water to thin it, but it was fluid enough for writing as it was.

Still kneeling before the chest, the cunning man raised a document case and untied the ribbon which closed it. Bowsmith placed the straight chair by the table, moving the rocker aside to make room. Then he watched over the cunning man's shoulder, finding in the written word a magic as real as anything Old Nathan had woven or forged.

"Not this one," the older man said, laying aside the first of the letters he took from the case. It was in a woman's hand, the paper fine but age-spotted. He could not read the words without his glasses, but he did not need to reread what he had not been able to forget even at this distance in time. "Nor this."

"Coo . . ." Bowsmith murmured as the first document was covered by the second, this one written on parchment with a wax seal and ribbons which the case had kept a red as bright as that of the day they were impressed onto the document.

Old Nathan smiled despite his mood. "A commendation from General Sevier," he said in quiet pride as he took another letter from the case.

"You fit the Redcoats et New Or-Leens like they say, thin?" the younger man asked.

Old Nathan looked back at him with an expression suddenly as blank as a board. "No, boy," he said, "hit was et King's Mountain, en they didn't wear red coats, the most uv thim."

He paused and then added in a kindlier tone, "En I reckon thet when I was yer age en ol' fools wuz jawin' about Quebec and Cartagena and all thet like, hit didn't

matter a bean betwixt them t' me neither. And mebbe
there wuz more truth t' thet thin I've thought since."

"I don't rightly foller," said Bowsmith.

"Don't reckon ye need to," the older man replied.
"Throw a stick uv lightwood on the fire."

Holding the sheet he had just removed from the
case, Old Nathan stood upright and squinted to be sure
of what he had. It seemed to be one of his brother's
last letters to him, a decade old but no more important for that. It was written on both sides of the sheet,
but the cuttlefish ink had faded to its permanent state
of rich brown. The paper would serve as well for the
cunning man's present need as a clean sheet which
could not have been found closer than Holden's store
in the settlement—and that dearly.

He sat down on the chair and donned his spectacles,
using the letter as a placeholder in the book in their
stead. The turkey quills were held together by a wisp
of twine which, with his glasses on, he could see to
untie.

After choosing a likely quill, Old Nathan scowled
and said, "Turn yer head, boy." When he felt the
movement of Bowsmith behind him, obedient if uncertain, the cunning man reached out with his eyes closed
and brought his hand back holding the jackknife.

Some of Old Nathan's magic was done in public to
impress visitors and those to whom they might babble
in awe. Some things that he might have hidden from
others he did before Bowsmith, because he knew that
the boy would never attempt to duplicate the acts on
his own. But this one trick was the cunning man's
secret of secrets, and he didn't want to frighten the
boy.

The knife is the most useful of Mankind's tools, dating
from ages before he was even human. But a knife is also
a weapon, and the sole reason for storing it—somewhere

else—rather than in a pants pocket was that on some future date an enemy might remove a weapon from your pants. Better to plan for a need which never eventuated than to be caught by unexpected disaster.

"Ye kin turn and help me now, Eldon Bowsmith," the cunning man said as he trimmed his pen with the wire edge of the smaller blade. "Ye kin hold open the book fer me."

"Yessir," said the boy and obeyed with the clumsy nervousness of a bachelor asked to hold an infant for the first time. He gripped the volume with an effort which an axehelve would have better justified. The shaking of his limbs would make the print even harder to read.

Old Nathan sighed. "Gently, boy," he said. "Hit won't bite ye."

Though there was reason to fear this book. It named itself Testamentum Athanasii on a title page which gave no other information regarding its provenance. The volume was old, but it had been printed with movable type and bound or rebound recently enough that the leather hinges showed no sign of cracking.

The receipt to which the book now opened was one Old Nathan had read frequently in the months since Spanish King had won his last battle and, winning, had died. Not till now had he really considered employing the formula. Not really.

"Boy," lied the cunning man, "we cain't git yer horse back, so I'll give ye the strength uv a bull thet ye kin plow."

Bowsmith's face found a neutral pattern and held it while his mind worked on the sentence he had just been offered. Usually conversations took standard patterns. "G'day t' ye, Simp." "G'day t' ye Mister/Miz. . . ." "Ev'nin', Eldon. Come en set." "Ev'nin' Mar' Beth. Don't mind effen I do." Patterns like that made a conversation easier, without the confusing precipices which talking to Old Nathan entailed.

"Druther hev Jen back, sir," said the boy at last. "Effen you don't mind."

The cunning man raised his left hand. The gesture was not quite a physical threat because the hand held his spectacles, and their lenses refracted spitting orange firelight across the book and the face of the younger man. "Mind, boy?" said Old Nathan. "Mind? You mind me, thet's the long and the short uv it now, d'ye hear?"

"Yessir."

The cunning man dipped his pen in the ink and wiped it on the bottle's rim, cursing the fluid's consistency. "Give ye the strength uv a bull," he lied again, "en a strong bull et thet." He began to write, his present strokes crossing those of his brother in the original letter. He held the spectacles a few inches in front of his eyes, squinting and adjusting them as he copied from the page of the book.

"Ever ketch rabbits, feller?" asked the cat as he leaped to the tabletop and landed without a stir because all four paws touched down together.

"Good feller," muttered Bowsmith, holding the book with the thumb and spread fingers of one hand so that the other could stroke the cat. The trembling which had disturbed the pages until then ceased, though the cat occasionally bumped a corner of the volume. "Good feller. . . ."

The click of clawtips against oak, the scritch of the pen nib leaving crisp black lines across the sepia complaints beneath, and the sputtering pine knot that lighted the cabin wove themselves into a sinister unity that was darker than the nighted forest outside.

Yet not so dark as the cunning man's intent.

When he finished, the boy and the cat were both staring at him, and it was the cat who rumbled, "Bad ez all thet?" smelling the emotions in the old man's sweat.

"What'll be," Old Nathan rasped through a throat drier than he had realized till he spoke, "will be." He looked down at the document he had just indited, folded his spectacles one-handed, and then turned to hurl the quill pen into the fire with a violence that only hinted his fury at what he was about to do.

"Sir?" said Bowsmith.

"Shut the book, boy," said Old Nathan wearily. His fingers made a tentative pass toward the paper, to send it the way the quill had gone. A casuist would have said that he was not acting and therefore bore no guilt . . . but a man who sets a snare for a rabbit cannot claim the throttled rabbit caused its own death by stepping into the noose.

The cunning man stood and handed the receipt to his visitor, folding it along the creases of the original letter. "Put it in yer pocket fer now, lad," he said. He took the book, closed now as he had directed, and scooped up the cat gently with a hand beneath the rib cage and the beast's haunches in the crook of his elbow.

"Now, carry the table acrosst t' the other side," the cunning man continued, motioning Bowsmith with a thrust of his beard because he did not care to point with the leather-covered book. "Fetch me down the strop uv bullhide there. Hit's got a peg drove through each earhole t' hold it."

"That ol' bull," said the cat, turning his head to watch Bowsmith walk across the room balancing the heavy table on one hand. "Ye know, I git t' missin' him sometimes?"

"As do I," Old Nathan agreed grimly. "But I don't choose t' live in a world where I don't see the prices till the final day."

"Sir?" queried the boy, looking down from the table which he had mounted in a flat-footed jump that crashed its legs down on the puncheons.

"Don't let it trouble ye, boy," the cunning man replied. "I talk t' my cat, sometimes. Fetch me down Spanish King, en I'll deal with yer problem the way I've set myself t' do."

The cat sprang free of the encircling arm, startled by what he heard in his master's voice.

It was an hour past sunset, and Baron Neill held court on the porch over an entourage of two of his three sons and four of the six grandsons. Inside the cabin, built English-fashion of sawn timber but double sized, the women of the clan cleared off the truck from supper and talked in low voices among themselves. The false crow calls from the look-out tree raucously penetrated the background of cicadas and tree frogs.

" 'Bout time," said the youngest son, taking a swig from the jug. He was in his early forties, balding and feral.

"Mar' Beth," called Baron Neill without turning his head or taking from his mouth the long stem of his meerschaum pipe.

There was silence from within the cabin but no immediate response.

The Baron dropped his feet from the porch rail with a crash and stood up. The Neill patriarch looked more like a rat than anything on two legs had a right to do. His nose was prominent, and the remainder of his body seemed to spread outward from it down to the fleshy buttocks supported by a pair of spindly shanks. "Mar' Beth!" he shouted, hunched forward as he faced the cabin door.

"Well, I'm comin', ain't I?" said a woman who was by convention the Baron's youngest daughter and was in any case close kin to him. She stepped out of the lamplit cabin, hitching the checked apron a little straighter on her homespun dress. The oil light behind her colored her hair more of a yellow than the sun would have brought out, emphasizing the translucent gradations of her single tortoise-shell comb.

"Simp's comin' back," said the Baron, relaxing enough to clamp the pipe again between his teeth. "Tyse jist called. Git down t' the trail en bring him back."

The woman stood hipshot, the desire to scowl tempered by the knowledge that the patriarch would strike her if the expression were not hidden by the angle of the light. "I'm poorly," she said.

One of the boys snickered, and Baron Neill roared, "Don't I know thet? You do ez I tell ye, girl."

Mary Beth stepped off the porch with an exaggerated sway to her hips. The pair of hogs sprawled beneath the boards awakened but snorted and flopped back down after questing with their long flexible snouts.

"Could be I don't mind," the woman threw back over her shoulder from a safe distance. "Could be Simp looks right good stacked up agin some I've seed."

One of her brothers sent after her a curse and the block of poplar he was whittling, neither with serious intent.

"Jeth," said the Baron, "go fetch Dave and Sim from the still. Never know when two more guns might be the difference betwixt somethin' er somethin' else. En bring another jug back with ye."

"Lotta durn work for a durned old plowhorse," grumbled one of the younger Neills.

The Baron sat down again on his chair and lifted his boots to the porch rail. "Ain't about a horse," he said, holding out his hand and having it filled by the stoneware whiskey jug without him needing to ask.

"Hain't been about a horse since he brung Old Nathan into hit. Fancies himself, that 'un does."

The rat-faced old man took a deep draw on his pipe and mingled in his mouth the harsh flavors of burley tobacco and raw whiskey. "Well, I fancy myself, too. We'll jist see who's got the rights uv it."

Eldon Bowsmith tried to step apart from the woman when the path curved back in sight of the cabin. Mary Beth giggled throatily and pulled herself close again, causing the youth to sway like a sapling in the wind. He stretched out the heavy bundle in his opposite hand in order to recover his balance.

"What in tarnation is that ye got, boy?" demanded Baron Neill from the porch. The air above his pipe bowl glowed orange as he drew on the mouthpiece.

"Got a strop uv bullhide, Bar'n," Bowsmith called back. "Got the horns, tail, and the strip offen the backbone besides."

He swayed again, then said in a voice that carried better than he would have intended, "Mar' Beth, ye mustn't touch me like thet here." But the words were not a serious reproach, and his laughter joined the woman's renewed giggle.

There was snorting laughter from the porch as well. One of the men there might have spoken had not Baron Neill snarled his offspring to silence.

The couple separated when they reached the steps, Mary Beth leading the visitor with her hips swaying in even greater emphasis than when she had left the cabin.

"Tarnation," the Baron repeated as he stood and took the rolled strip of hide from Bowsmith. The boy's hand started to resist, but he quickly released the bundle when he remembered where he was.

"Set a spell, boy," said the patriarch. "Zeph, hand him the jug."

"I reckon I need yer help, Bar'n," Bowsmith said, rubbing his right sole against his left calf. The stoneware jug—a full one just brought from the still by the Baron's two grandsons—was pressed into his hands and he took a brief sip.

"Now, don't ye insult my squeezin's, boy," said one of the younger men. "Drink hit down like a man er ye'll answer t' me." In this, as in most things, the clan worked as a unit to achieve its ends. Simp Bowsmith was little enough of a problem sober; but with a few swallows of wildcat in him, the boy ran like butter.

"Why, you know we'd do the world for ye, lad," said the rat-faced elder as he shifted to bring the bundle into the lamplight spilling from the open door. It was just what the boy had claimed, a strop of heavy leather, tanned with the hair still on, and including the stiff-boned tail as well as the long, translucent horns.

Bowsmith handed the jug to one of the men around him, then spluttered and coughed as he swallowed the last of the mouthful he had taken. "Ye see, sir," he said quickly in an attempt to cover the tears which the liquor had brought to his eyes, "I've a spell t' say, but I need some 'un t' speak the words over whilst I git thim right. He writ thim down fer me, Mister Nathan did. But I cain't read, so's he told me go down t' the settlemint en hev Mister Holden er the sheriff say thim with me."

He carefully unbuttoned the pocket of his shirt, out at the elbows now that his mother was not alive to patch it. With the reverence for writing that other men might have reserved for gold, he handed the rewritten document to Baron Neill.

The patriarch thrust the rolled bullhide to the nearest of his offspring and took the receipt. Turning, he saw Mary Beth and said, "You—girl. Fetch the lamp out here, and thin you git back whar ye belong. Ye know better thin t' nose around whin thar's men talkin'."

"But I mustn't speak the spell out whole till ever'thing's perpared," Bowsmith went on, gouging his calf again with the nail of his big toe. "Thet's cuz hit'll work only the onct, Mister Nathan sez. En effen I'm not wearin' the strop over me when I says it, thin I'll gain some strength but not the whole strength uv the bull."

There was a sharp altercation within the cabin, one female voice shrieking, "En what're we s'posed t' do with no more light thin inside the Devil's butthole? You put that lamp down, Mar' Beth Neill!"

"Zeph," said the Baron in a low voice, but two of his sons were already moving toward the doorway, shifting their rifles to free their right hands.

"Anyhows, I thought ye might read the spell out with me, sir," Bowsmith said. "Thim folk down t' the settlemint, I reckon they don't hev much use fer me."

"I wuz jist—" a woman cried on a rising inflection that ended with the thud of knuckles instead of a slap. The light through the doorway shifted, then brightened. The men came out, one of them carrying a copper lamp with a glass chimney.

The circle of lamplight lay like the finger of God on the group of men. That the Neills were all one family was obvious; that they were a species removed from humanity was possible. They were short men; in their midst, Eldon Bowsmith looked like a scrawny chicken surrounded by rats standing upright. The hair on their scalps was black and straight, thinning even on the youngest, and their foreheads sloped sharply.

Several of the clan were chewing tobacco, but the Baron alone smoked a pipe. The stem of that yellow-bowled meerschaum served him as an officer's swagger stick or a conductor's baton.

"Hold the durn lamp," the patriarch snapped to the son who tried to hand him the instrument. While Bowsmith clasped his hands and watched the Baron in nervous hopefulness, the remainder of the Neill clan eyed the boy sidelong and whispered at the edge of the lighted circle.

Baron Neill unfolded the document carefully and held it high so that the lamp illuminated the writing from behind his shoulder. Smoke dribbled from his nostrils in short puffs as his teeth clenched on the stem of his pipe.

When the Baron lowered the receipt, he removed the pipe from his mouth. His eyes were glaring blank fury, but his tongue said only, "I wonder, boy, effen yer Mister Nathan warn't funnin' ye along. This paper he give ye, hit don't hev word one on it. Hit's jist Babel."

One of the younger Neills took the document which the Baron held spurned at his side. Three of the others crowded closer and began to argue in whispers, one of them tracing with his finger the words written in sepia ink beneath the receipt.

"Well, they hain't words, Bar'n," said the boy, surprised that he knew something which the other man— any other man, he might have said—did not. "I mean, not like we'd speak. Mister Nathan, he said what he writ out wuz the sounds, so's I didn't hev occasion t' be consarned they wuz furrin words."

Baron Neill blinked, as shocked to hear a reasoned exposition from Simp Bowsmith as the boy was to have offered it. After momentary consideration, he decided to treat the information as something he had known all the time. "Leave thet be!" he roared, whirling on the cluster of his offspring poring over the receipt.

Two of the men were gripping the document at the same time. Both of them released it and jumped back, bumping their fellows and joggling the lantern dangerously. They collided again as they tried unsuccessfully to catch the paper before it fluttered to the board floor.

The Baron cuffed the nearer and swatted at the other as well, missing when the younger man dodged back behind the shelter of his kin. Deliberately, his agitation suggested only by the vehemence of the pull he took on his pipe, the old man bent and retrieved the document. He peered at it again, then fixed his eyes on Bowsmith. "You say you're t' speak the words on this. Would thet be et some particular time?"

"No sir," said the boy, bobbing his head as if in an effort to roll ideas to the surface of his mind. "Not thet Mister Nathan told me."

As Baron Neill squinted at the receipt again, silently mouthing the syllables which formed no language of which he was cognizant, Bowsmith added, "Jist t' set down with the bullhide over my back, en t' speak out the words. En I'm ez strong ez a bull."

"Give him another pull on the jug," the Baron ordered abruptly.

"I don't—" Bowsmith began as three Neills closed on him, one offering the jug with a gesture as imperious as that of a highwayman presenting his pistol.

"Boy," the Baron continued, "I'm going t' help ye, jist like you said. But hit's a hard task, en ye'll hev t' bear with me till I'm ready. Ain't like reg'lar readin', this parsin' out things ez ain't words."

He fixed the boy with a fierce glare which was robbed of much of its effect because the lamp behind him threw his head into bald silhouette. "Understand?"

"Yessir."

"Drink my liquor, boy," suggested the man with the jug. "Hit'll straighten yer quill for sure."

"Yessir."

"Now," Baron Neill went on, refolding the receipt

and sliding it into the pocket of his own blue frock coat, "you set up with the young folks, hev a good time, en we'll make ye up a bed with us fer the night. Meanwhiles, I'm goin' down t' the barn t' study this over so's I kin help ye in the mornin'.'"

"Oh," said Bowsmith in relief, then coughed as fumes of the whiskey he had just drunk shocked the back of his nostrils. "Lordy," he muttered, wheezing to get his breath. "Lordy!"

One of the Neills thumped him hard on the back and said, "Chase thet down with another, so's they fight each other en leave you alone."

"Thet bullhide," said the Baron, calculation underlying the appearance of mild curiosity, "hit's somethin' special, now, ain't it?"

"Reckon it might be," the boy agreed, glad to talk because it delayed by that much the next swig of the liquor that already spun his head and his stomach. "Hit was pegged up t' Mister Nathan's wall like hit hed been thar a right long time."

"Figgered thet," Baron Neill said in satisfaction. "Hed t' be somethin' more thin ye'd said."

Bowsmith sighed and took another drink. For a moment there was no sound but the hiss of the lamp and a whippoorwill calling from the middle distance.

"Reckon I'll take the hide with me t' the barn," said the Baron, reaching for the rolled strop, "so's hit won't git trod upon."

The grandson holding the strip of hide turned so that his body blocked the Baron's intent. "Reckon we kin keep it here en save ye the burden, ol' man," he said in a sullen tone raised an octave by fear of the consequences.

"What's this, now?" the patriarch said, backing a half step and placing his hands on his hips.

"Like Len sez," interjected the man with the lamp,

stepping between his father and his son, "we'll keep the hide safe back here."

"Tarnation," Baron Neill said, throwing up his hands and feigning good-natured exasperation. "Ye didn't think yer own pa 'ud shut ye out wholesale, did ye?"

"Bar'n," said Eldon Bowsmith, emboldened by the liquor, "I don't foller ye."

"Shet your mouth whin others er talkin' family matters, boy," snapped one of the clan from the fringes. None of the women could be seen through the open door of the cabin, but their hush was like the breathing of a restive cow.

"You youngins hev fun," said the Baron, turning abruptly. "I've got some candles down t' the barn. I'll jist study this"—he tapped with the pipestem on the pocket in which paper rustled—"en we'll talk agin, mebbe 'long about moonrise."

Midnight.

"Y'all hev fun," repeated the old man as he began to walk down the slippery path to the barn.

The Neill women, led by Mary Beth with her comb readjusted to let her hair fall to her shoulders, softly joined the men on the porch.

In such numbers, even the bare feet of his offspring were ample warning to Baron Neill before Zephaniah opened the barn door. The candle of molded tallow guttered and threatened to go out.

"Simp?" the old man asked. He sat on the bar of an empty stall with the candle set in the slot cut higher in the end post for another bar.

It had been years since the clan kept cows. The only animal now sharing the barn with the patriarch and the smell of sour hay was Bowsmith's horse, her jaws knotted closed with a rag to keep her from neighing. Her stall was curtained with blankets against the vague possibility that the boy would glance into the building.

"Like we'd knocked him on the head," said the third man in the procession entering the barn. The horse wheezed through her nostrils and pawed the bars of her stall.

"Why ain't we done jist thet?" demanded Mary Beth. "Nobody round here's got a scrap uv use fer him, 'ceptin' mebbe thet ol' bastard cunning man. En he's not right in the head neither."

The whole clan was padding into the barn, but the building's volume was a good match for their number. There were several infants, one of them continuing to squall against its mother's breast until a male took it from her. The mother cringed, but she relaxed when the man only pinched the baby's lips shut with a thumb and forefinger. He increased the pressure every time the infant swelled itself for another squawl.

"Did I raise ye up t' be a fool, girl?" Baron Neill demanded angrily, jabbing with his pipestem. "Sure, they've a use fer him—t' laugh et. Effen we slit his throat en weight his belly with stones, the county'll be here with rope and torches fer the whole lot uv us."

He took a breath and calmed as the last of the clan trooped in. "Besides, hain't needful. Never do what hain't needful."

One of the men swung the door to and rotated a peg to hold it closed. The candleflame thrashed in the breeze, then steadied to a dull, smoky light as before.

"Now . . ." said the Baron slowly, "I'll tell ye what we're going' t' do."

Alone of the Neill clan, he was seated. Some of those spread into the farther corners could see nothing of the patriarch save his legs crossed as he sat on the stall bar. There were over twenty people in the barn, including the infants, and the faint illumination accentuated the similarity of their features.

Len, the grandson who held the bullhide, crossed his arms to squeeze the bundle closer to his chest. He spread his legs slightly, and two of his bearded, rat-faced kin stepped closer as if to defend him from the Baron's glare.

The patriarch smiled. "We're all goin' t' be stronger thin strong," he said in a sinuous, enticing whisper. "Ye heard Simp—he'd gain strength whether er no the strop wuz over his back. So . . . I'll deacon the spell off, en you all speak the lines out after me, standin' about in the middle."

He paused in order to stand up and search the faces from one side of the room to the other. "Hev I ever played my kinfolk false?" he demanded. The receipt in his left hand rustled, and the stem of his pipe rotated with his gaze. Each of his offspring lowered his or her eyes as the pointer swept the clan.

Even Len scowled at the rolled strop instead of meeting the Baron's eyes, but the young man said harshly, "Who's t' hold the hide, thin? You?"

"The hide'll lay over my back," Baron Neill agreed easily, "en the lot uv you'll stand about close ez ye kin git and nobody closer thin the next. I reckon we all gain, en I gain the most."

The sound of breathing made the barn itself seem a living thing, but no one spoke and even the sputter of the candle was audible. At last Mary Beth, standing hipshot and only three-quarters facing the patriarch, broke the silence with, "You're not ez young ez ye onct were, Pa. Seems ez if the one t' git the most hed ought t' be one t' be around t' use hit most."

Instead of retorting angrily, Baron Neill smiled and said, "Which one, girl? Who do you pick in my place?"

The woman glanced around her. Disconcerted, she

squirmed backward, out of the focus into which she had thrown herself.

"He's treated us right," murmured another woman, half-hidden in the shadow of the post which held the candle. "Hit's best we git on with the business."

"All right, ol' man," said Len, stepping forward to hold out the strop. "What er ye waitin' on?"

"Mebbe fer my kin t' come t' their senses," retorted the patriarch with a smile of triumph.

Instead of snatching the bullhide at once, Baron Neill slid his cold pipe into the breast pocket of his coat, then folded the receipt he had taken from Bowsmith and set it carefully on the endpost of the stall.

Len pursed his lips in anger, demoted from central figure in the clan's resistance to the Baron back to the boy who had been ordered to hold the bullhide. The horns, hanging from the section of the bull's coarse poll which had been lifted, rattled together as the young man's hands began to tremble with emotion.

Baron Neill took off his frock coat and hung it from the other post supporting the bar on which he had waited. Working deliberately, the Baron shrugged the straps of his galluses off his shoulders and lowered his trousers until he could step out of them. His boots already stood toes-out beside the stall partition. None of the others of the clan were wearing footgear.

"Should we . . . ?" asked one of the men, pinching a pleat of his shirt to finish the question.

"No need," the Baron said, unbuttoning the front of his own store-bought shirt. "Mebbe not fer me, even. But best t' be sure."

One of the children started to whine a question. His mother hushed him almost instantly by clasping one hand over his mouth and the other behind the child's head to hold him firmly.

The shirt was the last of Baron Neill's clothing. When he had draped it over his trousers and coat, he looked even more like the white-furred rodent he resembled clothed. His body was pasty, its surface colored more by grime and the yellow candlelight than by blood vessels beneath it. The epaulettes on the Baron's coat had camouflaged the extreme narrowness of his shoulders and chest, and the only place his skin was taut was where the pot belly sagged against it.

His eyes had a terrible power. They seemed to glint even before he took the candle to set it before him on the floor compacted of earth, dung, and ancient straw.

The Baron removed the receipt from the post on which it waited, opened it and smoothed the folds, and placed it beside the candle. Only then did he say to Len, "Now I'll take the strop, boy."

His grandson nodded sharply and passed the bundle over. The mood of the room was taut, like that of a stormy sky in the moments before the release of lightning. The anger and embarrassment which had twisted Len's face into a grimace earlier was now replaced by blank fear. Baron Neill smiled at him grimly.

The bull's tail was stiff with the bones still in it, so the length of hide had been wound around the base of that tail like thread on a spindle. Baron Neill held the strop by the head end, one hand on the hairless muzzle and the other on the poll between the horns, each the length of a man's arm along the curve. He shook out the roll with a quick jerk that left the brush of the tail scratching on the boards at the head of the stall.

The Baron cautiously held the strop against his back with the clattering horns dangling down to his knees. The old man gave a little shudder as the leather touched his bare skin, but he knelt and leaned forward, tugging the strop upward until the muzzle flopped loosely in front of his face.

The Baron muttered something that started as a curse and blurred into nondescript syllables when he recalled the task he was about. He rested the palm of one hand on the floor, holding the receipt flat and in the light of the candle. With his free hand, he folded the muzzle and forehead of the bull back over the poll so that he could see.

"Make a circle around me," ordered the patriarch in a voice husky with its preparations for declaiming the spell.

He should have been ridiculous, a naked old man on all fours like a dog, his head and back crossed by a strip of bullhide several times longer than the human torso. The tension in the barn kept even the children of the clan from seeing humor in the situation, and the muzzled plowhorse froze to silence in her curtained stall.

The Neills shuffled into motion, none of them speaking. The man who held the infant's lips pinched shut handed the child back to its mother. It whimpered only minutely and showed no interest in the breast which she quickly offered it to suck.

Two of the grandsons joined hands. The notion caught like gunpowder burning, hands leaping into hands. In the physical union, the psychic pressure that weighted the barn seemed more bearable though also more intense.

"Remember," said the Baron as he felt his offspring merge behind him, two of them linking hands over the trailing strop, "Ye'll not hev another chance. En ye'll git no pity from me effen ye cain't foller my deaconin' en you're no better off thin ye are now."

"Go on, ol man," Mary Beth demanded in a savage whisper as she looked down on Baron Neill and the candle on the floor between her and the patriarch.

Baron Neill cocked his head up to look at the woman. She met his eyes with a glare as fierce as his own. Turning back to the paper on the ground, the old man read, "Ek neckroo say Üxwmettapempomie."

The candle guttered at his words. The whole clan responded together, "Ek neckroo say mettapempomie," their merged voices hesitant but gaining strength and unity toward the last of the Greek syllables like the wind in advance of a rainstorm.

"Soy sowma moo didomie," read the Baron. His normal voice was high-pitched and unsteady, always on the verge of cracking. Now it had dropped an octave and had power enough to drive straw into motion on the floor a yard away.

"Soy sowma moo didomie," thundered the Neill clan. Sparrows, nested on the roof trusses, fluttered and peeped as they tried furiously to escape from the barn. In the darkness, they could not see the vents under the roof peaks by which they flew in and out during daylight.

Baron Neill read the remainder of the formula, line by line. The process was becoming easier, because the smoky candle had begun to burn with a flame as white as the noonday sun. The syllables which had been written on age-yellowed paper and a background of earlier words now stood out and shaped themselves to the patriarch's tongue.

At another time, the Baron would have recognized the power which his tongue released but could not control. This night the situation had already been driven over a precipice. Caution was lost in exhilaration at the approaching climax, and the last impulse to stop was stilled by the fear that stopping might already be impossible.

The shingles above shuddered as the clan repeated the lines, and the candleflame climbed with the icy purpose of a stalagmite reaching for completion with a cave roof. Jen kicked at her stall in blind panic, cracking through the old crossbar, but none of the humans heard the sound.

"Hellon moy," shouted Baron Neill in triumph. "Hellon moy! Hellon moy!"

Mary Beth suddenly broke the circle and twisted. "Hit's hot!" she cried as she tore the front of her dress from neckline to waist in a single hysterical effort.

The woman's breasts swung free, their nipples erect and longer than they would have seemed a moment before. She tried to scream, but the sound fluted off into silence as her body ran like wax in obedience to the formula she and her kin had intoned.

The circle of the Neill clan flowed toward its center, flesh and bone alike taking on the consistency of magma. Clothing dropped and quivered as the bodies it had covered runneled out of sleeves and through the weave of the fabrics.

The bullhide strop sagged also as Baron Neill's body melted beneath it. As the pink, roiling plasm surged toward the center of the circle, the horns lifted and bristles that had lain over the bull's spine in life sprang erect.

The human voices were stilled, but the sparrows piped a mad chorus and Jen's hooves crashed again onto the splintering crossbar.

There was a slurping, gurgling sound. The bull's tail stood upright, its brush waving like a flag, and from the seething mass that had been the Neill clan rose the mighty, massive form of a black bull.

Eldon Bowsmith lurched awake on the porch of the Neill house. He had dreamed of a bull's bellow so loud that it shook the world.

Fuddled but with eyes adapted to the light of the crescent moon, he looked around him. The house was still and dark.

Then, as he tried to stand with the help of the porch rail, the barn door flew apart with a shower of splinters. Spanish King, bellowing again with the fury of which only a bull is capable, burst from the enclosure and galloped off into the night.

Behind him whinnied a horse which, in the brief glance vouchsafed by motion and the light, looked a lot like Jen.

When Eldon Bowsmith reached the cabin, Old Nathan was currying his bull by the light of a burning pine knot thrust into the ground beside the porch. A horse was tethered to the rail with a makeshift neck halter of twine.

"Sir, is thet you?" the boy asked cautiously.

"Who en blazes d'ye think hit 'ud be?" the cunning man snapped.

"Don't know thet 'un," snorted Spanish King. His big head swung toward the visitor, and one horn dipped menacingly.

"Ye'd not be here, blast ye," said Old Nathan, slapping the bull along the jaw, "'ceptin' fer him."

"Yessir," said Bowsmith. "I'm right sorry. Only, a lot uv what I seed t'night, I figgered must be thet I wuz drinkin'."

"Took long enough t' fetch me," rumbled the bull as he snuffled the night air. He made no comment about the blow, but the way he studiously ignored Bowsmith suggested that the reproof had sunk home. "Summer's nigh over."

He paused and turned his head again so that one brown eye focused squarely on the cunning man. "Where wuz I, anyhow? D'ye know?"

"Not yet," said Old Nathan, stroking the bull's sweat-matted shoulders fiercely with the curry comb.

"Pardon, sir?" said the boy who had walked into the

circle of torchlight, showing a well-justified care to keep Old Nathan between him and Spanish King. Then he blinked and rose up on his bare toes to peer over the bull's shoulder at the horse. "Why," he blurted, "thet's the spit en image uv my horse Jen, only thet this mare's too boney!"

"Thet's yer Jen, all right," said the cunning man. "There's sacked barley in the lean-to out back, effen ye want t' feed her some afore ye take her t' home. Been runnin' the woods, I reckon."

"We're goin' back home?" asked the horse, speaking for almost the first time since she had followed Spanish King rather than be alone in the night.

"Oh, my God, Jen!" said the boy, striding past Spanish King with never a thought for the horns. "I'm so glad t' see ye!" He threw his arm around the horse's neck while she whickered, nuzzling the boy in hopes of finding some of the barley Old Nathan had mentioned.

"Durn fool," muttered Spanish King; but then he stretched himself deliberately, extending one leg at a time until his deep chest was rubbing the sod. "Good t' be back, though," he said. "Won't say it ain't."

Eldon Bowsmith straightened abruptly and stepped away from his mare, though he kept his hand on her mane. "Sir," he said, "ye found my Jen, en ye brung her back. What do I owe ye?"

Old Nathan ran the fingers of his free hand along the bristly spine of his bull. "Other folk hev took care uv thet," the cunning man said as Spanish King rumbled in pleasure at his touch. "Cleared yer account, so t' speak."

The pine torch was burning fitfully, close to the ground, so that Bowsmith's grimace of puzzlement turned shadows into a devil's mask. "Somebody paid for me?" he asked. "Well, I niver. Friends, hit must hev been?"

Spanish King lifted himself and began to walk regally around the cabin to his pasture and the two cows who were his property.

"Reckon ye could say thet," replied Old Nathan. "They wuz ez nigh t' bein' yer friends ez anybody's but their own."

The cunning man paused and grinned like very Satan. "In the end," he said, "they warn't sich good friends t' themselves."

A gust of wind rattled the shingles, as if the night sky were remembering what it had heard at the Neill place. Then it was silent again.

The Box

"What 'm I bid what 'm I bid what 'm I bid?" Sheriff
Tillinghast rattled out like a squirrel complaining.
"Come on, fellers, a nice piece like this could set in
the finest parlor in New Orleens."

What a grotesquely carven chest like the one at
auction would be doing in any kind of parlor in New
Orleans was an open question, but a rough-hewn man
ahead of Bully Ransden and Ellie in the crowd called,
"I'll give ye a dollar fer the blame thing!"

"Bid a dolla bid a dolla bid a dolla!" the sheriff
caroled. "Who'll gimme two gimme two?"

He paused for breath and a practiced glance around
the gathering, checking for anyone who might be on
the verge of raising the bid. Nobody. . . .

The sheriff lifted the jug of whiskey from the table
beside him, where his clerk marked down the winning
bids against the lot numbers. "Who'll gimme two?" the
sheriff repeated. "A dram uv good wildcat fer the man
as bids two dollars!"

"Two dollars!" cried a fellow down in front. He probably didn't have the money to his name, much less in his pocket, and the auction was for ready cash . . . but the bidding was already too slow for the auctioneer to dare risk stifling the little life it had finally gathered to itself.

"Two dolla two dolla two dolla, who'll gimma three?" prattled the sheriff.

"Ugh!" said Ellie as she hugged herself closer to Bully Ransden. "Who'd hev thet ugly ole thing in their house noways?"

The Bully grunted without enthusiasm. He was present because Ellie had wanted to come, "t' pick up a purty fer the house," and he wasn't going to have his woman going to an auction alone. Next time, though, she could stay to home. . . .

The chest finally sold for three dollars and a half. Taxes had accumulated for many years on the Neill property, but neither Sheriff Tillinghast nor any of his predecessors had chosen to bring matters to a head while the Baron was in possession. When Baron Neill and his whole clan vanished—no one knew or cared where, so long as the Neills were gone for good—the sheriff had promptly set the tax sale.

There was a good crowd, 300 at least, swirling around the run-down cabin and sheds, but the bidding was slow. At the current rate, the auction wouldn't bring enough to cover the accumulated tax bills.

"I don't like this place airy bit," Ellie murmured, more to herself than to Bully. He grunted noncommittally and, though he didn't draw away from her touch, neither did he circle her with his strong right arm.

The sheriff wiped his brow with a kerchief. His assistants were Mitch Reynolds and Jeb Cage, a pair of idlers working for the promise of whiskey after the auction. Tillinghast motioned them to bring up the next lot.

This place had an atmosphere even after the Neills themselves were gone. It made folk uneasy and weighed down the bidding. Even the sheriff, spurred by the knowledge that part of the taxes he collected went directly into his pocket by law—and another portion arrived there by other means—was unable to raise a proper enthusiasm for his task.

Tillinghast's assistants grunted as they lifted a small travelling case containing a uniformly bound set of books. "Here we go!" the sheriff said. "Must be nigh twinty books right here, 'n a real jam li'l chest besides. Who'll start the bid at five dollas?"

"What're the books?" someone called from the crowd.

"Hit don't signify!" snapped Sheriff Tillinghast. "Why, they's so many I reckon thar's one uv airy thing a man might wish t' read!"

"They're Frinch," Jeb Cage said unexpectedly. If Tillinghast had known the blamed drunken fool could read, he would have told Cage to keep his mouth shut on pain of losing the promised popskull.

The crowd burst out laughing. A number of the folk here spoke French from keelboat journeys down the Tennessee, Ohio, and Mississippi to New Orleans. The vocabulary learned in the cribs of the French Quarter was not the language of Voltaire; and anyway, speaking was not the same as reading.

"Hey, Shuruff!" somebody called. "I figger you know now whur thet Frinchman disappeared on the way from Columbia back in twinny-siven, don't ye?"

"Some of the books, they may be Frinch, I don't know," Tillinghast said loudly in an attempt to retrieve the situation. He wiped his forehead again. "Now, this is a right fine chest. Who'll start the bidding at a dolla a dolla a dolla, who gimme a dolla?"

"Why, I reckon the Frenchman, he give the durn

thing t' Baron Neill fer free!" a heckler called from the crowd.

"Aye!" another chimed in. "An' he fed their hogs fer 'em in a neighborly way too er it's a pity!"

"Cull, I don't reckon I want t' stay much longer," Ellie Ransden murmured to the man at her side.

She'd dragged him to the auction for a change, and in the vague hope that something pretty for the cabin might be going at the slight price she and Bullie could afford. She'd ignored who—and what—the Neills were, though. You couldn't separate an object from its past, any more than you'd eat pork from a sow been grubbing in a grave. . . .

"I give ye a dolla," offered a farmer named Murchison. "Reckon the case, hit's worth sompin."

Tillinghast glanced around the personalty waiting for sale. He saw his chance to keep the bidding alive by throwing in an item he hadn't a prayer of selling by itself. He raised a cubical box some six inches to a side and placed it atop the chest of books.

"Hyar!" the sheriff called. "We'll sweeten the pot fer all you bettin' men out thar. This here box, hit goes with the books t' boot."

Ellie felt Bully Ransden stiffen as though he had been changed to a statue of oak. She looked at him in surprise. His mouth was slightly open.

"Waal, what's in the durned box, Shurrif?" someone demanded from the back of the crowd.

"Don't rightly know, Windell," Tillinghast replied smugly. "Don't rightly see how hit opens, neither. Reckon airy man with a drap uv sportin' blood'll want the box t' larn fer himse'f, though."

The box made no sound when it was shaken. Either it was empty or, just possibly, it wasn't a box at all: merely a block of wood less dense than it seemed from its hard surface to be.

The cube's base and top were smooth. A band around the center of the four sides was undercut in a pattern of vertical half-round sections. The patterning might have been sliced from lathe-turned dowels, but equally they could have been carved from the block's surface by an expert.

There was nothing in the box, or there was no box—but the object would do to spur the bidding.

"Thet's mine," said Bully Ransden. He pushed forward as though the people in front of him in the crowd were no more than stalks of barley sprouted ankle high. "I'll take hit."

"Cullen?" Ellie said. She caught at the big man's leather vest, more to stay attached than to restrain him. He hunched his shoulders and pulled away, oblivious to her touch.

"Cull, what're ye—"

Sheriff Tillinghast drew himself up stiffly, but he did not protest aloud. Murchison didn't face the specter of Bully Ransden, cold-eyed and broad-shouldered, bearing down on him like a landslide. He cried, "Hey naow, what's this? We're biddin' fer riddy cash, we are!"

Bully reached the front of the crowd. He shrugged, clearing a space with his elbows the way an angry bull sweeps his horns across the ground.

"I'll give ye cash," Ransden said in a husky voice that ripped like a saw through pinewood. His great, calloused hand dragged out the purse hanging by a thong on the inside of his waistband. He opened the throat and poured the contents of the purse, all coin and the savings of a lifetime, out onto the clerk's table.

Ellie gasped and covered her mouth with her hands. Her teeth bore down firmly on the first knuckle of her right index finger.

Bully Ransden took the box. Tillinghast quivered with a desire to assert his own authority, but he noticed how easily Bully's hands spanned six inches to grip the box between thumb and forefinger.

"Waal, what's the bid, thin, Shurrif?" Murchison demanded. "Might be I'd choose t' raise my own!"

Ransden turned and faced the farmer before Sheriff Tillinghast formed a response. "This box is mine, Murchison," he said in a voice hard as millstones.

"Three dollar and thutty-sivin cents," announced the clerk who had counted the spill of coins while the others concerned themselves with the human elements of the incident.

"Now, thet's a right good bid, boys," Tillinghast said in false camaraderie.

"You say airy word more, Murchison," Ransden promised, "en ye won't see t'morry dawn."

He struck his muscular right arm out to the side and raised his thumb as if he were gouging an eye. Nobody who had seen Bully Ransden fight doubted the truth of the threat.

The crowd swayed back from Bully Ransden the way a horse shies when he comes upon a corpse in the trail. From the rear of the gathering, a voice called, "Shurrif, hit's time 'n past ye did sompin about these carryins on!"

"There's enough here fer you too, Jake Windell, ifen ye want it!" Ransden boomed. He held the small box against his chest protectively as he glared out over the crowd. His eyes flashed, and his long blond hair caught a sunbeam to halo him.

"Bids closed," Tillinghast said. He rapped his gavel down. "And a right good bid hit was, too. The next item, now—"

Ransden strode back through the crowd that parted for him as the waters before Moses. Ellie managed to swiggle to his side, but Ransden gave every indication of having forgotten completely about her.

"Hey, Bully!" the sheriff called. "Them books, they're yours now too."

Ransden ignored him. After a moment, Tillinghast began calling out the next lot, a pair of European chairs on which the Neill clan had whittled with their knives.

Bully Ransden unhitched his horse and mounted. He blinked in surprise when Ellie finally caught his attention by tugging on his leg. He pulled her up onto the crupper behind him, then turned the horse's head toward home.

"Cull, sweetest?" Ellie asked in a small voice. "What's the box thet ye wanted hit so bad?"

Ransden carried his prize instead of giving it to the woman to carry as he would normally have done. He said nothing for a moment, then admitted, "I don't know quite what hit is. But it war my pappy's box en the thing he loved afore all others. And I reckon I'll larn why soon enough."

Two cardinals were plucking pokeberries near where Old Nathan sat with his back against a warm rock overlooking the valley. "Waal, is she goin' to make trouble?" one bird demanded of other.

"How 'n tarnation 'ud I know?" the second bird answered in the same harsh, peevish tones; not that anybody was likely to mistake a cardinal on the best day of his life for a songster. "Don't guess she is. They ain't ginerly, humans ain't."

Old Nathan turned his head. The outcrop was in the way of him seeing anything behind him unless he stood up. If the birds hadn't said "she," the cunning man might have been concerned enough to rise. As it was— he didn't much care to be disturbed, but he didn't guess any woman was likely to try for his scalp when she found him here.

From the outcrop on which Old Nathan sat, he

could see the smoke of six chimneys. The valley was open and sunlit. The cleared fields had been harvested, and much of the foliage had fallen from the woodlots and thickets.

"Hmph!" said a cardinal. "Don't even look et us. Does she think she's sech a beauty herse'f?"

Old Nathan's thoughts had been meandering down pathways in which alternate pasts shimmered as if behind walls of glass; untouchable now because of the decisions the cunning man had made, and the decisions fate had made for him. Some beautiful, some bleak; all void, and after seventy-odd years, all too many of them stillborn.

He didn't want to move, but if someone was coming, he had to. He rose to his feet, straightening his lanky limbs; carefully, because he was an old man and stiff, but with a certain grace yet remaining to him.

Sarah Ransden, coming around the rock with her head lowered, gasped and drew back at the motion.

"Hain't a bear, Miz Ransden," the cunning man said dryly. "En I was jest leavin' anyhow."

" 'Sarah' was a good enough name sixty years ago, Nathan Ridgeway," the old woman snapped, embarrassed at her instinctive surprise. "Reckon hit still might be."

She looked down into the valley. Sarah Ransden— Sarah Carmichael as she'd been when she and Old Nathan were children together—was a tall woman, though age had made her stoop. She had never been beautiful, though she might have been called handsome and indeed still was. Sarah hadn't married in her youth, which was a pity; and late in life she'd wed Chance Ransden, which was far worse.

The old woman shivered and drew her blue knitted shawl more closely about her. "Hit's goin t' storm, I reckon," she muttered.

Old Nathan frowned. The only clouds were some wisps of mare's tails standing out against a background of high-altitude haze.

The cunning man's index finger drew a figure in the lichen of the outcrop. He kept his eyes on the simple character as he muttered a phrase beneath his breath, then gestured Sarah's attention upward toward the sky.

Clouds shifted and began to chase one another with mad enthusiasm across the heavens. Light pulsed into darkness and gleamed again. The mare's tails thickened into a mackerel sky, ridge after ridge of gray-white against pale blue; but that cleared with a rush eastward toward the foot of the valley, leaving the air with a sheen as smooth as that of a knifeblade when the racing images darkened again.

Old Nathan rubbed his thumb across the lichen, eliminating the character. The sky reverted to the bright afternoon normalcy from which the cunning man's art had dragged it briefly.

"Thet's t'day and t'morry," Old Nathan said. "Don't reckon we need fear a storm fer thet while."

"You know what you know, Nathan," the old woman said. She shivered again. Her hand rested on the rock as she gazed out over the valley.

Old Nathan settled his broad-brimmed hat. "Waal . . ." he said.

Sarah looked at him sharply. "Ye needn't t' go, Nathan Ridgeway," she said. "I jest cloomb up t' look from a high place. Hit's a thing I do . . . but I don't see you here, ez a rule."

The cunning man shrugged. The cardinals had resumed their feeding, commenting in griping tones on the quality of the late pokeberries. The humans had shown themselves to be no threat, and therefore of no interest. . . .

"Sometimes," Old Nathan said in the direction of

the far horizon, "I think I might move on west. No pertikaler cause. Don't reckon I'll iver do it."

"Thet girl you had back along b'fore ye went off t' the war," Sarah said, also facing the western end of the valley. "Slowly, her name was. Ye think on her, iver?"

"Mebbe," said Old Nathan. "Sometimes, I reckon. But thet's over and done long since."

The sun was still near zenith, but its rays had little warmth now in late fall. When Old Nathan left the shelter of the outcrop to walk back to his cabin—he hadn't saddled the mule, hadn't wanted the beast's company or any company—the trail would be chilly.

Darkness would not be long in coming.

"My datter-in-law, Ellie . . ." Sarah Ransden said. She glanced at Old Nathan. "I b'lieve ye've met her?"

Old Nathan nodded toward the horizon. "I hev."

"Ellie reminds me a powerful lot uv Slowly," Sarah continued. Her tones were flat.

She turned her head away. "I don't see Ellie much." Bitterness tinged her voice. "Nor my son neither, not since he moved out. He allus figgered I should uv left Chance Ransden myse'f, 'stid uv waitin' till Cullen druv him out with an axe handle an' him jest a boy. Cull don't understand what hit is fer a woman married to a feller like Chance Ransden—"

She turned to meet Old Nathan's eyes, for the cunning man had turned also. "—and it could be thet I did do wrong, fer Cull and myse'f both. The good Lord knows I hain't been lucky with men, Nathan Ridgeway."

Old Nathan snorted. "I hain't been lucky with people, Sary," he said. "But I reckon the most of thet's my own doing."

His thumb had rubbed a patch of limestone free of lichen. He wanted to leave, but that would mean moving past the woman and he didn't much care to

do that either. In the forest above, a squirrel berated
a crow for startling him, and the crow offered to shit
in the squirrel's mouth if the critter didn't shut it. Life
went on.

"Chance warn't a bad man," Sarah Ransden said in
a tone that reminded Old Nathan of the days when
they had been children together. "Only thar was a divil
in him. I thought I was blest ez an angel that he picked
me, him so handsome and a sight younger. But the divil
rode Chance Ransden, harder an' harder iver' day till
the last time he tried t' take a strap t' Cull . . ."

She stiffened. In a flat, age-cracked voice she concluded, "Thet war the last I saw Chance Ransden, ten
year since. Figgered he run off t' the Neills, he were
thick ez thieves with thim. But I niver heard word one
uv him agin. Nowadays, I don't reckon I will."

"I reckon I'll be movin' on now," Old Nathan said.
He paused to clear his throat. "Good t' see you agin,
Sary."

He stepped toward the woman. Instead of edging
back to let him by, she put a hand on Old Nathan's
arm. Her fingers, tanned and sinewy, stood out against
his faded homespun shirt like tree roots crawling over
gray rock.

"You don't need a young gal, Nathan Ridgeway," she
said. "Ye need an old one what's worn inter the same
ruts ez you."

"I don't need airy woman, Miz Ransden," the cunning man said harshly. He lifted her hand away from
his arm. Their fingers were much of a kind, dark-
tanned and knobby at the joints. "You know thet."

"Thar's companionship," Sarah said. "Thar's hevin'
somebody t' say howdy to in the mornin'!"

Old Nathan pushed past her. His boots scuffed bits
of stone down the slope until they pattered to a halt
among the fallen leaves and pine straw.

"I niver figgered thet was enough t' offer airy soul, Sary," he said gruffly. "Thet's why I sint Slowly away whin I come back from King's Mountain."

He paused and looked westward again. "Thet's as fur as I've been, King's Mountain. Reckon the way thet turned out, I kin see why I hain't been travelin' since. . . . But I should hev gone, Sary. Comin' back here t' lick myse'f where iverbody knew me, thet was wrong. I should hev gone."

Old Nathan started up the trail. Nuthatches disputed sharply over a pine cone. The birds were not so much angry as asserting their kinship and mutual interests.

"Thar's a storm comin', Nathan Ridgeway," the old woman called from the overlook. "You know what you know . . . but my bones tell me thar's a storm coming."

"Cullen, honey?" Ellie said in a plaintive voice. "Hain't ye comin' to bed, sweetest?"

Bully Ransden sat at the table with his shoulders hunched. Though he faced in her direction, he didn't bother to look up to where his wife lay under the quilt's protection.

The threat of the season's first snow hung in the chilly night, but it was more than the temperature that caused Ellie to shiver.

"G'wan t' sleep," Bully said. He held the simple box he had purchased at the auction. His fingers moved over its surface like the blunt, questing heads of serpents. The fire had sunk to a glow, but an alcohol lamp on the table threw its pale, clean light over Bully's face and the object in his hands.

"Cull . . . ?"

"Shet it, will ye?" Ransden snarled. "Or I'll shet it fer ye!"

Three nights before, a strip along the bottom of the box had slipped sideways to display a hollow base.

Inside was a key, shaped from apple wood instead of metal and so cunningly fashioned that it hadn't rattled against its compartment when Ransden shook the box.

The key sat on the table beside him. He had still not found any sign of a keyhole.

Ellie began to cry softly.

Bully Ransden put the box down and pressed the knuckles of his two great fists together. "Ellie, honey," he muttered to his hands, "I'm right sorry I spoke t' ye thet way. But you jest get t' sleep 'n leave me be fer the while."

"Cull," the woman said, "why don't ye jest break hit open and come hold me? Hit's only a scrap uv wood."

"Hit's the only thing I've got uv my Pappy's, girl!" the Bully snapped in a barely controlled voice. "I hain't a-goin' t' smash it t' flinders!"

Ellie Ransden sat up in the simple bed and shrugged the quilt aside. She wore only a linen shift, but she had let her hair down for the night. It hung across her shoulders and bosom in a lustrous black veil. "Cull," she said, "you hated Chance Ransden, an' you were right t' hate him. You oughter take thet box and throw hit right straight into the hearth."

Bully looked up with anger bright in his eyes. His mouth formed into a snarl. The woman faced him, seated like a queen on her couch and for the moment as proud and fearless.

"Ye know what I'm sayin's no more thin the truth," she added in a tone of trembling calm.

He gave a shudder and looked at his hands again. "Tarnation, Ellie," he said. "Hit's jest a puzzle. Whin I figger it, I'll be over 'n done with the blame thing."

He spoke without conviction. Ellie's upper lip trembled minutely, though for the moment she retained her regal pose.

"I thought Ma, she hed done jest thet," Bully said

softly. His fingers began playing again with the box. "Throwed hit int' the fire, 'long with airy other thing thet was Pappy's whin I druv him out. Cain't figger how the Neills got aholt uv it. Pappy didn't have it whin . . ."

The young man swallowed. "Whin he left, thet is. And nobody seed him since."

Ellie got up from the bed and stepped toward her man.

"This box, hit set on the fireboard," Ransden murmured. "Time t' time, Pappy took it down and looked inside, but he niver let me nor Ma see what hit was there. . . ."

"Cull, honey—"

The upper portion of the box slipped smoothly for a quarter inch across the hollow base. As if a voice had whispered the secret to him, Bully thumbed down one of the half-round ornamentations now that it could clear the base.

Beneath the ornament was a keyhole.

"Oh, hon," Ellie Ransden whispered. She reached out as if to touch the box or the man; withdrew her arm and wrung her hands together instead. "Oh, Cull, don't do thet. . . ."

Bully Ransden inserted the key and turned it. As he did so, a gust of cold air raked through the cabin without disturbing the dim fire. The alcohol lamp flared wildly. The flame touched the thin glass chimney and shattered it an instant before the light blew out.

Silver radiance flooded across Bully Ransden as he lifted the lid of the puzzle box. It was gone in an instant.

Ellie screamed and tossed a knot of lightwood onto the hearth. The pitchy wood crackled into an honest yellow glare.

The box lay open on the table. It was empty. But

when the man turned to look at her, Ellie saw a glint
of cold light in his eyes.

Old Nathan woke up when his roan heifer bawled,
but he didn't catch the words. A moment later the cat
yowled at the cabin's front door, "Hey old man! Ye got
somebody messin' round yer shed with a gun!"

Old Nathan swung out of bed. He was wearing his
breeches and a shirt. The quilt on his bed with its
gorgeous Tree of Life pattern was down-filled and
thick, but on a cold night a thin old man didn't gen-
erate enough heat to adequately warm the cavity his
body tented within the cover.

His breath hung in the air. He stepped silently to
the flintlock rifle on pegs above the fireboard.

"I don't think thet feller oughter be here," the black-
patterned heifer called, speaking to her roan-patterned
partner but in a voice loud enough for all the world
to hear.

Spanish King was in the far pasture. The great
bull bellowed a question that was almost lost in the
wind.

There was a full moon this night, but it rode above
the overcast. The sash windows were gray rectangles
which scarcely illuminated the dusting of snow that had
slipped in beneath the cabin doors.

"Come on, old man!" the tomcat demanded. "He's
markin' yer patch!"

The hearth was cold, though the coals banked beneath
sloped ashes would bring the fire to life in the morning . . . if there were need for a fire.

Old Nathan loaded his rifle with controlled care. He
poured the main charge of powder into the bore and
followed it with a ball wrapped in a linen patch to take
the shallow rifling. Cold had stiffened the lubricant of
beeswax and butter, so the cunning man eased the

hickory ramrod home so as not to snap it in his haste to have a weapon in his hands.

He replaced the ramrod in its tubular brackets beneath the barrel instead of dropping the lathe-turned stick on the floor to save time. He might need to reload. . . .

Old Nathan's final act of the operation was to measure the smaller priming charge into the pan. Now it was ready to flash from the sparks the flint struck from the steel frizzen whenever the cunning man pulled the trigger.

When the task was complete, Old Nathan began to shiver with the cold.

He pulled on his boots one-handed. The cold leather scraped his heel and ankles, but the cunning man was scarcely aware of the contact. He would need the boots if he had to run any distance through the snow, hunting or hunted.

If there was only the one man his animals had warned of, Old Nathan expected to be the hunter.

With the rifle in his hands, cocked, and the bullet pouch and powder horn slung over his left shoulder, the old man slipped out by the cabin's front door to avoid warning the intruder in back. Snow swirled in crystals too tiny to have obvious shape. The cat had gone off into the night, though the marks of his paws remained on the drifted porch.

The night was gray rather than black, but trees were indistinct blurs from only a few feet away. Old Nathan moved away from the cabin so that the prowler would have no clue to the cunning man's whereabouts should terror cause him to shoot in desperation—

As Old Nathan intended that he should.

The gusting wind drowned any sounds the intruder might make in the creak of branches and moaning air. The heifers continued to complain but in lowered

voices, and the mule chose to be silent for reasons of
its own.

Old Nathan knelt, murmuring words under his
breath. He picked up a pinch of snow between his left
thumb and forefinger, spinning it into the air before
it could melt. The tiny vortex grew into a loose, twisting
funnel of snow. It glowed with the moonlight which
would have fallen on it had the night not been overcast.

The ragged cone slid off among the trees. It moved
in a pattern of arcs and reverse arcs, like a hound
following a scent trail.

Grinning at the proof of his art, the cunning man
sent two more snowy will-o'-the-wisps to follow the
first. They were man height but as soundless as the
transferred light that illuminated them.

Old Nathan squatted among the roots of a century-
old oak whose shade had cleared a considerable circle
in surrounding woods. Winter had stripped the undergrowth to blackened stems which would not interfere
with the cunning man's shot when his prey came in
view. . . .

The intruder's bawl of fear was as high-pitched as
the scream of a rabbit with its hind legs snared. A gun
banged an instant later, the sharp crash of a rifle rather
than the snap of a pistol's smaller charge. Even so, the
night muted the sound to merely another forest noise.

Wind-whipped snow crystals melted before they
reached Old Nathan's flushing cheeks. Anger and the
powers he had summoned warmed the cunning man's
flesh, though he knew there would be a price to pay
when the struggle was over. He trembled with anticipation.

There was a flicker through the treetrunks. A whorl
of moonlit snow reappeared, drifting like a ghost toward
its creator. Another funnel glimmered thirty feet to the

side, while the third was still hidden deeper in the woods where it prevented the intruder from breaking back.

The will-o'-the-wisps were only patterns of snow and cold light, but the purposeful way they moved regardless of the wind gave them an ambiance still more chilling than the night. They drove their quarry like hounds after a raccoon; and, as with coon hounds, a human gunman waited to finish the job the pack began.

Twenty feet away the prowler crashed through the brittle undergrowth like a panicked doe. His breath wheezed in and out. Old Nathan could still not see him for the gloom.

The cunning man muttered a command. A will-o'-the-wisp drifted directly toward the intruder. The third twist of frozen moonlight was now visible through the trees beyond.

The prowler screamed again and swung his empty rifle like a club. The butt slashed through the snow funnel with no more effect than it would have had in a running stream. On the other side of the target, the rifle stock hit a pine and shattered.

The swirl of snow and moonlight quivered closer yet, illuminating its quarry.

Old Nathan sighted across the silver bead of his front sight.

He did not fire. The face of the prowler was that of Bully Ransden, but its bestial expression was not that of anything human.

Ransden hurled away the remains of his rifle. His eyes were too fear-glazed to take in his surroundings, neither the cunning man nor even the will-o'-the-wisps which had driven him to what a finger's pressure would have made his last instant of life. The barrel clanged on a tree.

The funnels of snow settled because the cunning man no longer had the will to maintain them. Bully

Ransden blundered off in the darkness, bleating with fear every time he collided with a tree trunk.

Old Nathan shivered with cold and reaction. There was something badly wrong. The prowler wore the flesh of Bully Ransden, but Bully wasn't the man to skulk and flee. . . .

Old Nathan searched until he found the intruder's rifle. The barrel was kinked, and the stock had broken off at the small. Farther back along the prowler's trail in the fresh snow lay a saddle which the cunning man had hung out of the weather in his shed. The mule saddle was not quite valueless, but it would bring a thief little more than a couple drams of popskull from a crooked buyer.

Old Nathan stared at the saddle and the broken rifle. The yellow tomcat drew himself across the back of the cunning man's boots. "I'm not the one t' tell ye not t' play with things afore ye kill thim," the cat said. "But they hadn't ought t' git plumb clear. 'Specially—"

The cat twisted to look off in the direction Bully Ransden had fled. "—whin they're the size 'n meanness t' tear yer throat clean out the nixt time, old man."

"Whin I want yer advice," the cunning man growled, "I'll ask fer it."

When Old Nathan returned to his cabin, he didn't pull the load from his rifle as he usually would have done. Instead, he emptied the priming pan and refilled it with fresh powder, just in case snow had dampened the original charge.

When they came in sight of the Ransden cabin, the mule snorted, "Hmph!" and blew an explosive puff of breath into the chill, dry air. "Whutiver happened t' the horse whut used t' live here?"

Old Nathan frowned at the dwelling a furlong down the road ahead. Ransden's cabin seemed abnormally quiet, but a line of gray smoke trembled up from the chimney. "I reckon Bully Ransden rid off already this mornin'," he said. "Mebbe he figgered we'd come a-callin'."

Or the Shuriff would.

The mule snorted again. "Hain't no horse lived here these months gone," it said. "Don't smell sign uv airy stock a'tall, neither, though thar used t' be a yoke uv oxen."

The mule's forehoof rang against a lump of quartz beneath the inch of powdery snow. The cabin door quivered open a crack wide enough for a man to peer out and down the road.

There was a cry and a blow from within the cabin.

The cunning man's face hardened. "Git up, mule," he said and tapped back with both heels to show that he was serious.

Bully Ransden bolted from the cabin. His galluses dangled behind him and he had to hop twice on his own porch before his foot seated in his right boot. He ran across the road, into the unbroken forest which faced his tract of cleared land.

The mule had obeyed—for a wonder! The beast's racking trot precluded the slightest chance of hitting anything but air from a hundred and fifty yards. Even so, Old Nathan rose momentarily in his stirrups and sighted down the long, black-finished barrel of his rifle, obedient to the predator's instinct that always urged chase when something ran.

He settled again into the jouncing saddle. The muscles of his upper thighs were already reminding him that he wasn't as young as he once had been.

"Waal?" the mule demanded as it clopped heavily along the frozen ruts. "What naow, durn ye?"

"Pull up, thin," the cunning man muttered. He drew back on the reins with his left hand, though he continued to hold his rifle with the butt against his hipbone and the barrel slanted forward at an angle. "I don't figger we need t' go messin' through the breshwood lookin' fer sompin I don't choose t' shoot nohow."

"I don't figger we needed t' go harin' over the ice fit t' break a leg, neither," the mule grumbled as it slowed to a halt in front of Ransden's cabin. "Might hev thunk on thet afore ye roweled me all bloody, mightn't ye?"

"Mule . . ." Old Nathan said as he rose again in his stirrups to peer into the woods. The Bully was gone past the use of mere eyesight to follow. . . . "Ifen ye keep grindin' thet mill, I'll sell ye t' some fella who'll treat ye jest as you say I do."

The beast's complaint and the old man's threat were both empty rhetoric: the litany and response of folk who'd worn into one anothers' crotchets over the course of years.

The cabin door creaked. Old Nathan turned, swinging the rifle reflexively. Ellie Ransden stood in the doorway with her left hand to her cheek and a shocked expression on her face. She wore only a shift, and her fine black hair was tied back with a twist of tow.

Old Nathan swung his leg over the saddle, pretending that his threatening reflex was merely the first stage in dismounting. "Howdy, Miz Ransden," he called. "Thought I might hev a word with yer man, but I reckon I just missed him."

After a moment he added, "I could come back later ifen this time don't suit."

Ellie straightened. "Oh, law," she said, "I hain't got a thing t' offer ye, sir, but do—"

She looked down at the threadbare cotton shift that was her only garment. "Oh law!" she repeated.

She stepped back and pushed the door to. "Shan't be two flicks uv a cat's tail," she called through the closed panel.

"If I leave you be," the cunning man said to his mule, "you kin find a sunny patch in the lee of a wall 'n mebbe grub up some grass. But ifen ye wander off on me, I'll blister ye good er it's a pity. D'ye hear me, mule?"

"Hmph," said the mule. "I reckon with you runnin' the shoes offen me, up 'n down the high road, I got better things t' do than go gallivantin' somewhar er other on my own."

The barrel and splintered stock of Bully Ransden's rifle were strapped to the mule's saddle. By the time Old Nathan had them loose, Ellie threw the door open again. She wore a check-printed dress; an ornate ivory comb set off the supple black curves of her hair.

The girl's usual complement of additional tortoise-shell combs was missing. The red patch on her left cheek would become a serious bruise before the day was out.

"Come in, Mister Nathan," she said making a pass at a formal curtsey. "I'm all sixes 'n sivins, b-but—"

Her control broke. She didn't blink or avert her eyes, but tears started from the corners of them. "—the good Lord knows thet I'm glad t' see ye!"

Old Nathan mounted the porch steps with his own rifle in one hand and the remains of Bully Ransden's in the other. He paused in the doorway and eyed the trees again. No doubt the Bully was watching from conceal-ment like a fox circling to eye the hounds on his scent, but if he'd been willing to meet the cunning man he could have done so from the protection of his own walls.

Had the thing that looked like Ransden been Bully Ransden in fact, he would have died on his porch before he ran from any hundred men.

Old Nathan shut the door behind him.

The cabin was a wreck. All the furnishings had been damaged to some degree. The chairs' slatted backs were punched in, a boot had smashed the face panels of the storage chests, and the bed frame was missing so that the straw tick and blankets lay on the floor in a pile that Ellie had just attempted to arrange.

Someone had with systematic brutality broken the sturdy legs of the table. It stood upright due to repairs made with twine and splints of leather.

Bully Ransden was a better-than-fair journeyman carpenter. Repairs to the table were Ellie's work.

"Where's yer cattle, Miz Ransden?" the cunning man asked with calculated brutality. He set the broken weapon down on the table carefully, but the splints were firmer than he had feared.

Ellie faced him. "Drunk up er gambled away," she said bluntly. There warn't no point tryin' t' put a fine face on the bus'ness, not ifen ye wanted a cure fer hit. . . .

"Hain't like Bully," Old Nathan said aloud.

"Hit's like Cull these three months past," Ellie replied. Her face twisted into an expression Old Nathan had not seen on it before when she talked about her man. "Hit's like the Bully."

The porcelain plate that had held the place of honor on the Ransden's fireboard was gone. The only ornament there above the hearth was a nondescript wooden box with no evident hinges or keyhole.

For the first time, Ellie took in the shattered rifle which the cunning man had returned to its owner's cabin. "Oh," she whispered. "Oh, Mister Nathan, did he . . . ?"

The cunning man frowned in concern. When Ellie saw the gun, her mind had turned to ambush and murder.

"Naow," he said, "nothin' so turrible ez what yer thinkin' on. I heerd some noise in my shed last night, and the feller makin' it dropped this behind him. I thought yer man might know sommat about hit."

"I reckon he might," Ellie Ransden agreed coldly. She daubed unconsciously at the fist print on her cheek, trying it the way one might try a scab. In the same controlled voice she continued, "Last month, whin thet feller from Saint Louie was clubbed down on the Columbia road. . . . ?"

Old Nathan nodded. A traveller had stopped to relieve himself while the other men in his party rode on. One of his friends had gone back when he decided the night was too dark to leave a man alone on an unfamiliar trail. The sound of the companion's hoof-beats drove away a figure crouching with a knife raised to finish what a blow from behind had begun.

"Cull war out thet night," the girl continued. "Like he is most times now. Nixt day he come in 'n he hed a watch 'n chain. He—"

Her voice began to break. "He saw me look at it," she said, speaking faster and louder to finish the story before she lost control completely. "He a'mos' hit me thin, an' he told me not t' tell a soul what it was he had—" tumbling, word over word "—but I've tolt you now, Mister Nathan!"

Ellie turned so that her back was to her visitor. She was sobbing. In a small voice she continued, "Wax Talbot, he took a shot at Cull when his wife screamed out t' the barn whin Cull war s'posed t' be he'pin' butcher some hogs."

The cunning man still held his rifle. He was uneasy about many things. The only one to which he could put a name was the possibility that the cabin's owner would burst through the doorway with an axe raised, so the rifle's familiar touch was that of a raft to a drowning man.

He wanted to put a hand on Ellie's shoulder to comfort her, but he wasn't sure that wouldn't be a worse idea than any he'd had before.

"This been goin' on three months, Miz Ransden?" Old Nathan asked. "Why hain't ye been t' see me? Might be I could he'p."

Ellie wiped her face on her sleeve. When the cuff, decorated with home-style embroidery, slid up, Old Nathan saw that her wrists were bruised also. His face didn't change, but it was already set in the lumpy gray lines of a thundercloud.

"I don't guess no woman magicked my Cull this time, Mister Nathan," the girl said wearily. Her expression hardened momentarily. "Though I hear tell some uv the sluts hereabouts, they hain't so perticular as Adele Talbot was."

She shook herself. "He's changed, right enough. He ain't my Cull no more. He's jest comin' out like his pappy, the way folks allus warned me he'd do and I paid thim no nivermind."

"I knew Chance Ransden," the cunning man said uneasily. "Bully hain't no frind t' me, but he hain't noways his pappy."

The thing uv it was, Chance Ransden would hev acted exackly the way Bully acted now—cunning and cruel and as petty as he was deceitful. . . .

"I thought he warn't like thet," Ellie said. "But I was wrong, an' I'm payin' fer it, Mister Nathan, payin' fer bein' a f-f-fool!"

She put her hands to her face again, and this time he did put his knobby old arm around her, holding the rifle out to the side and him no kind of man since the Tory bullet gelded him like a shoat at King's Mountain back in '79. . . .

"Thet blamed old box!" Ellie sobbed against the cunning man's coat. "Thet's what set him off rememb'rin' his Pappy. I'd throw hit in the fire but hit's too late naow. . . ."

Old Nathan looked at the box on the mantelpiece. His face slowly lost its anger. He disengaged himself carefully from the young woman.

"This is the thing ye mean?" he said, leaning his rifle against the cabin wall so that he could take the box in both hands.

"Thet's so," Ellie agreed. The preternatural calm in the old man's voice stilled the trembling of her own.

"Thin mebbe," Old Nathan said softly, "you're wrong about the cause. . . . And hit might happen thet you're wrong t' think I couldn't be airy he'p besides."

The cunning man stared at the box in his hands. His concentration was so deep that though he heard the sound of a foot on the half-log floor of the porch, the possible meaning of the noise didn't register for an instant.

Ellie Ransden looked at Old Nathan, realized that he had slid beneath the immediate present, and snatched his flintlock rifle from where it leaned against the wall. "I hear ye there!" she called in a clear, threatening voice as she sighted down the barrel toward the door.

Old Nathan tore himself free of the walls of his trance like a beetle emerging from its chrysalis. The girl and the cabin's interior had both been present in his mind; now focus and solidity returned to them the way dough fills a biscuit mold.

"Ellie?" a woman called through the closed panel. "Hit's Sarah Ransden, and I'd admire t' speak with you fer a bit."

The cunning man rolled his shoulder muscles to

loosen them. For a moment, it had seemed that his fingertips were growing into the box; that they were becoming roots or that the knife-carved wood changed to flesh and began to pulse with a life of its own. . . .

"Who's with ye, Sarah?" Ellie demanded. She lowered the stock from her shoulder to her waist, but the gunlock was still roostered back and the muzzle aimed toward the door.

"She's alone, child," Old Nathan murmured. Something had broken—or turned—in Ellie Ransden since the time the Bully struck her face this morning.

"I'm alone, child," Sarah said bitterly. "I been alone these ten years gone, since my son left me. As you should know."

"Come in an' set, thin," Ellie replied. "Tain't barred."

She lowered the hammer and replaced the rifle where Old Nathan had set it. "I beg pardon, sir," she muttered sheepishly without meeting the cunning man's eyes. "I shouldn't hev took hit on myse'f t' do thet."

The cunning man sniffed. "En why not?" he said.

Sarah Ransden recoiled as she saw Old Nathan, though he was looking past her toward the empty forest across the roadway. "Mister Ridgeway," she said formally from the doorway. "I come t' speak with my datter, but I don't mean t' intrude."

"Come in er go out, Miz Ransden," Ellie said with evident hostility. "Thar's some uv us here warn't born in a barn."

Sarah flinched. The cunning man stepped to her and drew her into the cabin with his free hand. His boot pushed the door to until the latch clicked.

"I hain't yer datter," the younger woman said. "You let me know right plain thet I warn't good enough fer yer boy the one time I come callin' on ye. He turnt his back on you years ago, but I warn't good enough!"

"Ellie," Old Nathan said quietly, "thar's no call fer thet. Sarah, what is it brings ye here?"

"Yer Cull ain't good enough fer me now, Miz Ransden!" Ellie cried. Her right cheek was bone white, but the swollen print on the left flared like an August rose. "Ifen he don't hang afore he comes back, I'll leave."

The anger that had kept Ellie ramrod straight poured out through a memory, leaving her suddenly vulnerable. She touched her left cheek, then lowered her hand and stared at the fingertips.

"He niver hit me," she whispered. "He niver hit me afore naow."

"Oh, child," Sarah Ransden said. "I felt the storm comin' in my bones, an' the good Lord knows hit was true."

Sarah hesitated, from fear of being rejected rather than calculation, then put her arms around the younger woman's shoulders anyway. They hugged one another, both with their eyes closed and on the verge of tears.

Old Nathan looked away uncomfortably. His fingers began to probe the box again. A thin panel slid aside; the cunning man shook a wooden key out into his palm.

"Whar did ye git thet box, Nathan Ridgeway?" Sarah asked from behind his shoulder. Her tone was controlled and distant, the sort of voice one used to inquire of a stranger found staring over one's garden fence.

"Happen I found hit here on the fireboard, Sarah," the cunning man replied calmly. "What is it ye know about this thing, thin?"

The women stood side by side; both of them tall and striking, though Sarah forty years younger had never been the beauty Ellie Ransden was now. Their clothing, Ellie's check dress and the blue shawl Sarah wore over homespun, was worn and had been inexpensive when new, but there was an unmistakable pride in the women—at what they were, and in the fact that they were surviving.

"Chance had a thing like thet," Sarah said. "Hit opens up, though I niver knew how."

Old Nathan's paired thumbs slid the base of the box rearward. His eyes were on Sarah. In his mind trembled like a tent of shadows the joints and planes of the object with which he had almost merged.

"Like thet, I reckon," the older woman continued. She licked her dry lips. "The one time I asked, he told me his Pappy hed give it to him whin he come of age . . . en he hit me, which warn't new by thin."

Ellie put her arm around Sarah's shoulders.

"I burnt it," Sarah said softly. "I burnt hit whin Cullen run him off, but I swear t' God thet hit war the same box ez ye've got in yer hands."

Old Nathan uncovered the keyhole. As the women silently watched him, he inserted the key and opened the box.

The box was empty. He upended it. Ellie and Sarah relaxed palpably.

"We ain't out uv the woods," the cunning man murmured. "Not jest yet. . . ."

He set the box on the table and reached into the air above him. It was like fumbling on a shelf in the dark. If he looked up there would be nothing to see, only his knobby old fingers closing on—

The familiar, solid angles of a jackknife. The German silver bolsters were cool to his touch, and the shield of true silver set into one jigged-bone scale was cold.

He lifted the knife down without meeting the eyes of the women. There were things the cunning man did for show, when impulse or perceived need drove him, but he felt uncomfortable at the notion of showing off before this particular pair. The only reasons he could imagine for doing that were so childish—and so foolish in a not-man like him—that his mind danced around their edges like a pit.

Old Nathan held the knife between his thumb and forefinger so that the polished silver plate reflected down into the box. It showed—

Nothing. No hidden object, but not the coarse grain of the wood, either. It was as if the silver were mirroring a gray void . . . except that when the cunning man stared at the plate without blinking, he seemed to see flames flicker at the corners of his eyes.

He stepped away from the table and drew in a deep breath.

"No," he repeated, "we hain't out uv the woods. . . ."

Sarah slid a chair beneath the cunning man. He settled into it heavily, straining Ellie's jury-rigged repairs. What was there hed teeth, en it hed took a bite whilst he scouted hit out.

"What is it?" Ellie asked, looking from the box to the door as if undecided as to whence the danger could be expected. "What is it thet you see?"

Old Nathan rubbed his right biceps with his left hand, then raised his arm to put the jackknife away. There wasn't any wonder about the knife. Its blades were good steel, with a working edge on the larger one and on the smaller a wire edge that could serve as a razor at need.

The wonder of the place where Old Nathan kept the knife was another question, but it was a question to which the cunning man himself had no answer. It was like all the rest of his art, a pattern of things known but not studied; the way a clockwork toy moves without understanding in its spring.

And if the toy should cease to move, the spring would be none the wiser for that result either. . . .

Old Nathan sighed and ran a fingertip across the interior of the box. The wood felt as it should: vaguely warm because the cunning man's flesh was cold, and slightly rough because the board had been planed smooth but not polished.

"He found hit et the shurrif's sale," Ellie murmured, not so much to inform as to fill the silence in which she and Sarah Ransden stood with Old Nathan stepped along the pathways of his mind, open-eyed but unseeing. "I was a fool t' take him thar. The Neills was evil on the best day uv thar lives."

"They was evil," Sarah said grimly. "But Chance Ransden had Satan hisse'f livin' in his skull, en I know thet t' my cost."

"Earth 'n air . . ." the cunning man murmured.

He blinked, then shook himself fully alert. His eyeballs felt as though someone had ground sand into them. He rubbed them cautiously. There were risks going into a waking trance with his eyes open. One day the lids would stick that way and he would be blind as a mole; but it hadn't happened yet. . . .

The cabin door opened and closed; Sarah had gone out. Old Nathan looked at the panel, confused and still uncertain. He had dropped back into reality as though it were an icy pond.

Ellie threw another stick of wood onto the hearth. The billet looked chewed off rather than chopped. The axe had gone the way of the Ransden's cattle and seedcorn. The girl was reduced to cutting logs with the handaxe she had concealed in her mulch pile to keep it from being traded for liquor as well.

"Fire and water?" she offered to prompt the cunning man to say more.

"Did I speak?" Old Nathan asked in surprise. "Reckon I did. . . ."

Sarah came back inside. She carried the kitchen

knife she had used as a trowel and a cupful of dirt gathered into her lifted dress. She spilled the soil onto the table near the little box. "There's snow mixed in along with this," she said. "Or I reckon there's water in the jug by the fire."

Old Nathan looked from the older woman to the young one. Most folk he worked magic for, they were afraid of what he did and the fellow who did it besides. This pair was rock steady. Their minds moved faster than the cunning man was consciously able to go; and if they were afraid, it was nowhere he could see by looking deep into their eyes.

On the cabin eaves, chickadees cracked seeds and remarked cheerfully about the sunlight.

Mebbe the wimmen 'ud be afeerd if they knew more; but mebbe livin' with the Ransden men hed burnt all the fear outen thim already.

Ellie rose from the hearth with a long feather of hickory, lighted at one end. It burned back along the grain of the wood with a coiled pigtail of black waste above the flame. "This do ye fer fire?" she said as she offered the miniature torch.

"Aye," agreed the cunning man. "Hit'll do fine."

His right index finger traced characters on the table. They were visible only where they disturbed the pile of sodden earth or the wisps of ash which dropped from the hickory. The room began to rotate around the focus of Old Nathan's vision, but the walls and all the objects within them remained clear.

A driblet of mud and melt water curled from the table like a thread being drawn from a bobbin. The ribbon of flame from the hickory attenuated and slanted sideways, as though the strip were burning in a place where "up" was not the same direction as it was in central Tennessee.

There was a keening sound like that which the

wind makes when it drives through a tiny chink in a wall.

Old Nathan spoke in a soft, monotonous voice, mouthing syllables that were not words in a language familiar to his listeners. His eyes became glazed and sightless. His tongue stumbled. It was shaping itself to the sounds not by foreknowledge but the way a hiker crosses a shallow stream: hopping from one high rock to the next, then searching for a further steppingstone.

The elemental strands—earth and air, fire and water—wove together as do fibers in a ropewalk, coiling and interweaving into a single tube. It curved into the box, probing the wooden bottom—

And slid away, broken into its constituent parts, its virtue dissipated.

Old Nathan awoke with a start, jolting backward in his chair. His arms spread with the fingers clawed in readiness to meet a foe. His spasm flung the feather of wood toward the pile of bedding.

Sarah snatched up the burning splinter. In her haste she gripped it too close to the flame, but she carried it without flinching back to the hearth.

Ellie Ransden cried, "Sir!" and grasped Old Nathan's right arm, both to control it and to prevent the cunning man from tipping over with the violence of his reaction.

He glared at her. His face for a moment was a mask of fury; then he calmed and softened as though all the bones had been drawn from his flesh.

"Tarnation, gal," the old man gasped, pillowing his head against his left arm on the table. He seemed oblivious to the slime of ash and damp earth left on the surface by his attempt.

Old Nathan lifted himself again. He gave Ellie a squeeze with his left hand before he drew his right from her support. "I figgered with all creation t' push,

I'd hev thet gate open lickity-split . . . but hit warn't ready t' open."

The cunning man smiled wryly at the miscalculation he had barely survived. "I was betwixt the gate en' the push thet I'd drawed up myse'f."

"The bottom's false, thin?" Ellie asked, glancing toward the little box beside Old Nathan's hand. Her lips curled. "Cain't we chop hit open?"

"Hain't like thet, child," the cunning man said. Sarah Ransden eyed them without expression from beside the fireplace. "Thar's a gate, so t' speak, but not . . ."

He gestured, rubbing his fingertips together as if attempting to seize the air. "Not on this world. Not all this world—" his index finger drew a line across the dirt on the tabletop "—has airy bit t' do with what's on t' other side uv thet gate, so I couldn't force hit."

Without speaking, Sarah reached into the bosom of her dress. She drew a locket up and over her head. The ornament was suspended on a piece of silk ribbon so faded that its original color was only a pink memory.

Sarah opened the spring catch and held the locket out to Old Nathan. Inside was the miniature portrait of a man, painted on ivory. "Thet's Chance Ransden," she said in a distant voice. "Thet was my husband whin I married him."

Old Nathan set the locket down on the table and examined it. The artist had been skillful, not so much in the depiction of physical features—the face on the miniature was thinner than that of the Chance Ransden the cunning man remembered from ten years past— but rather in the sheen of the spirit glinting through the skin. No single detail in the painting was objectively right, but the result had the feel of Chance Ransden.

And the feel of hot, soulless evil.

Old Nathan stood up, moving with an exaggerated care. I'm too durn old fer sech goins-on. . . . "Blame lucky thing I hain't bruck yer table down, me threshin' about thet way," he grumbled aloud.

He stretched, feeling the tenderness of his muscles. They had locked rigidly against one another while the vortex of power the cunning man summoned tried to crush his mind against immovable blackness.

Mebbe there was a better feller somewhars t' do this thing; but less'n he showed hisse'f right pert, Nathan Ridgeway meant t' do whativer an old man could.

"Thankee, Sarah," Old Nathan said. "I reckon it might serve."

He touched the painted face softly, then raised the locket by its loop of ribbon. This time he would stand.

The locket twisted over the interior of the box while the cunning man mumbled not-words. The face glinted—spun behind the unpainted back—spun again. . . .

To the women facing one another across the table, it seemed as though the corners of the portrait's mouth were rising into a sneer.

Old Nathan saw nothing. Streaks like the beams of sunlight drawing water through the clouds slid blindingly across the surface of his mind.

The latch rattled an instant before the cabin door burst open. The women looked up. Ellie's hand thrust out, then froze. The long rifle leaned against the far wall.

Bully Ransden stood in the doorway, wild and disheveled. There was a glitter of madness in his eyes, and his powerful arms hung down like the forelegs of a beast.

Beams of light rotated and rotated back. The cunning man raced past them like a fish rushing along the in-slanting walls of a weir.

None of the four figures in the cabin moved. The locket ticked against the bottom of the puzzle box.

And vanished.

Old Nathan was naked. The damage wreaked on his privates at King's Mountain by a Tory musketball was starkly evident.

He stood at a portal whose upper angles stretched beyond conception. The surface beneath his feet was wood, coarsely finished but seamless. The gigantic door that stood ajar before him was patterned with the same grain as that of the lid of the puzzle box in another place and time.

When the cunning man glanced back over his shoulder, he saw a forest like that on the site where his cabin now stood—but from the time before young Nathan Ridgeway began girdling trees and clearing undergrowth with a brushhook.

"Come t' be comp'ny t' me, Nathan?" called Chance Ransden from across the threshold. He giggled in a fashion that Old Nathan remembered from life—

For wherever this was, it was not life.

Chance was naked also. His appearance was that of a powerfully built man in the prime of life, the way he had looked the night he disappeared. Allus hed the luck uv the devil, Chance did. Nairy a one uv the scars, not even the load of small shot Jose Miller put into what he thought war a skunk in his smoke shed, showed whin Ransden hed clothing on. . . .

"I hadn't airy scrap uv use fer ye whin ye were alive, Ransden," Old Nathan said coldly. He stood straight, facing forward. He could not conceal the ancient injury to his manhood, and to attempt the impossible would be a sign of weakness. "I'll be no comp'ny t' ye now, 'cept t' tell ye t' be off whar ye belong. Leave yer son be!"

Chance giggled again. "D'ye want to see my boy Cull naow, Nathan?" he asked.

The portal opened slightly. Hunched behind the elder Ransden was the naked, cringing figure of his son. The image of Bully Ransden was bruised and bloody, as though he had tried to fight a bear with empty hands. He threw Old Nathan a furtive, sidelong glance past the legs of his father.

"Ain't he the dutiful lad?" Chance cackled. "He warn't whin I last wore my body, but he's larned better naow."

"Git up an' fight him, boy!" the cunning man snarled. He felt sick in the pit of his stomach to see a proud man like Bully reduced to this. "He don't belong here. Drive him out!"

Instead of fighting, Bully Ransden launched himself at the crack between the doorpanel and the jamb, trying to reach Old Nathan's side of the portal. His father kicked him aside with contemptuous ease.

The landscape across the threshold was a lifeless gray. The occasional quiver of movement was only heat-spawned distortion.

"Cull, he war a very divil fer strength, warn't he, Ridgeway?" Chance Ransden said. His lips were fixed in a cruel sneer. "Whin strength warn't enough, he bruk like a China cup. He hain't airy more spunk thin a dog since I bruk him."

He dug his toes into the ribs of his son. The younger man whimpered and cringed away.

Old Nathan licked his lips. "Aye, you're jest the bold feller I recollect, Ransden. Come acrost here en do thet, why don't ye?"

"No, old man," Chance said, "you ain't gitting me over whur you stand."

He opened the portal a hand's breadth wider. "But you kin come t' me—ifen ye dare. And I'll let my Cull

here go across t' thet side. A soul fer a soul. Thet's
fair, ain't hit jest?"

He began to laugh. Behind him, Bully Ransden
huddled with his arms about his knees. He eyed Old
Nathan through the opening with a look of desperate
appeal.

"Cullen Ransden," the cunning man said. "Listen t'
me, boy! What is it thet ye want t' do?"

"I want t' get shet uv this place," the Bully whispered. "Please God, git me shet uv here."

He was afraid to look up as he spoke. As his father
had said, Cullen Ransden had broken. There was no
sign of the former man who crushed every opponent
with his fists and masterful will.

"Git me out, sir," Bully begged. "I swear, there
hain't nuthin' I won't do fer ye ifen ye only git me
free."

"A soul fer a soul," Chance repeated. "I'll let him
go across, s' long ez you pay him clear. Are ye thet
much uv a man, Nathan Ridgeway?"

The cunning man shuddered with desire for what
he knew he had no right to hope. The boy couldn't
know the price. Only the old man who had lived that
price for so many decades could understand it—

But Cullen Ransden knew what he was paying now;
and it was too much for him.

"Listen, boy," Old Nathan said. He tried to speak
gently, but his voice was full of too many emotions—
hope, fear, and the anger of years. Fate had played a
cruel trick on him when he was a youth younger still
than Bully Ransden. "Listen. If you come through that
door, you'll live out the rist uv yer life ez an old man.
As no man a'tall, by some ways uv lookin' et it. D'ye
hear me?"

Bully Ransden did not speak. His body trembled
as he readied himself for another dash toward the

opening—which Chance would stop as surely as his weasellike smile was cruel.

"Boy, ye won't niver git back," Old Nathan said with desperate emphasis. "You cain't know what a weak, pulin' thing ye'll—"

Bully sprang for the portal. His father's foot thrust him back. Chance's long toenails gouged like a beast's talons.

Old Nathan felt the calm of a decision made for him, in the clearest possible manner. *Warn't right, but warn't my choice neither.*

"Let him go, Chance Ransden," he said. "I'm comin' to ye, since thet's what ye think thet ye want."

Old Nathan stepped forward. The portal and the forest behind him vanished, leaving him alone on a lava plain with Chance Ransden.

The sky was pale and yellowish. The air was bitterly cold, with a tang of brimstone.

Chance Ransden stood arm's-length distant, grinning like a neck-chained monkey. He backed slightly away when the cunning man appeared before him. Bullets had puckered Ransden's flesh in a dozen different places, and a long pink scar snaked up the right side of his rib cage where a knife had just failed to let out his evil life; but he looked a fine, muscular specimen of a man for all that.

If he was still a man. If he had ever been a man.

"Cull, he made me a good dog, Ridgeway," Chance said. "You'll make me a better one."

The cunning man tested the surface with the toes of his right foot. The plain on which he stood was formed by ropes of lava spilling out to cool in arcs across the axis of the advance. Individual ropes lay one against the next in a series of six-foot hillocks, with sharp valleys between ready to break the ankle of an incautious man.

There was no animal life visible anywhere on the plain, and no vegetation save scales of lichen—white and gray and rusty orange—which slowly powdered even raw stone. Plumes of vapor marked cabin-sized potholes where rock bubbled, and the wind occasionally burned instead of cutting with cold.

"What I'll make you, Chance Ransden," the cunning man said softly, "is glad t' git off t' whar ye belong."

"You thunk I was afeerd uv ye, back t' thet world, didn't ye, Nathan?" Chance said. "Waal, I'm another guess chap thin ye took me fer."

Old Nathan stepped across the V-shaped trench between his hillock and the one on which Ransden stood.

Ransden hopped back. He raised his hand in the air. "Ye say ye're the Divil's master, old man?" he asked.

Old Nathan stared at the image of the younger, stronger man. "Aye," he said.

Chance snapped his fingers.

The rim of a fuming pothole ten yards behind Ransden began to move. Minerals deposited by steam shivered away in blue-green and saffron patches. Something was coming to life, the way the first rains cause toads to break free of the capsule of hardened slime in which they have survived summer and drought.

"Waal, Ridgeway," said Chance Ransden. "I say I'm the Divil's sarvint. Let's see who's the wiser uv us, shall we?"

The thing from the rock cocoon was gray and looked somewhat like an ape. It would have been taller than most men if it walked upright; instead it shambled forward in a crouch, occasionally touching down the knuckles of a slablike hand. Its upper canines were the size of a man's thumbs, and each finger bore predatory claws.

"Thar's nowhere t' run, old man!" Chance cackled.

"Ye kin run till Hell freezes over, en ye still cain't git away!"

The creature shambling forward was no ape nor any other living thing. The eye sockets beneath its deep brows were pools of lambent flame.

There were fears in the heart of every man. Chance Ransden's soul stood as naked as those of his son and the cunning man, but his master had offered him an ally. . . .

"I'm too old t' run, Ransden," Old Nathan said. He reached into the air. "B'sides, I warn't niver airy good at it."

His fingers crooked and—

—closed on the hard angles of his knife. There when he needed it, and he hadn't been sure.

But he was sure he would not have run. He'd known since the day the bullet struck and passed on at King's Mountain that there was nowhere to run from the worst fears, the true fears. . . .

The backspring clicked with assurance as Old Nathan opened the main blade. There was a faint sheen of oil on the steel.

Ransden looked startled and backed again. For the first time he may have realized that there was content to the cunning man's boast to be the Devil's master.

But steel wouldn't win this fight, any more than Bully Ransden's strength had done.

"C'mon thin, durn ye," Old Nathan muttered, to himself rather than to the ape hulking toward him. He stepped over a trough in the rock, then stretched his long shanks in a leap to close with the creature.

The ape lifted onto its hind legs to meet the attack, but the cunning man was already within the sweep of the long arms before they could grasp him. He held the knife with the cutting edge up. The creature's hide plucked at the point before giving way. Its breath reeked with an unexpectedly chemical foulness, like that of stale urine.

Old Nathan started to rip upward against the resistance of the gray skin and the belts of muscles beneath it. The ape bit into the top of his skull with a pain like nothing the cunning man had ever before experienced.

He was on his back. The creature was twenty feet away, patting at the gash in its belly and roaring like the fall of a giant tree. There was blood on its fangs, speckling the froth bubbling across the broad lips.

Old Nathan couldn't see out of one eye and his hands were empty. He sat up and only then realized how much his shoulders hurt. The ape's claws had raked furrows across him before the creature flung the cunning man away.

He wiped his left eye with the back of his hand, then blinked. That cleared enough blood from the eyesocket that his vision, though dim, was binocular again. He needed the depth perception of two eyes. . . .

The jackknife, slimed with a greenish fluid that was not blood, lay beside his right hand. The ichor crusted and turned black where it touched the silver set into one bone scale.

Old Nathan picked up the knife. The tacky ichor would give him a better grip. Despite dazzling flashes of pain, he got to his feet before the monster started toward him again.

The ape bellowed and spread both arms. There was blood on the creature's foreclaws also. Old Nathan stumbled when he tried to leap forward. That worked to his advantage, because his opponent's great hands clapped together above the cunning man so that he was free to stab home again within an inch of the first wound.

This time the sound the ape made was more a scream than a bellow. It drove its clawed fingers into

Old Nathan's sides like the tines of a flesh fork lifting meat to the fire. The cunning man shouted hoarsely, but he used the twisting power of the ape's own arms to tear the blade through rib cartilage that would have daunted mere human strength.

The creature flung Old Nathan over its head. For a moment the cunning man twisted in a kaleidoscope of yellow sky and gray stone, picked out occasionally by the sight of one of his own flailing limbs.

He hit the lava on his left side. His hip and hand took the initial impact, but his head struck also.

Old Nathan lay on the rock. He saw two apes turn toward him, but one image was only a faint ghost. The flap of skin torn from his forehead had almost bled his right eye closed again.

The creature's mouth was open. The cunning man could not hear the sounds directly, but he felt the lava tremble beneath him.

He sat up. The tear in the ape's belly was the size of a man's head. Coils of intestine dangled from the opening, and the fur of the creature's groin and upper thighs was matted by sour green ichor.

The ape lowered its forelimbs and knuckled toward its opponent.

Old Nathan found the knife beside him. The main blade had broken off at the bolsters when it struck the lava. He tried to open the smaller blade and found that his left hand had no feeling or movement.

The cunning man's vision cleared, though it remained two dimensional. He could hear the monster roar.

He gripped the jigged bone scales of the knife in his teeth and snicked out the smaller blade with his right thumb. When Old Nathan took the knife from his mouth, the taste of the monster's body fluids remained on his lips, but that could not be allowed to matter any more than the pain did.

The tiny blade winked in the jaundiced light. Old Nathan had honed its edge too fine to make a weapon, but it would serve until it broke.

"C'mon, thin," he whispered as he tried to lurch to his feet. His left leg would not support him. He fell back.

C'mon, ye ole fool. . . .

Old Nathan began to crawl forward on his hands and knees. The crystalline surface of the lava was bright with blood that leaked through his abraded skin.

The ape rose onto its hind legs again. It was trying to stuff loops of gut back into its belly, but each handful squeezed additional coils out of the knife-cut opening.

". . . whar ye b'long," Old Nathan whispered through the slime coating his lips. He had no peripheral vision. He could see nothing but the figure of the ape standing gray against the lighter gray background of a fumarole, and the edges of even that image were blurred and drawing inward.

"C'mon . . ."

The ape turned away.

"No!" screamed Chance Ransden from where he stood behind the monster. "Ye dassn't leave—"

The ape shambled on in its new direction. Chance leaped away.

Old Nathan transferred the knife to his teeth again. He needed his right hand to drag himself forward. White light pulsed at the center of his field of view.

Chance Ransden turned to run, then screamed as the ape caught him in the crook of one hairy arm. The creature stumbled over its trailing intestines. It took two further steps, then looked over its shoulder toward the cunning man.

The ape and Chance Ransden, howling like a stuck pig, plunged into the heart of a pothole crater. Mud so hot that it glowed plopped up, then sank again beneath a curtain of its own steam.

"C'mon . . ." a voice whispered in Old Nathan's mind as he lost consciousness.

Old Nathan woke up. He could hear the straw filling of a mattress rustle beneath him when he turned his head.

There was a quilt over him as well. Ellie Ransden sat in a chair beside the bed made up on the floor in lieu of a proper frame. It was morning. . . .

But not the same morning. Beside the bed was a pot with a scrap of tow burnt at the bottom of it. Ellie had melted lard into the container, then floated a wick in it as a makeshift candle by which to watch the cunning man's face while he slept.

Old Nathan tried to sit up. Ellie knelt beside the bed with a little cry and helped to support his shoulders.

His hands were bigger than they should have been, and the hairs along his arms were blond. He had awakened in Bully Ransden's body, as he knew he would do—if he awakened.

"Sarah took the—old man back t' the homeplace," Ellie said. "He'll be right ez rain, she says."

"Gal, gal . . ." Old Nathan said. "I—"

He stood up in a rush. Ellie scrambled, flicking the bedding out of the way so that it would not tangle the cunning man's feet.

Sparrows quarreled on the window's outer ledge. Their chirping was only noise, as devoid of meaning to him as it was empty of music. Nathan Ridgeway was no longer a wizard—

And no longer an old man.

Ellie Ransden put her arms around him. Her touch helped to support Old Nathan while he got his legs under him again, but it was offered with unexpected warmth. "Child, listen," Old Nathan said. "I ain't yer Cull. He changed place with me."

"Hush, now," Ellie murmured. "You jest hold stiddy till ye've got yer strength agin."

Old Nathan looked down at the supple, muscular arm that was part of his body. "Warn't right what I did," he whispered. "But Bully begged fer it . . . en' I warn't goin' t' leave Chance Ransden loose in the world no longer."

Chance Ransden loose, or Chance Ransden's master.

Old Nathan wore the dungarees and homespun shirt with which Bully Ransden had fled the cabin the morning before, and a pair of Ransden's boots stood upright at the foot of the bed. He detached himself from the girl and began to draw on one of the boots.

"Sarah said she'd keep yer animals, ye needn't worry," Ellie said. "She said she knew how ye fussed yerse'f about thim all."

Old Nathan looked at the young woman. Ellie had plaited her hair into a loose braid. Now she coiled it onto the top of her head, out of the way. Sarah Ransden knew more thin he'd thought airy soul did uv his bus'ness.

He hunched himself into the other boot. His head hurt as though someone were splitting it with the back side of an axe, but the easy, fluid way in which his young joints moved was a wonder and delight to him.

"What is hit thet ye intend, sir?" Ellie asked from where she stood between the cunning man and the door.

Old Nathan snorted. "With the repetation thet Bully, pardon me, thet Cullen hed aforetimes, en' the word thet's going on about him these last months whin his pappy rid him—I figger I'd hev to be plumb loco t' stay hereabouts, wearing the shape thet I do now."

Memories flooded in on him the way a freshet bursts

a dam of ice during the spring thaw. His body began to shake uncontrollably with recollections of what had been and what might have been.

"Might be," he said softly, "thet I should hev gone off after King's Mountain, 'stid uv settlin' back here en' fixin' a fence round me, near enough."

Ellie gripped his hands firmly. "Take me along," she said.

"I ain't Cull Ransden!" Old Nathan shouted as he drew himself away. What he wanted to do . . .

"I know who you are," Ellie said. She stepped close but did not touch him. "I know ye treated me decent whin others, they didn't. D'ye think I kin stay here-abouts, sir? Or thet I want to?"

Old Nathan turned away. There was a rifle on the pegs over the fireboard; his own. His mule gave its familiar brassy whinny from the shed, though there was no certain meaning in the sound.

Sarah Ransden en' her son 'ud be set up right purty, what with the two farms—

Or three, ifen Ellie wint off with the man who wore her husband's shape.

"I ain't special t' the beasts no more," he said musingly. "Reckon hit's better I try my possibles t' git along with men now, anyways."

He looked at the young woman. "I reckon if I warn't all et up with bitterness whin I come back from King's Mountain," he added, "I might hev thunk a man could be ez good a frind thin a cat. A man er a woman."

"I packed a budget," Ellie said. "Hit seemed t' me thet ye'd feel thet way whin ye come around."

She looked out the window. The sun was already high in the sky. "We kin wait till ye're stronger . . . ?" she said.

"Sooner we're away, the better," Old Nathan replied. The pain in his head was passing as he moved; and for the rest of his body—he hadn't felt so good in fifty years. . . .

Ellie handed him a sheepskin coat, cracked at the seams but warm enough to serve until his youthful strength earned him better. Soon—

He frowned, then took Ellie by both shoulders and held her until she met his eyes. "Thar's no more magic, girl," he said. "I'm a man en no more. I want ye t' understand thet."

She hefted the bundle of household essentials she had prepared. "Thet's what I wish fer," she said. "A man as treats me decint."

They walked outside into bright brilliant sunlight reflecting from the snow. Old Nathan left the cabin door open. Sarah could deal with the place whenever she chose; Sarah Ransden and the son who now kept her company. . . .

He saddled and bridled the mule, then rubbed its muzzle. The beast gave a snort of satisfaction and made a playful attempt to bite him.

"Git on up," Old Nathan said to the girl. "I reckon I'll walk."

He hefted the rifle he had leaned against the sidelogs of the shed, then crooked it into his left arm. He glanced to see that Ellie was in the saddle, then made a cautious pass through the air with his free hand.

Nothing happened. Old Nathan sighed and said, "Gee up, mule. We've got a passel uv country t' ride through afore we find airy place thet wants t' see us."

"We'll be all right," Ellie said.

She looked back once from the road. In the shadow of the shed, there was a faint glimmer as of fairy lights . . . but very faint, and the young couple had many miles yet to ride.